RUE DE PARADIS

Semiramis - Queen of Heaven
Book 1

JEENA MURPHY

ONE

Yvette

Mont-Saint-Louis, August 1933

Yvette wished she'd attached weights to Papa's arms and legs before she'd slid his drink-ravaged body into the water. If she had, he wouldn't have washed up further down the river. The fisherman who found him saw the gunshot to his head and concluded he'd taken his own life.

If Papa had disappeared, everyone would have assumed he'd wobbled down to his fishing spot and tumbled into the river. He'd have been declared missing when they found his rod and bait lying on the bank.

In that version, Yvette and her sister Janie would have held Papa's funeral at the parish's small stone church; its wooden pews would have been filled with people from their village of Mont-Saint-Louis, the congregation all around them, cosy and intimate, warmed by the light of hundreds of flickering candles, the sisters' grief soothed and smothered by hugs and kisses from family and friends.

Instead, they were standing around Papa's open grave in the most overgrown part of the cemetery, among broken and neglected tombstones, as far away as you could get from the well-tended plots of respectable families and the welcoming stoop of the church.

If anyone had known what really happened, then Yvette would have been absent from the graveside too. No one knew, no one suspected, and Papa was as good as buried.

They'd wanted to lay Papa to rest beside Mama, surrounded by the well-trimmed trees and hedges in the newer part of the cemetery. Yvette visited Mama every day to change the flowers and pluck out any weeds that dared push their way out of the ground.

The priest had refused but did agree to Papa being buried a war hero. In a compromise, he'd chosen this plot on the edge of unconsecrated ground, next to the long-forgotten soldiers. Their graves were covered in weeds, marked by tombstones so weathered, the identities were unreadable.

He chose it as a public statement of their disgrace, signalling that Papa's children must suffer for his sin. Yvette refused to feel guilty about Papa being apart from Mama.

Her tiny act of rebellion was to forgo black in favour of her best dress, which Mama had made her just before she died. It was a glorious sky-blue seersucker cotton that cinched in at the waist and flared out over her hips. It suited her olive complexion and dark hair.

The meagre numbers around the graveside reflected her fellow villagers' belief that she and Janie were sinners, tainted by Papa's act.

At least cousin Lila and baby Joseph had come, even though Lila seemed ready to collapse with the weight of him on her hip. The baby seemed bigger than ten months, mainly because of Lila's slight frame. The faded red dress that once showed off her curves hung from her like she'd dressed up in her mother's clothes. The bigger the baby got, the smaller Lily seemed, as if the child sucked the goodness from her body, leaving her hollowed out, like a shrivelled apple. Lila's sixteenth birthday was next week, and she looked like a middle-aged, worn-out farm worker. Her brown hair, once lush, was now stringy and thinning, and her face was sunken and gaunt. At least the baby thrived. Lila kept him well fed and warmly dressed.

At the foot of the grave stood the village patriarch, Patrick Aubert, and his wife. Aubert's brown eyes twinkled in his almost wrinkle-free face. He frequently reached up to smooth his perfectly cut silver hair. Not that it needed smoothing – it was always immaculate, just like his clothes and his small, muscular frame. Every time Yvette walked past the barber's, Aubert seemed to be in there. He loved his hair more than his lands, more than his wife, and more than his village conquests.

In contrast, Madame Aubert was shaped like a well-fed marmot, and waddled when she walked. No one was sure what she looked like, as she was never without a veiled hat. Yvette suspected she wore the veil to screen herself from the realities of their tiny village.

Two of Papa's drinking buddies, Messieurs Almon and Fubern, had creaked their way up to the cemetery with the help of their walking sticks. They'd managed to shave their craggy faces, brush the mildew from their moth-eaten black suits, and find black armbands to wear.

The priest frowned his way through the service. His tight purple biretta, pressed down on his florid forehead, accentuated his unruly eyebrows, making him seem more severe. Each word he read from his black book was uttered in a begrudging manner, as if Papa's death was an affront and had happened only to keep him from a mid-afternoon snooze.

The priest scowled at Yvette and cleared his throat. What on earth did he want from her? Was he about to comment on her dress?

Janie nudged her arm, and she remembered the lavender and jasmine bouquet. They'd picked the flowers on their way through the cemetery. She opened her hand and let them fall into the gaping hole, where they scattered across the lid of Papa's wooden coffin.

Janie had tied a lavender stem around her flowers to form a bouquet. She wore Mama's green and white spotted dress – it was still too big for her, but it made her look older than her thirteen years. Yvette had twisted Janie's curly hair into an almost-tidy chignon. Against Yvette's wishes, she'd put on Mama's matching green peridot earrings and necklace. She held the bouquet in both hands in front of her, like a bride ready to sprint up the altar.

Janie cast her bouquet into the grave with a flourish. It landed on the middle of the coffin with a loud thump and bounced the loose flowers off the lid.

Yvette looked up from the grave to find Aubert leering at Janie. That man – how could he do this at their father's funeral? Her stomach clenched. She'd done what was necessary to protect them from Papa, but the next threat was here at the foot of Papa's grave.

Aubert had turned his attention to her thirteen-year-old sister.

The knot in her stomach grew tighter as Janie smiled back at Aubert, apparently oblivious to who was standing next to her – Cousin Lila. And Joseph, Aubert's illegitimate son.

On cue, the baby bellowed. Lila jostled him on her scrawny hip to keep him silent. The girl had spent most of the funeral glancing at Aubert, but she and Joseph may as well have been invisible. His attention was anywhere except on her.

The veil on Madame Aubert's black mourning hat didn't appear to be interfering with her vision. She kept glancing at baby Joseph and Lila, each time clutching her prayerbook a little tighter in her sausage fingers. Yvette marvelled at how she managed to stuff those swollen fingers into her tight leather gloves.

Madame Aubert may have found this indiscretion harder to ignore because the baby's hair stood up the same way as her husband's, and his eyes were the same almond shape and the same shade of brown.

The priest scooped up a handful of dirt from the pile beside him and threw it into the grave, before continuing the committal. He picked up his thurible and stirred up the incense. Smoke twisted out of its holes like grey snakes as he held it by its long chain and waved it across the open grave.

As he droned the final blessing in Latin, the cloying incense mingled with the scent of lavender and newly dug dirt, leaving Yvette struggling to breathe.

'May God rest his soul.' The priest wiped his hand down the front of his cassock as if he were finished with Papa.

'God rest his soul,' Yvette murmured out of politeness.

Suddenly Lila turned to Aubert. 'You must acknowledge Joseph as your son,' she shouted.

Aubert and his wife pretended not to hear.

'Quiet, Lila. This is not the place,' chastened the priest, but she wasn't listening.

'Do not ignore me!' Lila's voice rose to a screech.

Aubert took his wife's arm and turned away, as if Lila were nothing more than a barking dog.

But Lila was unstoppable, just like when she'd smashed a shovel in the boy-next-door's face when he called her mother a whore. Yvette reached out to restrain her, but Lila was too quick. She rushed towards Aubert with baby Joseph held out in front of her like he was a ball she was about to throw at him.

Aubert twisted around with his arm up to deflect her. She hurtled into him and lost her grip on Joseph, who tumbled out of her arms. Yvette launched herself at the baby at the same time as Madame Aubert spun towards the falling child and knocked the shrieking Lila into Papa's grave, where she hit the wooden coffin with a thwack.

Yvette skidded across the ground with her hands outstretched Joseph plopped neatly into her arms. The baby blinked and let out a coo. He was perfectly unharmed, which was more than Yvette could say for her sky-blue seersucker. It would be hard to get rid of the grass stains.

She whispered *sorry* to Mama and hoped the dress wasn't permanently damaged. Tendrils of hair, dislodged during her dive to save the baby, brushed her face. She must look a mess, but she couldn't have let baby Joseph follow his mother into Papa's grave.

She looked down at Lila, curled up on Papa's coffin surrounded by bright bursts of flowers. The absurdity of it all bubbled up into Yvette's chest. She couldn't keep it in. Great guffaws of laughter rattled her body, surprising baby Joseph. His eyes stayed wide and his mouth opened in the shape of an O. He began to laugh too, a cackling baby chuckle that embraced his whole body.

Lila sat up and rubbed her head. 'Oh my god,' Lila hooted, hyperventilating. Then she too laughed.

All that needed to happen now was for Papa to burst out of his coffin and accuse Yvette of murdering him. She started laughing again, mostly from hysteria.

'Are you okay?' Janie called down to Lila.

'I think so.'

'Get out of there now,' the priest shouted down into the grave. His face had turned the same shade of purple as his robes. He'd forgotten about the thurible. As he continued shouting and waving his arms, smoke writhed about him like angry eels trapped in a pond.

No one moved to help Lila out of the grave. The priest would have been happy to bury her alive with Papa. It was up to Yvette to help her cousin again.

Yvette turned to pass the baby to Janie, only to find her between the Auberts, who each had an arm around her. Madame

Aubert seemed genuine in her sympathy – but she couldn't see her husband's hand move down to rest on Janie's budding breast. Smugness radiated from Janie's wide-set brown eyes.

How could the man be so brazen? Even if his wife couldn't see, the priest and others by the graveside could. She had to get Janie away from that man.

'Come and take the baby,' Yvette called out to her.

Janie hesitated, but Yvette had perfected the look that compelled Janie to obey. With more sass than was necessary, Janie stepped to the side, deliberately letting Aubert's hand stroke her body as she came to collect the baby.

Joseph's legs dangled to Janie's knees as she hoisted him onto her hip.

'Stop that with the old goat,' Yvette hissed at Janie. 'You'll end up with a baby of your own.'

'I'd never be as stupid as her. I know how to play the game.' Janie rolled her eyes and scuffed her shoe, sending dust towards Papa's open grave.

Lila's head appeared above the rim, and Yvette hauled her out, helping her to her feet.

'You are a disgrace. Your family is a disgrace. Leave this hallowed ground,' the priest bellowed at them.

It was a pity the priest wasn't referring to Aubert. Replies bubbled through Yvette's head, but she forced herself to stay quiet. In the coming days, they might need what little help the priest was prepared to give them.

Behind them, the village odd job man leant on his shovel, ready to fill in the grave. She'd only ever seen him in his shapeless, dirt-streaked trousers and the grimy shirt that may once have been white. He pulled a knife out of his greasy waistcoat to whittle a twig which he used to pick at what was left of his teeth. Then he ran his hand over his sparse hair and cleared his throat.

'Don't mean to hurry you,' he said, 'but I got to help with the harvest in Cochin Fields. I'll get paid for a whole day if I can get there in an hour.'

'Fill it in. We are finished,' the priest replied. He strode away from the graveside. Behind him, the thurible oozed disdain-laden smoke trails between the graves. The Auberts hurried away from the graveside in the opposite direction to the priest.

As the odd job man lumbered towards the pile of soil, Yvette stepped in front of him. The smell from his unwashed body and dirty clothes was overpowering. He was poorer than them, and a day's wages would mean everything to him, but Janie needed to say goodbye properly.

'Give us a minute. You'll still have plenty of time to get down to Cochin Field.'

He shrugged, then pulled out a tobacco pouch from the inside pocket of his filthy vest.

What did Yvette need from these final moments with Papa? She wasn't sorry for what she'd done. She'd only sped up his end. She'd lost count of how many times he'd said he'd kill himself. That night by the river, he'd pointed the gun at her, then at himself. He'd collapsed onto the ground wailing about mice crawling out of dead soldiers' eye sockets. The pistol lay next to him. She'd picked it up and he'd grabbed her hand. They'd struggled. She'd been surprised at how strong he still was. She'd pulled away...

She didn't need God to forgive her. What she needed was to forget.

'Let's say a prayer together,' Janie said, mistaking her silence for grief.

Janie began, 'Our Father, who art in heaven, hallowed be thy name ...'

Yvette mumbled along with the others, wishing the prayer to be over.

'Be at peace, Papa,' Janie said, looking down on their father's coffin.

She should say something like *God speed*, or, *we will see you in heaven*, though Papa wouldn't be heading up that way. And nor would she be, now.

There wasn't anything to say so she turned to the gravedigger. 'We are finished. You can fill it in.'

Janie seemed mesmerised by the chink of the spade in the dirt and the patter of soil, like rain, on the coffin. Dust rose out of the grave and Yvette tugged Janie away, not wanting to inhale it in case their father's disgrace further tainted them.

She moved like a sleepwalker after the trickle of mourners, through the weathered graves onto the gravelled pathway, a demarcation line that ran along the hedge separating the cemetery from the road. The mourners turned to mutter their goodbyes then shuffled past Aubert as he stood alone, like some gargoyle guarding the entry to heaven, next to the exit gate in the hedge.

Aubert wore a stupid smile that he clearly thought was benevolent. His intentions were anything but benevolent when he held his hand out to Janie. The silly girl stepped towards him. It was so matter of fact, no hiding his intentions, no pretending to care. Everything in the village was there for his pleasure, even her younger sister.

Yvette grabbed Janie's wrist and yanked her back. 'And how long will it be before she'll be living with Lila in that hovel?'

Aubert's expression hardened, and he spat on the ground. 'You will regret saying that to me. You will be out of my cottage by the end of the week.'

'We have paid up until next month.'

'Your father owed four months' rent. I am calling in that debt.' He shrugged and smiled at Janie, who simpered back.

Yvette would never let that man touch her sister. 'I will find the money.'

He inclined his head, pretending it didn't bother him. 'End of the week, then.' His expression changed and he smiled at Janie like a wolf might smile at a rabbit, willing it to jump into its mouth.

Bile rose up Yvette's throat, and she swallowed it back down. She wouldn't throw up in front of him.

'By the end of the week, then,' she managed to say.

'Five months' rent is due.'

He clicked his heels together and bowed towards them, then left by the exit gate, swallowed up by the hedge.

TWO

Yvette

___

As they walked towards Mama's grave, Janie pulled runs of jasmine from the hedges. She broke off pieces and passed them to Lila for Joseph to hold.

'Where are you going to find five month's rent?' Janie asked, twisting the vines around to form a messy bouquet.

'I have my ways,' Yvette said, with what she hoped was confidence. She had no idea where she'd get the money, but she wasn't going to admit that to Janie. She'd have to take in three times the amount of laundry, double her hours in Madame Sorve's boarding house, and find three more disabled neighbours, like Monsieur Rhodes, to pay her to help them. Even then she'd only scrape together two months' rent.

'Just let me go to the Aubert's,' Janie said. 'The food's way better there and you won't have to worry about feeding me. I'll convince him to let you off.'

'Haven't you noticed who's walking beside you?' Yvette flicked her hand towards Lila and baby Joseph.

'I can hold him off. I won't let him do *that* to me,' Janie said, implying Lila was an idiot to have got pregnant.

'You know nothing,' said Lila. 'He slipped something in my

11

drink one night and I woke up with him on top of me. He stopped coming round as soon as he'd got what he wanted.' She tickled Joseph under his chin. He cackled and grabbed her finger. 'But I got my little darling. Wouldn't be without him now.'

The sweet scent of jasmine wafted around them as they arrived at the family plot. When Mama was alive, she'd filled their home with vases of lilac, lavender, and jasmine.

Mama's name was at the bottom of the marble column. The year-old gold lettering hadn't yet been battered by the weather. Above her name, a long list of ancestors rose like rungs on a ladder heading towards heaven. There was no room left for more names under Mama's, so Yvette and Janie would have to make other arrangements.

Yvette traced the letters of Mama's first name, *Loriene.*

'Papa's gone, Mama. We're all alone,' Yvette whispered.

Janie started to cry. 'Don't say that. We're not alone, we have each other.'

Yvette hugged her. 'Yes, we do have each other. And I am not giving you up to Aubert.'

They sat by Mama's grave while Janie sobbed.

Mama had been their anchor stone, and after she passed, there hadn't been a day when Papa wasn't drunk. He'd rambled on about the war and accused them of things they hadn't done.

Two days before he died, he'd beaten Janie for stealing imaginary money from his wallet. And he'd chased the butcher's boy down the lane yelling that he'd robbed them. The butcher had intervened, and Papa had only stopped shouting when the butcher threatened Papa with a machete.

She'd avoided Papa as much as she could. It wasn't difficult, as he went down to the river every day with his fishing rod. If he caught anything, they never saw it as he traded it for booze, or for opium to ease his old injuries. If he wasn't at the river, he was at the Café Saint Louis drinking away what little money they had.

When Janie's sobbing eased, Yvette stood up. 'Dry your eyes. We're going to show the village they can't hurt us.'

They walked out the cemetery gate, and after giving Lila and Joseph a goodbye hug, continued down into the main street of Mont-Saint-Louis. The church, its buildings and the cemetery ran down one side of the road, and on the other, whitewashed houses with red tiled roofs buttressed together, holding each other up as they rambled down the hill.

At the bottom, the street widened out into a plaza where a statue of Saint Louis raised his marble arms to God, and the bronze fish around his feet bubbled out water into the base of the fountain. On special occasions water sprayed out from stigmata on the saint's hands and feet.

At Café Saint Louis, Messieurs Almon and Fubern were sitting at their usual table playing backgammon. They still wore their black armbands and had placed one over the back of the chair Papa had usually occupied.

Monsieur Almon pushed himself out of his seat and leant on his cane as they approached. 'Come over and join us. Let us toast your father.'

Madame Vitere, in her habitual war-widow black dress, bustled out of the café and stood, arms crossed, in the doorway, her mouth tight as if she'd been sucking on limes. Her eyebrows were permanently knitted into a scowl, which contracted further when she saw who the old men were speaking to.

'Don't encourage them in here.' She pulled a tea towel out of her white apron and flicked it towards Yvette and Janie as if to ward them off.

Monsieur Fubern struggled up. 'They're all right,' he told Madame Vitere.

'Don't you be telling me what to do in my own place, or you'll be out too.' She flicked him with the tea towel and deliberately knocked the black band off the unoccupied chair as she stalked back inside. Monsieur Fubern dropped back into his seat, looped the fallen band over the tip of his cane and replaced it on the back of the chair.

Yvette shook her head. 'She happily took our father's money every day, even when she knew he couldn't afford it, and now look at her.'

Janie tugged at her hand. 'Come on. It's not worth it.'

'Sorry, girls. We will visit you soon,' Monsieur Almon called out.

Yvette shrugged and followed Janie. Those two were supposed to be Papa's friends, and they couldn't even stand up for them against mean old Madame Vitere.

Further down the street, Madame Medon was sweeping her porch, the broom swinging like a metronome in her ample arms. Her usual genial expression disappeared when she recognised them. She crossed herself, kissed the little amulet around her neck, and held it up towards them.

It was too much. Yvette's hand came up and flicked forward under her chin. It was the rudest gesture she knew.

'You were happy to take Papa's eggs and provide him with wine, even when you knew he shouldn't be drinking. And now you treat us like we're the problem?' she yelled.

Madame Medon gasped and backed herself into her doorway, still holding out the amulet. As they passed her home, the kitchen door latch clicked shut.

'Was that wise?' Janie mimicked the gesture, her voice thick with sarcasm.

Of course, it wasn't. She felt better, though, for a few steps, until she felt the village watching as they continued towards their cottage. She looked straight ahead and imagined the villagers' judgemental expressions, because of their father and because they weren't wearing black.

Yvette didn't have a black dress and couldn't afford to buy one just for one day. It was a stupid tradition, anyway. Everyone knew their father was dead and he supposedly killed himself. What did it matter what colour she wore?

Janie's best friend Marie ran towards them, her straight blonde plaits bouncing beside her face like skipping ropes. Her mother's harsh rebuke stopped her in her tracks and her shoulders drooped. She held Janie's gaze as she made a heart shape with her hands across the front of her grey pinafore. Her mother barked at her again and she turned away, leaving Janie without comfort.

Yvette glanced at her sister. Tears were trickling down her face, and she looked far younger than her thirteen years.

'Wipe away your tears. Think about something else.' Yvette instantly regretted the harshness of her tone. She wanted to cry now too, but she wouldn't let these people know how much their rejection hurt.

Papa had fought for them, and this was how they repaid him, by shunning his children. She wanted to shout at them and shake them, just as she'd wanted to do with Papa.

As they reached their cottage, they saw the undertaker, Jean Robain, leaning on the fence. He stared up at the roof where a missing tile stood out like a blackened tooth in a tobacco-stained smile.

Monsieur Robain's complexion was as grey as the corpses that passed through his funeral home. For a man of nearly fifty, he kept himself trim, dressed neatly, and attended to his beard and hair.

Yvette could encourage his attentions, and even become his wife. But she found it unsettling how he never looked directly at her, or anyone else. He smelled of formaldehyde and blue cheese, and she was repelled by the idea that he would touch her intimately with hands that pulled out the innards of dead people during the day.

At his feet sat a woven basket covered with a blue and white checked cloth. Yvette's stomach gurgled in anticipation of the goodies inside.

As they reached him, he spoke. 'I can fix that for you,' he said, inclining his head towards the missing tile.

'Thank you for your kind offer. Monsieur Rhodes will lend me his ladder and I will do it tomorrow.'

Monsieur Robain offered her the basket, again not looking at her.

'Just a little something to say I am very sorry for your loss.'

'It's very kind of you to think of us,' Yvette murmured.

'Now you are without your father, you will need someone to provide for you. If you would accept myself as that person, and we can come to a formal arrangement, I can void your father's funeral costs.'

He glanced up as he thrust the basket towards her. She grasped it and tried to take a step back, but he clasped his hand over hers. She couldn't pull away or she'd drop the basket. Her stomach growled again. She wasn't dropping the basket.

'Is this a proposal of marriage, Monsieur Robain?'

'Yes, Mademoiselle Yvette. I am asking for your hand in marriage.'

'I am very flattered, Monsieur Robain. I will need to give this some thought, but you must understand it is difficult, having just lost my father. Thank you for your gift,' she murmured as she pushed the gate shut and dislodged his hand from hers.

She thanked him again as she followed Janie inside the cottage.

The basket contained bread, cheeses, cured meats, a bottle of wine and an envelope. She expected a condolence note, but it was the fee for her father's funeral. Another bill to pay.

She caught Janie by the hand and pulled her in for a hug.

'I'll sort it out. I'll make it right. Neither of us will have to end up with someone we don't want to be with.'

Janie began to cry, and Yvette joined in. How would they

survive? She had to find seventy francs just to pay back their debts, and that was without rent and other expenses for the months to come.

As she held Janie, she assessed their belongings. Was there anything they could sell, among the chipped plates and battered silverware? The edge of Papa's chest peeped out from under his bed. Now he was gone it was no longer off-limits and she could explore its contents.

One thing she already knew was inside was a letter from her cousin Daniel, who had moved to Paris three years ago. Remembering it, she felt a glimmer of hope for the first time since Papa had died, and the panic that gnawed at her insides receded.

THREE

Steffan

Paris, August 1933

Steffan topped up Madame Bruist's wine glass and stoked the fire every time she left the table to fetch something from the kitchen.

The dining room was stifling, made worse by the overabundance of tapestry wall hangings, sideboards and cabinets cluttered with toby jugs, crockery sets, and Limoges figurines.

Steffan wished he could dispense with the charade of having dinner every night in Madame Bruist's claustrophobic mausoleum when he all he wanted was to bolt out the door into Paris's intoxicating night. He consoled himself that each dinner got him closer to finding the fastest way to get her blind drunk so he could go out without her telling tales to Father.

It was only natural that a young man like him should be out every night enjoying what Paris had to offer. If Father found out, he would insist Steffan move into the single men's dormitory at the Blum Foundry where all the other workers would watch everything he did. Or worse, stay with the Blum family and share a room with his surly half-brother, Phillippe. No more late-night jaunts wandering the streets and drinking in the bustling ebb and flow of the city. Instead, a glass of port and a cigar after dinner, a game of backgammon or cards, and in bed by nine.

Sweat trickled down his back and beaded on his face. He peered at himself between the oxidised black spots in the wall mirror to wipe his nose and cheeks with a serviette and dab at his forehead. He avoided touching his pomaded hair. He didn't want to waste more time fixing his carefully constructed side-swept look, with two cowlicks that curled back directly between his dark eyebrows.

He took off his jacket and hung it on the back of his chair. If Madame Bruist noticed his jacket faux pas, he still had work to do.

It was difficult to think of Oscar Blum as Father. His new last name, Blum, felt foreign and spikey in his mouth when he said it. His mother's family name, Ossler, which he'd grown up with, was smooth and silky on his tongue, like an avocado.

After dinner, Steffan moved Madame Bruist's nearly empty wine glass into the sitting room. He shuddered every time he entered this room, as a whole wall was devoted to Madame Bruist's porcelain dolls. Their piercing black eyes seemed to follow Steffan's every move.

'You rest here, and I'll do the dishes.'

'You are such a good boy, just like a son,' Madame Bruist slurred as she lurched into the seat closest to the fire.

'I'll get you a fresh glass.' He rummaged through the kitchen cupboards, pulled out the biggest one he could find, and sloshed in half a bottle of shiraz. He took the empty glass from her hand and gave her the full one.

The wall of dolls glowered at him in an accusatory manner.

'My, that's generous.' She held the glass away from her and struggled to keep it in focus.

'You deserve to treat yourself.'

'I do,' she mumbled between sips.

Madame Bruist was fast asleep by the time Steffan finished drying the pots. He took the glass out of her hand and covered her with a blanket.

The drink had loosened her features and she appeared quite peaceful – not the angry woman he knew her to be.

Madame Bruist would never tolerate him going into the city at night, and if she caught him, he would be asked to leave, like the previous lodger.

'*A sin-soaked devil in human form*,' Madame Bruist had called him, repeated the insult every single day. And as the drink loosened her tongue, she said worse things about the poor man. Her colourful oaths surprised him. He hadn't expected respectable matrons to know bad words like gutter snatch and cocksucker. But she hadn't always been old, so maybe Madame Bruist knew a thing or two about life.

He glanced at her wedding photograph, which jostled for attention with the other paintings that hung from the picture rail around the room. She'd once been an attractive woman with a pleasant smile, standing respectfully behind her seated husband, her hand resting on his shoulder. She never mentioned Monsieur Bruist, and Steffan wasn't foolish enough to ask about him.

She'd almost caught him coming home in the early hours last week, but seemed satisfied with his explanation, that he'd heard a noise outside. From then on, he made sure she'd had at least a bottle and a half of wine before he settled her down by the fire.

By the time he slipped out of the house to *gad about down by the Seine with the whores and the sailors,* Madame Bruist was in a drink-addled coma.

On the farm, Grand-père raged at everything that smacked of fun – socialising, dancing, drinking, and gambling – a puritan through and through. Paris, or any town for that matter, was the Devil's city, founded on the ways of Babylon. According to Grand-père, no good ever came to anyone who lived in a city.

Steffan didn't believe Madame Bruist or Grand-père. Nothing

in the dazzling streets and sparkling parks had ever harmed him. He intended to make up for those lost years on the farm and experience all Paris had to offer. In the cafés and restaurants, light sparkled from glasses raised to ruby lips and from the jewels around ladies' throats. The tinkle and clatter of cutlery against porcelain was as overpowering as the liquor, even from outside. He could stand for hours leaning against the railings of the river watching Paris's inhabitants' promenade by – women and men dressed in clothes so fine they would have cost two years of his wages. The latest motor vehicles chugged past, their occupants honking the horn at people they knew.

He'd follow couples walking arm in arm until they strolled into the expensive arcades with their mirrored walls and gilt vaulted ceilings rising to cathedral heights, where he, with his workman's boots and rough wool coat, hadn't been welcome – until Father had insisted on him having a suit.

He shut the front door quietly and walked to the tram line which would take him across the Seine to the 6th Arrondissement to Place Saint Michel. Montmartre was closer, but he didn't enjoy drinking with men who hunted in packs, and he loathed the undercurrent of violence and lust that rippled throughout the district. He preferred the company of scholars from the Latin Quarter, and workers who loved to debate and sing, sometimes at the same time.

He was lucky to catch a tram straight away and sat next to a man whose mud-splattered trousers and threadbare jacket told his life story more than the calluses on his hands. Steffan hoped none of the mud would rub off onto his own trousers.

'All young men must have a good suit,' Father had said when Steffan first arrived in Paris.

He'd sent Steffan to his tailor.

When he picked the suit up the following week after work, the mirror had reflected a man transformed. Gone was the farm boy, and in his place was a young Parisian. The tailor had even made him a new hat that sat well on his head, hiding the fact that he needed a haircut, and bringing out the green of his eyes. He heard Grand-mère's voice saying, 'Such pretty eyes are wasted on a boy.'

The tailor had insisted he have a wash and wear it home, where even Madame Bruist complimented him, in her own way. 'Come up in the world now, haven't we? You'll be forgetting your people soon. I'll have to put up the rent for such a grand gentleman.'

Steffan would never *forget his own people*, and his life with Grand-mère, Grand-père and his sister Liselle. But he was here in Paris now, and intended to shrug himself into this new life, just like he'd put on his new suit.

Steffan alighted from the tram beside Fontaine Saint-Michel, where flocks of tourists were tossing coins into the water. Students, fortified with drink, timed each other climbing up the columns to kiss Archangel Michael's bronze cheeks and wish him luck for his eternal battle with the Devil.

In line of sight of the fountain was Steffan's favourite café, named after its owner, *Claude's*. The red canopy and red checked table clothes gave him a warm feeling of belonging. He preferred to sit outside to watch the trams rattling by and the automobiles circling the ring road around the fountain, like owls searching for mice in a field. The pavement was thick with strolling couples, and streetlights were reflected like stars in the visible sliver of the Seine.

Claude's interior walls were dark mahogany and covered with autographed serviettes and photographs of famous artists who'd visited the café. Down one side of the room were booths occupied by regulars from the neighbourhood. Steffan hoped one day he'd be considered a local and worthy of a seat in a booth.

Claude, stocky and balding with a beet red face, spent half the night playing the piano accordion accompanied by his son Leon, who had a voice that God himself would have envied.

Claude spent the other half working his way around the tables telling jokes and collecting patrons' life stories. Instantly likeable and charming, Claude remembered everyone's names and bellowed out especially loud greetings to Steffan, claiming he was his favourite. Although everyone seemed to be Claude's favourite.

Steffan wondered whether this special attention had something to do with Claude wishing to marry off his less-than-attractive daughter, Margot. Acne scars marred her wide, moon-shaped face, accentuated by her hairstyle of two plaits crossed over her head. As she lumbered past their tables, patrons held onto their dinners and drinks as her oversized derrière occasionally swept up plates and glasses in its wake.

'We'll find a spot for you inside soon,' Margot simpered, after she'd taken Steffan's order for a beer.

He couldn't stop looking at a blob of beef bourguignon Margot had spilled on her bosom. It wobbled as she spoke.

'I've never seen you here with a girl. A sharp-looking man like you should have a sweetheart,' she said, in an attempt at flirting.

'My sweetheart's back home. Her name's Rosalee and I'm going to call for her once I've made my way.' Hopefully the fictional Rosalee would scythe through any ideas Margot might have about him bestowing sweetheart status on her.

The sickly smile vanished from Margot's moon face. 'That's real nice for you. I haven't got a sweetheart yet, but Papa says it won't be long before the boys line up to take me out because I'm a real catch.'

Well, her father had to say that. The girl didn't have a lot going for her.

Margot hovered around his table for another minute, and when Steffan showed no inclination to abandon Rosalee for her, she gave up and went to get his drink.

Margot returned with his beer and looked ready to settle in

for a long night attempting to wear him down. Two men sat down at the table behind him, and Margot appeared miffed that they were interfering with her plans for Steffan. She tossed a menu at them so she didn't have to leave his side.

'I assure you, Mademoiselle, that we are just as witty and handsome as the young Monsieur you only have eyes for,' said a voice he recognised.

Steffan turned to see Daniel, the good-natured ivory carver from Blum Foundry, grinning at him.

'Not quite as witty or handsome as me, I'm afraid, Daniel,' he laughed. 'May I buy you a drink to make up for your lack of good fortune?'

'Only if you join us.' Daniel pulled out the empty third chair. People commented on Steffan's height, but Daniel, with his curly mop of hair, stood a good hand's width above him.

When Steffan had settled himself at their table, Daniel turned to his companion. 'This is my friend Ashlam Roan; Ashlam, meet Steffan Blum.' Cleary Jewish, Ashlam was smaller and darker than Daniel and would have fitted in nicely with the Blum family.

'What do you want to drink?' Margot was unimpressed that Steffan had joined them. She sighed and swayed from side to side as Daniel ordered a beer and Ashlam a Kir Royale, then ambled off to fetch their drinks.

'Steffan's father is Le Directeur at the Blum Foundry,' Daniel told Ashlam.

His emphasis on *Directeur* unsettled Steffan, but even more unnerving was how he didn't break eye contact with Ashlam. Daniel seemed to want his friend's approval.

Ashlam nodded and sized Steffan up for authenticity and value, rather like a potential buyer of one of the bronze figurines in the Blum Galerie.

'What does my father have to do with anything?' Steffan didn't know whether to be insulted or intrigued.

'Don't get me wrong, Le Directeur is a kind and fair man – for a petit bourgeois,' Daniel assured him.

Steffan had heard that phrase before and wasn't sure what it meant – some sort of slur communists made about anyone who had a bit of money?

'My father is not a wealthy man, and the Blum family live modestly,' said Steffan, feeling compelled to defend his father.

'The Blum family? You speak as though you are not part of them.' Ashlam appeared truly curious.

Daniel must have known his background, and since Ashlam was Jewish too, Steffan decided to speak freely. 'I am the oldest son, but my mother's family claimed me and my sister when our mother died. They didn't want their grandchildren growing up as Jews.'

Ashlam raised an eyebrow and Daniel watched Ashlam intently.

'My mother's family is Gentile,' Steffan added.

'Ah,' the other men said in unison.

'It makes sense now, all that bad blood between you and Phillippe,' Daniel said, finally looking at him.

'No bad blood from me. Just from him. He grew up thinking he's the eldest son. From what I understand, my father didn't prepare him for the possibility that either myself or my sister might return.'

'A not uncommon story. Hard for him to be usurped.' Ashlam took a long drag on his pipe.

Daniel shook his head. 'It doesn't give him the right to treat you like *merde*. It must upset you, some of the things he does.'

'It's more important that my father and stepmother accept me. My sisters are darlings too. That all makes up for it.' Steffan shrugged and hoped they might stop talking about this soon.

'Phillippe's a complete arse. His main purpose in life appears to be making trouble for Steffan. It's all very trying, especially when Phillippe acts like he's a cut above everyone else. Petit bourgeois through and through. We'll take him out for you, Steffan, when the revolution comes.'

Steffan laughed, but Daniel didn't join in. Perhaps he wasn't joking.

'No need. I can fight my own skirmishes,' he said, just in case Daniel was in earnest.

Ashlam finished his drink and called Margot over. She ignored him, having transferred her attention to another table.

Margot's brother Leon frowned at her and nudged her on his way to their table. Steffan heard him say, 'Keep up with your tables and stop mooning about.'

Margot shrugged and made a great show of pointing out items on the menu, even though the two men weren't interested in food.

After Ashlam ordered them another round of drinks, something unspoken passed between him and Daniel. Suddenly, Steffan was unsure about these two men. Something was going on that he didn't understand.

'I'd class you as a proletariat,' Daniel said to Steffan, but he was entirely focused on Ashlam, waiting for his reaction.

Leon arrived with their drinks, breaking the tension.

'Of course, he's a member of the proletariat.' Ashlam raised his glass and encouraged them to raise theirs.

'Should we ask him to join us, then?' Daniel had visibly relaxed.

'Do you wish to join us tomorrow night?' Ashlam asked Steffan.

'I'd like to know where you are going, before I agree to anything.'

'We're attending a meeting led by Monsieur Potiev,' Ashlam replied.

Steffan shook his head. 'I don't know who that is.'

'Monsieur Potiev is France's leading communist thinker. We're fortunate he's addressing our chapter.'

'Chapter?' Steffan didn't know what he meant.

'The artisans' chapter of the Communist Party, of course.'

'You are communists?' Steffan blurted out before he could stop himself.

Daniel laughed. 'Don't be so surprised, Steffan. Most of the carvers at Blum's are too.'

Grand-père used to rave about the bloodthirsty Bolsheviks who'd slaughtered their aunts and uncles. Steffan had always pictured communists with rifles slung over their red wool military coats, ready to skewer babies on their sabres as they galloped across the Russian tundra.

Good-natured Daniel would never skewer babies, or wear a rifle slung across his shoulder, yet he was a communist. As was Ashlam, who he could picture galloping across the tundra on a Siberian pony.

'Won't a lecture be boring?' Steffan asked to cover his discomfort.

'On the contrary; I have always found them interesting, as I am sure you will too,' Ashlam said.

What was the worst that could happen? He might get a little bit more sleep if it was boring, or he might learn something.

'I will come with you on your open-minded adventure.' Steffan raised his beer to Daniel's, and Ashlam's Kir Royale. The three clinked glasses.

'A toast to open minds.' Ashlam drank his Kir Royale in one gulp.

FOUR

Yvette
———

Yvette got up for the third time that night to empty the bucket catching the leak in the cottage roof. Papa's off-limits chest caught her attention. She was so tired she could have slept for two days straight, but there didn't seem much point going back to bed when she'd be up in twenty minutes to empty the bucket again. She might as well see what was inside the chest, and whether there was anything worth selling. She pulled the curtain across to screen their bed from the living area, so the lamp light wouldn't wake Janie.

When she reached under Papa's bed to haul out the chest, she almost expected his ghost to materialise and shriek at her to leave it alone. During his last couple of months, he'd become so secretive, checking and rechecking its position under his bed to convince himself no one had touched it.

After Mama died, he'd taken down every picture and photograph of her, as if he could hide from his grief by erasing her. Yvette had been so angry with Papa that she'd taken them out of his precious box and put them back on the mantel. When

28

Papa had seen them there, he'd slapped her so hard she had a bruise on her face for a week.

'Never touch my chest!' he'd screamed at her as he threw the pictures back inside his precious box.

She hadn't, until tonight. She'd open the chest because she wanted to – and because she could.

When Mama was alive, and Papa wasn't home, she'd run her hands over the rough iron chest, drawing circles with her finger over every one of the seventy-five metal studs that attached the outer metal lid to its inner wooden frame. Papa had refused to talk about the chest, but Mama told them he'd acquired it during the war. Mama sometimes opened the lid and insisted they take deep breaths of the scented air infused by the fragrant wood that lined the chest.

'You're taking a trip somewhere else when you breathe this air from far away,' she told them.

Yvette heaved the heavy chest onto the table and struggled with the clasps to see what else Papa had kept from them all these years. She forced open the lid and inhaled deeply, coughing and sneezing as the mildew spores hit her sinuses. Not a hint of fragrant wood was left.

Sitting in the removable top compartment was a flat red case. She opened it to find Papa's Croix de Guerre nestled on faded blue satin. She stroked the green ribbon, shot through with red, and enjoyed the textured weave on the whorls of her fingers.

Would it be wrong to sell the medal?

They needed to raise fifty francs in less than a week. She didn't have time to be sentimental, or earn it, not even if she took in twice the amount of washing, worked extra hours serving at the tavern, and took all the money Janie earnt as Madame Sorve's domestic. Then there would be next month's rent, and the month after that, along with helping Lila and baby Joseph. No charity for her and Janie – Papa had seen to that. And no charity for Lila. Patrick Aubert would not acknowledge baby

Joseph as his child. It seemed so unfair that the village shamed Lila when they should be shaming the old goat for forcing himself on her and getting her pregnant.

Yvette placed the medal to her left and started a *to be sold* pile.

She removed the chest's top compartment, revealing the binoculars Papa had used, more infrequently over the years, to bird watch. Yvette had never been allowed to touch them. She pulled the binoculars from their case and fiddled with the lens barrel until the table came into focus. She looked around the room and laughed as the door handle filled the lenses, bulging and round like a beetle.

They were battered but at least they worked. She put the binoculars back in their case and lay them next to the medal box.

Other items new to her were a silver teapot and serving tray, a pair of silver sugar tongs and a set of forks. The forks had swans engraved on the handles. She checked them all and could make out through the tarnish that all the pieces had the same emblem. Did her father acquire these in the war? Perhaps Monsieur Rhodes would know. They went onto the *to be sold* pile too.

The three pictures of her mother were next, and she placed them back on the mantel. Next, she unwrapped the cheesecloth that covered a picture frame and gasped as she turned it over. Her mother at the same age as her, standing straight and corseted in a ruffled blouse with a parasol in one hand and a metal sculpture of a scantily clad woman in the other.

Her younger mother wore her dark hair swept into a knot on the top of her head. Her skirt skimmed the top of her shoes, and she stood proud and full of anticipation of her life to come.

Yvette held the picture closer and scanned the image for any more information about the sculpture. Yvette had never seen anything like that in their home, or in anyone else's. Perhaps it was hidden in the box. She rummaged through the rest of the contents and groaned when she didn't find it, wishing she'd asked more questions about Mama's earlier life.

One thing she did recognise was the expression on Mama's face. The same determined countenance looked back at her every day from the damp-spotted mirror.

Why couldn't Papa have kept this photograph out for them to see? Why was his grief more important than theirs? She was their mother, not just his wife.

Yvette kissed the picture and put it on the other side of the table, the *keep* side.

At the bottom of the chest, she found a bundle of letters. Some were from her mother and father to each other – written during the times he went away for work. She opened one from her mother.

My darling,

I have missed you so much and can't wait for your return next month. Every day without you is an agony, and I know you must be away, but my heart is breaking that we are apart. I love you ...

She stopped reading, feeling as if she were overhearing intimacies between a couple that weren't her parents. The handwriting was her mother's, but the loving words written on the page were not something she'd ever heard her say to Papa.

She put the letter back into the bundle and placed it beside Mama's picture.

Apart from some carved animals, possibly made by Papa during the war, the only other interesting thing was a letter from Cousin Daniel. And this was what she'd really been searching for when she opened the chest.

She turned the envelope over and couldn't help smiling at the improbable address, *Rue de Paradis*. She didn't need to read the letter, as she'd memorised every word three years ago. Paris fizzed off the pages. He'd been on a riverboat that berthed near the cathedral of Notre-Dame, where he'd lit a candle for his family. He'd climbed the Eiffel Tower's 1665 steps to stand on top of Paris. He'd found a job at a foundry as an apprentice carver. Madame Blum made soup and bread for their lunch, along with cakes and biscuits for morning and afternoon tea. They drank real coffee.

They hadn't received another letter from him. Daniel might have moved on. Madame Blum might not know where he worked now. She could write to him and ask if he could help them to set up in Paris.

If she sold the medal, binoculars, and the silver, she might reach fifty francs. But she needed more money, and there was only one thing left to sell.

She grabbed the carving knife out of the kitchen drawer, prised open the loose floorboard under Papa's bed and pulled out a triangular object wrapped in oilskin. Papa's ruby pistol might be worth forty francs. It was risky selling it, but Papa was buried now, and no one was looking for the pistol. They'd all assumed it fell into the river with him when he shot himself.

Monsieur Rhodes could tell her how much she could get for each item. She'd sell them in La Montagne and no one in the village would need to know.

She wrapped her fingers around the pistol's hand grip and felt the weight of it in her hand as she pointed the gun at the photograph of Papa in his army uniform. She placed the pistol with the other items in the *to-be-sold* pile.

If she heard from Daniel and he agreed to help, they could buy train tickets from Montagne to Paris and leave before their next month's rent was due.

She put everything back in the chest, apart from her mother's photograph which she left on the table. She emptied the bucket and blew out the lamp. The raindrops joined together into a constant stream. Yvette had another ten minutes before she'd have to empty it again. She snuggled into Janie and pulled the covers close.

Janie's giggle carried across the garden. Yvette looked out the window to see the old goat Patrick leaning on their fence talking to her. As she continued to giggle, Janie moved towards him. Whatever she said must have been funny because he'd laughed and tucked an unruly lock of Janie's hair behind her ear.

Every nerve in Yvette's body jangled. The old goat had touched her thirteen-year-old sister. Even worse, the girl had enjoyed the attention and flirted back.

'Janie!' she shouted. Her voice sounded shrill.

Janie shot her a defiant look. 'What?' she asked, making it clear Yvette had interrupted her.

'You need to get to work.' Even to her it sounded lame.

'Shall we go?' Janie asked the old goat.

Yvette's knees just about gave way. Her sister was falling for the old goat's tricks.

'You've forgotten your raincoat,' she called after Janie, hoping to stop her.

'You know it doesn't fit,' Janie shouted, without even looking back.

Helplessly, she watched them walk around the corner out of sight. Yvette would not let him have her little sister. But she couldn't be with her all the time to protect her. They worked at different times and places. And the old goat, like his hands, seemed to be everywhere.

They would have to leave. They couldn't stay here. Janie had caught his attention and Janie liked it. Yvette would never let him near Janie. Never. They only had one option and that was joining Daniel in Paris.

FIVE

Steffan

____

Paris, August 1933

Steffan revved the Bierlet's engine and pressed the horn. Its bellow echoed from the buildings lining the narrow street but had no effect on the cart driver blocking the road. Only the horses responded, turning their heads to stare at him. The carter ignored him and continued lifting full sacks from the cart, carrying them into the storehouse. Steffan considered yelling at him to move the cart, or getting out and leading the horses to the side of the road to leave room for him to get past. The carter was older than him but about twice his size, and strong. Whatever he did, the carter would not take kindly to his interference. Country folk were like that, stuck in their ways.

Steffan smiled. A year ago, he would have been the carter moving sacks of grain with Grand-père. Here he was trusted to drive this nearly new truck that was twenty times more powerful than a team of horses.

He could back up the truck and go around the block, but the foundry was only 100 metres down the road. Instead, he got out of the cab.

'I'll give you a hand,' he said to the carter.

The carter mumbled his thanks.

The sack's rough exterior grazed Steffan's face as he hoisted it onto his shoulder. It was like a caress reaching out from his previous life. The weight of the sack and the tart aroma of barley filled him with longing for Grand-père and the years they'd worked side by side sowing, tending, and harvesting the crops.

By the time the carter took his seat behind the horses, Steffan had helped him move another twenty sacks.

He climbed into the truck, his back and shoulder muscles hot and burning from the exertion. He smoked a cigarette while he waited for the cart to move further down the road.

The thrill of driving the Bierlet truck through the Blum Foundry's archway never got old for Steffan. He loved how the courtyard captured the engine noise; how it echoed back at him when he put his head out of the cab to back into the loading bay. He never failed to complete a perfect manoeuvre, unlike Phillippe, who Le Directeur had banned from driving.

Le Directeur – Father. He was still getting used to that, along with his half-brother Phillippe. With their father in common, it was surprising they didn't look more alike. Phillippe had a Jewish, aquiline nose and was shorter in stature than Steffan. Phillippe's hair was dark and wiry, all over his body, while Steffan's took after his mother's family, his hair being finer, and lighter in colour.

Phillippe reminded him of a stunted male pheasant which lived in their lower field. The bird made up for its lack of size by being scrappy, loud, and harassing all the other males. It had worked for the pheasant, but Steffan wasn't so sure it worked for Phillippe.

The Bierlet's headlight and right mudguard had just been repaired because Philippe miscalculated the turn into the entranceway and damaged an arch stone. Father had to get the stonemason in to mend the entire foundry archway.

Steffan drove towards the courtyard's left wall and stopped when the lunchroom door lined up with the right edge of his windscreen. He heaved on the steering wheel until it could go no further to the right, then moved the gear stick into reverse. The Bierlet shuddered into the loading bay perfectly aligned, so he could open the cab door and step out onto the platform.

'Not bad, new boy.' Controleur Kubreck stretched up to clap him on the shoulder. The diminutive man was never without his blue worker's cap, and matching overalls he managed to keep pristine throughout the day.

Steffan forced himself not to smile, as Philippe was standing with the other men behind the truck waiting to offload the freight.

'Not bad for a mischlinge.' Phillippe tried to make it sound like a joke. He looked at the other men to rally support and got a couple of half-hearted responses.

Steffan could tell Controleur Kubreck wasn't happy with Phillipe and was grateful he said nothing to him. No need for Phillippe to have more reason to resent him.

With a flurry of hand gestures, Controleur Kubreck organised the men into teams to offload the truck's freight. Naturally Steffan and Phillippe were paired up and allocated the job of carrying the copper lengths. Phillipe ignored Steffan and stalked to the end of the truck so he would lead the way into the foundry. Steffan kept his expression neutral and moved to the other end of the copper bar. Controleur Kubreck held up two fingers, but Phillippe countered him by holding up three.

Controleur Kubreck glanced at Steffan.

Steffan nodded. He could lift three, but Phillippe would struggle. Controleur Kubreck must have thought this too because he held up two fingers. Phillippe stiffened but didn't challenge Controleur Kubreck. Much to Steffan's relief, Phillippe nodded.

On Philippe's count of three they lifted two copper lengths

and shuffled their way to the storage racks. The strain showed on Phillippe's face as they lifted the lengths into the rack.

'Let's just take them as singles,' Steffan suggested as they took a breather.

'I am no weakling, Michlinge,' Phillippe hissed at him. His red face and laboured breathing betrayed him.

Anger sparked inside Steffan; he was fed up with how Phillippe always had to compete with him. 'Don't call me Michlinge, Phillippe.'

'That's what you are, a Michlinge. You're a mongrel, not a full Jew.'

'And you might never have been born if my mother hadn't died. Or if you were, you would have been Michlinge too.'

'Why didn't you stay away? You've ruined everything.' Phillippe stood up and strode off to get the next load.

Steffan followed him back to the truck. Should he have stayed away? All he wanted was to know his father. He wished Phillippe could understand he wasn't a threat. He was family, his half-brother. Why was it so hard for him to understand that someone would want to find their family?

Phillippe counted to three again and they picked up the next copper lengths. Phillippe's back and arms strained against the weight and Steffan feared he might drop the load. Why was he so stubborn? He risked injuring himself for his pride. Phillippe wasn't losing anything. Steffan wanted nothing more than what was rightfully his. His father. Phillippe had his mother and sisters, and his father.

Steffan had his own family: his sister Liselle and her husband Bede. With Grand-père and Grand-mère gone, they worked the farm, and he was free to go back to regain his past life; the life he'd had before his mother died. A faded memory of her flickered like a sputtering candle in a draft.

When they arrived back for their third load, Controleur

Kubreck was waiting for them with the metal cart, a long trolley on wheels.

'This will make it quicker,' Controleur Kubreck said.

Phillippe grunted and moved to pick up the next length. The final six lengths of copper were the only items left on the truck.

'Use the cart, Phillippe. We have to load the truck so Steffan can meet the train.'

Phillippe glowered at Controleur Kubreck but did as he said. They loaded the rest of the copper, one length at a time.

When the last copper length clanged into the rack, Phillippe stretched his back.

'Everything is always about you. Steffan's truck, Steffan's loads. Take the cart back yourself.'

He glared at Steffan and strode into the foundry, the furnace's red glow an angry halo around him. He'd left Steffan to take the cart back, a cart designed for two people to use.

Controleur Kubreck came over to help when he jerked the cart back into the loading bay. 'Where's he gone?'

'Back into the foundry.'

'Le Directeur needs to be told.' Controleur Kubreck shook his head.

'Please don't. It only makes it worse.'

'Le Directeur needs to know. It's not only about you, Steffan.'

What he said was true, but Steffan would suffer the consequences. Just what those would be filled him with dread.

At the end of the day as Steffan headed for the locker room, Controleur Kubreck called out to him that Le Directeur wished to see him. Steffan braced himself for whatever trouble Phillippe had stirred up and entered the foundry. A wave of noise and heat hit him, along with the harsh smell of molten metal. Oscar Blum, Le Directeur – Father – stood with his back to him, his hands on his hips.

The furnace glow cast Father's shadow on the wall beyond and it danced and twisted as he called out instructions to four men attempting to join two parts of a plaster mould for a life-size bronze sculpture of a bear. Even his shadow betrayed his frustration.

When the workers had lined up the moulds, Steffan touched him on the arm. Le Directeur started at his touch and turned to look at him. Steffan regretted surprising him, but Father would have never heard him call out with this amount of noise.

The weighted lines of concentration and focus lifted from Father's face, and he smiled. For an instant, Steffan felt seared by belonging as Father seemed genuinely pleased to see him. Steffan often observed his father, to note their similarities and differences. He hadn't inherited his father's stature, and hopefully not his baldness. They did share green eyes and a mouth that seemed to be about to smile. Their hands were similar too, with long slender fingers and small palms. It made them both good carvers.

'I wanted to catch you before you go home.' Father put a hand on his shoulder.

Steffan braced for the *Philippe talk.*

'Bring your suit to work tomorrow. I want you to join us for a special supper for Rosie's birthday. Martje's arranged a surprise too.' Father leant towards him.

Steffan nearly sighed in relief that it wasn't about Phillippe, and almost missed his cue to reply. 'What's the surprise?'

'A trip up the Eiffel Tower AND a boat ride on the Seine.'

'She will love that.'

Rosie talked of nothing else but the Eiffel Tower.

'She will. Drop your suit off at the house before work.' Father waved him on and turned his attention back to the bear mould.

It didn't matter what Phillippe did, Father wanted him to be part of the family, so he would be. He didn't need Philippe to like him or even tolerate him, as long as he had his Father's approval, and that of his half-sisters, and stepmother.

Steffan spent the three long blocks walking back to Madame Bruist's planning what gift he'd give Rosie. He decided on a box of her favourite bonbons, only found in a little shop down by the Seine. Fortunately, the shop stayed open until late.

He'd have to start Madame Bruist drinking earlier this evening so he could get to the shop before it closed, then meet Daniel and Ashlam for the open-minded adventure.

SIX

Yvette

____

Yvette's shoulders relaxed as she walked the river pathway with her basket of food for Lila and baby Joseph. Usually, she relished in the privacy the trees offered her from the village and their prying and judging ways. Today her stomach churned as she practised what she'd say to Lila.

We're leaving, but we'll send you money. Too blunt.

It's not that I don't care about you, but he's noticed Janie. Too dismissive.

It's about giving Janie a future. I don't want her or me to end up like you. Too real.

She stopped to watch the bees moving unconcerned between the wildflowers and weeds on the riverbank. She wished she could be like the bees. Accept her life here in the village, keep working and moving between her little jobs and home, and store up honey for the winter.

Except she and her sister would never get the villagers' acceptance, no matter how she tried to continue the rhythm of their lives. Now Patrick's attentions were firmly on Janie, their only option was to leave, the sooner the better. It all made sense, but a flood of what ifs threatened to overwhelm her every time she imagined them stepping off the train in Paris.

Telling Lila kept it manageable. Just a little step towards the plan. She could be honest because she wasn't sure if Lila really appreciated what they did for her. Yvette came up here every week with food for them and found money to help Lila.

The basket swung faster, keeping tempo with her rising irritation and quickening speed.

Joseph's high-pitched cries greeted her as she left the lane and walked along the fence line to Lila's. Her home – a hovel, really – was little more than an animal shelter. When she visited, Yvette always thought of Joseph like baby Jesus in his manger. The old goat Patrick allowed Lila to live here when she couldn't afford the cottage rent any more.

Yvette shuddered as she imagined Janie in this lonely place, saddled with a screaming baby.

Lila's roof must leak more than theirs; she'd offer to help Lila thatch it before they left.

'Lila, it's me,' she called out, pulling the door open.

As her eyes adjusted to the smoky gloom, she located baby Joseph lying on the dirt floor, his bare arms bouncing up and down with each scream. Lila lay unmoving on what did for a bed, covered by a thin woollen blanket that Yvette recognised from her cousin's family home.

Yvette scooped up the baby and he stopped mid-screech, surprised into silence.

'What's Joseph doing on the ground? He's freezing,' she yelled at Lila.

She rummaged in her food basket and pressed a bread crust into the baby's grubby hand. He stuffed it into his mouth, and she rubbed his cold limbs.

'What on earth, Lila? Are you trying to kill him?'

Lila didn't answer. Yvette prodded her with her foot, and she didn't move.

'Don't play tricks with me.'

Yvette's anger evaporated as she understood her cousin couldn't respond. Yvette shook Lila's shoulder, and a small moan escaped her lips. Thankfully she wasn't dead, just unconscious.

Yvette looked around the tiny room and found a damp blanket to wrap around the baby. His cradle had disappeared, along with the chairs. She'd been so consumed with their problems she hadn't seen Lila in a week. There'd been four chairs then, and a cradle.

'Lila.' Yvette shook her, and she responded with a coughing fit. She poured some water from a jug on the table into a dirty cup.

'Sit up and drink this.' She pushed Lila up and rubbed her back until she stopped coughing and could take some sips. 'How long have you been like this? And where are the chairs?'

Stupid, asking about the chairs. She knew what had happened to the chairs. In this state, Lila couldn't gather wood.

It was a disgrace, Patrick expecting Lila to live in this hovel. It was a disgrace how Patrick treated her. It was a disgrace he wouldn't acknowledge Joseph as his own.

Out of breath, Lila slipped back onto the bed, too ill to remain sitting even with Yvette supporting her.

'I'm here now. We'll get something into you both and before you know it, you'll get your strength back,' Yvette said with more confidence than she felt. She stood up and took in the cold room. The fire was almost out, and there was nothing to burn. Lila would likely die if she stayed here, and what would become of Joseph?

Yvette found a cooking pot with remnants of mouldy oatmeal glued to its surface. She washed it outside in the stream, scouring it out with some leaves. She collected some fallen tree branches and dragged them back to the hovel to break them up with the axe that lay beside the chopping block.

Lila and Joseph's last hot meal must have been the one Yvette made them last week. Lila should still be breastfeeding the baby, but she figured her milk would have run dry.

She stoked up the fire and once it was burning, filled the pot with water and hung it over the flames. She had intended to make Lila an omelette with a salad, but she decided it would be easier to boil the eggs. Joseph could hold onto an egg, and they could keep them to eat later.

Joseph began to cry, and Yvette broke him off another chunk of bread. He grabbed it and his cries ceased as he stuffed it into his mouth.

'I've put the food I've brought on the table,' Yvette told Lila, more to fill the silence and stifle her mounting dread.

How long had Joseph been on that floor? Lila could not even sit up, let alone prepare food.

The water in the pot began to boil and she eased the eggs in, so they didn't crack.

First, she would feed them, and while she was doing that, work out what to do next.

Lila's illness would delay or stop their leaving. And what to do with baby Joseph while Lila was ill, and what if she died?

She scooped Joseph up again and sat outside in the sun while she waited for the eggs to boil. He could sit on his own now, and apart from being dirty, appeared to be healthy.

Her mind bubbled like the water boiling in the pot. She needed to calm down and think things through.

Lila couldn't look after herself, either. So, she had to be looked after, either here, or Yvette would need to bring her home. Was that the best thing to do? Take Joseph with her and come back for Lila? She could borrow Monsieur Rhodes' handcart. And then what?

Would she just be moving Lila to another place before she died? Or would some good food and medicine make her better?

Lila could make them all sick too, so it might be better if she looked after her here.

Joseph couldn't stay here with Lila. He'd have to come home with her until Lila recovered enough to look after him. The baby could still fit into the bottom drawer of their cabinet, which they could use as his cot.

Yvette pictured their francs spilling through her fingers as they paid for Lila's medicine and nursed baby Joseph. Damn Lila, her illness had put their leaving plans in jeopardy. What could she do, though? Lila was family, and Yvette had to help. But it wasn't fair that all this fell on her and Janie.

Where was Patrick? Whether he liked it or not, he'd fathered Joseph and should pay for his care. How horrible of him to expect Lila to live in this hovel and die here like a worn-out donkey.

After she'd sorted Lila and Joseph, Patrick would be getting a visit, and Yvette would tell him exactly what she thought of the situation.

Yvette encouraged Lila to eat two eggs and some bread, and she seemed to gain some strength. Yvette helped her outside to sit on the chopping block.

'The sun will be good for you.' Yvette tucked the blanket from the bed around Lila's legs. Like Lila, it smelt of sweat and sick. The straw mattress on the bed reeked too.

'I'm taking Joseph home with me and I'll bring the doctor back with me. I'll bring fresh straw and a fresh cover from home when I return.

Lila finally spoke. 'I can't pay the doctor.'

'I will pay him.'

'With what?' Yvette took it as a positive sign that Lila's usual stubbornness had flared up.

'I'm selling some things after Papa...' She hesitated, debating whether to say 'died' or 'killed himself'. This was Lila, after all.

'Another selfish man,' Lila murmured, but she didn't resist further.

'Has *your* selfish man been to see you? Does he know you are so sick?'

Lila said nothing, and for Yvette that was answer enough.

'Lila, I need to tell you something, but you can't tell anyone else.'

For the first time that day, Lila looked up and met her gaze. Her cousin seemed to have aged twenty years in the week since she'd last seen her, and the defeat hollowed out her voice when she answered, 'Who would I tell?'

The village would suck Yvette's and Janie's youth away too, which made it easier to say what she'd come to tell her. 'Janie and I are going to leave for Paris, to follow Daniel. You can move into our cottage and have our chickens and anything else you want from our place.'

'I am glad for you and Janie. Thank you for thinking of us,' Lila said, without any emotion.

Yvette supposed she couldn't feel anything, considering the state she was in.

'I don't want to leave you here. Once we are settled, we can send for you and baby Joseph.'

The offer didn't stop the guilt writhing around in her chest. For all she knew, she had just promised something impossible.

'It will be an easier winter for you with our chickens, and everything's ripening in the garden. We can cut plenty of wood before we go.' She talked because the silence was too awful.

Lila shrugged, clearly too tired to care.

'You are good to me, cousin,' she finally said, and gazed at Joseph when Yvette picked him up.

'I'm taking Joseph with me, and I'm bringing the doctor back to see you.'

'I can't afford to pay him.'

'Don't worry about that.' Yvette tried not to let it show how much she *was* worrying about that.

After taking baby Joseph home, Yvette made a bed for him from the bottom drawer of their sideboard. She padded it with a crocheted blanket, and covered the clean, fed, and sleepy baby with Papa's old cardigan. She picked up the makeshift cradle and took Joseph next door to her neighbour, Monsieur Rhodes.

Although his cottage was bigger than theirs, it seemed smaller because of all the clutter. Monsieur Rhodes, nearly eighty years old, fiercely independent and bent over like a question mark, liked everything close at hand. The only clear trail was a loop that ran through his piles of possessions from the door to the wood box, to the stove, to his seat at the table, from the table to the bedroom, and a clear run to his bed.

She knocked before opening the door, and found him sitting by his stove stirring porridge, one gnarled, arthritic hand gripping the wooden spoon, the other stabilising the pot. Today he wore the blue jersey he'd started wearing instead of his favourite brown cardigan, as the buttons must be too hard for him to manage.

Yvette ached to help him dish out the porridge into the waiting bowl. When she'd offered before, he'd refused, and things had become frosty between them. She didn't want that to happen again, so if she came in when he was struggling with his breakfast ritual, she usually left and came back later. Today, she wasn't going anywhere.

'Could I leave baby Joseph with you this morning while I get the doctor for Lila? He'll be no trouble. He's going down for his nap, so he'll just sleep.'

Monsieur Rhodes gripped the pot handle with his damaged

hands, pivoted on his seat and the pot landed in the centre of a wooden board on the table, just as he'd intended.

'I'd be delighted to have his company. We can take our morning naps together.'

'I'll pop him over here where he's out of the way.' She wedged the drawer between the coal bucket and the wood pile.

'I promise I won't mistake him for a piece of kindling.'

He tilted the porridge pot towards a waiting bowl and a reasonable portion slid its way across.

'I have to sell some of our things to pay Aubert our back rent. I was hoping you could tell me what they're worth.'

'Gladly ma chérie. We want you to get the best price possible if the money's going to that pile of *merde*.'

'I'll go and get them.' She hopped over the hedge and returned with her basket of *for-sale* items.

Yvette took each one out – the pistol, the medal, the binoculars, and the silver – and lined them up on the table, an odd assortment that summarised her father's life. Perhaps she should have put them in chronological order. Before she had a chance to rearrange them, Monsieur Rhodes nodded at the pistol.

'He kept it in good condition. You should be able to get forty francs for that. Are you sure you want it out in circulation, seeing as he used it on himself?'

'I found it on the riverbank.' Yvette spluttered out her answer. She studied him for any sign he might suspect she had something to do with his death.

'Leave it here while you sort out Lila, and I'll give it a good clean.'

'Thank you, I will. What about the other items?'

The medal's only good for scrap metal, maybe you'd get a franc.' He nodded to the binoculars. 'Do they focus properly?'

'Yes,' Yvette said, almost giggling as she remembered the doorknob that had turned into a beetle.

'You should get fifty francs for them.'

Monsieur Rhodes went back to concentrating on getting more porridge into the bowl.

'What about the silver?' Yvette figured ten pieces must be worth a bit.

He barely glanced at it. 'Your father stole that in the war. It's traceable. You'll only be able to sell it to the scrap dealer for fifteen francs.'

Part of Yvette wanted to know how Monsieur Rhodes knew about the theft, but he knew about a lot of things. Yvette didn't want to get side-tracked today.

By his estimates the items could put 106 francs in her purse. More than enough to pay Aubert's debt, buy train tickets and cover a few weeks' board in Paris.

'Guess you want to know where to sell it now?' Monsieur Rhodes asked. He'd succeeded in getting another large dollop of porridge into the bowl.

'Yes please.'

'Ask for Anoud Tremben at Les Metaux in La Montagne. Tell him I sent you.'

'Thank you, Monsieur Rhodes.' She was in tears as she packed up the items.

'Everything will work out, ma chérie.'

His damaged hand found its way on top of hers. His way to comfort her now wasn't a gentle squeeze. He couldn't do that anymore. Instead, he pressed down on her hand, and she found it soothing.

'We will have to leave.' She couldn't look at him.

He pressed down on her hand again and she looked up.

'As you are supposed to. This village is far too small for someone like you.'

He went back to his porridge.

Yvette should say something in response to his kindness, but she didn't trust herself to speak as tears welled up in her eyes.

She remembered the statue in her mother's hand and the determined expression on her face. She came from a line of women who wanted more from life, even if Mama had settled for Papa rather than her art.

She fussed about Joseph's makeshift crib until she was sure she wouldn't burst into tears.

'Thank you for letting me leave Joseph here. I should only be a couple of hours. Janie knows to come here to get him if I'm not back by the time she finishes work.'

Monsieur Rhodes puffed on his pipe. 'We will be napping.'

'That should keep you out of mischief.'

'But what will keep *you* from it? You seem very determined to complicate your life further.' He laughed.

'What can I do? Lila's family.'

'And not your responsibility.'

'She will die if I don't help her.'

He shrugged. 'It is the way of the world, ma chérie. You must learn to toughen that big heart of yours.'

Monsieur Rhodes was a fine one to talk. Here he was helping her, so who was he to criticise her for faults of a big heart?

She hurried across the village to the doctor's home, located in a wealthier area where they had running water, a flush toilet and paving right up to the front door. He answered the door himself, his shirtsleeves rolled up, with a tea towel in one hand. Had she caught him in the middle of drying the dishes? Yvette tried not to giggle at the improbable idea of the doctor's long fingers wiping crockery dry.

Everything about him was long – his face, his ears, his limbs, and his fingers. He was like a runner bean vine that had surged up its support pole after a week of rain.

'Yvette.' His clipped tone made him sound curt, although she had never found him to be that way.

'Lila is very ill. I need you to visit her with me.'

The doctor sighed. 'Lila has not paid me for the baby's birth yet.'

At the prospect of losing even more of their meagre funds, Yvette said, 'And you will not see any of it if she dies.'

His eyes narrowed.

Worried she had overstepped the mark, Yvette continued, 'I will pay for this visit and help work out payment for her debt to you.'

'This visit is one franc.' He stared at her unblinking.

Twice the usual price. She fought the urge to barter him down.

'I agree to that price,' she said, and deliberately didn't blink.

The doctor nodded his agreement. 'I'll get my medical bag.'

Yvette broke into a trot every now and again to keep up with him. She supposed he did a lot more walking around the village than she did, and his legs were way longer than hers.

He had a bicycle too, but she didn't want to break the silence between them by asking why he wasn't using it today. She felt awkward enough, considering how Papa had died, and didn't want to talk to him any more than she had to.

The doctor took charge the moment they entered Lila's dwelling. He treated Yvette as his servant. Heat more water. Hold these instruments. Get the stethoscope out of the bag. Take her other arm and walk her around the room.

Yvette considered charging him half a franc for the work he'd asked her to do.

He tapped Lila's back, listened to her lungs front and back with the stethoscope, and asked her to breathe in and cough several times.

'Good news. You do not have pneumonia. Bad news is you do have some fluid build-up in your lungs and swelling around your heart.'

Swelling around her heart sounded terrible.

'Can you make her better?' Yvette blurted out.

'There are many things we can do to make her more comfortable. It is not unreasonable to believe she will make a recovery of sorts.' The doctor didn't shift his concentration from Lila, his expression neutral, not giving away any information.

He clearly promised nothing, yet Yvette took comfort from his words. Hope still lived.

He settled Lila back into bed and asked Yvette to come outside.

'Where is the child?'

'We thought it best he stayed with us until Lila is well again. We didn't know if he could catch it, and she can't look after him.'

'It is not contagious. She has fluid on the lungs and a heart problem. Her father had it. I treated him too, and he lived a good life, although we lost him not long after he turned thirty-five.'

Yvette said nothing, knowing it would come out sounding sarcastic. Hurrah, she wouldn't die immediately, but dying at thirty-five didn't seem like a good life.

'If she continues to live in this –' He looked around, trying to find a word to describe Lila's hovel, settling on, '– place, she will not survive. She needs a warm fire, a home where the wind doesn't whistle through, and good food.'

'If she had all those things, how long before she recovered?'

'She would need a month.'

A month? They couldn't wait a month. The old goat would have got to Janie by then.

'I will make a heart tincture that will help and bring it to her later today. That will be one franc for the consultation, fifty centimes for the tincture.' He held his hand out.

'Bring it to our cottage. I will move Lila down to our place now we know she isn't contagious.' Yvette fished in her purse and pulled out the coins.

He took them and slid them into the small change pocket in his trousers. 'As you wish.' He nodded toward Yvette and called his goodbye to Lila.

Yvette returned later that day with Monsieur Rhode's handcart to take Lila back to their place.

'I am fine here.' Lila's stubborn streak made an appearance again.

'Don't be silly. You can't look after yourself. Le Docteur said you must come home with us so we can look after you.' What part of *you will die if you stay here* was she not understanding?

'I don't want to be a burden on you. You've enough going on.'

'You are family. It's no trouble.' It could affect their plans, but Yvette hoped Lila would recover enough for them to leave within the month.

Yvette helped Lila outside to sit on the chopping block and found another set of clothes in the drawer of the only other piece of furniture in the hovel. She also found two sets of Joseph's clothes that would still fit him in the other drawer. She put the clothes in a clean flour bag she'd brought with her and looked about for anything else worth bringing. Apart from some chipped crockery and the iron cooking pot, Lila had nothing else. Yvette sighed, deeply saddened by how reduced Lila's circumstances had become. She was expendable, a throw-away girl with a throw-away baby. This would be their lives too, if they stayed here and Patrick got his hands on Janie.

Yvette placed the flour sack in the bottom of the barrow and helped Lila sit on top of it. Her legs dangled out over the barrow's front edge; apart from that, she seemed comfortable and stable.

'I'll try not to tip you out.'

Lila's attempted laugh at Yvette's joke ended in a coughing fit.

'Hold on tight.' Yvette raised the barrow handles and wheeled Lila down the rutted track towards the lane. Lila's head bobbled back and forth with every judder, but she sat firm. They made it to the lane without the barrow capsizing and Yvette relaxed as the ground became more even.

'I haven't seen the river for weeks,' Lila said.

'You'll see it every day at our place.' Yvette smiled, glad her cousin appeared well enough to notice her surroundings.

Janie opened the cottage garden gate for them when they arrived.

'Here comes Princess Lila in her gilded carriage,' she said, ushering them through.

Janie's smile disappeared as Lila doubled over in another coughing fit brought on by her chuckling at the joke.

Yvette manoeuvred the barrow as close to the front door as possible and they helped Lila stand. Janie mouthed to Yvette, 'She's skin and bone.'

Lila almost fell as her trembling legs gave way. They half-carried and half-dragged her inside and sat her down in Papa's rocking chair beside the fire. Lila didn't have the strength to hold herself in the seat and would have slid out if Janie's quick reflexes hadn't kicked in to grab her.

Janie propped pillows around her and, once satisfied she wouldn't fall, beckoned Yvette outside. 'She's really bad. Do you think she's going to...?'

'Die?' Yvette finished for her. 'It's possible. She is very ill.'

'How will she look after Joseph?' Janie raised her arms.

'Is he still with Monsieur Rhodes?' Yvette felt her irritation rising. 'If Lila can't look after him, then of course it will be us.' She refrained from saying, *It will be good practice for you because you'll be exactly where Lila is in nine months if you keep carrying on with the old goat.*

'I know we will be looking after Joseph,' Janie said with a shrug.

Yvette took in her worried face and was glad she hadn't said what she'd been thinking. 'Just go and get Joseph.'

Janie vaulted over the fence into Monsieur Rhodes' garden.

'Janie. Use the gate to bring him back.'

Her sister just laughed and disappeared into their neighbour's cottage.

Yvette went back inside to check on Lila. She seemed more unconscious than asleep, which gave Yvette a chance to give her a good once over.

Lila had always been slight, but this illness had drained her of any reserves, and Janie was right, she was nothing but skin and bone. Her skin had a yellow tinge, and her dark hair hung in stringy clumps. Yvette put the kettle on to heat. A good wash and a change of clothes would make a difference. While she waited for the doctor to return with the tincture, Yvette busied herself making Lila a bit more presentable.

She looked up as Janie returned with Joseph, and her heart squeezed as the baby seemed huge in her small arms. Next year it could be Janie's baby in her arms. She had to keep going with her plan.

'Monsieur Rhodes says you need to come back for the ladder and the roof tiles. It's all in his shed.'

Yvette nodded. Another job to add to the mounting responsibilities that snuck uninvited into her life.

SEVEN

Steffan

Paris, August 1933

Daniel led the way down a side street a couple of blocks from Place Saint Michel, then turned up an alleyway where the buildings leant together above them, blocking out any chink of light. Daniel became nothing more than a shadowy figure in front of Steffan, while Ashlam shuffled behind him like an old man who could no longer lift his feet.

For a moment Steffan feared he'd been tricked into this backwater only to have Ashlam knife him in the back and Daniel rummage through his pockets for money. Something brushed his hand, and panic tightened around his chest like a barrel band. He stopped moving as the urge to turn around overcame him, and Ashlam smashed into his back. It knocked the wind out of him.

'Are you all right, Steffan?' Ashlam asked.

'Yes...' he gasped and staggered after Daniel. He held his arm out so he wouldn't run into Daniel if he suddenly decided to stop.

'We're here,' Daniel told them.

Steffan jumped when Daniel banged his fist on wood. The door opened and let out a crack of light that backlit a surly male face.

Daniel announced them, 'Comrade Foucart and Comrade Roan. We have a guest with us – Steffan Blum.'

The door opened a notch further and the surly face surveyed them as though they were possible assassins. They passed whatever assessment the doorman had made of them and he pulled the door open, indicating with a flick of his head that they should go up the stairway behind him.

They filed into the cramped entrance, Daniel leading the way up the steps. Steffan had no choice but to follow him as Ashlam and the doorman blocked the only visible exit. The stairs creaked under his weight and Steffan worried his leg might crash through the wood, leaving him stuck up to his groin in the rotting structure. To his relief, he made it up without incident and found himself in a small hall.

The dark, stained, wooden walls were lined with paintings, and on pedestals dotted around the hall were sculptures in stone and bronze. A polished circular wooden table took up most of the room with a removable segment positioned at the front of the hall like a magnet had sucked it away. It reminded Steffan of King Arthur and the Knights of the Round Table. A fitting metaphor as they were in an artisans' guildhall, about to attend a lecture from a communist.

A young man with parted and well-greased hair stood in front of the curved table segment at the front of the hall in animated discussion with two men. Something about the way he held himself, his confidence and passion, made Steffan certain that this was Monsieur Potiev. Another twenty or so men were clustered in small groups around the circular table and in the rows of benches behind. They were all talking; some seemed to be talking at, rather than to each other. There were also several young women, though it was difficult to see their faces because of the size of their hats and the shadows leaping up from the gas lamps.

'Let's go over,' Daniel said, in a tone that suggested he wasn't worthy to meet Potiev.

Ashlam led the way and Potiev greeted him with a kiss on each cheek.

'These are your comrades?'

Potiev's grip crushed Steffan's hand, but he didn't wince or show any discomfort. Daniel's fingertips turned white when Potiev grasped his hand. A silly sense of pride overcame Steffan as his friend gave no sign of how much pain he must be feeling. Ashlam avoided the handshake by moving away to greet someone else.

'I am honoured that you've come to my talk.' Potiev performed a small Germanic style bow that seemed out of character for a communist. He ushered them to a seat at the circular table, where Ashlam joined them. Steffan would have preferred to sit near the back so he could observe others in the audience. At least he had a good view of Potiev, who wore a grey wool suit of slightly superior quality to his own. He wouldn't have been surprised to learn that Potiev used the same tailor as the Blum family.

When everyone had found a seat, Potiev began. His voice was strong, and surprisingly loud for a small man. He moved comfortably as he spoke, clearly used to public speaking.

If Steffan ever had to give a speech, he was sure he'd be a bag of nerves, stumbling and stuttering over each word and too shy to make eye contact with the audience the way Potiev did.

'We common Frenchmen, and Frenchwomen, are the glue that keeps this country together. We, the workers, we the proletariat bake the bread, tend the fields, construct the buildings, and run the trams and the Métro.

'We are the makers of Paris and the rest of our country. It is we who are the means of production. It is we who are our country's wealth. We are entitled to our share.

'It's time to end the Bourgeoisie tyranny and terminate their lazy and greedy ways. They exploit us for our labour and rob us and our comrades of our equality and the basic means of living.

'When was the last time you walked down Montparnasse, filled with its brothels, drunkenness and degradation? Our comrades are forced to live in squalor. What did we fight for in the revolution? Is that what our grandfathers and grandmothers sacrificed themselves for?'

All around him were grunts and exclamations of agreement. Steffan's head reeled with ideas so foreign, yet Potiev's arguments made sense.

'The bourgeoisie holds France back by keeping the wealth to themselves, just like the aristocracy of old. The bourgeois should be removed from the garden like the weeds they are.'

Potiev caught them up with his tornado of ideas, spiralling them up with a string of words that bound them together as one in a chanting crescendo.

'Vive La France, Vive le communism.'

Dramatic piano cords rose above the chanting and soon the crowd began to sing. Steffan strained to catch the phrases from Daniel's clear baritone, *'For reason in revolt now thunders.'*

He couldn't make out anything else until the chorus that everyone sang with fervour.

> *'So, comrades, come rally*
> *And the last fight let us face*
> *The internationale unites the human race.'*

At each chorus, Steffan sang with more confidence, surrounded by a room of others roaring their togetherness. Some men held their open palms over their hearts, some were visibly moved to tears, and others clapped their hands and stamped their feet.

And for the first time since he'd come to Paris, Steffan felt he totally belonged. It seemed so obvious; communism was such a needed thing, the answer to making a better world, a perfect world that he could embrace. And this world would embrace him too, as his comrades Daniel and Ashlam did tonight as they sang together, in unison.

EIGHT

Yvette

While she waited for the train, Yvette fussed over the basket's covering to make sure the pistol remained hidden. She stayed up the far end of the platform, away from the station guard's office so she didn't have to interact with anyone. Not that she had to worry. Madame Jervois was the only other traveller on the platform, and she'd buttonholed the guard, who seemed to have fallen into a trance as she subjected him to a barrage of words about her brother's lung disease, her husband's bad heart and her niece's pregnancy woes.

The train arrived belching smoke and steam, and the brakes filled the platform with the smell of grease and metal. The conductor swung down from the last carriage and wrestled Madame Jervois's bulk and her bulging valise into the carriage.

Yvette took advantage of the pair clogging up the front carriage entrance and nipped up the back stairs. She sat down behind a lady with a large feather hat, hoping it would shield her from Madame Jervois. She need not have worried – Madame

Jervois was too busy berating the conductor over the placement of her valise on the overhead rack.

Yvette settled herself beside the window with her basket on the seat next to her. She rechecked its contents were covered and secure. The train lurched forward. Before she could stop it, the basket tumbled from the seat and spilt its contents across the floor. The gun lay in the aisle in plain view of everyone.

The gun that took her father's life was lying in the middle of the train.

She scrambled from her seat to pounce on the pistol, but a gloved hand on a uniformed arm reached it before she could.

She hadn't even left the station and the worst had already happened. Her trip today would end with her arrest. She looked up, expecting to see the conductor's angry face, to feel the tug of his arm pulling her up to frogmarch her off to whatever passed for a jail on the train. Instead, she met the gaze of the young conductor who had helped Madame Jervois. Under the stiff-peaked cap that had hidden most of his features, she now saw the scattering of freckles peppering his nose and cheeks. They gave him an impish air as he smiled at her, offering her a hand up while discreetly shielding the pistol from the other passengers' eyes.

'Let's get you sorted,' he said as he picked up her basket. He dropped the gun inside and placed it back on the seat.

'Are you not going to arrest me?' The words raced out of her mouth before her brain engaged.

'Last time I checked the municipal rail guidelines, it wasn't an arresting offence to drop a basket.' He placed the binoculars and the medal back into the basket, motioning her to sit back down.

'What about...' she didn't want to say the word 'gun', so she just looked at the basket.

'The cutlery? How many pieces were there? I'll make sure we pick them all up.'

Yvette didn't know whether to be annoyed that he seemed to be making a game out of her incident, or relieved he didn't seem worried about the gun.

'Fourteen pieces, all with a silver swan insignia,' she said.

He indicated she should count how many pieces were still in the basket. 'Take your time. I've done everyone in this carriage, except you. Usually four people get on here, but only the two of you today. Sometimes there's eight.'

With all the numbers he'd rattled off, she lost count. 'You did that deliberately, didn't you?'

He laughed like he'd just performed the funniest prank in the world. 'Pass them to me as you count. I'm good with numbers.' He seemed so earnest that she relented, and he repeated every number she said when she passed the piece of silver to him.

'Fourteen. That's them all,' she said.

'So, they're all accounted for, along with the gun.'

His expression became serious, and he took on the air of someone of authority. She stared back, feeling like a mouse that a cat had bluffed into a corner.

She tried to explain but nothing came out of her mouth, except a stuttered, 'It's… it's…'

'Where are you going?'

'La Montagne,' she managed to say. There was no point in trying to cover her tracks or tell him something different.

He held onto the seat back to steady himself and leant in so close she could smell the beeswax and pumpkin seed oil of his pomade. 'It is an offence to carry a pistol on public transport.'

'I am sorry, I didn't know,' she stammered. She fought the urge to move away. If she did, it would offend him.

He straightened up and reached into his jacket. Did he have a gun he was about to pull on her? With a flourish he retrieved an official-looking notepad that he flicked through until he found a blank form. 'I am supposed to fine you fifteen francs for carrying a concealed weapon.' He paused to gauge her reaction.

Fifteen francs was almost half of what Monsieur Rhodes said the pistol was worth. Tears threatened to well up into her eyes. She willed them back. She wouldn't be so weak as to cry in front of this man.

'You said supposed to, so maybe you won't?' She hoped she'd picked up on his cue.

'The train back leaves at four o'clock, and I finish my shift at two. If you agree to meet me at Café Loire by the railway station for coffee, I will waive the fine.'

She could just agree, and not show up. No one else had seen the pistol. If she managed to sell it, she wouldn't have it when she came back to the station. It would be just his word against hers.

'You want me to have coffee with you?'

'Don't seem so surprised that I have eyes in my head and can see how lovely you are.'

No one had called her lovely before, and she sat there with her mouth open. Here he was, coercing her to meet with him. Yet, he seemed sincere, like he really did think she was lovely.

'Twenty centimes for the return fare. It's cheaper for a return as it's fifteen centimes one way.' He held out his hand.

Glad of something practical to do, she reached into her pocket and dropped the coins into his outstretched palm.

She surprised herself by saying, 'If I am going to have coffee with you, I need to know your name.'

'Eric. *Et tu?*'

He'd used the familiar *tu*. She did like his cheeky smile, and he had made the pistol into a joke. Yet he was using it to his advantage to make her meet with him.

'I'm Yvette. Okay, I will see you at Café Loire, if you buy the coffee.'

'Of course, I am a gentleman.'

'Oh, good. Then you will also be happy to buy me a fancy pastry with my coffee.'

Eric's smile flickered for a second before he regained his polished façade.

'Naturally. Until two o'clock, Mademoiselle Yvette.' He passed her the ticket and touched her hand before he moved on into the next carriage.

If Café Loire's pastries did not look good, she might change her mind about whether she'd meet with him.

No one else in the carriage had noticed the basket mishap or her exchange with Eric. Madame Jervois seemed preoccupied by the contents of her purse, which clearly did not live up to her expectations as she tutted and muttered to herself.

Yvette tried to enjoy the trip, but her stomach fluttered and trembled like the fields of wheat and oats beside the tracks as they bent and swayed, disturbed by the speeding train. She pressed her face to the window looking further ahead. The fields reminded her of the patchwork quilts on the beds at Madame Sorve's tavern – she'd washed enough of them.

She ran through the instructions Monsieur Rhodes had given her to find Les Metaux. *From the railway station, turn right on the main road Rue De La Republique, turn left down Rue de la Belgique, and right into Rue Violin.* Les Mataux was in the middle of the block, and she was to ask for Anoud Tremben.

What if she couldn't find the shop? And if she could, he might not want what she had to sell.

The patchwork countryside gave way to whitewash houses with dark tiled roofs, and gardens facing the railway lines. Every garden that flew by was filled with neat rows of corn, tomatoes, and cabbages. Now there were workshops and businesses, where men and women toiled at their various crafts. As the train slowed down, Yvette marvelled at the number of businesses they passed. If a small town like La Montagne had so many, surely Paris would have more opportunities for her and Janie.

The train pulled into La Montagne. The station, built of the same red brick, was longer than the one at Mont-Saint-Louis, and had a second storey. Yvette was first to leave the train, as she didn't want to get tangled up with Madame Jervois. She sped across the platform, hurried down the steps beside the station building then turned right onto the road.

As she walked by Café Loire, she slowed, and gave them a tick for the red checked tablecloths and the well swept footpath. She'd stop on her way back to inspect the pastries.

She walked further down the road, feeling small beneath the three-storey buildings stretching up above her on both sides of the street. At ground level, most were shops and businesses with writing on their windows advertising what they sold or the service they offered.

The heavy basket dragged on her arm, so she stopped for a rest in front of a window display filled with brightly covered hats. They reminded Yvette of wildflowers in a field. She saw a sky-blue hat that would match her seersucker dress. But a hat like that would have to wait until they got to Paris. Standing here mooning over hats wasn't getting their goods sold.

In the distance was the signpost for Rue de la Belgique. She carried on to the corner of the street, which was much wider than the main street of her village. A continuous stream of motorised vehicles, carts and people on bicycles passed by and she hesitated to cross. She swapped the basket to her left side as she waited for the next motorised vehicle to pass. Her tired right arm felt light and floaty, as if it didn't belong to her.

She left the footpath at a brisk pace. Two bicycles flew past, their bells ringing.

'Watch where you are going!' one rider shouted.

She clutched her basket in front of her, terrified she might be knocked over and her possessions would scatter across the street. These people might not be so kind to her if a pistol ended up in the bicycle lane.

Rue de la Belgique's tall buildings continued on each side of the road and on past the intersecting street, Rue Violin. Yvette imagined a cluster of violinists playing just for her as she rounded the corner. In contrast to the raucous tunes that filtered out of Café Saint Louis, they would be playing the delightful, lilting music that seeped out from under Madame Sorve's door when she took her afternoon rest.

No such music awaited, but the street was lined with trees, and she enjoyed the shade they provided from the sun. Each shop she passed had a metal theme – a cutlery and silverware provider, a copper pot maker, fancy wrought iron gates and railings, and a business that made spokes and wheels for motorised vehicles. Not a violin in sight.

Just as Monsieur Rhodes had said, above the next building creaked a black metal sign with *Les Metaux* written in gold script. The shop door, like every other frontage she'd passed, had windows on each side. Les Mateux's left window housed a muddled display of silverware, and the right window contained an equally confusing jumble of metallic orbs, rods, and frames. She hoped Monsieur Rhodes was right about his friend, as the messiness of his shop frontage didn't fill her with much hope.

Yvette pushed the door open, and her nerves jangled in time to multiple shop bells. Inside the shop she stepped around iron rods leaning against walls, large rusting metal containers, and giant spools of copper wire. Silverware and other unidentifiable objects lined shelves around the walls.

She couldn't see the counter and called out to Monsieur Tremben.

'What may I do for you, Mademoiselle?'

She jumped as an elderly man with a face like a withered apple appeared beside her. His voice sounded as rusty as the iron stacked behind him.

'Are you Anoud Tremben?'

'*Oui*, Mademoiselle.'

Monsieur Tremben was younger than Monsieur Rhodes.

Unlike her neighbour, his body was strong and wiry, and his hands moved freely.

'Monsieur Rhodes from my village, Mont-Saint-Louis, said you could help me.'

Monsieur Tremben's eyes disappeared into his wrinkles as he laughed. 'Did he now? Glad to hear the old rogue is still alive and kicking.'

'He is well, apart from his arthritis. That slows him down.'

'Old age gets us all one way or another. Now, you have something to show me in that basket of yours?'

Yvette placed the basket on the counter, and for a moment she didn't want to remove the cloth covering her goods. What kind of person was she, selling her father's possessions with him just fresh in his grave? But she was here now, so she unpacked the medal, binoculars, and pistol. Monsieur Tremben motioned for her to leave the silver in the basket.

Yvette watched him closely for any indication of approval as he picked up the pistol, checked the barrel and aimed it at the wall. What would he do if he knew the pistol had taken her father's life? Would he throw it back in the basket as if it were cursed, or offer her half its value?

'Good condition,' he said.

Relief untied one tiny knot in her stomach. Perhaps it would be okay.

He fingered the medal. 'Your father's?'

Yvette nodded.

'You don't want to keep this?'

She shook her head instead of speaking, afraid she wouldn't be able to hide the anger in her voice. Her father didn't deserve that medal after what he'd done to her and Janie.

Monsieur Tremben placed the medal by the pistol. He inspected the binoculars and focused them on the door behind Yvette. He grunted and put them down next to the medal.

Turning his attention to the basket, he picked up a spoon, turned it over and ran his thumbnail over its markings.

'From the de Woelmont family.'

He picked over the contents of the basket. 'Most of this old family silver we turn into scrap, but the original family might buy it. They generally pay to have what's theirs returned. Your father left you a useful legacy.'

He gazed at the pile for so long that Yvette thought he'd forgotten how to speak, and she blurted out, 'So will you buy it?'

He looked up, and she realised her mistake.

'Thirty-five francs for the lot,' he said.

Why hadn't she waited for him to speak? Now she was at a disadvantage. She forced herself to wait, counting slowly to fifteen before she replied. 'Monsieur Rhodes' estimate was one hundred and thirty francs.' If she aimed higher than he'd suggested, she might get closer to what he thought they were worth.

'My old friend's been out of the game for a long time.' He drummed his fingers on the counter. 'Because he referred you, I can give you a special price of forty-five francs.'

That wasn't even half of their worth.

'Monsieur Rhodes has a good eye and would not steer me wrong. But as he is your good friend, I am willing to reduce my asking price to ninety-five francs.'

The amusement disappeared from Monsieur Tremben's lined face, and Yvette felt exposed under the weight of his scrutiny as he sized her up.

'My final offer is seventy francs.'

She needed more. Lila needed medicine for her care. She had to pay rent in advance before they left, and goodness knows what else would happen to drain the money from her purse.

'You said that you can sell the silver back to the family, and there's far more than twelve francs-worth there.'

'Yes, I can sell it back to them through an intermediary who will not ask questions and will take his cut. I would hate to have to ask you where you came by the silver, Mademoiselle ... What did you say your last name was? No matter, I can check against the medal.'

As he reached for it, Yvette changed tack. 'I understand your position with the silver. The pistol and the binoculars were legitimately owned by my family, and Monsieur Rhodes told me I would expect to get eighty francs for both.'

Monsieur Tremben shrugged his shoulders and started packing the items back into the basket. 'I wish you every success, Mademoiselle, but seventy francs was my final offer.'

He wasn't bluffing and he'd finished bargaining. She could walk the length of Rue de Violin and try every other scrap-metal dealer, but this was the only one she had a connection with.

'I will take it,' she said, hoping he wouldn't try and push the price down further.

'*Bon.*' He shook her hand.

Something inside her released a little as she helped him move the items out of the basket and onto the counter again.

After he'd counted out the money and she'd placed it securely into her purse, she said, 'At least the de Woelmont family will be happy to get its silver back.'

He shrugged. 'If there's any of them left. Losing the family silver might have been a small price to pay compared to others.'

He picked up her father's medal. 'Your father paid dearly for this, as I am sure you must know.'

'He never talked about the war.' But he had acted like he was still stuck there, in hell.

'No one did.' He held the box out to her. 'Keep this in his honour. He fought for France.'

As she took the medal, tears welled in her eyes. It was the first time since he'd died that she felt grief about his passing.

Mama had held them all together, including Father. Living without his wife was a step too far for Papa.

She thanked Monsieur Tremben and left the shop before she dissolved into tears.

NINE

Yvette

———

Every couple of blocks on her walk back to the train station, Yvette checked inside her basket to reassure herself her purse was still tucked safely under the cover. She'd never had so much money before. It seemed a fortune that could easily support them on their journey to Paris, yet it would quickly disappear if she was not careful.

Yvette arrived at Café Loire before the train, and the scent of fresh croissants and coffee drew her across the threshold. The inside of a café was new territory, as her mother had refused to waste money on something so frivolous.

The brightly coloured array of cakes and pastries attracted her to the display cabinet. As she read the labels, each sounded more tempting than the one before. The tartelette à l'orange was decorated with a candied orange slice balanced on its edge. Merely looking at the creation conjured up bursts of citrus with the tartness of marmalade, and saliva exploded into her mouth.

'*Bonjour*, Mademoiselle. Would you like to sit inside or outside?' Yvette started when the waitress greeted her. She'd been so busy drooling over the cakes, she hadn't heard her approach.

The outside tables at the café in Yvette's village were always taken by groups of men who drank whiskey and played backgammon. Her father had sat there every day with them, drinking their money away.

She could continue and easily get on the train before Eric saw her. But she wanted to sit outside to drink coffee and eat taelette à l'orange with a fancy dessert fork.

Yes, Eric had coerced her into this, but what could he do to her? She was winning by having him pay for afternoon tea.

'Outside, *merci*,' she said, with perhaps too much firmness.

The waitress smiled and led her to a table between an elderly couple and a mother with two small children.

'I won't order yet. I'm waiting for someone who's arriving on the train,' she told the waitress with more confidence than she felt.

'Not long to wait. It will be here in a few minutes. I will return when the other member of your party arrives.' The waitress returned inside the café.

It sounded so proper, *other member of your party.* Something fizzed and bubbled up inside her, like soda water. It was strange and unexpected, and it took her a few moments to realise what it was – excitement. Since Mama had died, dread and worry had churned inside her. She missed Mama so much, and watching Papa fall apart like a storm-ravaged tree was agony. Hiding from him what little money they earnt to pay the rent, searching for him when he didn't come home after the café closed, his frightening outbursts and accusations.

She was in a café for the first time in her life, here to meet a boy. Yvette felt like an adult, a lady. What would her father have to say about that? Damn Papa, always sneaking into her head when she didn't want him there.

'The train's almost here. Can you hear it in the distance?' the mother at the table next to Yvette asked her children.

She heard the whistle, and soon the belching train stack shuddered in behind the station building. The platform bustled with people disembarking and others scrambling onto the train. Even with his back to her, she recognised Eric by his purposeful movements as he stood in the luggage wagon and passed valises and packages down to the passengers leaving at La Montagne.

Without a beat, he swapped to receive boxes of produce that he placed in the carriage. He moved as if he were in control of his surroundings, as if nothing could rock his belief in his own abilities.

When he'd loaded the last of the packages, he vaulted down onto the platform and swung the wagon door closed. It clanged shut like a bell tongue clapping against its ringer, echoing off the cobblestones and the buildings clustered about the square. Eric signalled the end of his shift by removing his hat. He tucked it under his arm like a soldier.

Eric looked good with his hat on, but even better without it. She got the impression he knew it too – he couldn't seem to stop using his fingers as a comb to push back his curly hair from his forehead, leaving rivulets of wavy curls across his scalp.

Yvette's stomach did little somersaults as he walked closer.

He'd seen her sitting outside, waiting for him, and his face lit up in a grin. He sped up, almost but not quite running.

There wasn't much she could do now he'd seen her. She'd just have to stay put.

He was slightly out of breath as he reached the table. 'I am so pleased you're here,' he said.

He kissed her on both cheeks like a long-lost friend, and she caught a whiff of his pomade, now mixed with engine oil and tobacco. She gave him only the lightest peck, as she didn't want him taking liberties.

'What would you like to drink?' He sat down, facing her but also slightly angled so he could see the street.

She was about to confide it was her first time in a café, but decided against it as he might mock her. She didn't want this first experience ruined. At Café Saint Louis, when they weren't shouting for cognac, she'd heard people ordering café au lait.

'May I have a café au lait?'

'Exactly what I am having, since it's too early for Kir Royale.' Eric signalled to the waitress and gave her their order.

'Anything to eat?' the waitress asked.

Eric raised an eyebrow at Yvette.

'Yes please. I'll have a tartalette à l'orange.'

Eric glanced in the direction of the cabinet and seemed to make a decision. '*Bon.* I will have one too.'

Yvette was relieved he didn't seem at all put out that she'd ordered a fancy cake.

'Do you live in Mont-Saint-Louis, where you got on?' Eric asked.

'Yes, I've lived there all my life. What about you?'

'I live here in La Montagne, about a fifteen-minute walk that way.' He waved over in the direction where Yvette had come from. 'Our train runs from Nantes to Saint-Brevin-les-Pins. I do the run from La Montagne to Saint-Pere-en-Retz. I swap over trains and go back from Saint-Pere-en-Retz, where we picked you up today from Mont-Saint-Louis, and I keep going to Bougeunais, where I swap and come back.'

Yvette struggled to keep up with all the long town names. 'Don't you go to Nantes?'

'Oh yes. The trains run from start of the morning to late evening. We guards live all along the route and only do part of the run. I'm hoping to get a promotion next year and move to Nantes. Then I'd get to do the Nantes to Paris run.'

'Paris,' she said with a sigh.

'You want to go there too?' he asked.

'Yes. My sister Janie and I are going to leave soon to stay with my cousin Daniel who works in a foundry. They make bronze statues.' She instantly regretted telling him so much about their plans.

'I'm going to help my uncle with his political career,' said Eric. 'He's going to run in the elections next year for his party, Croix de Feu. He's a war veteran and he wants to make France great again. All these immigrants and Jews are ruining our economy.'

Yvette's mind went completely blank, and she couldn't think of a sensible thing to say. What did she know about politics? The waitress arrived with their order, saving her from answering, and Yvette admired the swirls on top of the coffee.

'What were you doing in La Montagne today?' Eric asked as he gulped his drink. He didn't even glance at his coffee.

'I was disposing of my weapon. I can't risk it falling out of my basket while I climb the Eiffel Tower.'

Eric laughed. 'You could have given it to me to pass on to my uncle.'

'Wouldn't that be arms trading? I could have been arrested.'

'Arrested for a good cause.' Eric laughed at his own joke then stared off into the distance as if he were mulling over something of great importance.

'Are you going to catch the next train home?' he asked.

Yvette nodded. She didn't want to take the coffee cup away from her face. She'd been slurping the last of the coffee from under the foam and was sure she'd have a little moustache.

'You could catch the late train, the one at eight o'clock, and spend the afternoon with me. There's a lovely spot down by the river – we could go for a stroll. There's a band playing in the park later this afternoon too. We could take some beer with us,' he said, barely drawing a breath.

His suggestions puffed around her like the train steaming out of the station.

'I can't be home too late, because of my sister.' She imagined Aubert strolling down their lane on the pretext of visiting Lila, his face lighting up when he noticed Yvette's absence.

Not looking at him in case he didn't approve, she spooned up some froth from the cup. The bubbles tickled as they popped in her mouth.

'Oh, I talk a lot. That's my job. Sorry, I haven't given you any time to think about anything.' He even had the good grace to look sorry.

'Is there a train after this one, before the late one?'

'There's one at five. We could still go for a stroll down by the river and maybe stop and listen to the band. They start playing at four,' Eric said in the most earnest way.

She spooned up some more bubbles to avoid answering him.

'I'm talking too much again. Eat your cake first.'

The forkful of tart filled her mouth and sinuses with a burst of orange and an underlying flavour of walnut.

'This is delicious,' she said as she filled her fork again.

This mouthful she chewed slowly, relishing the flavours. A hint of vanilla and a pop of fennel balanced the sweetness. The tart and coffee were so good, and she'd just made her mind up to agree to Eric's offer when an angry voice called her name. She turned to see Madame Jervois, who'd shared her carriage on the way here, marching towards their table.

'Yvette, you will miss the train. You must come with me now.' Madame Jervois linked her free arm through Yvette's and pulled her to standing. The partridge feathers on her maroon cloche trembled with indignation in support of their mistress.

'What are you doing?' Yvette cried out.

'Pick up your basket. We are leaving.' Madame Jervois held Yvette's arm so tightly there was no escaping.

'I am having coffee,' Yvette protested.

'Precisely why you are leaving.'

Yvette stammered a goodbye, leaving Eric gawping after her, as Madame Jervois dragged her off towards the train.

'I am doing your poor dead mother a favour, girl. That young man is nothing but trouble.'

'I was only having coffee, Madame Jervois. It was nothing else.'

'Nothing else? Nothing else? That young man has a girl at every railway station. I should know, I travel on this train enough to see what he gets up to. You get mixed up with him, and your chance to leave is gone.'

Had she heard right?

'How do you know we are planning to leave?' she blurted out, before she could stop herself.

'My maman lives across the road from Les Metaux. Monsieur Tremben takes luncheon with Maman every day and of course he told us of your visit. I put two and two together and came up with twenty-two.' Madame Jervois laughed at her joke.

'Please don't tell anyone in the village.' She pictured Madame Jervois accosting every soul she came across, spreading Yvette's news faster than the smoke threading from the priest's thurible.

Madame Jervois stood still and let go of her arm. 'I had my adventures in the Great War, most of which I would never tell my dear husband. I don't want you and Janie to be stuck in our little village. Your mother wanted much more for you.'

At the mention of Mama, tears sprang into her eyes. 'I didn't know you and Mama were friends.'

Madame Jervois smiled. 'We didn't rub it in people's faces. But yes, we were friends. She asked me to look out for you, and I just have.'

'Is he really that bad?' she asked.

'I'm afraid so.'

As they reached the train station, Yvette glanced back to Café

Loire. Eric had left their table. He'd seemed quite nice, a bit chatty, a bit pushy. But not exactly bad enough to be dragged away from in such a dramatic way.

Madame Jervois made her sit beside her on the platform bench. 'Don't move,' she ordered.

Yvette sighed at being trapped with Madame Jervois, but at least she could ask her some questions about Mama.

'I found a picture of Mama when she was young. She was holding a beautiful statuette. Would you know anything about that?'

'Oh yes. Your mother had quite the life before meeting your father. She studied to be a sculptress. Quite ahead of her time. That was probably one of her pieces.'

'Why did she not tell us?' There'd never been a hint of Mama's past life.

'Why would she? It's in the past. It wasn't like she could sculpt there in the village. Imagine how they would have reacted.' Madame Jervois laughed at the incredulity of a something like that happening in the village.

'Your mama came with her papa to repair the Mont-Saint-Louis statue after it was damaged in the war. Then she met your father, and that, as we say, was that.'

'How did I not know this?' Yvette's head reeled from this new information about her family.

'A drunken German soldier shot off Saint Louis' face. Your mama did a great job of restoring it. Never would have known it was such a mess.'

'If you were such good friends with Mama, why didn't you come to Papa's funeral?'

Madame Jervois patted her hand. 'Your father was such a lovely young man. The war changed him, sent him down a bad pathway.' She tapped her head. 'Not even your mother Loriene could save him in the end.'

As they readied themselves to board the arriving train, Yvette took one last look at Café Loire. Eric was back in his seat with a small glass in his hand filled with something red. He gave her an enthusiastic wave, toasted her with his drink, then blew her a kiss. Madame Jervois wasn't watching so she waved back with a tad less enthusiasm. She didn't blow a kiss in return because that seemed too forward.

TEN

Steffan

Paris, August 1933

Father said Steffan was a family member and didn't have to knock before entering the Blum home. Last time Steffan had walked in, he'd surprised Philippe and side-stepped a roundhouse punch. He did apologise, but he figured Philippe would use any excuse to try again.

Since then, he'd knocked, called out, and waited for an answer. If Martje, Rosie, Sarah, or Father called back, he let himself in. If no one answered, or only Philippe was home, he waited.

Today Martje called out, 'Come in.'

He pushed down the bronze handle. Father's house was bigger than his grandparents' home, with higher ceilings and many more windows. His favourites were the two small leadlight sunburst windowpanes beside the stairs, one with a red sun and orange rays, and the other in reverse colours. Before Paris, he'd only ever seen windows like this in a church.

'Have you brought your suit?' Martje yelled from the kitchen.

'Yes, I have.' He found her working in the kitchen.

Martje did everything with an unconscious grace. Wrapped in her brown calico apron with her hair scraped off her face, she flowed about her kitchen, whether selecting ingredients, stirring bowls, or washing dishes. She made the most domestic task a joy to observe.

She was in her forties, but men still stopped what they were doing to watch her walk by on her way to the foundry. She didn't seem aware of her effect on men. Steffan liked her even more for it. No wonder Father had fallen for her.

Martje wiped her hands on her apron and held her hand out for his jacket. 'Does it need pressing?' She greeted him with a kiss on his cheek. She smelt of oatmeal and cinnamon.

'I don't think so.' Steffan shook his head.

Martje held the jacket up and laughed. 'Look at all the wrinkles. Have you been sleeping in it?'

Of course he hadn't. But he wasn't going to tell Martje it had fallen off its hanger and had been sitting in a heap on the floor for several days.

'Trousers too, please.' Martje held out her hand.

Steffan rummaged around in his knapsack and pulled out the rumpled trousers.

Martje shook her head, and he grinned as an apology.

'Just as well I asked for them. You can't go out looking like a hobo.' She strode towards the kitchen, calling over her shoulder, 'There's coffee in the pot and oatmeal on the stove.'

Steffan followed her in, relieved Philippe was absent from the table. He helped himself to coffee and a bowl of oatmeal, spooning sugar and cream into both.

'Does Madame Bruist not feed you?' Martje asked, as she placed the irons onto the range to heat.

'Madame Bruist provides very well for us. She's up well before us, making our breakfast.' A total lie, as Madame Bruist was always hungover and didn't rise until mid-morning. But if Martje knew, she'd insist he came to stay with them. 'I'm particularly hungry today,' he added, to justify his supposed second breakfast.

Martje busied herself with pressing the suit while she ran through the evening itinerary.

'Be here by four thirty to have a wash and change into your suit. Rosie insists we go by tram rather than the Metro. She must take every opportunity to see the Eiffel Tower, even at a distance. The river boat is booked for six, up the Eiffel Tower at seven, dinner at eight.'

'Where are we eating?'

'You men. Always thinking about your stomachs.'

'I'm unable to think of anything else!'

'Les Deux Magots. A favourite of the artists, therefore a favourite of your father's.'

'Place Saint-Germain des Prés.'

He'd walked past the green-canopied restaurant many times. The waiters wore crisp, white formal shirts with winged collars, and waist-length black jackets. Les Deux Magots had a new neon sign and the fluorescent red name blinked on and off all night above the entrance and apparently could even be seen from the Eiffel Tower.

'It's time for me to go to work. I can't have Father scolding me for idleness.'

'See you at luncheon.' Martje smiled as she lifted the iron from the stove top.

Steffan made to take the bowl and cup to the sink, but Martje indicated he should leave them on the table.

'I'll clear it once I've finished this.'

'Thank you, Martje. You are very kind to me.'

Martje gave him another of her heart-warming smiles.

As he walked the short distance between the Blum's home and the foundry, he vowed not to take his good fortune for granted. Apart from Philippe, his father's family accepted him and treated him like he'd always been with them. The only time he felt adrift was during Jewish ceremonies, like Rosh Hashanah or Shavout. Father hadn't expected him to actively worship, but he did want to know more about being Jewish.

Philippe usually scowled his way through any celebration Steffan attended. Everyone else ignored Philippe's *silly jealousies,* as the girls dubbed it. It bothered Steffan how his half-brother didn't accept him.

When he reached the foundry, the Bierlet's black hulk blocked his entry from the archway like a giant bear trapped in a tree stump. It seemed wedged against the courtyard wall. He couldn't see Controleur Kubreck but he could hear him swearing, even using some phrases that were new to him.

Only one person could have got the truck this stuck. Philippe's unhappy face was the first thing that confronted him as he scooted under the chassis. Even worse, the truck's load was scattered across the courtyard with most boxes bent and broken.

At first, he thought Controleur Kubreck was unwell as his small body twitched and trembled.

'Look at the mess the boy has made,' he said, straining to keep his voice calm. His face was tight with anger and a nerve twitched on his jawline, making his waxed moustache writhe like a beached eel.

Part of him was glad it was Philippe who'd made the mistake. He would have wanted to shrivel up and disappear if he'd done this.

'Just leave it to us,' said Steffan. 'I'll help Philippe tidy up.' He risked a glance at his half-brother who, for once, wasn't glaring at him.

Controleur Kubreck balled up his fists towards the heavens. His moustache didn't stop in its attempt to leap from his upper lip.

'You will clear all this up. I will be back in thirty minutes. I expect a spotless courtyard and no vehicle blocking our entrance.'

He strode off, anger rising from him like steam from a newly poured cast.

'Shall we clear the courtyard and then move the truck?' He asked the question in such a way that Phillippe could agree or make another suggestion, then it would sound more his idea than Steffan's.

Philippe nodded, and Steffan retrieved the trolley from the loading bay. He helped Philippe straighten the boxes nearest the truck and they loaded them up on the trolley in a neat rectangle.

'Were you coming or going?' he asked.

'Going. I got a bit stuck.'

He sure had, but Steffan wasn't going to say that out loud.

'Once we've got everything on the trolley, shall we load it back onto the truck in the loading bay?'

'If you could sort the truck out, I'll move the trolley onto the loading bay,' Phillippe said in a civil tone.

'What's going on?' Daniel yelled from the other side of the truck. 'I can't get in.'

'You'll have to go under the truck,' Steffan called out.

Daniel crawled out from under the chassis into the courtyard.

'You call this parking?' he said to Steffan.

'I do my best.' Steffan shrugged.

Daniel laughed. 'Hope you make a better carver than a driver. I'll give you a hand to tidy up.'

Daniel stacked up two boxes and placed them on the trolley. 'Hope what's in here's not broken.'

'They're brass light fittings, so they're unbreakable,' Philippe answered in a tone that implied Daniel was a moron.

Steffan tried not to visibly wince.

'So, you did this, not Steffan?' Daniel stood holding the box he'd just hefted onto his shoulder.

When Philippe didn't answer, Daniel pushed the box at him, forcing him to take it.

'Good luck, Steffan.' Daniel picked up his bag, walked across the courtyard, and disappeared into the ivory carving room.

'He helped when he thought it was you, but now he won't because he found out it was me.' Philippe banged the box down on top of the other two on the trolley.

Philippe didn't seem to understand that if he were nicer to people, they would be nicer to him. Steffan could have pointed that out, but they still had a lot of work to do, and he didn't want to risk Philippe throwing another tantrum. He congratulated himself for choosing to say nothing.

They finished loading the fallen boxes. The trolley was too heavy for just Phillippe so they pushed it together up the ramp to the loading bay.

'Instead of me getting the truck unstuck, would you like me to guide you to do it?' Steffan offered, in the hope it this might help towards mending things between them.

'I would appreciate that,' Phillippe answered without looking at him.

Phillippe entered the truck passenger-side and shuffled over to the driver's side. Steffan swung himself up to sit beside him.

'First thing you'll have to do is heave the steering wheel as far as you can to the right. Just ease your foot off the clutch and creep as far as you can from the wall.'

Phillippe followed the instructions.

'Stop now. Put her in reverse and force the wheel the other way. Just ease her back slightly.'

After ten manoeuvres the Bierlet crept out into the courtyard like a timid rat. More importantly, Phillippe remained calm.

'Now, drive the truck towards the lunchroom door and stop when the right edge of your windscreen obscures the door jamb. Turn the wheel as hard as you can to the right, then back into the loading bay.'

Phillippe backed the truck smoothly, lining it up perfectly

with the loading bay. Steffan suppressed the urge to cheer. He nodded his approval to keep it low key.

Together, they reloaded the freight back on the truck.

'Can you help me get the truck through the archway?' Phillippe asked, again not looking at him.

'Sure, I'd be happy to.' He tried to make it sound casual, like it was a little thing. It wasn't, but it was a small step in the right direction.

Don't get too excited, he told himself, but he wanted to burst into the song they sang when their fields were harvested before the hay was safely stored for winter. A little victory. Steffan tried not to grin.

ELEVEN

Steffan

Paris, August 1933

As the family assembled on the doorstep ready for their night out, Philippe behaved as if Steffan had never helped him with the Bierlet. He stood as far away from Steffan as he could and refused to make eye contact.

Damn him. If that's how he was going to behave, then Steffan would ignore him too. It was Rosie's birthday, and her coming of age, and he would help her have a great evening, never mind what Philippe did. Rosie looked pretty in her pale blue dress and her matching hat, much older than her thirteen years.

Steffan felt a little shiver of belonging. He belonged with these people. He was part of this family. Of course, there would be a Bat Mitzvah ceremony, which he knew nothing about. He'd be asked, along with the rest of the Jewish community, unless it was a private ceremony. The only blight to his fully belonging was Philippe. One day he might come around, but clearly not tonight.

Father slammed the front door. It had the same effect as a starter gun going off at a running race. The family sped off down the steps, talking non-stop to each other, leaving Steffan still standing by the door. He caught up and linked his arm through Rosie's.

'You left me behind. Don't you want me to celebrate your big day?'

'Dawdling donkey. You caught up.' She squeezed his arm. 'Of course, I want my new BB here with me.'

Steffan glowed – in Rosie speak, new BB translated to new big brother. He felt protective of her, just like he had with his sister Liselle when she was Rosie's age. As Liselle got older, she'd become fed up with Steffan 'buzzing about her'. He hoped Rosie wouldn't feel like that too.

They got to the tram stop just as one rumbled to a halt. The factory workers hadn't finished work yet so there were plenty of seats for the family to sit together as a group. Steffan sat next to Rosie, and Father and Martje sat front of them, with Philippe and Sarah behind.

'Why do we always have to take trams when the Metro is faster?' Phillippe complained.

'No view,' Steffan and Rosie said in unison. They turned to each other and giggled.

'What are you looking forward to the most, Rosie?' Father asked.

'Eiffel Tower. What a silly question.'

Father laughed. 'There it is, Rosie. Your true love.' He pointed out the tower in the distance.

Steffan got a little thrill every time he saw it. He wished he'd been born to witness the building of Paris's most special symbol. Not only was it an engineering feat, but it also summed up Paris's beauty, mystery, and strength. He'd walked around the base many times but tonight they were going inside, and up.

The tram rattled its way through the shabbiness of Montmartre, the glittering world of Place de Vendome, the strolling families in the Jarden des Tuileries, and to the Place de la Concorde where they disembarked by the Seine. Martje ushered them on through the mix of motorised vehicles, horse-drawn carts, and bicycles, to the line for the river cruise.

As Steffan looked around for the ticket office, Martje shook her head. She opened her handbag and took out the tickets. She'd already bought them.

'You don't need to pay for me,' Steffan said to her.

'Nonsense. You are family. This is a family celebration.'

Steffan thanked her.

'Family, like hell,' Philippe whispered behind him so no one else heard.

After Steffan's kindness today, how could Phillipe say something like that? He took some deep breaths, fighting down the urge to shout at him to leave him alone.

He helped Rosie onto the open-topped riverboat, and she opted to sit in the middle seats that looked towards the Eiffel Tower.

Steffan tried to block out Philippe's insult, but it buzzed inside his head like a mosquito. He didn't want to let Philippe ruin his evening, but in a way he already had. Philippe constantly reminded him he didn't really belong. He would always be an outsider staring through a glass window into a world he couldn't quite understand.

The riverboat moved off downstream towards Notre Dame and Île de la Cité, away from the Eiffel Tower. Rosie sat transfixed by the view in front of her, and Steffan tried to do the same. But Philippe's presence, like a swarm of angry bees buzzing nearby, left him guarded and on high alert that something would happen.

Notre-Dame came into view. Its arches, spires, and stained-glass windows watching over Paris calmed him. Notre-Dame had stood on this island in the Seine for centuries while Paris grew around it through all its highs and lows. It put things in perspective. Steffan's quarrel with Philippe was a disturbance in the water, an eddy where they were spinning around each other. In time, Philippe would accept him, and like the great river, they would eventually drift downstream, all the currents merging as one.

The boat turned before they got to the Seine-Marne river confluence, and they worked their way back up on the other side of Île de la Cité where people walked by the riverside or sat in groups sharing picnics. The whole city celebrated being alive, along with him. The Eiffel Tower grew closer and Steffan traced the steel girders and giant rivets that created the lattice effect up the tower.

Father leaned over to Steffan. 'Isn't she a beauty?'

'She is a wonderful construction and very beautiful.'

'She caused an uproar when she first went up. We very much backed Monsieur Eiffel, and why wouldn't we? Good with paying his bills was Monsieur Eiffel.'

'We know, Father. We've heard this story a thousand times,' Philippe said.

'There's a bit of Blum Foundry in that tower,' Father reminded him. 'Anyway, Steffan doesn't know all the history yet.'

Steffan did want to hear more, but he didn't want to inflame Philippe further. He could find out more from Father when they were on their own.

'The Eiffel Tower is the best thing in Paris,' Rosie said.

'What about Sacré-Cœur or Sainte-Chapelle?' Martje asked.

'No. Definitely the Eiffel Tower, Maman.'

'It's your day. So, today I will say the same.' Martje smiled at Rosie.

Rosie laughed. 'If every day could be like this, I would always get my way.'

'Just as well it isn't. Every day would be consumed with Eiffel Tower discussions. There's only so many conversations I can have about rivets,' Martje answered.

'I love to talk about rivets,' Father quipped.

'You and Rosie can converse about rivets then.' Martje shook her head.

Rosie shushed them as they approached the Eiffel Tower's base.

'What difference does it make if we talk, Rosie Posie?' Philippe came to stand beside her.

'It does seem like a religious experience.' Steffan immediately regretted saying it.

Father laughed and Steffan relaxed. What he'd said hadn't offended anyone.

'If only she were as attentive at temple,' Martje said.

'Please. I need quiet,' Rosie told them as they moored just downstream. She gazed up at the tower as if it might bend over and embrace her.

Philippe stifled a laugh and Steffan caught Martje and Father exchanging an amused look. He wondered if Father and his mama had ever done that when he was a child.

The boatmen jumped onto the jetty and held onto the mooring ropes from the stern and bow. Hand over hand with ropes in unison, they pulled the vessel into the shore.

Another boatman positioned the gang planks so they could climb across onto the jetty.

'Time to disembark,' Philippe called out.

The family shuffled forward with Rosie in the lead, Sarah next, Father and Martje and finally Steffan.

Just as he reached the gangplank, someone gave him a mighty shove, sending him sideways. He grabbed the riverboat's rail to stop himself falling, but the momentum spun him to the outside of the boat. Ignoring the pain in his wrist, he swung his body across and grasped the rail with his other hand. Pain shot through his left wrist.

As Philippe offered him his hand, their eyes met. Steffan held his gaze and ignored his outstretched hand. No way was he falling for that trick.

Phillippe broke off eye contact and stepped back from the railing. Anger surged through Steffan propelling him back over the rail onto the boat.

'You did that on purpose,' Steffan yelled at Philippe. As he brushed himself down, he noticed a tear in his left trouser leg. Blood oozed onto the material.

'Absolutely not. It was an accident.' Philippe tried looked as if he meant it.

Steffan had spent the past months learning how to read Philippe. The bastard gave himself away by rubbing his neck.

Behind him the family called to Steffan. He stepped across the gangplank acutely aware of the tear in his trousers and his smarting knee.

Martje and Father caught him up and hurried him to a seat. Father sat with his arm linked in his while Martje inspected his damaged leg.

'Just a scrape, not too deep,' Martje pronounced.

'I don't want anyone to make a fuss.'

'Really, Steffan. You almost landed yourself in the Seine. Of course, we are making a fuss.'

'Sarah, ask the boatman for some iodine and a strip of fresh cloth,' Father said.

She hurried over to the nearest boatman who strode across the gangplank and disappeared into a cabin.

Martje eased up Steffan's trouser leg to get a better look at his knee. 'Not too bad. We should be able to stop the bleeding.'

Sarah returned with a bottle of iodine and a roll of bandage and gave them to Martje. 'They were well stocked. They said it's not uncommon for things like this to happen.'

Martje tore a piece from the bandage and poured iodine onto it. She dabbed it onto Steffan's knee and he sucked in his breath, surprised at how much it stung. He wouldn't show it though, not with Philippe hovering near Father.

'I'm using the iodine again, so brace yourself.'

It did hurt more, even though Martje worked quickly, with her usual precision. She soaked another bandage strip in iodine and placed it across the cut, then wound the bandage around his knee, tearing its end to tie it off.

She eased his trouser leg back over the bandage. 'The tailor can fix that tear so no one will ever see it. It will look as good as new.'

But it wouldn't be good as new. Philippe had ruined his father's gift to him. He'd torn more than just the fabric. He'd torn at the love of his family.

Steffan stood up to test that bandage and took a few steps. 'Thank you Martje. It will hold well.'

Steffan noticed Rosie standing a little way off from the family, staring up at her beloved Eiffel Tower. He called over to her. 'Rosie, I'm sorry I slowed down your ascent.'

'Are you ready now?' Rosie reached out to him, and he came over. 'Let's go,' she said, tugging at his hand.

A bolt of pain raced up Steffan's arm. 'Easy, Rosie. I think I hurt my wrist too.'

'You have another.' She let go of his hand, grabbed his right one, and was off running across the concourse, dragging him with her to the Eiffel Tower's entrance.

'Martje has the tickets,' Steffan called out to her.

'Then they'll have to catch up.'

Steffan twisted to look back. The family half walked, half ran behind them. Philippe straggled behind.

'What took you so long?' Rosie teased when they caught up.

Martje handed the tickets to the attendant who counted them off as they entered the Eiffel Tower's base. Rosie rushed them over to stand in a queue.

'We are waiting for an elevator. It's newly built and it's going to take us up on a diagonal to the second platform,' she explained. They edged forward when the people in front of them entered a small white room. The attendants pulled across a metal lattice that clicked into place.

'Keep your hands, fingers, and bags inside the barrier,' an attendant said to the group caged inside.

A man younger than Steffan stuck his hand out of a diamond shape in the lattice and was rewarded with a rap across his knuckles from the attendant's cosh. He squawked and pulled his hand back in.

The whir of a flywheel accompanied the sudden jerking of the makeshift room, then abruptly it moved sideways and upwards to a chorus of surprised cries from the people inside and in the queue. Even though he hadn't meant to, Steffan cried out too as the elevator disappeared from the first level, then tracked up to the second level high above them, guided by a series of pulleys.

'How fortunate we are to witness this miracle of modern technology,' Father said. He'd come to stand beside Steffan.

'It is like a miracle,' Steffan agreed, who'd been so caught up in the elevator's progress he almost didn't register his father's words. For once, he wasn't the only person disoriented by something he'd never encountered before. He found himself enjoying this feeling of equality and group wonder. It made him feel part of something bigger, larger than just family. Even Philippe's attempts to sabotage that hadn't worked.

After disgorging its human cargo high above them, the elevator crabbed its way back down to the tower's base. The attendants rattled back the latticed gate, and it was their turn to enter.

Martje insisted the family hold hands on the way up, just in case. Steffan found himself between Rosie and Father. When was the last time he and Father had held hands? Perhaps when he was a child, standing between his mother and father. He was acutely aware of the calluses across his father's fingers pressing onto his skin. He struggled to focus on the movement of the room upwards as his father's closeness and touch overwhelmed him. It was as if his sense of self held its breath as he stood, hand clasped with his father, in this timeless place, feeling like both a child and a grown man.

The room shuddered to a stop on the second level and the occupants, including his family, let out a cheer and clapped. Steffan turned to Father, hoping he would be looking at him. Father was laughing with all the family, including Steffan. It was as it should be, but Steffan couldn't help feeling disappointed that Father hadn't looked at him first.

There was no time to ponder further as they were ushered out to survey Paris from above. The sun's last golden light ebbed away as night unfolded. Paris spread out around them in every direction, as far as they could see. In the distance was the pale dome of Sacré-Cœur, and he traced the main railway line out from Gare du Nord as it cut a channel through the city.

'Come on, everyone, we have to get to the top before it's dark,' Rosie called out.

A hand came down to cover Steffan's, where he held onto the railing.

'Before we go on, I want to tell you something,' Father said. He paused as if struggling to find the right words, then continued, 'I fought for you and Liselle to stay with me. You may not be aware, but the law always sides with Gentiles in matters of custody. It broke my heart, losing you both, especially after losing your mother too. I hoped you would return when you were older. I am so very glad you have.' He squeezed Steffan's hand and gestured for him to follow.

And follow he did, easily climbing the hundreds of iron steps, buoyed up by his father's words of acceptance. The pain in his knee and wrist was just a minor niggle.

. . .

When they arrived at Les Deux Magots, the maître d' greeted Father by name. Steffan enjoyed the other patrons watching as their family was led to a prime outside table beside the main entrance.

Steffan kept as much distance as possible between himself and Philippe. It worked – Father sat between them, meaning he and Philippe couldn't see each other unless they leant forward.

The waiters glided past carrying drinks and plates of food on trays. Steffan's stomach grumbled as the aroma from a still-sizzling steak wafted past.

Father ordered Champagne, but Steffan would have preferred to gulp down several glasses of beer to dull the throbbing in his wrist and knee. He took a menu from the waiter to be polite, even though he had already decided on the steak.

Madame Bruist allowed generous portions at supper, but she usually cooked stews and casseroles. Grand-mère cooked two, if not three, roasts a week and only made stews out of the left-over meat. Steffan hankered for a meal where the meat wasn't turned into mush.

The waiter returned with the Champagne and Father waved him towards Rosie saying, 'The birthday girl must be served first.'

Rosie blushed, pleased to be the centre of attention. She watched every drop of Champagne froth out of from the bottle into her fluted glass.

Father nodded to the waiter to pour everyone else's drinks. Steffan enjoyed the way the Champagne fizzed against the glass as the waiter poured his, and when he moved on to Father, Steffan leant down to sniff the aroma. The air released by the popping bubbles touched his face like a caress, and he inhaled the yeasty sweetness.

Father tapped his knife against his glass to attract everyone's attention. 'A toast to our darling and delightful Rosie. Happy birthday to the most beautiful flower to grace our table. You are the light of our lives.'

They toasted Rosie and clinked glasses. The taste of the Champagne exploded in his mouth, a mix of grapes, sunshine, and freshly cut reeds. He'd always wondered why people made such a fuss about Champagne, and now he knew. If he was offered it again, he wouldn't turn it down for a glass of beer.

When the waiter came back to take their orders, Steffan requested steak *au poivre vert*.

Father stood up and greeted a balding, middle-aged gentleman dressed in a smart black suit, accompanied by a much younger woman in a green coat.

'Monsieur and Madame Chiparus.' He kissed them both. 'Let me introduce my family. Of course, you know my wife Martje. My children, Steffan, Philippe, Sarah, and Rosie.'

Father had introduced him as the eldest – the first born.

Philippe would make him suffer tomorrow, but tonight Steffan glowed from his recognition as eldest in the family.

Monsieur Chiparus smiled. 'Monsieur Blum, you have such a handsome family. It is an opportune meeting. I have some work for you.'

'We would be honoured. I shall send Steffan over when it is convenient.'

'Yes, send him Wednesday.'

The maître d' led the couple away and Father sat down again.

'A very good restaurant. A fine choice, Martje. We always meet someone to make it even more worthwhile.'

Father called the waiter over again and ordered another bottle of Champagne.

'What work will he have for us, Father?' Steffan asked.

'Monsieur Chiparus is the finest sculptor in Paris. His work is exquisite, is it not Martje?'

'It is very fine. Decorative figurines, usually. His work always sells,' Martje said.

Their dinner arrived and Steffan didn't think he could feel happier. Father had acknowledged him in public and had chosen him over Philippe to collect a distinguished artist's work.

Philippe had tried to humiliate him tonight. Steffan's physical injuries would heal. His suit could be repaired. And Philippe had failed because Steffan had won Father's approval. He'd been acknowledged as the eldest son.

Steffan was over being treated badly by Phillipe. He wouldn't put up with it anymore. Philippe needed it made clear to him that his place in the family had changed.

He took another sip of Champagne. Steffan would enjoy being the one to put Phillippe in his place.

TWELVE

Yvette

As Yvette waited in the lofty foyer of Madame Jervois's home, she understood her ally did not consider her an equal. Madame Jervois would help her get out of the village but that was it. Yvette wouldn't be invited into the living room to be served coffee. She was left to wait for the lady of the house beside the musty winter coats that the maid had placed on airing racks.

Madame Jervois appeared at the top of the stairs. She clutched the handrail while one foot, followed by the other, made it safely onto the same step. Her pleated bronze dress and matching satin hat gave her the appearance of a *canelé* decorated with a swirl of ganache. Madame's maid bumped a large suitcase down the stairs behind her.

'You can place the suitcase there and I will call you when I am ready to go.' She dismissed the maid without looking at her.

Thankfully the maid, a snooty girl two years older than Yvette who'd lived on the better side of the village, showed no interest in Yvette and hurried off down the hallway.

'Have you settled on the day for your travel?' Madame Jervois asked, stuffing her plump hands into a pair of mustard kid-skin gloves. The colour didn't match her dress and when her hands came close to her face, it gave her a sallow appearance.

'A week from today,' Yvette said with more conviction than she felt. All the things she had to do hovered above her like rain clouds.

'I enquired about the fares, and they are five francs each from Montagne to Paris.'

Yvette pulled out the required notes and gave them to Madame Jervois who secreted them in her purse. She almost jumped when Madame Jervois placed a hand on her arm. She hadn't been expecting that.

'You are doing the right thing.'

Yvette nodded. She wanted to confide in Madame that she worried Lila might die, that they might not find Daniel, that Janie might refuse to go. Her throat felt swollen and her mouth was so dry, she couldn't even squeak a reply.

'I will keep an eye on Monsieur Rhodes and Lila,' Madame reassured her.

Yvette nearly giggled as she imagined Monsieur Rhodes and Lila lined up as Madame Jervois inspected their cottages, critiquing them for tidiness and presentation. Neither would dare disobey her and she would consider either of them becoming unwell a moral affront.

'I will be back on the four o'clock train. Come by after that to pick up your tickets,' Madame added.

As Yvette left, Madame's barrage of instructions to her maid followed her down the pathway. If it hadn't been for her encounter with Eric, she'd have never found out about the calm patch of good inside Maman's friend. She'd be trying to work out all the arrangements herself, along with keeping the old goat Patrick away from Janie. Or was it keeping the young kid Janie away from the old goat?

On the way home, Yvette took a detour through the village

square so she could stop at the statue of Mont-Saint-Louis to have a closer look at her mother's handiwork. It gnawed away at her that she'd walked past this statue just about every day of her life and no one had thought it important to tell her that Maman had repaired it. Not even Maman had told her. She brushed away tears that welled up in her eyes. Maman must have had her reasons, and it wasn't like she could ask her.

'If I ever do anything as great as my mother, I will never keep it from my children. And I will make sure the village always remembers she fixed you,' she told the statue.

The saint had been fixed and life had continued as if some drunken soldier had never shot its face off and changed the course of her mother's life. Maman wasn't unimportant, and Janie wasn't unimportant, and Yvette wasn't either. She picked up a pebble and threw it at the statue's head where it hit its ear with a satisfying ting. The statue stared past her as if it couldn't wait to leave the village either.

'Sorry,' she whispered to the statue. She reached up to pat its arm. 'I just want to leave too.'

She continued down their lane to find Monsieur Rhodes sunning himself in front of his cottage on his favourite seat, sipping his morning coffee.

'Why didn't you tell me Maman fixed the saint's face?' she asked him.

'Not a bonjour? Not a pleasantry? Straight into it?'

'You owe me an explanation.' She came and sat beside him.

She waved away his offer of a coffee. She wasn't in the mood to stand by watching him slop it all over the stove as he struggled to get it into the cup.

'I had no idea you didn't know. One makes assumptions that parents tell children these sorts of things.'

'I did know about the soldiers shooting the statue. But Mama never said she worked on the saint.'

'After the war, the town council asked for help to fix the

statue. Your mama and her father answered the call. Once the repairs were done, your grandfather went back to his home and your mama stayed to marry your father.'

'Stay there.' She rushed next door and brought back the photograph of her mother with the nude statue. 'What do you know about this?'

Monsieur Rhodes studied the photograph. 'I haven't seen this before, but from what I knew about your mother, I would say that was one of her pieces.'

'You think she made this?' Yvette stroked the sculpture in the photograph. It was a wonderous thing, and she struggled to imagine her mother creating such a piece.

He nodded. 'She had talked in passing about sculpting.'

Yvette stroked the picture again. 'It's quite beautiful.'

'It's a shame she didn't keep it up. I don't want to speak ill of the dead, but your father was a somewhat inflexible man.'

Monsieur Rhodes wasn't telling her anything she didn't know.

As if on cue, baby Joseph began to wail. 'I'd better go and help Lila.'

Monsieur Rhodes shook his head. 'Sit a bit longer. Lila will have to do this on her own soon.'

She sighed and shrugged. 'I need to help her.'

Monsieur Rhodes watched her as she went back to her cottage. She couldn't shake off the feeling he was disappointed in her.

Lila gasped for breath as she moved out into the garden, Yvette shuffling behind her carrying Joseph. Lila settled herself into the seat under the tree, and as she reached for the baby, he launched himself out of her arms into his mother's, where he landed with a thump on her chest. Lila coughed up half a lung but stayed upright. She manoeuvred the wriggling child onto her breast.

The baby's whole body was longer than Lila's torso. As he

suckled, Yvette pushed away the thought that he was draining away her lifeforce. Lila seemed so frail and not more than a child, incapable of caring for herself, let alone a baby. It didn't seem possible they could leave her in two weeks. But they had to be gone before the autumn harvest festival. Her chest tightened as she imagined the old goat trotting up to Janie during the festivities and coaxing her into the woods.

She couldn't protect her or watch over her all the time. When the old goat visited Lila, Yvette followed his gaze as he gawped at her breastfeeding the baby. But his desire seemed to wane. He'd spoilt that fruit; he wanted something ripe and ready for the picking, and she would stop him tasting another tender peach from her family.

She heard his whistling in the distance and groaned, wondering if all her brooding had drawn him to them. She tried not to think about him, but he was ever present, like a teetering mudslide ready to engulf her family and sweep Janie away from them.

Lila's face lit up as the whistling grew louder. Yvette suppressed the urge to shake her. Why could none of her family see through this letch and understand what motivated him?

As he came into view, he took off his cap to greet them. It wasn't out of politeness; it was just to show off his full head of silver hair. Everything about him seemed staged to get what he wanted: the hair, the politeness, the pretence of caring.

'We've had good summer so we're going to pay you two months' rent in advance.' The words were out before she could stop herself.

Aubert put his cap back on; his mouth opened slightly, and his eyes crinkled up, giving him a weasel-like expression.

'Now Lila's living with you, it's only fair the rent goes up another eight francs a month.'

Damn, she'd left herself wide open, and he'd stepped right up to raise their rent by half again.

'You could say we were looking after her on your behalf, so perhaps the rent should go down?' She held her breath and hoped she hadn't pushed too far.

He laughed like it was a joke, but she could tell by the way he clasped his hands together, then let them go, that her comment had hit home.

'There are the two of them, which doubles the number in the cottage, so fifty per cent is fair.'

He was all business, and it didn't seem to matter to him that one of the extra people was his son.

'More like fifteen per cent.' A tingle crept up her neck as she eased into the bartering. It was like wrapping herself in a well-worn shawl.

'Thirty per cent, then.'

'Twenty per cent and we'll pay you a week early.' The last thing she wanted was for him to discover they were leaving. He might even try to charge them a subletting fee.

'Done.' He held out his hand.

She squeezed her hand around his as hard as she could to crush his fingers. She was rewarded when a muscle twitched in his jaw. She forced herself not to smile.

Another two francs and forty centimes gone from the fund, leaving just under thirty francs. They'd have to find work fast when they got to Paris.

Aubert leant on the fence ready to have a chat. His demeanour changed when Yvette excused herself to prepare lunch, to which she didn't invite him.

After the meal she settled Lila in the sun behind the cottage and tucked Joseph into his drawer cot.

The laundry was dry, so she unpegged it from the washing line. She loved the aroma of freshly dried sheets and the crisp sound they made when she pulled them taut to fold. If someone could make that smell into perfume, it would be very popular.

She finished the folding and placed the laundry in piles for her deliveries.

She swept the floor, polished the kitchen table, and when there were no more tasks to complete, made herself a coffee and sat beside Lila until she heard the train whistle that meant Madame Jervois would be on her way home.

She eased the two large bags of clean laundry into her wheelbarrow. After dropping the first bundle off at Madame Sorve's hotel, she headed straight to Madame Jervois's.

The maid met her on the pathway and scooped up the laundry bag containing clean sheets, tablecloths, and night gowns.

'Is that Yvette?' Madame called from inside.

The maid frowned at Yvette. 'Yes, she's delivered the laundry.'

'Tell her to come into the drawing room.'

The maid sighed. 'You heard her. Leave that there.' She pointed to the wheelbarrow.

'Do you really think I'm so silly that I'd bring it inside?'

The maid's sour expression made her instantly regret her comment. She followed her into the foyer.

'Take those off before you go any further.' The maid looked at her dusty shoes.

She slipped them off without comment and entered the drawing room, where Madame sat in a lavender-coloured armchair with her feet up on a matching footrest.

Yvette had expected the room to be cluttered with furniture and ornaments, but the only other pieces were a mahogany coffee table, two china cabinets and a large black leather sofa. The wallpaper was neutral with an embossed fleur-de-lis pattern, and the curtains matched the lavender armchair.

Madame Jervois had a cup of coffee on the table beside her, along with a plate of small cakes, each iced in a different colour. Perhaps she'd purchased them at Café Loire.

Yvette's mouth began to water as she glanced at the cakes.

Madame didn't offer her one. Instead, she held out a small envelope.

Yvette stepped forward to take it from her. She opened it and pulled out the tickets. They were dated Friday 12 September 1933. Carriage 6, seats 41 and 42. Her stomach somersaulted because it was real now. They had tickets, they were leaving this tiny village and going to Paris.

'So, a week from today, your train leaves Nantes Station at two in the afternoon. You will need to be at Nantes well before two. It's a three-hour journey to Nantes from here, so you will need to be on the nine a.m. train.' Madame instructed her as if she were a small child who understood nothing.

'I understand, Madame Jervois. Thank you for all your help. We won't miss the train. But I'd be less nervous if I'd heard from Daniel.'

'It's a leap of faith situation. You just need to have faith.' Madame Jervois shrugged.

The flower arrangement on the coffee table held wisps of jasmine and orange geraniums. The aroma from the two competing scents overpowered anything else nearby. It became difficult to breathe.

'I am not sure we can leave just yet.'

Madame Jervois froze, her coffee cup suspended between her saucer and mouth. She stared at Yvette as if she'd blasphemed against God.

'It's Lila. She still can't look after herself,' Yvette continued.

Madame Jervois shook her head. 'That girl is nothing but trouble. I promised your mother I'd do good by you. I will not be vexed by that little ne'er do well.'

She seemed to care more about getting her own way than helping them.

'I'm not sure what I can do. She's still too sick to look after Joseph properly...'

Madame's cup clattered back onto the saucer and Yvette's explanation deflated like an under-cooked sponge.

'I am determined that you leave when we said you would. We have already paid for the tickets.'

She had paid for the tickets, not Madame. But she wasn't going to correct her. 'I am worried about leaving her. She may still die, and what would happen to Joseph?'

'Is she still with you in the cottage?' Madame Jervois tapped her fingers against the saucer.

'Aubert knows she's there. I've paid him two months' rent so he can't put it up or throw her out.'

'I won't hear of you staying longer. My maid will take Lila her breakfast and bring the baby here during the day and we will tend to him until she is well enough to look after herself and the baby.' She tapped her foot twice on the floor to signal her decision.

'But you don't even like her,' Yvette blurted out.

Madame Jervois laughed. 'I like Patrick Aubert even less. And this will incense him. It's time someone stood up him. He may act like it, but he doesn't own this village.'

Yvette viewed the offer like a crystal hanging in a window, the light sending colours in all directions, each one with a potential consequence. What would the price for this be?

Three short weeks ago it hadn't seemed possible that Madame Jervois would be the one to help them. All she'd ever been to Yvette was a busybody and a gossip. How people could surprise you.

'If you will do that for us, I won't disappoint you. I'll send the rent money every month, so Lila won't be evicted. Could I ask one more favour? Could you make sure the old goat doesn't get near enough to Lila to plant another baby?'

'With pleasure.'

Madame Jervois rubbed her hands together, clearly thrilled at the prospect of further thwarting Aubert.

As she left Madame Jervois's home, Yvette's stomach continued to somersault. This could be one of the last times she walked through her village.

She had a wild sense that life was truly about to begin, until she rounded the corner and saw the old goat and the young kid holding hands as they walked down the lane. She broke into a run, intending to separate them with her wheelbarrow.

THIRTEEN

Steffan

Paris, September 1933

Steffan sat down beside Daniel on the bench outside the Blum Foundry break room to soak up the morning sun. On the farm he'd spent every day outside, and it was something he missed.

The bench also gave him a good view of the latest project under construction in the foundry. Today, they were assembling two life-sized bronze horses for the entrance gates of a wealthy client. Four workers heaved on ropes to haul up the horse head and neck to suspend it more than a metre above the ground. They wheeled over the horse's prone body and set about disagreeing with each other as to how to best join the two pieces.

Daniel tucked his precious newspaper, *L'Humanite*, under his derrière and pulled a letter out of his vest pocket.

Steffan didn't know why Daniel read the newspaper during their break, most of which he then wasted scrubbing the ink from his fingers before he could re-enter the carving room.

'Letter from home?' Steffan asked as he rolled a cigarette.

'From my cousin. She wants to move to Paris with her little sister.'

'Be nice to have family around.'

Steffan wished he were closer to his sister Liselle and her growing family. The last time he'd seen his nephew he'd begun to walk, and his niece was still a baby. A niggle of regret squirmed in his chest when he pictured his next visit and the children hiding behind their mother, afraid of a stranger.

Daniel turned the last page over and sighed. 'Yvette wishes to stay with me. It's not like they can bunk down with us.' He waved towards the single men's dormitory.

'Surely you can help them find somewhere else?'

Daniel frowned as he stuffed the letter back into his vest pocket. 'It's a crucial time for the party and I can't be distracted. It's out of the question.'

'Wouldn't it be fun, showing your cousins around Paris?' Apart from the incident with Philippe, the day he'd spent celebrating Rosie's birthday was one of the best experiences he'd had in the city. He couldn't think of anything better than being the tour guide. What a great reason to go up the Eiffel Tower and take a cruise on the Seine.

'We have enemies at our door. I don't have time for frivolity.' Daniel retrieved *L'Humanitie* from under his backside and opened it.

Steffan almost laughed, until he took in Daniel's shut-down expression. He wasn't joking, and he would not help his cousins.

'You enjoyed the meeting last month?' Daniel asked, without looking up.

Daniel's reluctance to help his family didn't sit right with Steffan, but he understood that if he pushed it any further, it might harm their friendship. The party meant everything to Daniel, and Steffan would need to choose his words carefully.

'A revelation. I see that Potiev is right, that we must unite to make this a better place for all of us.'

Daniel smiled at him.

Steffan took a gamble and said what he really thought. 'I

don't think it's the Blum Foundry he means when he talks about exploitation of workers. I mean, Le Directeur is fair to us, and his family aren't living in the lap of luxury.'

Daniel's eyes were still soft, and he leant towards Steffan. 'It's the real bourgeois, the ones who live in those fancy apartments by the Seine and in the enormous homes in Avenue Montaigne and Trocadero. They're the ones who are the problem.' He paused for effect then continued, 'Your father is an honourable man. I would certainly not call him bourgeois. The fight for us is to unite the left and create an equal society for all. That may mean some of the rich will lose their wealth. It needs to be redistributed.'

Controleur Kubreck bustled into the courtyard and rang the bell to signal the start of the day. For a small man he could whip the bell into a swinging frenzy. One day the metal holding it to the rope would wear through and the bell would tumble across the courtyard to flatten some poor worker.

Daniel folded *L'Humanite* as if it were made from the finest tissue paper, a treasure to be pressed and preserved. For all Steffan knew, that was exactly what he did with them. Daniel seemed to view the paper with the same reverence as the Torah meant to Father, or the Bible to Grand-père.

He followed Daniel into the washroom where they donned their white calico artist smocks, scrubbed their hands to remove anything that could mark the ivory, then backed their way into the carving room, careful not to contaminate their hands. Steffan stood next to Daniel at the bench, where in front of each of them was a 30-centimetre ivory sliver held taut in a vice.

With great patience and a lot of wastage over the past two months, Daniel had coached Steffan on how to turn a piece of bone into a voluptuous woman's leg, or the chubby arm of a baby. Now, he could follow the grain in the bone with his fine instruments and carve out the muscles of a calf and the fibres of a bicep.

The last time Le Directeur had come in to check his carving against the artist's mould, he'd made Steffan start again. After he'd gone, Steffan had complained that his leg looked exactly like the artist's. Daniel had taken the discarded carving and held it up to the plasteline model.

'*See the difference? The model's leg has a small blemish here on her calf. See how it's pocked in on the model?*'

It seemed such a little thing, a tiny detail that appeared unimportant.

As if he reading his mind, Daniel had said, '*It's the detail that takes this from a statue and transforms it into a work of art. Le Directeur wants nothing less than a masterpiece. It is our job to take the artist's vision and faithfully render it in bone.*'

Until that moment he'd thought Daniel only cared about the proletariat, but he cared also about their work.

In their own way, the foundry workers were artists too, transforming base materials like bone and metal into women, men and children, captured in the beauty of suspended movement. A child on a windy day who would forever roll a hoop along a road; a dancer's outstretched leg suspended in the air, poised to take her next step.

The legs this week were for the Dolly Sisters series. The pair were well known on the dancing and vaudeville circuit, and Martje said the statues sold well.

Swirling, knee-length bronze skirts met the sisters' legs mid-thigh, where bone screwed into bronze. It took hours to etch their flat, bobbled pumps with only a fine-pointed chisel, so delicate it seemed no thicker than an eyelash and could only be completed under a magnifying glass. When he left the carving room on Dolly Sisters days, his eyes would be smarting and blurry. At this rate, he'd need spectacles. He didn't mind, as he was sure it would give him a sophisticated air.

He began to enjoy the work, delighting in the details that changed a statue into objet d'art. Each precise cut into the bone, an individual act, built together to make a whole. He'd never seen himself as a patient person, and in some ways the work didn't require patience. It required stamina to complete a statue. A leg was just a leg, but a leg attached to a body, and the body attached to an arm, until all the pieces were assembled into a finished product... he was taken by surprise when the bell rang for their morning break. He'd become so engrossed that three hours had gone by in what felt like three breaths.

They removed their smocks and went out into the courtyard where the sun beat down as they rolled their cigarettes.

Controleur Kubreck rushed towards them, the tension in his shoulders and back making his chin jut further forward, like his head was eager to get to his destination before his body.

'I've just had a message from Monsieur Chiparus. He has some models and I want you to pick them up immediately. We don't want another foundry getting their hands on them.'

The other workers came out of the break room clutching steaming mugs of coffee and handfuls of langues de chat. Any errands would have to wait until he'd got his fair share of biscuits.

Controleur Kubreck stepped in front of the break room door. 'Chiparus will have sent messages to other foundries. You must go now.'

Steffan stepped around the small man. 'I'll go after I've had my break.'

Controleur Kubreck gripped his waistcoat, holding him back from his morning coffee. 'You need to go *now*. We must acquire the work.'

'Fine, I will go now.' He couldn't keep the annoyance from his tone.

Controleur Kubreck pushed Steffan towards the truck.

'I'll save you some biscuits,' Daniel offered.

'You will go with him to help carry the pieces.'

Daniel shrugged. 'As long as I get to drive.'

. . .

Daniel navigated the Bierlet through the streets to Chiparus's studio, all the while cursing the elitist bourgeois, as the homes became bigger and fancier as they approached Rue de la Faisanderie.

Chiparus lived in a colonial-style home of cream stone, set back from the street, surrounded by a solid wall with a sturdy black wrought-iron gate.

The double-doored vehicle entrance was a bonus, as they could back the truck into the courtyard to load the heavy crates directly onto the deck.

Daniel gave a disapproving shake of his head. 'This place could house ten families.' He slammed the black door knocker up and down with such force it reverberated through the courtyard.

When Chiparus's wife opened the door, Steffan wouldn't have recognised her from the night at Les Deux Magot. She wore her hair in plaits wound around her head, like the women from his village, and he felt instantly at ease with her, even though she must have been at least fifteen years his senior. Her serene face broke into a smile, her mouth twitching at the corners and a little dimple forming on her left cheek.

'You wish to see my husband?' she asked.

'We are from the Blum Foundry; Monsieur Chiparus sent us a message,' Daniel replied.

'I am glad you got here first, before the Barbedienne Foundry.' She waved them into the courtyard and pointed to a small building to the right of the main house. 'Go along the pathway,' she said, and went back inside.

'Is the Barbedienne Foundry actually competition?' Steffan asked as he followed Daniel down the white pebbled pathway.

'If they'd got here before us, it wouldn't have been worth getting out of the truck.'

Steffan stood back from Daniel as he knocked at the door. It was only Steffan's second time picking up work. On his first, the artist, Landowski, had bellowed at him for breaking his concentration. Daniel could take the brunt if that happened again, although Chiparus hadn't appeared the yelling type when he'd met him at the restaurant.

'*Entrez,*' a clipped male voice called.

Daniel pushed open the door, Steffan on his heels. They were confronted with a muddle of stone blocks, partially completed sculptures, and lumps of hardened clay and tools scattered over the floor and work benches. Paintbrushes soaked in jars of liquid, and cloths, sandpaper, and pots of paint packed the shelves lining the walls and were gathered in clusters about the floor. Books and magazines were strewn among the other objects, all open at pictures of dancing girls. The place smelt of turpentine and women's perfume.

'Are you two from the Blum Foundry?' the clipped voice said.

Steffan stepped past a block of marble taller than himself and found the voice's owner. Without his hat and overcoat, Monsieur Chiparus was slight and balding. He was sitting in front of a turntable, hunched over a red plasteline sculpture, a girl with two Afghan hounds. He kept his focus on his scalpel as he worked on the figure's legs. The curls of plasteline fell to the ground where they sat like fat, red ringlets around his feet.

'I am happy Blum Foundry arrived first. I do enjoy working with Le Directeur and his lovely wife. I have four figurines ready.'

Monsieur Chiparus did not look up but inclined his head towards the right where the statuettes waited on a bench. Even from a distance Steffan could see the detailed work on each piece. A girl held a book behind her back with a reflective expression on her face. Skirts whirled around raised limbs as the two Dolly Sisters danced another routine. But the one that got him excited depicted two lovers merged together in a dance.

'You have the truck?' Monsieur Chiparus's voice shook him out of his daze.

'*Oui*, Monsieur Chiparus,' Daniel replied.

Steffan didn't know if he was capable of uttering anything. Being in the presence of such a great artist made him so nervous he was afraid his voice would come out as a squeak.

They picked their way over to the bench through the discarded magazines and upended paint pots. Pencils and hardened curls of clay scrunched under their feet.

Even as plasticine sculptures, Steffan knew they would become the best pieces the foundry had worked with.

'We need to wrap these well.' Daniel had appraised the pieces too, but from a different perspective. 'May we please clear a pathway to safely remove the artwork?'

'Of course, let me help. What a mess I've made.'

Monsieur Chiparus unfurled from his turntable and set about picking up discarded tools, sketches, and magazines. The other foundry workers said artists were selfish, forgetful, debauched, and very rude. Monsieur Chiparus appeared to be none of those things.

Steffan extracted a broom from beside the bench and made good inroads into creating a clear, smooth track among the debris. Daniel returned with two crates stuffed with burlap.

'Can you back the truck into the courtyard and bring in the other two crates?'

By the time he'd returned, Monsieur Chiparus had wrapped two of his works in separate canvas sheets. With the love of a doting father, Monsieur Chiparus guided Daniel as he lowered one of the wrapped statuettes into the crate. They fussed about packing the burlap around the statuette, filling up every gap so it was fully protected.

Once he was satisfied, he allowed Steffan and Daniel to move the crate. It was surprisingly heavy and Steffan did not want to shame himself by staggering. He let Daniel take the lead and they shuffled out of the cluttered studio; he was careful not to bump himself or drop the load.

By the time the fourth crate was on the truck, Steffan's arms felt like they were made of clay and three times longer.

Daniel covered the cargo with a tarpaulin and strapped it down while Monsieur Chiparus puffed on his pipe and examined all the ties.

'Come back in three weeks. I'll have another four in the series finished,' he called out.

Steffan caught a last glimpse of the artist as he closed the gates behind the truck. He seemed sad, and Steffan understood it must be hard to let go of your work, handing it over to another where things could go terribly wrong.

Steffan insisted he drive back instead of Daniel, as he wanted to be the one to bring the statues into the foundry. Le Directeur waited on the loading bay with the other workers as he backed the truck without any corrections. The perfect manoeuvre was even more satisfying when Philippe, his face sulkier than usual, appeared beside Father.

When Steffan stepped out of the truck, Le Directeur kissed him on both cheeks. It was something he rarely did with other men, and Steffan had never seen him greet Philippe that way. Chiparus's work must be very important to him.

'He gave us four and he's working on another four. He told us to come back in three weeks,' he said to Father. He never knew what to call him in front of the workers. 'Father' seemed too familiar, like he wanted favouritism, and 'Le Directeur' was too formal. Usually, he could get away with not calling him anything.

'Ah, well. It is good to have four, it would have been better to have had more. No matter, let us see the beauties.'

Steffan swung up onto the truck bed to move the first crate to find Philippe beside him, his face, disfigured by hatred, only centimetres away. He could smell coffee on his breath and the acrid coal ash on his jacket.

'Anyone can pick up moulds from an artist. You are not that special,' Philippe hissed at him.

Steffan's fist closed, ready to punch him in his pathetic little face. He took a deep breath and uncurled his hand. With the whole foundry watching, hitting Philippe would be the worst thing to do.

They moved the crates from the truck to the moulds bench that ran the length of the foundry wall. When Steffan had come to Paris a year ago, they had been so busy, the bench full of thirty or more art works. The four they added today made a total of seven moulds.

He'd asked Daniel about the downturn, and he'd said, 'Decorative arts weren't a priority when the fascists were kicking down your door.'

'Please unwrap our beauties,' Papa said to Steffan and Daniel.

The wrappings fell to reveal a girl holding a book behind her back. Like the bellows in a furnace, the workers' voices erupted, and they yelled at each other about what could be cast as one piece, whether the book should be separate from her hands, and whether her legs should be bronze or ivory.

They went on to unpack the next one, a man and woman clasped in an embrace.

'Rudolph Valentino and Natacha Rambova,' Le Directeur shouted, like he'd won the lottery.

The workers cheered in response and continued yelling design ideas at each other.

Steffan recognised the late male film star's slicked-back hairstyle.

The third and fourth crates revealed more dancing girls. The workers crowded around, inspecting the pieces.

Someone pushed past Steffan to get closer to the figurines.

Steffan stumbled and lost his balance; he pitched forward and put out an arm to stop himself falling. His hip collided with the bench and his arm connected with Book Girl. The statue wobbled on its base. He tried to steady her, but his forearm collided with her head, and she plunged off the bench. Steffan's heart almost stopped as the precious statue careened to the floor, smashing into four pieces.

The excited conversation around him stopped, as if he'd put his head under water. He could feel everyone's eyes on him, and he didn't want to look up to see the expressions on their faces.

As he scrabbled around on the floor scooping up the broken pieces, the workers shuffled back into the foundry like defeated men.

Someone knelt beside him to pick up Book Girl's head.

'Nice one, michlinge. Made us all proud,' Philippe said.

Father stood in front of the bench with his back to the other statues. As Steffan placed the broken base back on the bench, he was dismayed to see tears trickling down Father's face.

'I will make this right,' Steffan said, in a clumsy attempt to comfort him.

Father shook his head. 'It feels like an omen. The bench is nearly empty, and our best piece is broken. We don't have enough work.'

'I'm sorry – it was an accident.'

Father nodded. 'I don't blame you, son.'

Philippe brought another piece of the shattered statue to the bench. He placed his hand on Father's shoulder. 'It's all right, Papa. We'll go and see Chiparus. He's a clever man. He can repair this.'

Father shrugged. 'What does it matter? Who's going to keep buying these things? They make it harder and harder for us to survive. They attacked Rue de Braque this week. People are scared to do business with us.'

Philippe nodded and rubbed Father's shoulder.

It was if Steffan's view of the world changed, like looking

through the telescope at the top of the Eiffel Tower and everything coming into focus. He hadn't known the foundry was under threat, but Philippe had. Stupid, because the evidence was there on the bench in front of him, the dwindling number of works. Maybe people weren't buying statues as much, but it seemed more than that. Philippe could comfort Father because he knew this world, knew the perils that came with being Jewish. Steffan hadn't seen what was right in front of him. He'd never felt more alone, an outsider, someone who didn't understand the world he lived in now. Unable to comfort Father, unable to find the right words, any words.

Father drew himself up and brushed away the tears with his sleeve. 'Put the pieces back into the crate. Tomorrow, we will take it back to Chiparus to repair. We will offer him a higher rate on the piece to compensate him for his additional work.'

Father left them to collect the broken pieces.

'Is it really as bad as Father says?' Steffan asked Philippe.

'Yes, I think so.' Philippe kept on picking up chips of plasteline from the floor.

'Are you worried?'

Philippe shook his head. 'Papa and Mama always find a way.'

What if they couldn't, this time? What if his breaking the statue was the beginning of the end? He was being silly. It wasn't as if one event could change everything ... but maybe it could.

'I wish we could get on better,' he blurted out, before he lost his nerve.

'You are a fool. Tidy up your own mess.' Philippe stood up and walked away.

Like Father, Steffan wanted to cry too. He didn't want to be an outsider any longer. It was bewildering not understanding what was going on around him.

He needed Philippe to accept him as a brother. He'd do anything to make that happen. Anything.

FOURTEEN

Yvette

Nantes, September 1933

Someone called out her name as Yvette and Janie started down
Nantes Railway Station's front steps. She didn't bother stopping;
they didn't know anyone here. She didn't want to lose her footing
either. The bags were heavy, and one started to swing, causing
even more momentum that propelled her down the steps.

Just as they reached the bottom, a man grabbed her arm.
Twisting around ready to lash out, a familiar freckled face smiled
down at her. She knew his face, the dark hair carefully pomaded
to sweep back from his forehead, those lively green eyes, and the
impish smile. And her instinct telling her to be careful.

'What are you doing here? Are you on your way to Paris?' he
asked.

His voice jogged her memory and she blushed. It was Eric,
the train conductor who Madame Jervois had dragged her away
from in La Montagne.

'Eric,' she stammered, then winced. If only she could have
said his name with confidence, then it wouldn't have been so

apparent he'd not crossed her mind since their coffee together in the café.

'Janie, this is Eric, we met…' Janie wasn't by her side. 'Janie's gone,' she squawked, turning from left to right like a broken windmill, searching for her. They'd only just left the village and she'd lost her at their first stop.

'The girl you were with is just over there.' Eric pointed across the plaza.

Janie stood holding her suitcase staring up at the cathedral to their right. Its arches and white columns soared high above them into a pointed bell tower.

Yvette hurried over and plucked at her sleeve with her free hand. 'Please don't wander off. We need to stick together.'

'You were just over there,' Janie said, dismissing her concerns, all the time staring entranced at the cathedral. 'Isn't it wonderful? So big, so tall, so white. Can we go inside?'

Yvette checked the clock on the station façade. Even though the train didn't leave for forty minutes, she worried about missing it.

'If you're catching the Paris train, you've got plenty of time,' Eric said.

When she looked at the clock again, he continued, 'It leaves from platform two. Don't worry, I'll take you there.'

Since they had so much time, it would seem silly not to go into the church. She couldn't face Janie's grumbling or a repeat of the hurt-puppy expression Eric had worn when Madame Jervois dragged her off.

'Let's go then.' Her voice came out confident, even though she didn't feel it.

Janie's face lit up with a big smile. Before she could introduce Eric, he did the honours himself, shaking Janie's hand. 'I had the pleasure of being your sister's train conductor from Mont-Saint-Louis to La Montagne. We even attempted coffee, until that

Madame Jervois whisked your lovely sister away, no doubt telling her all sorts of stories of my misdeeds.'

'She did say to stay away from you. Said you were nothing but trouble.'

Eric shrugged. 'She's all dried up. No sense of fun.'

As they walked towards the cathedral's vaulted mouth, she wanted to tell Eric about how kind Madame Jervois had been to them, and that he was wrong about her. She'd led a colourful life before and during the war, much like Maman. But she remained quiet, as Eric wouldn't see it as she did. No point in causing friction where the wheels turned freely.

They entered the church, and it surprised Yvette how long and narrow it was. The columns rose around them, stretching up to form a rib cage on the ceiling. The rows of wooden seats led them towards the altar, a lattice of white carved lace peppered with saints, flowers, and gilded candle holders.

She stopped to absorb the coloured light from the stained-glass windows and marvelled at this beautiful house of God. Eric's presence beside her kept dragging her back to more earthly matters. He held himself with such confidence and ease, and although his face was masculine, there was a female quality to his lips and around his eyes. The hairs on her arms rose as she imagined his face on one of the marble angels looking down on them.

Instead of mooning over how well Eric was assembled, she should be focusing on how men had been inspired to build this divine and wonderous place to worship God. It wasn't the place to be thinking sinful thoughts. Yet her hand twitched from the effort of not reaching out to touch him.

Eric stopped under a stained-glass window in a pool of coloured light, as if God had singled him out.

Something moved quickly to her left. She flinched back, but not fast enough to step out of the way of a running child who crashed into her. As she staggered to stay upright, two ragged children tugged her bag from her shoulder. She hung onto her suitcase, which stopped the bag from disappearing with the children. The bag upended itself and its contents, including her purse, tumbled out, scattering across the church floor.

One urchin launched himself onto her purse, scooping it up in one fluid movement. The other child let go of her arm to scuttle away.

'Stop him. He robbed me,' she shrieked, pointing in the direction of the tiny robber who zig-zagged around people in the crowd and disappeared into the forest of bodies.

Eric startled into action and sprinted after the children. Janie burst through the crowd, elbowing people out of the way.

Yvette could barely breathe, her vision focused on the floor in front of her as she scrabbled around picking up her scattered possessions with her one free hand. She wasn't letting go of the suitcase for a moment. She wasn't losing anything else, now all their money was gone. They had nothing, apart from ten francs she'd sewn into her coat, and the five francs in Janie's.

How were they going to survive? They wouldn't even have enough to last a week when they got to Paris.

She screamed as a hand came down on her shoulder. It was just Janie.

Her sister stood above her, shaking her head. 'We couldn't find them.'

Yvette sunk further onto the floor. They hadn't even made it to Paris, and she'd failed. She'd let them get robbed.

Eric ran up from behind Janie. He offered his hand to Yvette. 'Let me help you up.'

She would have preferred to continue wallowing in failure on the floor, but she could do that standing up. Tears pricked her eyes. Somehow, crying in front of Eric seemed so much worse, so she tried to make a joke. 'I hope my possessions ending up on the floor in front of you is not going to happen every time we meet.'

'If you still had your pistol, you could have shot the little shit.'

His comment surprised her so much, she laughed.

'We'd have to find them to do that. Did you see them? Should we report them?'

Eric shrugged. 'No sign of them. It would take hours to report it and you'd miss your train. Even if we found them, your purse would be long gone.'

'There's no way to get it back?' Even as the words came out, she knew it was a silly question.

He shook his head. 'How much did you lose?'

'Thirty francs.' She didn't tell him or Janie about the money sewn into their coats.

'I have twenty I can lend you right away.'

She couldn't take it from him, they'd be indebted. He'd have something over them, and they'd be no better off than they were in the village. She opened her mouth to tell him no, but Eric cut her off. 'It's a loan. You can pay me back a little at a time.'

Even during a good week in the village, the most she'd managed to save up was one franc. It would have taken her at least six months to pay Eric back. But if they got work in Paris straight away, she could pay him back in three months or less.

The sun came out again and lit Eric up in a beam of orange light reflected through the stained-glass windows. Yvette took it as a positive sign that even if Madame Jervois had doubts about Eric, God indicated it would all work out.

It could do, if he really was fine with her paying it off a bit at a time. 'How would I get the money to you? I'd want to try and pay you every week.'

'We could meet when I start my run to Paris.' Eric looked away as he added, 'I'd have something nice to look forward to, seeing you every week.' Then he shrugged. He didn't seem to be in any dire need of getting the money back straight away. He kept his head down, but his eyes glanced up at her to gauge her response. It made him seem endearing, the hurt puppy again. Yet, his response felt a little like a performance he'd perfected it over the years. Madame Jervois had already warned her he had a 'girl in every train station'.

God bathing him in orange light could also mean Eric knew exactly where to stand. She'd promised Madame Jervois she'd be careful.

'Meeting you at the station might not work out when I get a job. Could you give me your address, and I can send money to you when I get paid?'

He looked at her directly now. 'Certainly. I will give you my address when I get you two safely onto the train. Let's do one more thing before we head back to the station. I think you both need this, after being robbed.' Eric led them over to a cloister and dropped three coins into the collection box so they could each take a candle. They took them to a side altar and Eric passed her a lit taper, which she gave to Janie.

Her sister took her time lighting the candle and counted twelve places in and two up. She changed the placement after each birthday, moving it one over for every year.

Yvette didn't care about such things. She chose an empty spot in the first row of candles. Eric took the taper from her and made a big show of lighting his candle and placing it next to hers.

Yvette prayed to Mama and to God to keep them safe.

It didn't surprise her when Eric asked them, 'What did you pray for?'

'Special prayers are just like wishes. If you tell someone, they won't come true,' she and Janie replied in unison, then laughed.

When Eric looked puzzled, Yvette explained, 'Mama always said that.'

Eric dismissed their superstition with a wave of his hand. 'I prayed I will be joining my uncle soon in Paris to help him with his important work in the Croix de Feu.'

Before Yvette could ask more about his prayer, Eric turned

them back through the cathedral, and acted like a boat prow, cutting a pathway through the crowds and into the bustling railway station while Yvette, with a firm hold on Janie's hand, followed in the calm water of his wake.

He warded off other travellers from bumping into them, and Yvette only had one heavy bag bash her shin. Eric blew on his whistle to avoid all of them being run down by a luggage trolley pushed by a sweating porter.

They stopped in front of the entry gate at platform 2. Eric took their tickets and presented them to the guard who greeted him.

As Eric escorted them through the milling crowd, Yvette felt like a fish moving from a swift current into the quiet eddies of their stream at home. Eric's shrill whistle eventually cleared a pathway down the platform to carriage 6. He pushed them up the carriage's steep steps and followed with their bags.

The inside of the train felt serene after the noise, the pushing, and all the people on the platform. Working their way along the aisle they found their seats on the left side of the train, numbers 41 and 42.

'Good seats.' Eric lapsed into guard mode. 'You'll get great views of the Seine and Paris.'

He stashed their suitcase and bags in the luggage rack above. 'Keep the clasps to the carriage wall so no one can take anything. Remember to do that every time you get something from your bag.'

Janie scooted in by the window and pressed her forehead against the glass. Yvette placed their food bag on the floor between their seats.

Eric nodded his approval. 'It's full enough to last till you get to Paris. Don't buy anything on the train, it's too expensive.' As an afterthought he said, 'Except coffee – you can buy coffee from the cart.'

He took out his wallet and passed her 20 francs. He flicked

open his conductor's notebook, wrote his address onto a page, ripped it out and pressed it into her hand. 'Don't lose it. I will come and meet you in Paris.'

Eric Granger
2 Rue De La Vallee
La Montagne

Yvette took his hand. 'Thank you for looking after us.'

'My pleasure. I'll ask one thing in return.'

Eric leant to whisper in her ear, and suddenly his lips were on hers. It was so unexpected, and his lips so sensuous on her mouth that she kissed him back. It wasn't a proper thing to do in public, but her body took on a life of its own and pressed against his.

For a moment, all she wanted was to be a girl on a train kissing a boy. She could be who she wanted to be. Her new life had started the moment the train pulled out of Mont-Saint-Louis.

What would Madame Jervois know? Eric might be right, that life had sucked her dry and she'd forgotten what being truly alive felt like.

The long train whistle blast separated them.

'Where are you staying in Paris?'

Yvette hesitated, still unsure of how much she wanted Eric to know about their lives.

Janie took the decision away by answering, 'We are meeting our cousin, Daniel Foucart, who works at Blum Foundry, 29 Rue de Paradis.'

She should have corrected Janie, as Daniel might not even be there anymore. She didn't want her to fret, though. Yvette would carry the worry for them both.

Eric frowned. 'Jewish foundry.' Then his face lit up. 'Rue de

Paradis sounds wonderful. If you don't write, I will come searching for you there.'

Yvette smiled, still holding on to the address and money as he left the carriage.

She sighed with relief as the train lurched forward and shuddered out of the station. No one could stop her and Janie. She couldn't second guess her decision to leave Lila with Monsieur Rhodes and Madame Jervois as her guardians.

She rummaged through her bag and found a secure place for the 20 francs, and put the address in the back of the framed picture of her mother holding the statue.

She imagined Daniel's Blum Foundry at 29 Rue de Paradis as having a modern starburst above the door and wrought-iron gates. If Daniel had moved on, surely they would know his whereabouts.

If they couldn't find him, she'd figure out what to do next. Maman had survived in Paris before she came to live in Mont-Saint-Louis. If Maman could do it, then so could her daughters. Paris was a big place with lots of opportunities. They would find work and send money back for Lila and Joseph – and Eric. The list grew longer.

She settled into the seat beside Janie. Losing the money had been awful. Eric had helped them, but they weren't obliged, and she'd pay it off as quickly as possible. If she saw Eric again, it wouldn't be through obligation, it would be because she wanted to. And if that happened, she'd need to be very sure he had only one girl in one city – Yvette in Paris.

FIFTEEN

Steffan

Paris, September 1933

At Claude's, Steffan secured an inside table next to the coveted booths. He greeted a regular sitting in the closest booth and made small talk until Daniel arrived.

Daniel had no interest in the 'booth crowd' and on many occasions had made clear his disapproval of Steffan trying to wheedle his way in. Unlike everyone else in the foundry, Daniel also didn't seem to care that Steffan had broken the statue. The foundry workers began to call him *doigts de beurre*, and he feared butterfingers would be become his nickname.

Margot swept over and made a great show of taking their orders. Tonight, she wore her hair rolled under at the nape of her neck and a topaz pendant hung between her ample breasts. Much to Daniel's annoyance, she hovered over the two men much longer than necessary.

'Can we get our drinks soon, as we're off to a meeting?' Steffan said before Daniel was rude to her.

Margot frowned at him and said, her tone accusatory, 'You're off to the music hall, aren't you? You want to watch those girls shake it all about.'

Daniel sighed loudly. 'It's a political meeting. No one is shaking anything around, apart from the status quo.'

Margot sniffed at them and turned on her heel to steam away across the café.

'Don't upset her. We won't get our drinks in time now.'

'We'll be fine. She really wants to shake herself all around with you.'

'I don't think so,' Steffan said to be polite, knowing full well that Margot wanted nothing more than to drag him into a dark corner.

When she returned with the drinks, she placed Steffan's in front of him without a drop spilt, then slammed Daniel's onto the table. Daniel swore when the contents slopped over him.

'Oopsy,' Margot said. Her attempt at an innocent smile came off as a grimace.

Daniel wiped his waistcoat with his handkerchief while they gulped their drinks.

When they left, Steffan took notice of their route to the Artisan Guildhall. This time he felt comfortable entering the dark alley where before he'd feared he'd be knifed. He even recognised the Guildhall's ill-lit entranceway.

The same surly face opened the door and eyed them with the same amount of suspicion. Daniel showed him his Artisan Guild card, which he scrutinised with such intensity that Steffan wondered if he could read. Finally, he let them in.

'We've an important guest here tonight. Can't be too careful,' he said by way of explanation.

They made their way up the rickety stairs and into the dark room. Steffan recognised some of the men standing around in small groups from his last visit. This time several women were clustered near Potiev, and another man, who wore an expensive black suit and puffed on a long-stemmed pipe. As he chatted with Potiev, the man's inquisitive expression left no doubt he was taking in everything happening in the hall.

Daniel clutched Steffan's arm. 'Edouard Herriot,' he whispered in awed tones.

While Steffan tried to bluff his way through not knowing who he was, Daniel continued, 'He's the founder of Cartel de Gauches. Kept those fascists out of power.'

Of course, such an important man, and a member of Parliament. Steffan stood a little straighter, ran his fingers through his hair, and brushed down the front of his jacket.

Monsieur Herriot drew on his pipe and blew out perfect smoke rings above the heads of the two women next to him. He held himself as straight as a copper rod, as if his back were braced. His dark, prominent eyebrows gave him an air of severity, until he laughed at a comment from one of the women. Herriot's amusement was infectious and Steffan couldn't help smiling, along with everyone else.

Potiev led Herriot to the front of the room where they stood in front of the curved table. He motioned for everyone to be seated.

'Monsieur Herriot needs no introduction from me, as you will all be acquainted with his work and his commitment to the proletariat.'

Everyone else in this room knew about the man standing in front of them, except Steffan. He felt so out of place, and questioned why he was even sitting among them, until Herriot began to speak.

'Adolf Hitler knocks on the door to our freedom while he assembles troops near our border. Do you want to lose our way of life, our heritage, our religions? He might say he's for workers. He's not. He's an empiricist like the Kaisers before him; he wants to roll through Europe destroying our fragile peace and hard-won equality. And for what? For the ego of a zealot and the misplaced patriotism of Teutonic Germany.

'The champions of the proletariat and the working man must fight against this cancerous thinking. Here in our beloved country, here in the halls of our ministries, we must persuade these misguided comrades who swing right, that their faith in fascism will lead to nothing but destruction of our way of life, and unending oppression for our people. It offers nothing but tyranny and death.

'If we thought the Great War was horror incarnate, then we must pray the fascists do not gain a foothold here. For they will bring upon us unimaginable suffering and the destruction of our total way of life.

'We urge you to take part in the *La Marche Contre le Fascisme* with our comrades to show our support for the communist movement and our distain for fascism. The left must further unite and show our solidarity and strength to the Fascists.'

The room burst into applause and whistling, and a babble of noise shaped itself into a chant: '*Vive Parti Communiste, Vive Francaise.*'

Monsieur Herriot punched his fist in the air and chanted along with the room.

The idea of walking along Avenue de Champs-Élysées and waving a red flag appealed immensely, until Steffan imagined Father's disapproval if he found him at a rally. Half disappointed and half relieved, Steffan remembered Sabbath celebrations on Saturday with the Blum family.

He whispered to Daniel, 'That's me out then, what with the Sabbath.'

Daniel swore under his breath and shook his head. 'The duty to your fellow comrade is much greater than to your religion.'

Ashlam appeared beside him. 'If you are coming on the march, Blum, it's time to sign up as a party member.'

He took Steffan's stunned silence as consent and frogmarched him over to a thin man with trembling hands who stood behind a desk covered with Communist Party leaflets.

'This young man wants to join up.'

'I need some time to think about it.' Steffan tried to back away.

'Nonsense. Time's run out. Only now matters. Sign him up, Chavier.' Ashlam pushed him into a strategically placed seat.

Chavier observed Steffan through narrowed eyes as he placed an application form and a fountain pen in front of him. With Ashlam's hand pressing into his shoulder, saying no didn't seem an option.

Chavier's ink-stained, trembling finger pointed out a line on the form. 'Write your name there, your address there, age, occupation, and signature.'

Steffan guessed he could always change his mind later, when he wasn't being press-ganged into joining. He picked up the pen and filled in his information.

Chavier's finger moved down the page and he glanced at Ashlam. 'That's where you sign as his nominee. Who's going to be his second?'

'Daniel,' Ashlam said.

Chavier called Daniel over. 'Sign here as his second.'

Daniel wrote his name and signed it with an uncharacteristic flourish.

'All we need now is two francs and you're done. The committee's meeting in the next thirty minutes and I'll give it to them to review.'

Steffan reluctantly gave him the money. Chavier must have taken his half-annoyed expression for concern. 'It's just a formality. The committee will approve your application straight away. You've got two top men vouching for you.'

He placed the application with several more and bustled away with the sheaf of papers towards the group conversing with Herriot.

'Thanks for that, comrades,' Steffan said.

'You needed a nudge towards the left.' Daniel laughed at his joke.

'You won't have any regrets,' Ashlam assured him.

Steffan didn't share his confidence. He already regretted being pushed into something he wanted more time to think about.

'I might head off,' he said to Daniel.

'Don't go yet. Chavier puts the applications as the committee's first agenda item. He'll be out soon with the good news, and we'll have a celebratory drink.'

The mention of the drink won him over, and soon Chavier was bustling back into the hall from a side room. 'We want to welcome the following to our chapter: Comrade Steffan Blum, Comrade Petier ...'

Comrade Steffan Blum. It came as a shock that he'd be referred to that way. Ashlam and Daniel grabbed his shoulders like he'd won some award, while others in the room shook his hand and welcomed him.

After several brandies bought for him by complete strangers, he decided he quite liked being a comrade.

'It's time to unleash our artisanal skills.' Chavier pushed some tables together and produced some black damask.

'What are we making, Comrade Chavier?' Steffan liked calling everyone comrade now.

'Banners, Comrade. Banners.'

Under Daniel's direction, Steffan undertook his first communist endeavour, which depicted Lady Liberty holding a hammer in one hand and a sickle in the other.

SIXTEEN

Yvette

Paris, September 1933

Yvette woke on high alert. It took her a moment to realise the train wasn't moving. Janie was asleep by her side, and their bags were still above them. She leaned past Janie to make out the station's name – *Versailles*. Was this Versailles as in the palace? Mama had told her about a visit, describing gold-leaf statues, fountains in the gardens and the Hall of Mirrors.

As the train lurched forward and cleared the station, the palace gardens came into view. They had been landscaped to create the illusion of an intricately woven tapestry, and Yvette had never imagined they would be so vast. As she focused on them, like turning the lenses on Papa's binoculars, the gardens were revealed as consisting of four segments bordered by low box hedges in swirling fleur-de-lis patterns. Avenues of cone-shaped topiary lined the edges of each quadrant to form a cross, with a circular pool as the centrepiece. Yvette was disappointed that the pool did not have a fountain. As her eyes turned to the palace, she struggled to determine whether it was one building, or many nestled up against each other.

A twinge of guilt tickled her that she hadn't woken Janie to view the splendour. She shook it off. They could visit Versailles once they were settled. Yvette had done enough for now. Not only had she pried Janie away from the old goat, she'd also got them to Paris.

As the train approached the city, Yvette looked out at the warehouses, shops and homes lining the banks of the Seine, and the colourful houseboats moored against the jetties. Plainer, sturdier boats were transporting goods up and down the river.

The city was just finishing its day – men and women were walking out of the factory gates, and farmers were selling the last of their produce to hungry workers at small markets on street intersections. She saw a young lady on a bicycle, her skirt clipped to her stockings so it didn't get caught in the chain. A fancy motor vehicle with a red leather roof passed her, splashing her with muddy water from a puddle, and Yvette giggled when the cyclist shook her fist and yelled something at the driver.

Maybe Yvette could get a bicycle to go to work. And it looked as if there was plenty of work.

The train moved further into central Paris, where the streets were teeming with people, bicycles, and motor vehicles. She'd never seen so many people before – ten times, a hundred times the number of people in her village and La Montagne combined. The buildings became taller; long lines of them in straight rows, all of them white and cream with black wrought iron balconies.

The train slowed to join other rail lines all heading for their destination, Gare Montparnasse. When it halted, Yvette waited for the other passengers to clear the aisle before lifting their bags down from the luggage rack. They made their way off the train onto the platform that seethed with people. She was nervous without Eric's guidance; she squeezed Janie's hand tight. Her sister yelped and shook herself free.

'Keep your bag close to you, and stick with me,' she said to Janie.

'I'm not stupid.' Janie stood with her hand on her hip.

Janie's stance reminded her so much of their mother, she couldn't help but smile. 'I know. I'm just nervous. We've already been robbed once.'

'*You've* already been robbed, not me,' Janie teased.

'You win. Come on, let's find the right exit.'

They followed the crowd from the platform into the vaulted centre of the station. Its architecture was so like Nantes that she felt her tension ease. At Nantes, the ticket sellers and guards had been on the left side of the station, so she led them in that direction.

'Could you tell us which is the best exit for Rue de Paradis?' she asked two guards on a smoke break.

They looked her up and down, and the older one replied, 'You will need to take the Metro to Gare du Nord. It is over there.'

Yvette had heard about the underground trains in Paris, but travelling below the ground seemed impossible.

'I can show you how to get onto the Metro,' the guard offered.

She hesitated. She didn't want another train guard following them around Paris, but he seemed genuine and just wanted to do his job.

'Thank you. We would appreciate your assistance.'

The guard took them over to the ticketing counter and instructed them to ask for Metro tickets to Gare du Nord, before taking them down a flight of steps where they walked for what seemed like hours though white-tiled tunnels to the correct platform.

'It's twelve stops, and the end of the line. You can't go any further. It's a short walk to your destination from there.' He left them and disappeared back into the tunnel.

The train swept into the platform, disgorged its passengers, and they pushed their way into the carriage where Janie secured them seats near the sliding doors.

Janie amused herself by predicting how long it would take to reach the next Metro station then counting the seconds out loud. Yvette couldn't shake the feeling they would never reach their destination because they'd be crushed to death when the tunnel roof collapsed.

When they finally exited Gare du Nord, she said a silent prayer, thankful they had lived to see the sky again. They asked directions from an old lady selling flowers outside the station. She sketched a map with the end of her cane, using the cobblestones as street blocks, and assured them it was only a ten-minute walk. She gave them a sunflower for luck.

Yvette hurried after Janie as she strode off down the street. 'Three blocks this way, then we turn to the left,' she called to Yvette over her shoulder.

Small engineering workshops and metal trades lined the streets. The cafés and bars at the end of every block were filling up with men who'd finished work for the day. Some called out as they hurried by, but none followed them. She was relieved that Janie didn't seem to notice.

They turned into Rue de Paradis, and halfway along the road found number 29. It was another cream stone Parisian building, with a horseshoe-shaped entranceway that led into a large internal courtyard. Two intricate wrought-iron gates blocked their way in. On the left of the gates was a shop window filled with small bronze statues, mainly of dancing women. As Yvette moved closer, she noticed their ivory limbs, and the extraordinary detail on their bronze costumes. One statue was a perfect representation of a lady hunched over on a cold night with the wind whipping at her coat.

The statues were like the one Maman held in her photograph. She opened the clasps on her bag to pull it out and was so focused on wanting to compare the picture to the statues in front of them, she jumped with surprise when Janie spoke.

'Shall we go in?'

Yvette felt stupid. They'd come all this way to find Daniel, and here she was fiddling around in front of a shop window, transfixed by some statues.

'Yes, of course. Let's go in.'

Janie tried the door. 'It's locked.'

They had got here too late. The foundry had closed for the day. They peered inside the shop and couldn't see anyone moving about. The courtyard was deserted too.

'What should we do now?' Janie asked.

She'd never thought about what they would do if the foundry was shut. 'I guess we'll have to come back tomorrow.'

'Where will we sleep?'

'I don't know. How do you expect me to have all the answers?' Her response was out before she could stop herself. She'd insisted they come to Paris to escape their inevitable fate if they stayed in the village. She didn't have the answers, apart from knowing they needed to leave.

'I thought you might have a plan.' Janie's voice had taken on a lightness that she recognised as her way of trying to smooth over the situation.

'I'm sorry, Janie. We'll find somewhere to sleep, even if we must go back to the station.'

Yvette sat down on the bench outside the foundry, while Janie peered into the shop window. She kept up a running commentary of all the statues she could see – a naked lady holding a lamp, a lady with two dogs, two ladies dancing, boys chasing balls and hoops, and girls twirling skipping ropes.

When a door banged inside the foundry, Yvette rushed to the gates and peered inside. 'Anyone there?' she called out.

A tall, thin young man came into view, whistling a tune she didn't recognise as he did up the buttons of his black wool jacket. He flicked his fringe across his forehead as he adjusted his cap to hold his hair in place. Looking up, he caught sight of her, and stood in the courtyard with the assuredness of someone who belonged. The intensity in his expression nearly caused her to turn and run.

'Can I help you?' he asked. The warmth and sincerity in his voice surprised her. She'd never imagined she'd find this in Paris.

'We're looking for Daniel Foucart. He's our cousin. We wrote to tell him we were coming, but we didn't hear back. Does he still work here?' She tried to stop herself babbling but words kept spilling from her mouth.

At the mention of her cousin's name, the young man's face lit up in a radiant smile. 'Yes,' he said, 'Daniel said he got a letter from you. He's not here at present.'

'Could you tell us where we can find him?'

The young man seemed to weigh up the question. 'Well, he's at a meeting and won't be back till late. He lives in the single men's quarters behind the foundry. Can you come back in the morning?'

His smile disappeared when she couldn't muster one in return. 'You have nowhere to stay?'

She shook her head. 'I guess we could go back and wait the night out at the railway station.'

'That is not a safe place for two young ladies. My stepmother Martje will know somewhere. She lives just around the corner.'

Before she could ask any questions about who he and Martje were, the young man had stepped through the gate and clanged it shut. He held out his hand to her.

'I'm Steffan Blum. My father owns the foundry.'

Warning bells sounded in Yvette's head, reminding her of Madame Jervois's tales of disreputable men who'd drug them and sell them to brothels. Still, she couldn't help herself reaching out to shake his hand.

'I'm Yvette and this is Janie.' Her sister gave him a small wave as she lingered by the shop window. 'You know Daniel?'

Steffan laughed. 'Of course. He's teaching me to be an ivory carver. He's very good at it.' He turned to Janie. 'He carved most of the ivory pieces on those statues in there.'

Janie peered into the shop again and Yvette couldn't help being drawn over to the window.

'Could we look inside?' Janie asked.

'We can go in tomorrow when it's open,' Yvette said. 'We don't want to bother Steffan.'

'It's no bother.' Steffan produced a bunch of keys from his coat pocket and opened the door with a flourish.

'*Entrez*, mademoiselles.'

They stepped into the shop, where the walls were lined with wooden shelves displaying dozens of bronze and ivory statues and lamps. In the centre, larger sculptures of bears and tigers stood on plinths.

Steffan led them over to the series of dancing women. 'These are the ones Daniel and I have been working on in the last month. We carve their arms and legs and connect them to the bronze pieces.'

Yvette pulled Maman's photo from her bag and showed it to Steffan. 'Do you think it's possible our Maman could have made this?'

He took the picture from her and spent some time examining it. 'It's definitely made from bronze. Have you asked her about it?' He passed the photo back to her.

'She left us a year ago.' Yvette fought back the tears threatening to spill down her face. She wasn't going to cry in front of a stranger.

'I am sorry about your Maman. We can show the photo to the staff tomorrow. They might know more about the sculpture.' He moved towards the door. 'I'm sorry, we do need to go now, before they sit down for dinner.'

Steffan led them down Rue de Paradis, and as they turned a corner, the orderly stone buildings gave way to a hodge podge of single- and two-storey wooden houses with tiled roofs. All were grimy from factory soot, apart from the two-storey one they stopped in front of. Its roof was clean, and the walls were painted yellow.

Steffan pushed open the pristine wrought-iron gate, which glided open on well-oiled hinges without a sound. The tiny front garden was a riot of colour, with masses of geraniums competing with clusters of daisies and bursts of irises. The gardener, who Yvette presumed was Martje, had hung baskets of red and pink geraniums either side of the door.

'Just wait here,' Steffan said, letting himself into the house.

He left the door slightly ajar, and Yvette could hear the murmur of voices and the clink of cutlery. Suddenly she felt nervous, and wished they'd just gone back to the station. She didn't want to be the reason these people had to interrupt their dinner.

Steffan reappeared, holding a folded note which he waved at them in such an endearing way, Yvette couldn't help but giggle.

'Martje knows everyone. We're off to Madame Bissette's. She's *very* deaf, which is why Martje gave me a note.' He hustled them out the gate.

'She has somewhere for us to stay?' said Yvette.

'Oh yes. She's a concierge in an apartment block. Martje's related to her somehow. They caught up today and she mentioned some rooms for lease.'

They hurried back past the foundry, and Janie began to lag behind. Yvette was about to hurry her up when Steffan noticed too and took her bag. He offered to take hers, but she refused, even though her arms felt like they'd been stretched to twice their length.

Yvette barely registered the businesses and shops they passed, but she kept track of the street names for their return tomorrow. *Left at Rue d'Hauteville and left again at Rue de Petites Ecuries.* She was so busy concentrating on keeping track of their surroundings that she ran into Steffan when he stopped.

'We're here,' he said.

'Here' was 200 Rue de Petites Ecuries, a five-storey, cream-coloured apartment block with the same wrought iron covering the windows. The entranceway's stone steps were worn in the middle from years of residents' comings and goings. The green wooden doors sported a bronze knocker with a zig-zag motif. Steffan hammered on the door with so much force Yvette feared the knocker would break.

A hunched lady with a wispy grey bun opened the door and gave Steffan a full up and down stare. He introduced himself and handed her the letter, which she held very close to her face to read. Not only a little deaf, but maybe a little blind too?

The elderly lady nodded at the contents of the letter and croaked, 'We have a vacancy.' She opened the door to let them in.

Steffan moved to enter, but Madame Bissette's arm shot out to block him. 'No men allowed with single girls.'

He shrugged. 'Come to the foundry tomorrow at nine o'clock to see Daniel,' he said to Yvette. 'Martje wants to meet you too. Bring your Maman's photograph.'

He said goodnight and sprinted off down the road.

The spotless lobby had a worn, black-and-white flagstone floor, and there were green-fronded plants in big pots around the walls.

Madame Bissette got straight down to business. 'The rent is twenty francs per month. Do you have that on you?'

Yvette opened the back of the photograph and handed Madame Bissette the money.

She squinted at it to check it was the correct amount, then folded it into her apron pocket.

'No men in your room ever, and you must be quiet and respectful of the other tenants. You must pay your rent on time and clean your room thoroughly once a week. The bathroom and toilet are at the end of the floor. You will share it with other tenants. Please, no excessive use of hot water or taking too long in the bathroom. Your apartment is on level three, room twelve. This is the key to the front door, and this is the key to your room. You can see yourselves up.'

Madame Bissette waved her hand to dismiss them and went back into her apartment.

Yvette didn't care if room 12 was a broom cupboard, she was so relieved they'd found somewhere to stay.

Once they'd struggled up the stairs to the third floor she gave Janie the key, and her sister raced down the corridor to find room 12. She waited until Yvette got there before turning the key and opening the door. Yvette wasn't disappointed. The room was clean and tidy with whitewashed walls. The double bed looked comfortable, and the room had a small round table with two chairs. A wood-fired stove they could cook on and keep warm by was nestled in the corner. A set of drawers and a coat stand made up the rest of the furniture.

Janie pointed to a switch by the door. 'Electric lights,' they said together, and laughed. Janie switched it on and off for good measure.

The window let in plenty of light and could be opened. They had a view over the street too.

'We could grow plants.' Janie pointed out the window boxes in the building across the road. Some were full of flowers, while others held herbs and vegetables.

'Great idea.'

Yvette hugged Janie. 'We've done it. We're here.'

'And we've got electricity.'

Janie pulled out the photograph of Maman and placed it on the table. 'Now we belong.'

Yvette sank into the nearest chair and smiled at her little sister, marvelling at how quickly she'd adjusted to the idea of living in Paris. 'Shall we unpack, or find food first?'

'Food, I'm starving.' Janie spun around the room.

'You'll need to pass me your coat.'

Janie shrugged it off and held it out to her. 'Why do you want it?'

She lifted the lining up. 'I hid some money here.'

She began unpicking the seam to release the 10 francs note as Janie scurried about the room finding homes for their meagre possessions.

SEVENTEEN

Yvette

Paris, September 1933

Next morning Yvette and Janie returned to Rue de Paradis, where the Blum Foundry chimneystacks bellowed smoke over the street. They passed a cabaret advertising a Vaudevillian variety show, and nestled beside the foundry was a shop called Lalique, filled with the most delicate pieces made entirely of glass. Yvette lingered over a crystal perfume bottle in the window with two perfectly formed glass anemones as a stopper. She smiled at the long-haired women who danced their way around a glass tumbler, before moving on to the Blum Foundry Galerie window, where she was again mesmerised by the small bronze statues they produced. She marvelled how the men who worked inside the foundry could produce such exquisite art.

When they entered the shop, a young woman not much older than Yvette stepped past the plinths to greet them in a way that implied they were in the wrong place. She was dressed in a light-green woollen dress that accentuated her waist, and the leather on her ankle boots was embossed with flying birds.

Yvette had never felt more conscious of her shapeless brown

coat and hat, but she would have to appear confident or the young woman might usher them out thinking they were beggars.

'We are here to visit our cousin, Daniel Foucart. We met Steffan Blum here last night. He told us to come back this morning.'

Much to Yvette's relief, the puzzled expression on the woman's face changed to a smile.

'Steffan said you would be coming this morning. I'm his stepsister, Sarah. I will take you to the break room and have them meet you there.'

Apart from Sarah's hair being a similar brown to Steffan's, Yvette couldn't see any other family resemblance. They followed Sarah out of the shop into the courtyard, where a burst of heat and noise hit them as they passed the open doors of the foundry. Inside the building the furnaces glowed orange, like the sun at dusk in the village. She could make out the silhouettes of men pouring molten metal from pots.

Sarah led them away from the heat and noise and into the break room. Yvette had expected a mess, but the room was clean and tidy with whitewashed walls, well-scrubbed wooden tables, and bench seats. A kettle simmered on the coal range, next to a coffee percolator and a simmering pot of food. The metallic tang of the air in the courtyard was replaced by the delicious aromas of coffee and a rich stew. Freshly baked bread still steamed on the tables, along with plates of langues de chat.

'Is there a celebration?' Janie asked, surveying the loaded table.

Sarah smiled as she placed two steaming mugs of coffee and a plate of biscuits in front of them. 'Mama and Papa insist our men have full stomachs. The work is hard, and we want to show our appreciation of what they do for the foundry. I will get Daniel and Steffan.'

Sarah left Yvette and Janie alone with the food.

'These are so nice, I'm having another one.' Janie put the whole biscuit in her mouth.

'Stop that, you're being a pig.'

'Those men will eat everything when they arrive. They won't miss the few we have.'

Janie was right, and Yvette didn't have the heart to scold her again. Janie stood up to inspect the room, and a cord hanging from the ceiling knocked into her face. She batted it away.

'Is that an electric light cord?' Yvette asked.

Janie caught the cord and tugged on it, and as if a miracle had occurred, the bulb of light glowing above them turned off.

'I want to try it.' Yvette tugged on the cord and the light went on with a click. She turned it off and on four more times.

The door opened again, and Daniel came in. Yvette's cousin was taller than she remembered, and wore his dark hair swept over into a fringe similar to Steffan's. He was clean shaven and wore a white smock that he took off and hung on a peg by the door. His tailored brown waistcoat was good quality, as were his white cotton shirt, woollen trousers, and sturdy boots. Her gangly cousin had turned into a handsome young man.

'It's so good to see you both.' He embraced Yvette, then Janie. 'And haven't you grown, little Janie?'

'Not so little anymore.' Janie messed up his swept-over fringe.

'Watch it, you little troublemaker.'

He stood back, taking them in. 'Are you here for a visit or ...?'

Yvette said, perhaps too quickly, 'Mama died last year and Papa a few months ago, and–'

Daniel spoke before she finished, 'Yes, I am sorry. You said in your letter. Are you wanting to stay in Paris?'

'Stay. We want to stay.' Yvette tried not to burst into tears, though they welled in her eyes.

Daniel poured himself a coffee and sat down with them. 'Steffan told me you arrived last night. He helped you find somewhere to stay?'

'Yes, he was very kind to us.'

'I meant to write to you. I live here in the single men's quarters so you can't stay here. It's good you've found somewhere.' Daniel popped a biscuit into his mouth.

'You can show us around, though?' Janie asked. She took another biscuit too.

Daniel shrugged. 'It's great to see you, but I've got a lot going on with the Party, so I'm not going to have a lot of time for sightseeing.' He made a face when he said 'sightseeing'.

'What's the Party?' Janie asked, before Yvette could shush her.

Daniel seemed to come to life. 'The Communist Party. I'm a member of the Artisan Guild. When you've been here for a while, you'll see there are serious threats to our way of life that we must fight against.'

Purpose and conviction radiated from Daniel as he continued to speak about his Party. Yvette didn't understand most of what he was talking about, so she remained quiet. She followed Janie's lead and ate more biscuits.

Steffan stepped into the break room. 'There they are. Did Madame Bissette treat you well and give you a good room?' His friendliness took the edge off Daniel's intensity.

'Thank you for your kindness last night, Steffan. Our room is very good.'

'I've come to take you both to meet Martje.'

Yvette jumped when a clanging bell started up in the courtyard.

'Let's get out of here before men clutter the place up.'

With Steffan leading the way and Daniel following up at the rear, they ventured out into the courtyard where men appeared out of doors all around the yard.

A grinning man in overalls yelled out, 'Hey, Daniel, aren't you going to introduce us to your sweethearts?'

Several men wolf-whistled and another called out, 'Hey butterfingers, don't let these two slide out of your hands.'

Neither Daniel nor Steffan reacted, so Yvette didn't either. It was no different than being eyed up and down by the old goat, or the other men in their village. Though she was relieved when Steffan opened a door on the other side of the courtyard and ushered them up a set of stairs away from the curious stares and the heckling.

On the landing, Daniel moved past them and opened a door into an office. An older man with a neatly trimmed beard and moustache looked up from the papers on his desk.

'What have we here? Two visions of loveliness and Steffan and Daniel.' He laughed at his own joke.

'This is Monsieur Blum,' Daniel said. 'These are my cousins, Yvette and Janie.'

'Bonjour, Monsieur Blum,' Yvette said.

'And you are from the same village as Daniel?'

'Yes, sir.'

'Please, not sir. We are family here. We don't stand on ceremony.'

Yvette wasn't sure what to say, but Daniel came to the rescue. 'Yvette and Janie just came to the city last night and are looking for work. I thought you and Madame Blum might have some suggestions.'

Monsieur Blum nodded. 'What can you do?'

'I can sew,' said Yvette, 'and I helped run our local guest house. Janie worked as a domestic for a well-to-do family in our village.'

'That's not what I see you doing. You have such a beautiful face, and you move like an angel.' Monsieur Blum stared off into the distance.

Was he talking about her? Confused, Yvette turned to Daniel, who shrugged.

Monsieur Blum opened the door behind him and called out,

'Martje, you must come in here and meet Daniel's cousins, Yvette and Janie.'

Madame Blum entered the room. She was petite, with well-manicured nails, and wore the crispest white blouse Yvette had ever seen. She'd matched the shirt with a simple red pencil skirt that accentuated the length of her legs and the shape of her calves.

'Walk around the room, Yvette,' Monsieur Blum commanded.

Unsure if she should, she looked to Daniel, then to Steffan, for reassurance. They both nodded. She took four paces, turned when she arrived at the door and walked back.

'Very good. Very good.' Madame Blum clapped her hands together. 'You hold yourself beautifully. And those legs of yours...'

Did they think it a miracle she could stay upright? Why was Madame Blum looking at her legs?

'Madame Blum thinks you would make a fine model for our sculptors,' Daniel explained.

'Yes, yes, exactly,' Madame Blum agreed.

A model? Or did that mean something else? Possibly these were the people Madame Jervois had warned her about.

'It's nothing underhand. It's a very respectable profession,' Daniel reassured her.

'Is the pay reasonable? I'd have to make enough to pay for rent and to look after myself and Janie.'

'Of course. If you are popular, you can set your price. I feel you will be popular.' Monsieur Blum smiled at her and the gnawing, tight feeling in Yvette's stomach eased.

'Would you like me to make some introductions?' Madame Blum asked.

Yvette didn't know whether she wanted her to or not. But she understood that Madame Blum wanted to help her, and Daniel seemed to trust her, so she nodded her agreement.

'*Bon*. Come here tomorrow at nine, and I will take you to the Académie de la Grande Chaumière.'

Monsieur Blum must have taken her silence as a sign she wasn't willing. 'It's the artists' school where they come to learn to draw and paint,' he said. 'If you can get a position there, it will launch your career. Martje modelled there. That's where we met.'

Madame Blum nodded. 'We could visit Chiparus too. He's been looking for a new model.'

Yvette wanted to talk to Daniel without the Blum family being present. He seemed to think this was a good idea, but he might be agreeing only because these were his employers.

Steffan turned to Yvette. 'Why don't you show us your mother's picture? The one where she's holding a sculpture.'

She took the photograph from her bag and passed it to Madame Blum, who studied the photograph intently. 'What was your mother's name?'

'Loriene Gauthier. Her maiden name was Provon.'

Finally, Madame Blum smiled. 'Of course. I remember her now. She came to L'Académie. She worked with her father. Yes, that will be one of their pieces.'

'Hers?' She wanted Madame Blum to say yes.

'I can't say. We can show the photo to Monsieur Chiparus. He will remember the Provon family.'

As she passed the photograph back, Madame Blum squeezed her arm, a tender gesture that had the tears threatening to well up again. She distracted herself by stuffing the photograph back in her bag.

'I'll take you to L'Académie tomorrow, then we'll visit Monsieur Chiparus.'

As soon as they appeared back in the courtyard, the workers greeted them with a barrage of wolf whistles and indecent suggestions. Yvette hardly noticed, as the prospect of working as a model, and her mother's earlier life as a sculptor, competed for space in her head.

EIGHTEEN

Steffan

Paris, September 1933

Steffan was glad to leave the smoked-filled guildhall for some fresh air. He'd been tasked with purchasing further red and gold embroidery thread. Their banner had started out a simple affair, with comrade Madame Liberty holding a hammer in one hand and a sickle in the other. Then Potiev suggested embroidering Comrade Madame Liberty's sleeves with the red rose buds, the flower of the revolution. The idea found favour with the other guild members.

Steffan wasn't sure additional embroidery would make the banner more revolutionary, just overly ornate. It had been assumed Steffan would fund the embellishments. Since he was the newest member, he held his tongue and did their bidding.

He bypassed the nearest shop and went instead to Coen's Haberdashery, five blocks over. He enjoyed chatting with Monsieur Coen, who reminded him of Grand-père with his halting speech and his attention to detail. This also allowed him the opportunity to promenade about central Paris in the daytime, rather than in the evening. Sunday was his usual day to explore, but he'd been lunching with his family, to try and win over Philippe. It wasn't working. He still wanted to punch Philippe in his smug face in retaliation for the riverboat incident. Since that wasn't possible, he sought revenge when they played cards after lunch. He made sure he was never on Philippe's team. It was so easy to win against Phillipe, but he could never keep his feelings from his face. The win was more satisfying when Phillippe threw down his cards and left the table in a huff.

As Steffan came closer to haberdashery quarter, the smell of charred meat and burnt fabric became so strong it stopped him in his tracks. He covered his mouth and nose with his cap, but couldn't protect his eyes, which were smarting from the ash pattering down on him like snow. He kept moving, wiping his eyes and looking about, trying to work out what was on fire and whether he was in danger.

As he rounded the corner into the haberdashers' street, he was confronted by burnt-out shops and glass strewn over the cobblestones, and a god-awful smell. He let out a cry of shock, then suddenly he was back there, running across their big field to reach the burning barn. His horse, Bernie, was screaming and crashing in his stall, stuck inside the inferno, and the roof was melting inward.

The smell here was so much worse than the fire on the farm. He gagged; his diaphragm contracted and spasmed, and his head felt woozy, and he thought he might faint. He closed his eyes and breathed through his cap until he felt sure he wouldn't throw up or collapse.

Broken glass crunched under his feet as he forced himself to walk further down the street. Coen's Haberdashery hadn't been burnt, but horrible words shouted at him from the boarded-up windows:

Fuck off Jew
Burn in hell
France for the French

Coen's neighbour had tried to cover the hateful words scrawled across his shop, but the insults showed through the black paint.

Someone had desecrated the *Fermé* sign on Monsieur Coen's battered door with a stencilled skull and crossed swords.

The sign gave Steffan hope, that Monsieur Coen hadn't been hurt when the attack happened.

The next two shops were burnt out. The windows that had held colourful reels of cotton and fabric swatches were now gaping, empty holes, displaying only blackened, unrecognisable remnants.

Near the end of the street, a shop owner with a green apron wrapped around his stout body was rearranging stock on an outside display stand. The apron was the only colourful thing left on the street. He wasn't as old as Monsieur Coen, but he moved stiffly, as if he suffered from arthritis.

As Steffan crunched towards the open shop he disturbed the ash, which swirled up around him, catching in his throat. By the time he reached the shopkeeper, all Steffan wanted to do was run from this place before the ash and smell of death leached into him. He made himself stop.

'When did this happen?' Steffan asked the man.

'Two nights ago.' The man didn't look up from his task.

'But why would they do this?' As he spoke the question aloud, he realised how stupid it sounded.

The man looked up. His face was set in a permanent frown, and deep lines had formed across his forehead. He appeared to assess Steffan to decide whether such an idiotic question needed an answer. 'Same as everywhere. They want the Jews out.'

It didn't seem fair that an unknown 'they' wanted the Jews to leave. Where were they supposed to go? Could this happen to his family?

'Did anyone get hurt?'

The man nodded, and continued to arrange his wares,

moving each small bottle on a shelf slightly to the right. 'Two families who lived above their shops.'

'Whole families?' Steffan wanted him to reply but dreaded the answer.

The man only said, 'Yes.'

Families meant children, parents, maybe grandparents. Maybe the smoke had crept into their rooms and they'd died without waking. He shuddered, remembering his horse's screams.

'Many more suffered breathing problems from the smoke, and burns,' the man added, like it had happened a long time ago and he had to dredge up the details from his memory.

'I am sorry this happened.'

The man finished straightening the row and looked directly at Steffan. His expression betrayed his grief. 'They might believe they are only hurting Jews, but we've worked here side by side in our street for decades. They have attacked our whole community. They have attacked France, not Jews. And they have the audacity to think they are helping France.'

'And Monsieur Coen?' Steffan didn't want to say the words 'injured' or 'dead'.

'He wasn't physically injured. I cannot say the same for his spirit. I am not hopeful he will open again.'

'Oh, I am glad he wasn't injured. Maybe in time.' In time what? Monsieur Coen had had his livelihood taken from him and was too old to start again.

'Were you here to make a purchase from his store?' The man seemed to come back to life at the possibility of a sale.

'I wanted to buy some red and gold embroidery thread, strong enough for use on a damask banner.'

The man gestured to the shop door. 'Please come inside and we will provide you with what you need.'

Steffan followed him in and felt like he'd stepped inside a rainbow. Cottons, embroidery threads, buttons, zips, and other sewing accoutrements were arranged around the room by their colour. Red items began on the left-hand wall, one rainbow hue merging into the next, ending in purple on the right wall. After the horror outside, he felt instantly at home with the orderliness inside. They used the same colour palette shades in the Blum Foundry painting room.

A faint smell of burnt fabric permeated the shop. Steffan hoped it would fade in time.

The haberdasher helped him choose the best thread and the right amount for the job. A small basket of red rosettes sat on the counter, and he bought a dozen for his comrades to craft into Artisan Guild emblems. Mostly he bought them to help the haberdasher.

Steffan burst into the Guildhall and delivered his news with a strong steady voice. 'We need to do something, comrades. Two Jewish families were murdered.'

He felt emboldened by the heads nodding in agreement. Ashlam collected the thread from Steffan and passed it to the volunteer stitchers.

'Ashlam, surely it must outrage you what is happening to your people.'

'*Our* people, Steffan. What is happening to our people.'

He'd said it like he wasn't a Jew, yet he was. 'Of course, Ashlam, our people, and that is what makes me so angry. We need to fight back, comrades.'

Ashlam threaded the embroidery cotton onto his needle. 'Did you get any information about who did it?'

Before Steffan could answer, another comrade interrupted. 'This government can't control the gendarmes. They need to operate from more communist principles and purge the right-wing elements.'

'Don't you think that would make it worse? If they started

purging the constabulary, wouldn't that just whip up further hatred towards the Jews?' Ashlam replied.

'And there would be fewer gendarmes to attend to any unrest,' Daniel added.

Potiev wafted over on the pretext of admiring their stitching. 'You are quite right, Daniel. We'll use the law of attrition, and as the old guard retire, we'll recruit new men whose beliefs align with ours.'

Ashlam plunged his needle into the damask. 'That's a long-term answer. We need change now. Mobs are out there burning down hard-working people's livelihoods based on race.'

'If it was a mob, it was organised by someone. I did see this drawn on a shop.' Steffan turned over the rosebud pattern a comrade had sketched as a basis for their design. He drew the flared cross, the skull, and the swords that crossed under the skull.

'Croix de Feu!' Potiev exclaimed.

'You know it?' Steffan asked.

'Set up by François de La Rocque as a veterans' movement. It's turned somewhat political.'

Steffan found it difficult to imagine a group of old, broken-down men tottering through the haberdashery quarter, setting Jewish businesses on fire and murdering people.

His expression must have said as much because Potiev continued, 'They've recruited plenty of others to their movement. *France for the French, work for the French, not the foreigners.* The disaffected and the dullards find it irresistible.'

'Don't assume they are all disaffected and dullards.' Ashlam pulled his needle through the cloth.

'I'll wager that a number in the movement have eyes on a political career.'

Ashlam sighed. 'Just what we need. More nationalists teaming up with the bourgeoisie to keep trampling over workers.'

Daniel picked up the drawing and traced the cross with his finger. 'This was stencilled on the damaged buildings?'

'It was on Monsieur Coen's shop front. I didn't notice it on the others.'

'Best we keep an eye out for that symbol, then.'

'Best we do,' Ashlam agreed.

Daniel turned the paper over and repositioned it so that everyone could see where to place Madame Liberty's rosebuds. Only five more days before her first outing.

NINETEEN

Yvette

Paris, September 1933

Yvette woke early, her whole body itching to move so the time would speed by until she met with Madame Blum. She found a bakery and purchased four plump croissants, along with butter and berry compote, for their breakfast. She brought a kilo of coffee beans and watched while the café owner, a thickset woman in middle age, ground them. A man behind the counter tried to catch her eye, but she ignored him. As if she'd flirt with a café owner whose waist was as thick as his wife's.

His expression reminded her of Patrick, who behaved so shamefully and blamed all the young women for tempting him. Poor Madame Aubert, married to that letch.

Who did these men think they were? And why did their wives put up with it? She smiled with sympathy at the coffee grinder, who thrust the coffee bag at her with a glare and swished her out of the shop with a wave of her hands, as if she were a bothersome fly.

As she arrived back at their apartment building, the

concierge shuffled out with her swatch broom to sweep the front steps.

'Would you have a spare coffee pot I could borrow until we purchase one today?' Yvette asked. 'I will sweep the steps for you every morning this week in return.'

The tiny woman peered at her. '*Les femmes* from Madame Blum.' She seemed pleased with herself for identifying Yvette and went back to her sweeping.

'Would you have a spare coffee pot?' Yvette asked again. The concierge ignored her.

A gentleman dressed in a fine wool coat and an immaculate grey Homburg hat came out of the building. 'She's very deaf. Is there something you wanted from her?'

'A coffee pot. We arrived yesterday and haven't got one yet.'

'She wants a coffee pot,' the man yelled at the concierge with such force that Yvette stumbled on the steps.

'Sorry to startle you,' the immaculate man said. 'Think it did the trick, though.'

The concierge peered at Yvette again. 'Yes, I can lend you a coffee pot. I need it back by tomorrow morning.'

Yvette nodded her agreement and the old lady shuffled off, returning with a battered coffee pot. She thanked her and rushed up the stairs to their room, where Janie was still asleep.

Yvette banked up the fire and filled the pot from the jug of water they kept for washing and drinking.

Soon the room was warm and filled with the aroma of coffee. She lay their croissants on the table and roused Janie.

'You've been up for ages. Why didn't you wake me?'

'You needed your sleep.'

Janie rolled out of bed and plonked herself into the other kitchen chair. 'Oh my, they look lovely.' She inhaled deeply. 'Smells lovely too.'

Yvette poured the coffee into the two chipped mugs she'd

found in the cupboard and placed the croissants on plates with glaze so cracked it was impossible to see what the pictures were.

'Are you nervous about today?' Janie asked.

'A little. I'm worried they will think me too much of a country girl, not sophisticated enough for their Parisian ways.'

'Everyone in the village said how pretty you are. They will probably only see that.'

Had she misheard? Janie did have a mouth full of croissant that muffled her voice. But she hadn't misheard.

'Surely they weren't talking about me. Or if they were, they'd be saying I was the girl whose father disgraced his family.'

Janie shrugged. 'No. Always about how pretty you are.'

No one had ever called her pretty. Perhaps Janie said that now to help her nerves.

'I wish I had a better coat though.' She eyed up her brown threadbare hand me down as it sagged on the coat stand.

'Let's see if we can find a market.'

Yvette shook her head. 'Not until we've got some work. We've got to make our money last.'

At least her green dress could pass for respectable. She could take off her coat when they arrived at L'Académie.

Even though the walk had taken them only twenty minutes yesterday, they left by 8.15am. What if they took the wrong turn or somehow got held up? Yvette needed to make a good impression with Madame Blum.

Despite her nerves, she took in more of their neighbourhood. A bakery's array of cakes and pastries was as colourful as Monsieur Rhode's rose garden. Every second shop seemed to be something to do with food: a cheese shop, a shop that sold nothing but olives and olive oil, a delicatessen with a fine display of pastrami, salamis and smoked meats. More food in one place than she'd ever seen in her life.

Further down the road, the delicatessens and patisseries gave way to shops selling art supplies, and there were picture framers and galeries where paintings, smoky-pink glass vases and bronze sculptures of naked women filled the window displays. Yvette shivered at a painting of a kaleidoscope woman with a split face. She hoped never to have to pose for something as ghastly as that.

When they arrived at the Blum Foundry Galerie, Madame Blum was there with Sarah to greet them. Sarah surprised Yvette by embracing her and kissing her on both cheeks. She smelled of rose water and furniture polish. Madame Blum greeted her with kisses too. With her it was like being embraced by a whole garden. Madame Blum wore a fitted red coat that flared out from her tiny waist. Her matching hat, shoes and gloves were a colour that reminded Yvette of the delicate rosé wine her mother would drink on special occasions.

Yvette felt embarrassed by her shapeless brown coat, but Madame Blum's smile put her at ease.

'Janie can stay here with Sarah and help in the shop.'

When they stepped out on the street, Madame Blum surprised her by linking arms with her. 'Please don't be nervous,' she said. 'Visiting L'Académie will be fun. They will take one look at you and fall in love with your sweet face and those beautiful legs.'

No one had ever said anything at all like this to her. Not even lecherous Patrick. She might have expected an eager young man to express himself so, but not someone like Madame Blum. She was a mother, a wife, a respectable lady, and she spoke about her in an intimate way.

Before she could ponder this further, they arrived at the stop and clambered onto the tram.

'After we secure you a place at L'Académie, we will visit Monsieur Chiparus and win him over too.'

'Who is Monsieur Chiparus?'

'He is our finest sculptor. All those beautiful bronze sculptures in our galerie are his work.'

'I am grateful for your kindness and your help.'

'Once you are known at L'Académie, other artists will ask you to model for them. Some will appear kind and helpful but will try to take advantage of you. So, I want you to work with someone like Monsieur Chiparus who is a gentleman and very clean living. You will be treated very well by him.'

'Janie and I are fortunate to have met you. We had an important man in our village who said he wanted to help our family. It led to the ruin of my cousin.'

'I am so sorry to hear that. Monsieur Chiparus is responsible for my husband and me meeting and eventually marrying. They were friends and he encouraged him to come to L'Académie. My husband is an artist at heart but being the eldest, the foundry came first.'

Alighting from the tram, Yvette followed Madame Blum into a small side street where a small bronze plaque on the pavement announced *Académie de la Grande Chaumière, Peinture Sculpture*. The 'u' letters were carved as a Latin 'v', just like the lettering in their village church.

The steps up to the blue door were worn from years of artists' feet. Something swelled inside her, knowing so many people had mounted these steps and entered this building for the express purpose of making art. That knowledge calmed her nervousness, and she eagerly followed Madame Blum into the foyer with its orderly mosaic tile floor, a wall of neat lockers, the sharp smell of paint, and the hum of voices from further inside the building.

They were intercepted by a small, bespectacled man in a voluminous calico smock.

'Madame Blum!' He rushed towards her and swallowed her up in the folds of his garment. 'Who is this? Is she for us?'

Madame Blum squeaked a greeting before he let her go and pulled Yvette towards him.

'Off, off.' He motioned for her to take off her coat, which she did.

'Turn, turn.' He made spinning movements with his hands.

She glanced at Madame Blum who nodded, so she did as he asked.

The man clapped his hands together. 'That face, those legs. Magnificent.' He turned to Madame Blum. 'Please let us have her.'

'It's up to Yvette as to whether she wants to work here.'

'What would I be doing?'

'Come.' He led them down another set of well-worn steps towards the murmuring voices. They entered a workroom soaked in light from a bank of long windows. A cluster of artists in white calico smocks stood around the room in front of canvases mounted on easels. In front of them was a small stage on which a woman was reclining on a chaise, a shawl draped over her hips. Yvette stopped dead at the sight of her bare breasts.

Some of the artists looked up, and she realised she must have gasped out loud.

Heat rose in her face as she hurried out of the room, followed by Madame Blum, who took her arm to stop her running for the door.

'I don't know what type of girl you think I am,' huffed Yvette, 'but this is not what I came to Paris to do.'

'I know it took you by surprise, but this is a very noble profession. You can choose what you wish to show of yourself.'

The bespectacled man bustled out of the workroom. 'My dear. Do not fret. We will start you off clothed. It is only the artists who ever see your beauty. If you only wish to show that pretty face and those beautiful legs, then it is so.'

They both leaned towards her, their faces registering concern.

'Can I talk to the woman on the stage?' She wanted some breathing space.

'*Mais oui.* I will get Felicity.' The bespectacled man bustled back into the workroom, returning with the woman, who now wore a silk robe.

'Madame Blum brought us this angel who I fear will fly away. I beseech you to calm her worries and tell her how well we treat our muses.'

The woman smiled and motioned Yvette to follow her across the hallway into another smaller workroom. She shut the door and offered Yvette a stool, taking one herself.

'I am Felicity, and Tave and I run L'Académie. I only model now when we have no one else.'

Yvette found it difficult to pick Felicity's age, but the way the skin crinkled around the corner of her eyes suggested she must be at least thirty-five.

Felicity continued, 'I can understand you may be concerned, but this is a very respectable place. I can't always vouch for what the artists do outside these walls, but while we are here you will always be safe. No one will ever make you do something you don't want to.'

'And I wouldn't have to show...' Yvette motioned towards Felicity's breasts.

'Only as much as you are comfortable with. But in time.'

'I don't think so.' She didn't even want to consider that. 'How often would I work and how much will you pay me?'

'We will trial you for a couple of days and if all goes well, we can offer you a position here four days a week, Thursday to Sunday. The morning session is from nine to noon; afternoon from two to five and the evening session from seven to nine. We pay three francs a day. Most models pick up more work directly with the artists too.'

She could make twelve francs a week, triple the amount she made in the village. It seemed extraordinary she could make that much for lying about on a couch. It would pay their rent with four francs left over for food. With extra money she earned by working for other artists, she could easily buy a new coat. A pretty one with a cinched-in waist like Madame Blum's, in a beautiful cornflower blue, like the hat she saw in La Montagne. But that would be after she sent money home and made her weekly payment to Eric.

Yvette reached into her bag and pulled out the photograph of Maman. She passed it to Felicity. 'Did you know my mother? Did she come here.'

Felicity studied the photograph as if she might reproduce it on canvas. Finally, she smiled. 'It's a long time since I've seen lovely Loriene. She came here for a couple of years.'

'Do you think the statue is her work?'

Felicity stroked the photograph. 'Yes. I am certain it would be. She had an exhibition of her work, with your grandfather, of course.'

Maman must have stood in front of someone like Felicity to shape the statue. If her mother had felt comfortable being here, then she would be as brave as Maman had asked her to be.

'I will accept. When would you like me to start?'

Felicity sprang from her stool to hug her. 'Tomorrow morning. We will trial you on the morning and afternoon sessions.' She ushered Yvette back into the hallway. 'It is done. She starts tomorrow.'

Madame Blum and Tave clapped their hands together in unison. Madame Blum embraced her and kissed her on both cheeks.

Tave gathered her up too. 'You will never regret choosing to enter into the artist's world.'

'Be here tomorrow at eight a.m. and you will learn the ways of L'Académie,' Felicity said over her shoulder as she returned to the workroom.

Yvette followed her and stood with the artists as Felicity stoked the pot belly fire and disappeared behind the stage screen. She reappeared with the shawl wrapped around her, hiding her body. She gracefully reclined onto the chaise, and rearranged the shawl over her hips, once again exposing her breasts.

As the artists moved back to their canvases and picked up their brushes, Yvette left the workroom and joined Madame Blum and Tave in the corridor.

'Come. We shall celebrate with coffee and macarons.' Madame Blum hugged Tave and strode towards the foyer leaving Yvette to squeak a hurried thank you and rush after her.

Madame Blum stepped out onto the sidewalk with the confidence of someone who belonged in this world. Yvette's head spun as she trotted to keep up with her. She'd just been offered a job. Not any job, but an artist's model in the respectable Académie de la Grande Chaumière.

They stopped at a disappointingly small café with a faded red canopy, and secured the last battered table.

'It looks nothing, but it makes the best macarons in all of Paris,' Madame Blum said as she stripped off her silk gloves, exposing her long fingers. The middle fingers of each hand sported dazzling rings, each with a different coloured stone.

'What lovely rings,' Yvette felt moved to say.

Madame Blum laughed. 'These are reminders of my previous life, where I did exactly what you are about to do. They are all gifts from appreciative artists who considered me their muse.'

Suddenly Yvette felt uncomfortable. Had she had affairs with these men?

Madame Blum reacted to her shocked look. 'Oh no. Not that. I inspired them only. They did try, but once I met Oscar, my heart belonged to him.'

The waiter appeared jend Madame Blum ordered them the macaron special and café au lait.

'Did he attend your sessions at L'Académie?'

'He did. He came to console himself in art.'

'A failed romance?'

'More than that. His wife died not long after his second child was born. His wife's family came and took the children, on account of him being Jewish.'

'How could they take them?'

'All they had to do was find a judge who disliked Jews to rule in their favour. In Paris, that's most judges.' Madame Blum sipped her coffee. 'He didn't lose them forever. Steffan found his father last year and we have met Lisette and her family.'

The waiter brought their order, an array of seven brightly coloured macarons arranged like a rainbow on a rectangular plate that seemed specifically designed for the purpose.

'First choice is yours,' Madame Blum said.

Yvette took the red one. Her teeth cracked through the firm shell and the sharp zing of raspberry burst into her mouth, followed by the satisfying creaminess of the filling. She'd thought they made good macarons at home, but they were nothing like this. She forgave the café it's shabby appearance and vowed she'd be here every day until she'd tried all their flavours.

Madame Blum offered her another macaron. This time she chose the blue one. It wasn't quite cornflower blue, but near enough.

'Would you know of a tailor who could make me a coat in a style like yours, but in blue?'

'After we visit Monsieur Chiparus, I will introduce you to our family tailor.'

TWENTY

Steffan

Paris, September 1933

When they broke for lunch, Daniel motioned Steffan to stay behind. Daniel waited for the others to leave before he spoke. 'Can you borrow the truck now? Ashlam's found the headquarters of Croix de Feu and they're having a meeting today.'

Steffan put his smock on the hooks. 'Easy. I'll tell Le Controleur Papa wants me to pick something up.'

Le Controleur was nowhere in sight when they got outside.

'Let's just do it.' Steffan sauntered across the courtyard to the truck, which was in its usual place backed into the loading bay. He glimpsed Philippe's silhouette inside as they pulled out and imagined his thwarted expression. He didn't care if Philippe told Papa. He'd just say someone else asked him to get something. No one else, apart from Daniel, had quite the same flair for driving as he did. He'd become the main drivers for the Bierlet, much to Phillippe's annoyance.

'Turn right and head towards Boulevard Haussmann. We're

looking for the Figaro Building.' Daniel lit a cigarette and dangled his arm out the open passenger window.

The ugly, triangular, yellow stone building squatted on an intersection, and Steffan pulled the truck over just before the corner. A large man stood outside the double doors and greeted men as they approached the entrance. He wore a royal blue sash, but they were too far away to see whether his lapel bore the Croix de Feu emblem.

'How do we know it's the Croix de Feu's headquarters?' asked Steffan.

'Ashlam said it was here. He's usually right.'

More well-dressed men greeted blue sash and entered the Figaro Building.

'He's not just the building doorman, is he?' Steffan said.

'Ashlam lives nearby and only sees him on days when they have the Croix de Feu meetings.'

Steffan wondered where Ashlam lived. It must be somewhere very nice if he walked past here often. And how exactly did he know where and when the Croix de Feu met?

'Blue sash is the muscle,' Daniel said, in a tone that was supposed to convey authority. But he sounded as if he wasn't quite sure. 'I've got an idea.' He opened the truck door and hopped onto the street. 'Stay here, I won't be long.'

'What are you doing?' Steffan couldn't keep the anxiety out of his voice.

'Watch and learn. When I walk away, wait a minute, then pick me up around the corner.' Daniel gave him a cheeky grin and shut the door.

He walked toward blue sash with purpose in his stride. Anyone observing him would be convinced he belonged on that street. Daniel stopped in front of blue sash, shook his hand, and they chatted away like old friends.

What on earth was he playing at? Daniel was no match for blue sash. One punch and he'd be laid out on the pavement.

After what seemed like an eternity, Daniel shook hands again with blue sash, walked past the double doors, then disappeared around the corner.

Steffan counted slowly to sixty then eased the truck out into the traffic. He spotted Daniel smoking a cigarette at a tram stop and drove past him. He pulled over further down the road to wait.

Daniel vaulted into the passenger seat. He radiated energy as he rolled a cigarette.

'Are you and blue sash best friends now?'

'I'm an interested party who wants France for the French. It wasn't too difficult to get him talking.'

Steffan shook his head.

'I asked the doorman about evening meetings. Apart from this meeting during the day, they meet every Wednesday evening. He said we're most welcome, we just need to wear a suit.'

The symbol of those people inside was emblazoned onto a building where families had been murdered. Steffan had to see for himself who those monsters were.

'Just as well we both have suits then,' he said, as he swung the truck back out into the traffic.

TWENTY-ONE

Yvette

Paris, September 1933

All the way to Monsieur Chiparus's home, Yvette worried they would be intruding. Even Madame Blum's reassurances didn't shift her uneasiness, which increased when they entered the artist's opulent street, Rue de la Faisanderie.

Again, Madame Blum led the way, rapping the brass knocker firmly on the door. The slim, plainly dressed woman who answered was not what Yvette had expected of an artist's wife. At the sight of Madame Blum, her eyes lit up and a dazzling smile made her eyes dance and a little dimple appear on her cheek, transforming her into an attractive woman quite a bit younger than Madame Blum, who she greeted with a kiss on each cheek and an ample hug. When she released her, she asked, 'This is the model?'

'Yvette,' Madame Blum replied, encouraging her to step forward.

Madame Chiparus assessed her from the top of her head down to the tips of her shoes; she even walked around her in a full circle. Yvette felt like a nanny goat at the stock yards being inspected for her pedigree by a prospective buyer. She hoped her hooves were in good enough condition and her eyes shiny.

Finally, Madame Chiparus nodded her approval. 'Just the characteristics we are looking for. My husband will be pleased.'

Her comment didn't help Yvette's sense of unease.

Madame Chiparus abruptly turned and strode towards a small, whitewashed building. They followed her down the white pebbled pathway, and she tapped on the door and entered without waiting for a reply.

Yvette stepped into the gloom. It took a moment for her eyes to adjust and for the shambles within to come into focus. If this had been *her* husband, she would have made sure he worked in an ordered and tidy studio. Every tube of paint; every brush, water pot and rag would have a permanent home on a shelf or bench. And at the end of every day, she'd sweep the studio, remove all the curls of clay, pick up the scalpels and put his current work in pride of place at the centre of the studio.

Yvette had to restrain herself, so she didn't snatch up the nearest broom and sweep all the mess out the door.

Monsieur Chiparus was so engrossed, crouched over the block of clay on his little turntable, he didn't notice them until his wife said, 'Dimi'.

At the sound of his name, he rose from the emerging sculpture like an uncoiling spring and focused his attention on the newcomers in his domain.

'Always a pleasure to see you, Martje.'

'Likewise, Dimi. I have brought Yvette to meet you. Oscar said you were looking for a new model for your next series.'

He didn't appraise her like his wife had done, or obviously look her over. Instead, he met her gaze and asked, 'Have you modelled before?'

She shook her head.

'Do you think you have the patience to stand balanced on a single leg and hold a pose?'

Yvette drew herself up on the ball of her foot and pointed her other foot out in front of her. She'd seen a dancer posed this way in a painting on the wall of childhood friend's parlour. She silently counted to sixty without wobbling and knew she could do at least another two minutes. The village girls had competed to see how long they could stand on one leg, imitating the painting. She always won, and she'd win today too.

'Very impressive. Can you hold this pose?'

He showed her a picture of a woman holding her arms outstretched above shoulder height, her upper back arched a little from her waist, and her left foot tucked up by her knee.

Yvette imagined how her body would feel in this pose. She slid her left foot up her calf to nestle beside her right knee, raised her arms and arched her head and spine backwards. She'd counted to ninety when the artist called time.

'Do you think you have the stamina to do this for several hours?'

'I think I do.' She wanted to ask about payment but worried that this was too forward.

Madame Blum rescued her by asking on her behalf, and it surprised Yvette when the artist's wife replied, 'Three francs for a four-hour session.'

Triple the amount she could make at L'Académie, for a third less time.

'How many sessions a week would you require?'

The wife looked across at the husband.

'Three times a week for ten weeks,' he said.

The wife took longer to calculate the ninety francs than Yvette. She nodded her assent and came up slightly in Yvette's opinion. The wife held the purse strings and Yvette felt certain she would be paid.

'I would be very happy to take the work, as long as we can work around my hours at L'Académie.'

'Of course. I will leave it to my wife to make the

arrangements.' Monsieur Chiparus gave them a tight little bow, picked up his scalpel and coiled himself over his turntable once more. Yvette admired his focus. A marching band could have circuited the room three times and he would not have looked up.

Madame Chiparus ushered them from the studio, and they stood on the white-pebbled pathway. 'What days do you not work at L'Académie?'

'Monday to Wednesday.'

Yvette wondered if Madame Chiparus would make a big show of deciding whether these dates were suitable. She didn't, though, just nodding. 'Yes, that will work. Let's start eight thirty on Monday morning.'

Yvette quickly agreed. She was used to starting work before the sun rose.

'Thank you so much for your help,' Yvette said as they walked back to the tram.

'It's my pleasure. And it keeps us nicely connected to Monsieur Chiparus.'

So, this hadn't been about kindness at all. Madame Blum had seen an opportunity to get more business from Monsieur Chiparus. Yvette didn't know whether to be offended or admire Madame Blum for her ability to see opportunities where others couldn't.

Although, it left her wondering just how much she really could trust her new benefactor.

TWENTY-TWO

Steffan

Paris, September 1933

When the end of the day bell clanged, Steffan waited with Daniel and his young cousin Janie in front of Blum Galerie for Yvette and Martje to return.

He'd never seen Yvette in anything other than her shapeless coat. Even that threadbare garment couldn't hide that she moved like a dancer, flowing from one step to the next, her head balanced in perfect harmony above her spine. If Chiparus accepted her as a model, he'd carve the shape of her limbs. And her facial features, if he'd graduated to carving heads by then.

Janie walked ten paces up the road, stood for a moment waiting for her sister to round the corner, then when she didn't, paced back past them to check the other end of the street.

'They've been gone a long time. Do you think she's all right?' Janie asked.

'Sit down, Janie. You're making me feel sick,' Daniel said.

Janie dismissed him with a flick of her fingers and kept pacing, coming to a halt, then pacing back again.

The girl didn't have her sister's grace, but she did have her features. Her heart-shaped face emphasised her full lips and wide eyes, and the corners of her mouth sloped upwards. The girl radiated good cheer. Wisps of curly brown hair escaped from her chignon, hinting at the spirited young woman who might soon emerge.

'Yvette's fine. Madame Blum will look after her,' Daniel said.

'Maybe she didn't get the job and Madame Blum had to take her somewhere else.'

'They were going to L'Académie and to Monsieur Chiparus's home. It's quite a distance between the two.'

Janie sighed and flopped onto the bench.

Daniel nudged her and said, 'Madame Blum doesn't like to travel on the Metro. The tram and the bus take longer.'

'I understand you have been offered a job too,' Steffan said to distract her.

Janie smiled, ramping up the cheerful. 'Yes, helping in the galerie. Four francs a week.'

Not so long ago, Steffan would have been happy to work for the same amount of money. Now he had to pay for his board, his visits to Claude's, and his weekly subs for the Communist Party.

Janie leapt up. 'Here they come.'

Steffan jumped up too, and his stomach fluttered as he waited for Yvette to round the corner.

And there they were. Madame Blum faded into the shadows cast by the light that seemed to surround Yvette. She didn't walk down the street, she flowed effortlessly, as if the pavement cushioned her feet. Her heart-shaped face lit up when she saw her sister. One day he hoped Yvette might look at him like that.

Yvette hugged her sister, and listened intently as she described her day and her new job. When Janie had finished, she said, 'I had a successful day too. Four days a week at L'Académie and three days with Monsieur Chiparus.'

'Is the money good?' Janie asked.

'Very good. More than enough for us, and we can send money back for Lila, Joseph, and Monsieur Rhodes.'

'That's great,' Steffan said.

Yvette stared at him, seemingly perplexed he'd joined the conversation.

Daniel followed her gaze and shrugged. 'Steffan's fine. We're comrades.'

She continued to stare at him until he felt compelled to say, 'I'm Daniel's comrade. It's all good.'

'Steffan's family,' Martje said. 'Is your father still in the foundry?'

Steffan shook his head. 'He left about half an hour ago.'

Martje said goodbye and headed home.

Yvette passed Janie a rainbow of wool swatches. 'Madame Blum took me to her family tailor. She said we need new coats for winter, so I picked out these colours.'

Janie rubbed her thumb over each swatch as she sorted through them, eventually selecting two – olive green and light blue.

'The green for me and the blue for you,' Janie said.

'Exactly what I thought.' Yvette plucked the light blue swatch from her sister's hand.

The colour perfectly matched Yvette's eyes. Steffan imagined escorting her to the Musée d'Orsay in her new coat, every passer-by stopping to admire her as if she were one of the artworks on display. If she shrugged on that new coat before he got to know her, he'd have no chance at all.

Steffan took a deep breath and made his move. 'Should we celebrate your good fortune?'

Janie clapped her hands together. 'Can we have dinner out? Can I order canard? I've only had it once.'

'Of course. Steffan and I will treat you two,' Daniel said, without waiting for Yvette to agree.

'You are very good to us, cousin,' Yvette said.

'We haven't paid for you yet. We might change our minds if you are dull company.'

'It might be you who are the dull ones,' she replied with a laugh.

'I'm the one who's been out and about meeting new people and organising two jobs. What have you three been doing?'

'I got a job too,' said Janie.

'I did some damned fine carving,' Daniel said.

'Me too.' Steffan hoped he didn't come across as too desperate to be accepted by the sisters.

'Let's find some canard for the young lady,' Daniel said.

They meandered down a cobblestone lane lined with restaurants where waiters in formal black waistcoats, jackets and bowties attended to well-dressed patrons seated under the black and red awnings.

In the next road they hurried past a group of workers who'd tumbled out of a bar to place bets on two drunkards about to fight.

Around the corner, Daniel stopped at the third café, its green awning standing out from its neighbour's red ones. The patrons, a step up from the previous streets, sat on wobbly chairs on the uneven pavement. The tables were laid with slightly stained green and white check tablecloths, and on each sat a posey of geraniums in a small preserving jar.

The waiter greeted Daniel in the same manner as Claude welcomed Steffan and offered them a seat outside. They were protected from the cool breeze by a canvas attached to the awning but could still watch people stroll by.

'A glass of Champagne for the lady, a grenadine for Mademoiselle, and two beers,' Daniel told the waiter.

'Can I have a glass of Champagne?' Janie asked Yvette.

'You can have a sip of mine,' she replied.

Daniel shook his head and told the waiter, 'Let's have a glass of Champagne for Mademoiselle instead of the grenadine.'

Yvette attempted to protest, but Daniel said, 'It's a special occasion.'

Janie smirked at her sister.

'The place doesn't look much, but the food is fantastic,' said Daniel. He steadied the wobbly table with his knee as he pointed out the canard on the menu to Janie. She gasped at the prices.

Steffan nearly dropped his menu when Yvette touched him lightly on his hand. 'I haven't thanked you for helping us when we arrived. It should be us paying for your meal to repay you for your kindness,' she said.

'I know how confusing it can be arriving in a big city. Daniel's been very good to me, so I'm happy I could help his family.'

Yvette nodded, her expression sympathetic. His jaw tightened as he realised Martje had told her about him. It was his story to tell, and he should be able to choose who he told it to. Yvette had already formed an opinion about him being an outsider in his own family. He'd just have to prove her wrong.

Before Steffan could reply, Daniel held up his glass. 'Let's raise a toast to your parents, my aunt and uncle. I am sorry that you've lost them both.'

They clinked glasses and took a sip.

'Papa made it impossible for us to receive any help, which is why we are here,' said Yvette.

'Did he...?' Daniel drew his finger across his neck.

Yvette glanced at Janie, then pointed her fingers to her temple and pretended to pull the trigger.

Daniel nodded. 'Mama said he was never the same after the war. Damned shame.'

'I am sorry that happened to you,' Steffan said. A war veteran had taken his life in their village, and his family had eventually been turned out from their holding because no one would help. It was more a curse on the living than a sin for the dead.

'Let's not talk about such maudlin things,' Daniel said. 'What about Lila?'

'You didn't want to talk about maudlin things,' Yvette answered.

'Okay, now you've started. I want to hear about it.'

'It's not good. Lila's very sick and she has baby Joseph now. He belongs to that old goat Patrick, not that he'll acknowledge the boy. He had her living in an animal shelter on his land.'

'He's always been a miserable devil.'

'Patrick's all right,' Janie said, sipping her Champagne.

Daniel and Yvette exchanged a look that Janie seemed not to notice.

'How he's treating Lila isn't all right,' said Yvette.

'She shouldn't have got pregnant.' Janie held her hand over the glass to feel the bubbles popping on her skin.

Yvette dismissed her sister with a wave of her hand. 'You know nothing.'

'Will Lila be all right now you're here?' Daniel asked.

'Oh yes, very much so.' Yvette laughed. The corners of her eyes crinkled in a way Steffan found endearing. 'Lila and the baby are staying in our cottage and Monsieur Rhodes and Madame Jervois are looking out for them.'

Daniel burst out laughing. 'Madame Jervois helping Lila in an alliance with that ratbag Rhodes? Well, I never. How the winds shift in our little village.'

The waiter arrived to take their order and Janie persuaded them all to have *canard à l'orange*. Steffan had eaten far too much *canard* on the farm, nearly breaking his teeth on the buckshot. But he agreed, to keep Janie happy, and he wasn't disappointed.

Afterwards, Daniel insisted they should have a nightcap – a *bonnet de nuit*. He ignored Janie's yawns and Yvette's protests.

'I start work tomorrow, so we need to go home now,' Yvette said, putting on her gloves.

Like Daniel, Steffan didn't want the evening to end, but he could see how tired the sisters were. 'Perhaps we could dine again after work, and you can tell us how your first day went,' Steffan suggested.

'We've got a party meeting after work tomorrow,' Daniel said, scuppering his idea.

'Thank you for buying us dinner,' said Yvette. 'It was lovely to meet you again, Steffan. Janie and I will reciprocate when we receive our first wages.'

She hugged and kissed Daniel. Steffan hung back, half-hoping she'd kiss him too, but not wanting to push himself onto her. He nearly floated out of his body when she leant towards him. She smelt of oranges and Champagne, and her lips were soft and light against his cheek. He had to restrain himself from touching his cheek where his skin tingled.

After they left, he asked Daniel, 'Do you think Yvette would be interested in me?'

Daniel laughed. 'You'd better hurry up and make a move, because as soon as she starts work at L'Académie, the competition's going to be fierce.'

Not if he were there too. He'd have a fighting chance. He could easily look in on the L'Académie when passing by during his deliveries, or even on his day off.

Before he could ask his friend's opinion, Daniel had struck up a conversation with a comrade at the next table, about the benefits of demonstrating for workers' rights. There'd be no interrupting that for matters of the heart.

TWENTY-THREE

Yvette

Paris, September 1933

Yvette stood behind the flimsy screen in L'Académie's big studio. She took deep breaths to calm her nerves as she listened to the artists setting up their easels and murmuring to each other. She did some of the warm-up stretches Felicity had shown her, wriggling her shoulders and swinging her arms. It didn't help; the sleeves of her robe shook along with her trembling hands.

She peeked around the screen to see ten artists standing at their canvases, backlit by the skylights, waiting for her to take her place on the stage. She repeated Felicity's instructions. *It is up to me to show however much of my body I wish to.*

When she left the safety of the screen, she would wear the robe until she sat down on the chaise, then would drape the shawl across her breasts and hips. Her skin felt cold and prickly, and she struggled to keep her breathing under control.

What if Madame Jervois heard of this? What would she think? She'd stop supporting Lila. There was no way she *could* hear about it, though. And it wasn't as if Yvette was prostituting herself, or dancing without underwear, like the women in Montmartre.

What made her think she could go out there? It seemed so wrong, yet everyone here thought it completely normal that strangers were about to inspect every part of her body.

As if on cue, Felicity appeared behind the screen. 'Everything all right, Yvette?'

'I can't go out there.' The words stuck in her throat.

Felicity gave her a sympathetic smile. 'The first time is always the hardest. Let's go out together.'

She needed this work. This was her one opportunity to follow in her mother's footsteps. But those steps wouldn't lead back to her village.

'Okay,' she answered. It came out high pitched and squeaky.

Felicity took her by the arm and escorted her onto the dais. She felt like Marie Antoinette being taken by her guard to the guillotine, her execution about to be painted by ten eager art students.

Felicity positioned them in front of the chaise and announced, 'This is Yvette. She is new to modelling, so I ask you to be kind and welcome her to L'Académie.'

A chorus of *Bonjour Yvette* greeted her from around the room.

Felicity motioned for her to sit down, then guided her when Yvette couldn't respond. She arranged her on the chaise, lying down with her top leg slightly forward, so she inclined towards the artists. Finally, she draped the shawl just as Yvette would have, across her chest and hips.

'There we go, you are ready.' Felicity stepped off the stage, leaving Yvette alone with the full attention of the artists. As her panic receded, and she got her breathing under control, she observed them while they studied her.

Only two were females, both over sixty; four men about the

same age as the women, and four younger men ranging from early thirties to around fifty.

None of them looked at her like men did when she walked down the street, as if she was a tasty little duckling and they were hungry eels. These artists studied her shape to capture it on their canvas, more like tradesmen trying to replicate another's work. Except she was a one off – not even Janie her sister was the same. Unique, that's what she was. The artists were capturing their own idea of her as an individual.

To pass the time, she imagined the tailor stitching her beautiful blue coat, cutting out the pieces, adding the stiffening, then sewing on the lining. She had her fitting at the end of the week. Perhaps the tailor would finish it by next week. She saw herself turning men's and women's heads as she walked past wrapped in the colour of the sky.

Her stomach gurgled and her thoughts turned to what she'd cook for supper. Something light, like potatoes dauphinoise, as Janie would have eaten her midday meal with the Blums. During her break she would go to the café that Madame Blum took her to last week. The other customer had been eating more than just macarons, although Yvette could eat macarons for her midday meal if she so wished. She suppressed a giggle, almost forgetting she was under the scrutiny of the artists.

Time trickled, and Yvette fought off sleep by counting the sploshes of paint on the handrail between her and the artists.

Finally, Felicity called the session to an end and helped Yvette shrug on the robe while still covering herself with the shawl. Yvette kept glancing at the artists, but they were all busy packing up their easels, hanging up their smocks and rearranging their sketches so their work was on display for the next class.

As her next sitting wasn't for two hours, Yvette went behind the screen and put her clothes back on. When she came out, all the artists had left, except for an elderly man with a forest of coarse grey hair sprouting from his nose and ears. He'd changed out of his smock and wore an expensive, black, three-piece woollen suit.

'Mademoiselle Yvette, may I escort you to lunch?'

He loomed over her as if she were a new flavour of macaron he hadn't had the pleasure of tasting.

'Thank you for your kind offer, Monsieur but I am dining with my uncle and aunt. They live just around the corner.'

He seemed satisfied with her refusal, and she congratulated herself for reading the situation correctly.

'You must allow me another time. Perhaps I can escort you to your aunt and uncle's home?'

'You are too kind. But I am due for some instruction with Felicity before I go,' she lied.

'Next week, then.' He reached out, attempting to kiss her hand, but she neatly side-stepped him, hurrying down the corridor to Felicity and Tave's office.

She tapped on the door and burst into the room as soon as she heard Tave call out, '*Entrez*'.

Tave was swamped by the large writing desk he perched behind, and he seemed even smaller than before, as the desk was marooned in a sea of overstuffed leather sofas, and coffee tables covered in empty wine bottles, smeared glasses, and peanut shells.

'Goodness are you being hunted?' he said.

'I believe so, and this is my sanctuary.'

'Of course, this is your sanctuary any time you feel under threat.'

'Hopefully it won't be too often.'

'My dear, you are new to L'Académie. You will be making frequent visits to this office until certain artists understand you will not give in.'

'That sounds tedious.'

Tave's laugh echoed around the room. 'Although necessary,

from L'Académie's perspective. We want them coming back, even if it is to pine for you from afar. So do give in to the odd invite for coffee. In public, at a café. Never go anywhere else with them, though!'

'Can I wait in here until the old goat is gone?'

'Of course you may. But next week you need to say yes to a quick drink.' Tave returned his attention to the document in front of him, continuing to write in short bursts, like a telegram operator sending a message.

Yvette heard the elderly artist hobble down the hallway and close the front door with a slam.

Tave shook his head. 'He will shake the glass from the door pane. It's so expensive to replace. He's done it once already.'

'Why not stop him from coming, if he's such a nuisance.'

'He happens to be a founding member and one of our most generous benefactors.'

'I'll just have to keep him at arm's length, then.'

'And if you want to continue to do so outside these walls, avoid Café de la Rotonde to the right. Turn left and you'll find Le Bistrot des Campagnes. Delightful place with a delightful host.'

'Thank you. I will heed your advice.'

'Enjoy your repast.'

She followed Tave's instructions and spotted Le Bistrot de Campagnes, its dark exterior and gold-leafed windows conspicuous between the lines of cream-coloured buildings that flanked it.

The host lived up to Tave's description. He welcomed Yvette, gushed appropriately when he heard Tave had recommended him, and guided her to a table with a good view of the street and the passersby. He left her with the menu and she agonised over the options, so many tempting things. She couldn't decide, until an apple tart passed by on its way to another diner. She nearly swooned at the aroma of baked apples and perfectly cooked pastry.

'I must have the apple tart,' she told the waiter.

'Excellent choice, Mademoiselle. A glass of Liqueur de Noix goes beautifully with the tart.'

Yvette accepted his suggestion. For the first time since arriving in Paris, she felt very grown up. Her mother wouldn't have approved of her drinking, but she would have been proud of her courage and her ability to look after Janie.

The drink arrived before the tart, so she had a sip. It smelled like the diesel exhaust from the trucks that rumbled by as she walked about the city. The liquid hit the back of her throat, the fumes seared her nose, and she fought back a cough and the reflex to spit it out.

Don't be a baby. Take another sip. If she was a grown up, she needed to act like one.

The waiter appeared with her tart, bringing the scent of home when her mother had baked with her preserved fruit. The dish came with a large dollop of cream that she tasted with her finger when the waiter left. Combined with vanilla and sugar, it was a perfect match with the tart.

She started off taking little lady-like bites. The spoonfuls increased in size until she was shovelling the tart into her mouth, not caring what anyone thought of her. She was ravenous – not for food, but for something that shimmered at the edge of her mind, something without a name or a shape, and as she ate, it chewed away inside her.

She scraped the plate clean, savouring the flavours remaining in her mouth. Then she stared at the liqueur, wishing she hadn't ordered it. But she didn't want to waste it, now it sat in front of her.

She caught the waiter's attention and asked him to bring her a coffee noir. When it arrived, she took a sip from the coffee and a gulp from the liqueur. Three gulps later it was finished.

She had a few minutes before she needed to be back at L'Académie, so she stopped outside a bookshop and stared at the window display – she'd never seen this many books before. Her mother had had a small collection, which her father had given to Madame Sorve in exchange for drink. Madame Sorve kept them secreted away behind the firmly shut door of her parlour. Yvette had only ever managed to snatch a glimpse when she took Madame her afternoon tea on a tray.

She would save the bookshop for another day.

When she returned, someone had wedged open L'Académie's door. She supposed Tave did it to keep his precious glass safe from door bangers like the 'old goat'.

More than twenty artists were cluttering up the hall, fluffing about with their lockers. A dozen others syphoned off into the studios with most heading to hers. Still not used to being in crowds of people, Yvette kept her head down, weaving through the throngs of feet, until she was safely behind the screen.

She changed into her robe and listened to the artists talking to one another, setting up easels and putting on their smocks.

Felicity spoke from the other side of the screen. 'It's time to start, Yvette. Are you ready?'

'I am ready.' She came out from behind the screen and followed Felicity onto the stage. At least this time she felt more confident and less like Marie Antoinette.

Once again Felicity introduced her, and once again the artists greeted her.

When Felicity finished arranging the shawl over her torso and limbs, Yvette studied the people observing her. Twice as many artists were at this session, with a greater number of younger people, and six women.

In the back row was a tall young man, partly obscured by his canvas. The way he held himself seemed familiar. When he lifted his head to look at her, she almost screamed. What was Steffan doing here? She was nearly naked in a room with a man she knew.

Their eyes met and he winked. If she hadn't needed to stay still, he'd have received the hardest slap she could muster.

For three hours she fumed inside, but her face remained calm and serene, while Steffan looked from her to the canvas and back again.

Finally, the clock chimed, and Felicity reminded the artists to thank Yvette.

Yvette removed herself as quickly as she could from the stage to the safety of the screen. She only came out when Felicity called her name, and the room was empty.

'The young man in the back of the room. Was that his first time here?'

Felicity shook her head. 'It's about his third week. Do you know him?'

The tension in her stomach relaxed. It was a coincidence he'd been here, not something he'd engineered.

She was a little disappointed Steffan wasn't waiting for her outside L'Académie when she stepped out into the street.

TWENTY-FOUR

Steffan

Paris, October 1933

As they got closer to Place de la Bastille, more workers joined the march from side roads, emerging from nearby workplaces, some still in their leather aprons, with metal filings and wood dust stuck to their clothes. Comrades from other guilds and worker groups unfurled banners and walked side by side with the starving scarecrows newly arrived in Paris.

Steffan hoped to unveil the Lady Liberty banner somewhere where she reminded Paris about the atrocities happening in her streets. He could still feel the crunch of broken glass underfoot and taste the bitter embers from the burned shops.

Place de la Bastille was a fitting destination, but the rag tag bunch that trailed behind their banner disappointed him. Their voices were weak and straggly during the chants, and little more than a mumble when they sang.

He didn't begrudge the Artisan Guild supporting comrades arriving from the provinces to protest rising prices and the scarcity of food, but he'd have preferred his banner's first outing to be about something with more fervour.

Another guild member took the banner pole from him, and he dropped back to walk with the country folk. The man next to him had no shoes and shuffled along with his feet wrapped in rags. It was impossible to tell how old he was; his hollowed-out face and dull eyes gave nothing away. The man stumbled on a cobblestone and lurched towards Steffan, who caught him under the arm, stopping him from falling. He weighed nothing, less than a newborn calf, his arm as thin as a shepherd's staff.

'When was the last time you ate?' Steffan asked him.

The man shook his head, seeming too weak to even talk, or maybe he just couldn't remember. Steffan helped him over to the pavement and sat him under a tree outside a bakery.

'He can't stay there. He'll scare away other customers,' the red-faced, rotund baker yelled from his shop doorway.

'You will make him a customer and give him something to eat.' Steffan moved towards the baker, who turned a deeper shade of red and backed into the shop. Steffan put his foot in the door before the man could close it.

'Go away, I don't want any trouble.' The baker's voice had turned high and shrill.

'Just give me a basketful of bread.' He thrust some money at him.

The baker's wife, as rotund and red faced as her husband, appeared to snatch the money from Steffan. She counted it and shoved loaves of bread, brioche, and croissants into a wicker basket. She elbowed her husband out of the way and thrust the basket at Steffan.

'Bring it back once it's empty,' she growled at him.

Steffan placed a loaf of bread in the exhausted marcher's lap. He stared at it as if he didn't think it was real.

'Eat, comrade,' Steffan said.

When the man raised his head, tears trickled down his face. He nodded his thanks.

Steffan rejoined the crowd, then turned back to check on the man. He was holding the loaf in both hands, his face buried in it like it was a corncob.

The procession slowed as ravenous men stopped to take the bread he was handing out. One man sank down onto the road as he stuffed the food into his mouth.

He finally understood why the Guild had agreed to take up this cause. The workers' plight wasn't as violent and obvious as a burning street; it was slow, cruel, and pitiful. He'd volunteer to organise a clothing and food drive for the men. Perhaps they could even put some of them up in the Guildhall.

Other onlookers were also taking pity on the starving marchers – bakery workers with large baskets began weaving through the hungry marchers, handing out bread.

But the food turned the march into a beast with energy to heckle the well-dressed passersby. Only one man challenged their taunts, calling out that they were troublemakers and Jew lovers. Two marchers tore off his fine wool jacket, leaving him dazed on the ground as they ran away holding the garment above their heads like a trophy. The beast roared its approval.

They circled the Place de la Bastille like a flock of dishevelled pigeons and finally settled in front of the July Column, on top of which the winged figure of the *Spirit of Freedom* was poised on one foot, like one of Chiparus's dancers. Beneath the gold leaf, the statue would be bronze, and Steffan wished it were closer to the ground so he could examine the joins, and how it was attached to the column. A single fixed point, rather than two, seemed risky at such height.

A man who introduced himself as 'a member of the Friends of the Rural Poor Committee' mounted the steps at the base of the column. He fired numbers and percentages into the ragged crowd like projectiles, but his tailored wool suit, the pressed creases in his trousers, and his embossed leather shoes told a different story. Steffan couldn't take him seriously.

Nor could the crowd, and the beast woke up. It rumbled and

swayed, searching for release, until the committee member allowed a protestor to speak. The man was standing beside Steffan, and he had the same gaunt appearance as the other country folk but was better dressed and his boots still had soles. He was from a small town 100 km from Paris, he said. His lilt reminded Steffan of the village an hour's walk from their family farm.

'Our crops failed in last year's drought,' the man began, his voice so low and faltering that Steffan had to lean forward to hear him. 'We had nothing to feed the cattle, so we butchered them.' Tears trickled down his face.

The beast settled and the crowd turned its full attention to the speaker.

'Once the meat was gone, we caught rabbits and birds, until they were gone. We scoured the countryside for every dandelion leaf, acorn, and fennel bulb. Until they were all gone too.'

Another man close to Steffan called out, 'In our village as well.' He clutched a picture frame to his chest.

The speaker sobbed now. 'My children cried as their stomachs ached, and stopped when they were too weak. No one came to help. We buried all four of them.'

The second man held up the picture towards the speaker. 'My family is dead too.' Steffan reached out to comfort him, but the man was too distraught to notice his gesture.

Steffan imagined his sister Liselle and her husband Bede thin and sick, searching their barren and empty pastures for anything to eat; Liselle's baby dead in her arms and her husband digging its grave, Bede so weak he had to rest after each shovelful of earth.

Around him men called out the names of their dead loved ones, spoke of their dead cattle and losing their land. Country folk shouldn't be having it so hard. They produced France's food, and here they were, starving.

Anger boiled up inside him. He needed to do something more than listen to speeches.

He leant over and whispered to Daniel, 'Shall we cause a little mayhem?'

Daniel raised an eyebrow. 'What did you have in mind?'

'Rattling the Croix de Feu's cage.'

'Figaro Building?' Steffan drew an imaginary hammer and sickle in the air between them.

Daniel smirked. 'We'll get some paint on the way.'

'Blood red,' Steffan insisted.

'Of course, Comrade.'

Daniel whispered to a cluster of Artisan Guild members. By the time the next speaker climbed the steps of the July Column, ten of them had slipped out of the crowd.

As soon as they were far enough away, the men around him erupted into action, planning slogans, where to get the paint, and which masks to use to hide their identities.

Daniel led them into a small park a block away from the Figaro building.

'We'll need paint, brushes, and masks to hide our faces. Anything else?' Daniel looked around the group.

'Could we make stencils?' Steffan suggested. The group's enthusiasm encouraged him further. 'We can cover the building with dozens before anyone works out what we are doing.'

'Great idea. Let's add thin boards to the list,' Daniel said, holding out his arms to demonstrate their size. 'We could get two or more stencils from each sheet.'

Two men who worked at the glass factory next to Blum Foundry left to hunt down paint and brushes, while two others from another foundry volunteered to bring back the masks and the boards.

While they waited, the rest of the group shouted out words for the stencils, and eventually agreed on using just the hammer and sickle.

'We walk down the road in pairs, then cover the building in slogans,' Daniel said, his voice full of assurance.

'Shouldn't we wait until it's dark?' Steffan asked.

Daniel waved away his concerns. 'We're all good runners and our faces are covered.'

Two comrades returned with a rucksack full of paint and brushes.

'How many paintbrushes did you bring?' Steffan asked.

The guild member rummaged around in his rucksack. 'Eight.'

The other comrades returned with a bag of balaclavas, and the boards.

'Draw as many stencil outlines as you can,' Daniel said to Steffan.

Steffan estimated he could draw two hammer and sickles on each board. He didn't have any tools, apart from his knife and a pencil.

'Do we have enough knives to cut out the stencils?' Steffan asked.

The men searched their pockets and bags, and enough pulled out small knives like his.

With a firm hand, Steffan drew the image, proud that Daniel had faith in him to do a good job, especially when he was surrounded by men who were much more experienced.

He passed each completed board to an artisan; Daniel claimed the last one.

To anyone passing by, they were just a group of men whiling away the afternoon with some group woodworking activity. The men who weren't cutting out the stencils moved about smoking, making sure no one else got too close.

A restless comrade pulled out a balaclava from the sack and tried in on. It had a slot for his eyes and the material covered his mouth.

'Take that off – you're attracting attention,' Daniel growled.

Steffan almost laughed. As if they were going to draw any more attention to themselves. They'd been sitting there for an hour, carving out stencils surrounded by rucksacks of paint and brushes. He busied himself picking up the wood shavings.

When the first stencil was finished, Daniel held it up against a nearby tree trunk. 'One comrade will take responsibility to hold it against the building, and another will apply the paint.'

'We'll break up into pairs?' Steffan tried to say this with conviction, and cringed a little when it came out as a question.

Daniel nodded. 'Great idea. Let's all pair up.'

Daniel wasn't looking at Steffan, though. He meant to pair up with the burly man who'd returned with the balaclavas.

The other balaclava gatherer nodded at Steffan, so he asked, 'Would you like to hold the stencil or wield the brush?'

His new partner made a painting motion. Steffan didn't mind being the stencil holder.

They rejoined the group and Daniel explained the plan. Steffan's stomach fluttered as they gathered in a tight group to walk the block to the Figaro Building. He was amazed no one seemed to notice them. If everyone was as hyped up as him, they must be glowing. They weren't just a group of workers off to complete some job, but revolutionaries about to attack their enemy.

Daniel stopped them twenty paces away from the Figaro Building.

'Stick with your partner. Try for two stencil applications. Run as soon as anyone comes out of the building. Take off your balaclava after you dump your stencil and paint. If you get separated, check you're not being followed. When you're clear, make your way back to the Guildhall.'

'Comrades ready, balaclavas on,' Daniel called out.

Steffan pulled the strange covering over his head, the wool scratching his face as he adjusted it. The fibres caught on his lips, so he closed his mouth and breathed through his nose.

On Daniel's signal, they moved forward. As Steffan ran towards the other side of the building, he checked his partner was following him. At any moment the large Croix de Feu doorman could burst out of the building and knock him to the ground. He didn't care; he could take on anything and anyone coming his way.

He rounded the corner and slammed the stencil up against the cream blockwork near the front door. His partner ran the brush down the stencil twice, covering Steffan's thumbs in red paint. He pulled the stencil away, pleased with the two red hammer and sickles they'd made. His heart drummed in his chest and his throat burnt from the paint fumes. He wanted the Figaro doors to burst open; he wanted to punch someone. They painted three more stencils before Daniel called out to scatter.

He turned back towards the park, so he could see their handiwork. Dozens of red hammer and sickles dripped around the Figaro's entranceway. He laughed as he ran with the others, flinging the stencil into nearby bushes. After he passed a group of startled pedestrians, he ripped off his balaclava and used it to wipe the paint from his fingers.

He jogged all the way back to the Guildhall, checking he wasn't being followed. He rushed up the Guildhall stairs hoping Daniel and the others had made it back safely. As he emerged into the hall, comrades cheered and clapped, and slapped him on the back like he'd won a gold medal in the Revolutionary Olympics.

Daniel hugged him, thrust a beer into his hand and held up his other arm. 'Comrade Blum's first successful mission.'

He couldn't stop grinning. It had been his idea and they'd been successful, sticking it to the Croix de Feu. He raised his glass and drank deeply, not only quenching his thirst but also his desire to avenge what had happened to Monsieur Coen and the haberdashery quarter.

TWENTY-FIVE

Yvette

Paris, October 1933

As Yvette emerged from the Metro a block away from Chiparus's home, she felt transported into a different city. In contrast to the Rue de Paradis, where factory smoke mingled with the aroma of baked bread, the sharpness of roasting coffee, and the delicious meals produced from the nearby cafes, here the air smelt fresh. She was surrounded by trees, and the river ran close by.

As she walked down the long avenue of cream buildings punctuated by black and blue doors, she didn't pass a single factory, shop or person. What if she met someone coming the other way who meant to harm her? Would anyone open their door if she knocked and cried for help? She shook her head to dislodge the thought. No one seemed to be on the streets in this respectable neighbourhood.

Yvette relaxed once she turned into Chiparus's street and the buildings became detached. Individual homes weren't as intimidating as towering great blocks of stone. She found comfort in the glimpses of green lawns and flowering gardens behind wrought-iron palings.

The gate to Chiparus's home stood open, so she continued down the white pebbled path to knock on the studio door.

'*Entrez,*' Monsieur Chiparus's clipped voice replied.

She pushed open the door to see the same jumble of paints, clay, and stone blocks.

'Bonjour, Monsieur Chiparus. I am here for our session.' She winced as her voice came out hesitant, like she wasn't supposed to be there.

'Of course,' he answered.

She followed his voice and found him in front of his sculpting table, staring at an unformed column of clay.

'Bonjour, Yvette,' Madame Chiparus called out. She materialised from behind a large block of white marble and held up a flimsy cream costume that she shook out to show Yvette.

Yvette snuggled further into her coat. She looked about for a stove but couldn't see one in the jumble. She'd be very cold standing in one place all day in that flimsy and floaty costume. Still, she would earn four times what L'Académie paid for the same length of time.

'You can change behind here.' Madame Chiparus led her to a plain wooden screen. She swept the dress over the top, then indicated Yvette could leave her bag and clothes on a chair wedged into a corner. 'Come out once you are changed.'

Behind the screen, Yvette took off her coat and placed it beside the dress. Goosebumps prickled over her limbs as she removed her blouse and skirt. All she wanted to do was throw her coat back on.

She held the dress up against her, for the first time noticing the splits that ran up the front. She took a deep breath.

Just put it on. Don't make a fuss. It's not like I need to parade down the main street of my village wearing it.

She slipped the dress over her head. The silk slid over her skin like the whisper of river water on a hot day. Turning to the mirror behind her, Yvette didn't recognise the woman in the flowing dress. Her hands flew to the tops of her thighs to hide where the splits revealed too much skin.

Madame Chiparus spoke. 'Do you need any assistance?'

Yvette had almost forgotten they were waiting for her. She couldn't go out there holding the fabric together to hide her thighs. She let it go and twisted her hips. The skirt flared around her, the silk caressing her legs.

'Yes, I am ready,' she said, stepping out from behind the screen.

A smile spread across Madame Chiparus's face. 'You are perfect. Come.'

The floor was so cold, she followed Madame Chiparus on tiptoes trying to keep her feet from freezing. She stepped over dropped rags, discarded papers, and scrolls of clay.

Madame stood on a piece of carpet next to a stool and motioned for Yvette to join her. 'You will stand here with one leg forward. You can keep your hand on the stool for balance.'

She moved away to stand beside her husband. For the second time, Yvette felt like a sculpture being inspected for its merits, rather than a model.

'More leg,' Monsieur Chiparus said.

His wife nodded and fussed about, arranging the folds of the skirts around her thigh. Yvette tried not to cringe away from her cold hands when she touched her skin. Madame kept checking with her husband then fiddling with folding the material until he finally gave a nod of approval. Yvette almost sighed with relief when she stepped away.

'Look into the distance,' Monsieur Chiparus commanded her.

She followed his direction until he put his head down to concentrate on the clay. Then she looked directly at him, a small act of rebellion for having to stay so still. She made a game of moving her eyes just as he began to look up.

After twenty minutes, she yearned to stretch her back leg. Would the artist really expect her to stand in one place for the whole session? Her calf muscle screamed at her to move as ten more minutes crawled by. Monsieur Chiparus remained hunched over his work, completely absorbed in his sculpting.

She gave an experimental wriggle while he looked down. He must have sensed a movement – he looked up just as she looked away, but she saw him notice. She wasn't fast enough. She didn't move again, or play the looking game, even though her legs were about to freeze off, along with the rest of her, and she wanted to collapse on the floor.

She needed this job. They had rent to pay, food (and a sky-blue coat) to buy. She almost giggled at the silliness of her standing here freezing so she could buy a coat. Yet standing still in the cold was 100 times better than scrubbing floors on aching knees, or doing other people's washing with hands chafed from the lime and the cold.

What seemed like an hour later, Madame Chiparus returned with a morning tea tray and a big pot of coffee. 'You may take a break.'

Yvette shook her legs, letting the blood flow back through them, and scampered over to the screen to grab her coat. She threw it on then retrieved her shoes from behind the screen.

By the time she came back, Madame Chiparus had poured her husband his coffee. She offered Yvette a cup, and she accepted with gratitude. She inhaled the aromatic steam as she clasped the cup to let the heat thaw her freezing hands.

The Chiparus's murmured over the lump of clay on the turntable. Yvette watched their heads bent together like a pair of bonded swans. She wondered what it felt like to be so in tune with another person.

Another model at L'Académie had told her the Chiparus's weren't married, yet she wore a wedding band and called herself Madame Chiparus.

When Madame Chiparus caught her staring at her wedding ring, she straightened her back and placed her hand on her

Monsieur Chiparus's shoulder. She stared down Yvette, as if challenging her to say something.

Yvette smiled instead, all the way up to her eyes. The Chiparus's had their reasons for not marrying – who was she to judge, especially after all she'd gone through with Lila.

Madame Chiparus raised an eyebrow at the empty carpet, and Yvette followed her cue. She removed her coat and shoes and took up position by the stool.

'Would you like me to help arrange her?' she asked her husband.

Chiparus shook his head, and Yvette was grateful the woman's hands wouldn't touch her skin again. As she looked Yvette over one more time, her gaze fell to where the fabric tumbled away from her thigh.

'I will leave you to get back to work.'

Yvette kept her head still, only moving her eyes, so she could watch her leave. She walked with her shoulders back and her spine straight as she carried the tray out of the room.

Yvette entertained herself by counting the objects on the floor. She counted five scalpels scattered around the turntable's base, seven pencils, two splintered and squashed from a careless boot, eight turpentine jars filled with paintbrushes, with another on its side, the turpentine dried in a greasy rainbow over the floor.

Finally, Chiparus unfurled to stretch his back. 'I am finished,' he said.

Yvette shook out her legs then sat on the stool. 'May I see your work?'

Chiparus appeared surprised she wanted to see it. He spun the turntable around to face her. She gasped. Her face, serene and relaxed, stared out of the clay. She made out the shape of her right shoulder and arm, and the curve of her leg. She had the impression her image was pushing itself out of the clay.

'I like it very much,' she said.

He laughed, and it somehow made him approachable. 'It is only the beginning, my dear. Wait until it has completely revealed itself.'

'My mother was a sculptor before she got married. I have a picture of her holding one of her pieces.'

'I would like to see that picture. Can you bring it next time?'

'Certainly. I was hoping to learn to sculpt too, like my mother.'

Taking in her words, Chiparus seemed to see her, like she'd just snapped into focus as a person, not just a model.

'Would you teach me?' It was out of her mouth before she could stop herself.

He picked up a cloth to wipe his hands.

When he still hadn't said anything, she added, 'You could pay me less money for the same amount of time, and I could stay afterwards for an hour's tuition.'

She braced herself for his rebuff.

'Yes, I can teach you. And those terms are agreeable.'

On the Metro ride back, she thought about the sculpture always being there in the clay.

A man in her village had a way with horses. He could calm beasts that responded to no one else. She'd overheard him telling her father, 'It's in them to be calm. You just have to find the trigger to bring it out.'

Chiparus did this with clay. He found the piece inside the clay and brought it out.

Tomorrow she would have her own block of clay and would explore what was inside waiting to come out. As she stepped off the train, she imagined herself as the sculpture emerging from the clay, just as she was moving onto the platform, first her leg stepping off, her hand appearing, followed by her arm, her hip, then her upper body.

Outside the Metro, a shop owner was scrubbing black insults from his wall.

Filthy jews leave France now.

He didn't look much different from anyone else, apart from the small black cap on his head. He looked up, then quickly looked away when their eyes met. She recognised the same embarrassment she'd felt in her village at being singled out for something her father did to them.

'I am sorry this happened to you,' she told the man.

He mumbled his thanks as he kept on scrubbing.

Other shops further along had skulls with silver crosses drawn on their windows and walls. The owners were also doing their best to remove them.

She'd seen that symbol before, not on a wall but somewhere else. Something about it made her feel uneasy, like it was an omen of things to come, an unknown lurking ready to swoop in and upset their lives. She shivered. Today wasn't the day to think about that though. Today Monsieur Chiparus had agreed to help her follow in her mother's footsteps.

TWENTY-SIX

Steffan

Paris, October 1933

Steffan knocked on the door of the Blum family home and entered, not waiting for answer. He found the family eating breakfast at the table while Martje buzzed about in the kitchen. His stomach fluttered at the sight of Yvette, with Janie, seated at the table too.

Phillippe stopped talking to Yvette when he saw Steffan. He made an excuse and left the table.

'Sit down and have breakfast,' Martje said and waved him towards the seat Philippe had vacated. It happened to be opposite Yvette, who gave him a welcoming smile.

Steffan smiled back, knowing it would infuriate Phillippe. He could feel him scowling at him from the doorway. He resisted the urge to glance his way. Instead, he helped himself to brioche and cheese while Martje poured him a very strong coffee.

'Are you working with Chiparus today?' he asked Yvette.

'I've got a big day. An early start with Monsieur Chiparus and two sessions at L'Académie.'

He really should go to the Guild meeting to plan their next

action after the success of the Figaro Building. He may have to rethink that, now he knew Yvette would be at L'Académie tonight.

'How's it going with Chiparus? That man is such a superb sculptor, and so exacting. I've had to redo several sets of legs that weren't up to his standards.' He stuffed the brioche in his mouth to stop himself burbling on.

Yvette reached under the table and pulled out a framed photograph of a woman holding a statue. 'I'm taking him this photo of our mother. She was a sculptress, and I think this is one of her works.'

Martje studied the picture, shaking her head. 'I don't recognise her. Monsieur Chiparus might, though.'

Yvette passed the picture to Steffan. The young woman who stared back from the frame had the same almond-shaped eyes as both Yvette and Janie. Wisps of hair escaped from her chignon the way that Janie's did. The black and white photograph gave few clues about the construction of the sculpture, except that it must be bronze.

'I've got some other news too,' Yvette said. 'I asked Monsieur Chiparus to teach me how to sculpt.'

The conversation around the table stopped and everyone stared at her.

'You never told me you wanted to sculpt,' Janie scolded.

Yvette shrugged. 'I didn't know until I watched him work and found out about Maman being a sculptor.'

'Did he agree?' Martje asked.

Yvette clapped her hands together. 'Yes, he did agree. At least an hour a week.'

Suddenly the room felt very distant, as if Steffan was floating out of his body. He wanted Chiparus to teach *him*, not Yvette. It was silly because it hadn't ever occurred to him that he could ask for tuition. He tried to sound sincere with his congratulations.

'He will be very patient, and you will learn a lot,' Martje said.

Steffan didn't trust himself to say anything and left the conversation to the others. After breakfast, he walked the short distance to the Blum Foundry with Janie, Sarah, and Yvette.

'Do you think you will come to L'Académie for this evening's session?' Yvette asked him.

He couldn't see her expression, but by her tone it sounded like she wanted that.

'Yes, I can come ... if you would like me to.'

He held his breath through her silence until she finally said, 'I would like you there. It's nice to have someone I know among the artists.'

'I would be delighted to come, then.'

'My session starts at six.'

'I'll be there.' Definitely doable, though he'd have to fend off Daniel's communist fervour by reassuring him he'd be attending the meeting later in the evening.

As they rounded the corner, Rue de Paradis bustled with the foundry men and workers from other businesses scrubbing graffiti from the buildings.

'Not again,' Sarah said to one of the men.

Even though the workers had scrubbed most of the insults away, the outlines were still visible. It was the same depressing stuff he'd seen scrawled over the desecrated Haberdashery Sector.

The best Jews are dead Jews.

Fuck off from France greedy Jews.

Stencilled everywhere was the Croix de Feu's silver cross and skull emblem. He hadn't seen them use a stencil before and he hoped it wasn't because of their attack on Le Figaro. Did someone from Croix de Feu know they did it, or had they just copied the stencil idea?

'Who would do such a horrible thing?' Yvette exclaimed.

Before he could tell her exactly who had caused it, Sarah

answered. 'Many people would dance in the streets if every Jewish family was forced to leave.'

Yvette's hand shot out and she grabbed Janie's arm.

'Stop it, Yvette.' Janie shook her hand away.

'It's only natural she's worried for you,' Sarah said to Janie, in a tone that conveyed years of calming down younger children.

To Yvette, she said, 'These people are cowards and won't confront us. They just skulk about in the dark polluting our walls with their foulness.'

Steffan wasn't so sure she was right. The Guild had raided Le Figaro during the day. If they had provoked this, then it was likely the Croix de Feu could come here during the day too.

He didn't want to be the cause of a mob rioting in Rue de Paradis. They'd been careful and would carry on being careful. Any mob would be outnumbered by the street's workers, many of whom were as strong as their foundry workers.

Sarah underplaying the attack didn't seem to ease Yvette's concerns. Her back was tense, and her arms were crossed defensively across her body. He wanted to wrap his own arms around her to reassure her that Janie was safe with them. But she wouldn't tolerate that, so he offered the next best thing.

'I could take the truck to L'Académie, then bring you back to the foundry to pick up Janie and take you both home.'

Yvette visibly relaxed. 'You don't mind doing that?'

'It's no bother. You can tell me about your sculpting lesson with Monsieur Chiparus,' Steffan added.

Janie rolled her eyes. 'Honestly, you are all the most tiresome fusspots. I am quite all right.'

She did seem pleased about the fuss they were making over her, though.

The girls entered Blum Galerie, while he watched Yvette walk to the corner. She had a damn fine derrière.

TWENTY-SEVEN

Yvette

<hr>

Paris, October 1933

It seemed inevitable that Yvette would find herself standing in front of an easel with charcoal in her hand. And the more she drew, the less she wanted to be the model.

During the breaks between her L'Académie sessions, she attended other classes to watch the models and study their poses, both for aesthetics and for comfort. Last week her arm had been so numb at the end of one session, she could hardly move her hand. She wiggled her fingers and still felt the tingle in her elbow. That never seemed to happen to Felicity, who today had arranged herself on the chaise longue, draped her orange shawl across her hips, and left her breasts exposed. She exuded comfort and grace, with her upper body well supported. Yvette decided to use Felicity's pose in her next session – her own version though, without the exposed breasts.

The artists assessed Felicity, then turned that intensity to the parchment in front of them. Their charcoal scritched against the paper, reminding Yvette of cricket song during summer afternoons in their village garden. She moved behind the artists as their charcoal strokes assembled themselves into muscles, hair, breasts, buttocks, limbs, hands, and feet. On some canvases Felicity emerged, in others she was merely a collection of parts.

When Yvette posed now, the desire to draw became so powerful, she fought with herself to keep still. She felt she was wasting time, a rock in a stream with life moving past her, leaving only her edges wet. While she modelled, she wasn't immersed in life.

She buzzed with possibility when she held the charcoal onto the parchment, each stroke leaving fine dust along the edge of her fingertips. She let it settle, knowing she'd apply it to the parchment later when she shaded in texture and depth.

Felicity's session finished and the artists who were leaving placed their easels at the end of the studio. Those who stayed found fresh parchment.

Yvette went behind the screen to remove her dress and slip on the dressing gown. Steffan should be here by now, and she hoped she could be brave enough to show a little more of herself.

Felicity popped her head behind the screen. 'All ready?'

Yvette nodded and came out onto the dais. A dozen artists in the studio were fussing about with easels, struggling into smocks, and selecting the correct parchment.

Steffan was standing by his easel in the middle of the studio. His face lit up when he saw her. Yvette grinned at him, and a warmness radiated out from her stomach into her chest.

She set herself up on the chaise the way Felicity had, except with her back to the artists, curling one leg up under her and leaving the other long, then removing the shawl to expose her back and buttocks. It was thrilling and freeing, especially knowing Steffan was studying her body. Yvette longed to turn her head to catch the expression on his face.

Instead, she pictured herself in front of the easel, assessing her own body and directing the charcoal to translate her form onto the parchment. By the end of the session, she'd imagined the whole picture, every heavy stroke, each lighter one, and exactly where the shading would be most effective. She had perfectly imagined it, and she could barely stay still, she was so desperate to draw it.

The second Felicity clapped her hands, Yvette jumped behind the screen and shrugged on her dress and calico smock. Plucking an easel, she planted it beside Steffan.

She surprised herself by kissing him forcefully on the lips. 'I have to get this down before I forget.'

Felicity and Steffan stood behind her, watching her work. Within five minutes, her self-portrait shaped itself from her memory onto the canvas. She stepped back from her work and Steffan put his hand on her shoulder.

'Beautiful, Yvette.'

She shivered when he kissed her neck. It was unexpected, soft, and goosebumps tracked down her arms. He smelt of copper and tobacco.

'Impressive,' Felicity said.

She'd captured herself, the roundness of her buttocks rising from the chaise, the nuisance curl that always escaped at the base of her neck, and the slight turn of her head as if she were listening for Steffan's rendition of her coming alive under his charcoal.

She glanced at his work. It was good, there was no doubting that. Her own picture was great, though, markedly better. She tried not to show her pleasure at the discovery.

'I think it through while I'm modelling, so I'm ready to go. I've already made the strokes, so it feels like I'm just drawing over the top of them.'

'It's wonderful. You are a natural.'

Tears welled in her eyes when Felicity touched Yvette lightly on the shoulder and moved on to the artist beside her. How foolish. Felicity did that with everyone.

It had reminded her of her mother's touch when she brushed

her hair, warm and comforting, signalling she'd finished by resting her hand on her shoulder. She hadn't thought of her mother in weeks. She wished she'd drawn her instead.

Steffan put his easel away. 'You must be starving. Let's go and get something to eat after we've picked up Janie.'

As soon as Steffan said it, her stomach grumbled. They hung their smocks up and moved through the groups of artists who had stayed behind to chat, smoke, and share some wine. An older man with tufts of hair escaping from his ears and nose, and with the wildest eyebrows she'd ever seen, stood in her way.

'Mademoiselle Yvette. Please stay and share a glass of wine with us. You are L'Académie's most celebrated muse.'

Steffan had already passed through them, and she lost sight of him as the group closed in around her.

She shook her head. 'Thank you for the offer, but I am leaving.'

'Stay for a drink.' A younger man stepped towards her and put his arm around her waist. She froze, the way she did back home when the old goat would touch her knowing she couldn't push him away.

The man's friend swayed in front of her, blocking her way, then reached out and grabbed her breast. She swatted his hand away, but he just laughed and did it again. She wasn't back in her village, and she didn't have to put up with this. As Yvette raised her fist ready to punch him, he lurched sideways into the man with his arm around her waist.

Steffan appeared in the gap. 'Yvette said she is leaving. With me.' He seemed taller, and threat rolled from him, so much so that the first man stepped backwards. Steffan took her hand to escort her through the group, like they were annoying thistles in a field.

She couldn't keep the smirk from her face. The moment they were outside and the door shut, she reached up and kissed him again.

'Can't let anyone take liberties with you,' he said. 'They must treat you with respect.'

'That was impressive,' she murmured.

He laughed and they started to walk.

'I learnt my stand-over tactics from watching the rams. My favourite, Charles, only had to move his head towards the others and off they scattered.'

'You seem so confident that I forget you're a country person like me.'

He took her hand. 'Probably why I feel very comfortable with you. We see the world the same way.'

'Sometimes I feel unprepared for living in a city. There's so many different types of people and they are very hard to understand.'

'You had chickens, didn't you?'

She nodded, wondering where this was going.

'People are just like chickens. They are fighting to be on top, to get the best piece of food, to sit in the warmest spot in the roost.'

'You think I should just treat people like flocks of chickens?'

'Exactly.'

'So, if they get stroppy, I should just hold them upside down until they calm down, so they know who's in charge?'

'Now you put it like that. Yes, why not.'

'We can go around tipping unruly men upside down and holding them there until they agree to obey us.'

'I like that plan. It's a good plan.'

She couldn't think of a time when she'd ever been this happy. Here she could draw, sculpt, and walk down the road with an unmarried man. She had enough money to pay the rent months in advance, to feed herself and Janie, and she could even send money home for Lila and Monsieur Rhodes, and repay Eric, of course.

When they reached Steffan's truck, he made to open the passenger door then stopped. 'Can I ask a question?'

His expression was so serious, she held her breath, wondering what was to come. She nodded.

'Since you've kissed me twice now, do you think we might be dating?'

She laughed. 'I didn't know what you were going to ask. I am glad it's that, though.'

'Don't leave me hanging. What's your answer then?'

She didn't hesitate. 'Yes. I think we can say we are dating.'

'I'll seal it with another kiss then.'

He leant forward until his lips touched hers. She moved towards him, his arms wrapped around her, and hers around him. It was delicious, and delicate, and she could have stayed in his arms all night.

He broke it off and smiled down at her, then opened the door and helped her up into the seat.

After swinging himself into the cab, he said, 'Let's go get Janie.'

TWENTY-EIGHT

Steffan

Paris, October 1933

Steffan didn't want to listen to another of Potiev's pep talks, he just wanted to roll out their Lady Liberty banner across the narrow street to the Artisan Guildhall. It was THE MARCH, the one where they would go head-to-head with the Croix de Feu. He wanted to get moving, confront them, maybe crack some heads.

It was easy for Potiev to call for a calm and peaceful march. He hadn't witnessed the destruction of the Haberdashery Quarter. Steffan wanted someone to pay for destroying Monsieur Coen's business and murdering his neighbours.

At last, Potiev stopped pontificating and motioned them to fall into line. Steffan and Daniel pushed to the front of the march to roll out Lady Liberty. Newly arrived comrades ducked underneath to squeeze behind them into the narrow street.

'Comrades, please. Get yourself organised. We are leaving in two minutes,' Daniel yelled.

A red-faced man with a circular drum strapped to him pushed past Steffan and stood in front of the banner. A trumpeter and another comrade with a kettle drum joined him. The drumming gained momentum and thrummed through his chest, while the trumpet reverberated up through the buildings.

He stepped forward in unison with Daniel to carry the banner into the road, melding with other protesters who greeted them with great whoops that soared into the sky, chasing the trumpet bursts.

Steffan's heart thumped in time with the drums and his breath grew ragged from screaming out the chants that rolled up and down the lines of men. His leg muscles cramped from speeding up as the march surged forward, then suddenly stopping before he crashed into the backs of the men in front.

Chants raced up and down the lines like the wind rattling through a barley field. No sooner had *Vive La France* left his lips than *Workers Unite* crashed down on them, and they replied with a snatch of the Artisan Guild anthem.

As their numbers grew, so did the din. He'd never been anywhere so noisy. His head swam as if he'd downed half a bottle of brandy, yet he'd never felt so alive. Everything sparkled, and he inhaled the salty smell of sweat from the men surrounding him.

They spilled out onto Cours la Reine and moved towards Pont des Invalides to cross the Seine, shuffling along like old men scything the field, careful not to step on the comrade ahead, until they slowed to a standstill as the march narrowed to cross the bridge.

The crowd behind them kept moving forward, pushing into Steffan. He struggled to keep his balance as his feet were nearly swept out from under him. He had to keep standing or he'd be pulled under and trampled.

In front of them two comrades pushed their way through the crowd like eels swimming against river weed.

'Gendarmes won't let us through,' they shouted. 'Croix de Feu coming the other way. They want us separate.'

Someone yelled, 'Fuck the Croix de fascist shitheads.' The crowd took up the chant.

Another chant started. 'Pont Alexandre.'

The crowd surged again, and Steffan had no choice but to continue the shuffle along Port des Champs-Elysees to the next bridge. A line of gendarmes blocked their way. The men lined up in front of them spat in their faces and screamed insults. For a while the gendarmes stood their ground, then in unison they lifted their batons to smash at the faces, shoulders, and backs of the front row.

Caps flew off heads, and there were sprays of blood as men tried to dodge the blows but were pushed back up against the gendarmes by the crowd. Steffan cried out as an injured man collapsed and disappeared under the feet of the people around him. He wanted to help the man but could barely move, wedged in by the shoulders of other men.

Keep it together, concentrate on keeping upright.

He heard what sounded like a distressed horse and, thinking he was imagining things, shook his head to clear his hearing.

The crowd roared. To his right, three mounted gendarmes forced their frightened horses through the press of men. If he reached out, he could touch the panicked horse. It reared away from the mass of people, its eyes rolling back in fear, its hooves lashing out to connect with heads. The gendarme held onto the bridle with one hand to keep his balance. In his other, his baton crashed down on anyone within reach.

As the horse reared again, Steffan's warning shout to Daniel was drowned out by the din. He jerked Daniel towards him but wasn't quick enough to stop the horse's hoof glancing Daniel's head. The man next to him took the full force of the slashing hooves. Blood spurted from his ruined face. Steffan reached past Daniel and grabbed the man's coat to stop him toppling over. The horse reared again. It pawed the air and crashed down on the man. The forced ripped him out of

Steffan's grasp. He disappeared, swallowed up by the sea of bodies.

If he didn't do something now, Daniel would be crushed. He spun the banner pole in one hand to roll up the fabric, drawing the poles together, then jabbed the poles into the horse, which shied away.

'Across us,' he yelled at Daniel, flipping the poles crosswise in front of them.

Daniel understood immediately and grasped the banner to his chest. Steffan linked his arm with Daniel's and pushed forward into the crowd. The banner poles bound them together, giving them traction, even when they stumbled over the soft bodies under their feet. Steffan couldn't think about those men; they just needed to push forward like two bullocks in a yolk. They struggled past the causeway onto Ponte Alexandre, where dying men were held upright by the density of the crowd that seethed and surged like an angry sea.

Blood oozed from Daniel's head where the hoof had grazed him, trickling down his face into his right eye. His skin was as white as the bone they carved. But they mustn't stop.

'Push, Daniel.' Steffan had to keep Daniel moving. If he went under, he'd be lost.

They moved faster now, ploughing their way through the protesters who parted in front of them.

Less resistance, fewer men. Then they were out, stumbling across the cobblestones.

The other side of the bridge was blocked by lines of dark grey uniforms. Brass buttons and buckles caught the light like fireflies. They pushed their way back up the avenue, away from the mounted gendarmes and the angry crowd. Steffan led them to a patch of garden on the edge of Jardin du Petit-Palais and sat Daniel on a bench beside a pond. He hid the banner in the bushes. He wasn't going to lose Lady Liberty.

Steffan ripped off his shirt tail and dipped it into the pond.

'No, you're not touching me with that!' Daniel waved a hand in protest.

'You can't walk down the road covered in blood; you'll be arrested straight away.'

Daniel sighed like a burst feed sack. He let Steffan cradle the back of his head while he wiped away congealed blood. More oozed from a long cut along his hairline.

'If you press the cloth to your head, it should stop the bleeding in a few minutes.'

'I don't think we have a few minutes. We need to get going.'

Steffan turned in the direction Daniel faced. More injured protesters were stumbling out of the march as it roiled its way towards them.

'Yep, let's do it.'

They walked quickly away through the park, but even on the other side could still hear the marchers shouting and the horses screeching.

When they had the palace between themselves and the march, he forced Daniel to rest, worried by his pallor and how subdued he was.

'Does your head hurt?'

'Worse than the meanest hangover I've ever had.'

It must have been bad, then.

Steffan's hands were shaking so much, it took him several attempts to roll a cigarette. He passed one to Daniel who sat in a trance. Steffan nudged him until he finally took it.

'Maybe we should have stayed,' Daniel said, once he'd taken a long drag.

'And get our heads caved in? I don't think so.'

'We shouldn't have left our comrades.'

They both took another drag on their cigarettes. 'Wasn't a lot we could do.'

Despite his shaking hands, Steffan felt weirdly exhilarated. 'That was something, wasn't it?'

Daniel started to laugh. 'It sure was something.'

Steffan joined in. The laughter was a fizzy release, like he was a shaken-up bottle of beer which had just had its cap knocked off.

'Let's go back to the Guildhall,' Daniel said.

'What about the banner?'

'We'll come back for it when it's dark.'

As they jumped on a passing tram, Steffan looked around for any of their comrades. The tram's passengers were all tired workers on their way home from another gruelling day.

TWENTY-NINE

Steffan

Paris, October 1933

The buildings on either side of the lane to the Guildhall bowed towards each other, cutting out what little light the day let in. It was as inviting as a wolf den, and Steffan still felt apprehensive entering the lane, even more so with the possibility of arrest.

Daniel strolled in, so sure of himself that he never considered anything bad could be waiting for them.

They both exclaimed when Ashlam opened the Guildhall door.

'Where's...?' Steffan didn't know shovel-face's name.

It didn't seem to matter, as Ashlam replied, 'He's still out on the march. What's it like?'

'Pretty bad. We're going to have lots of injuries.'

Ashlam stopped at the top of the stairs. 'I couldn't go because of Shabbat, so I volunteered to stay behind and patch everyone up.'

A few comrades had made it back before them. Two had bandages around their heads. Another three sat at a table, each with an arm in a sling. It didn't stop them raising a glass to their lips. Near the back of the room two others lay in makeshift cots.

Someone hammered on the door.

Ashlam pointed at the casualties as he walked towards the stairs. 'Get them all a round of brandy.'

Steffan found the bottle behind the bar, along with five glasses. He filled them up and handed them out to the injured men.

He checked on the two lying down. 'Shouldn't we take them to the hospital? That one looks like he's been kicked in the head by a horse.'

Daniel shook his head. 'Not today. The gendarmes will be waiting there. They'll just get arrested and receive another beating in the cells. Their chances of survival are much better here.'

Ashlam returned with another group, two bleeding comrades being carried by the other four. As soon as Ashlam had pointed out where to put them, he rushed back downstairs to answer the door.

'Just stay down there and open the door. We'll take care of things up here,' Steffan yelled down.

He inspected the new arrivals. The first man had a deep cut on the side of his head, while the other couldn't bear weight on his right foot.

Steffan poured some water into a small tureen and cleaned up the man's face. Instead of helping the injured, Daniel was helping himself to several glasses of brandy. It surprised Steffan that Daniel had reacted this way. Perhaps he'd never had to deal with injuries like Steffan had. He'd set his dog's broken leg, sewed up Liselle's torn knees more than once and delivered countless lambs and calves.

'Can you find me a needle and thread and bring me a bottle of that brandy and a glass?' he called to Daniel.

When Daniel returned with the items, Steffan poured brandy

into the glass and handed the injured man the bottle to drink. 'I don't want you flinching when I'm trying to sew you up.' While the man gulped from the bottle Steffan threaded the needle and immersed it into the glass of brandy.

'I thought that was for you to drink,' Daniel said.

'It's to clean the needle and thread.'

He waited until the alcohol slackened the man's face, then began to stitch the wound. The man winced when Steffan doused the stitches in brandy.

'There you go. Give you something interesting to boast about to the girls. Can you ask Ashlam where we can get some ice?' he said to Daniel, moving on to the next injured comrade. 'We need it for the head injuries.'

Steffan registered Daniel's boots going down the stairs as he plied the comrade with brandy, poured some on his arm, then cleaned away the blood to reveal a long slash across the forearm. By the time he'd sewed up the wound, Daniel had returned with a washing tub of ice.

Steffan showed him how to smash up the ice and make up compresses out of the cloth they had on hand. He placed compresses on any man who had a head injury, a foot or ankle injury or any swollen limb. Once they'd distributed the compresses, twenty injured comrades filled the hall.

'Are you sure we can't send the badly injured ones to hospital?' he asked Ashlam.

'We have to wait until tomorrow.'

Steffan pointed to the man he suspected had been kicked by the horse. 'What about this one? He's unconscious. Surely, they wouldn't drag him out of the hospital.'

'It's likely they would. He's better here with us. We need your help with some splinting.'

Steffan worked with Ashlam to splint two broken arms, a broken wrist and four fractured legs. He stood up and stretched his aching back. He'd been caring for the injured since they'd come back, hours ago. He needed some air, and was comforted to see the shovel-faced doorman back at his post when he got down the stairs.

Steffan's knees nearly gave way when a large hand clamped onto his shoulder. 'You are a true comrade,' Shovel-face said. It was the first time he'd ever heard him speak, and his low, pitted voice suited him.

Steffan nodded his thanks and stepped into the alley. He went to walk towards the road when Shovel-face's hand clamped on his shoulder again. He was holding out a jacket. 'Can't go out like that.' He indicated Steffan's front.

He looked down and realised his shirt was covered in blood.

'Thank you.' He couldn't call him Shovel-face, and he'd been coming here for too long to ask him his name now.

With the jacket firmly buttoned up, he came out onto the main road to smoke his cigarette. It didn't seem right that happy couples strolled by, and music played in nearby cafés, while his comrades were injured, some dying, just behind them.

He heard the hoof beats just before the gendarmes turned into the road. He had to let the others know, but his legs seemed to have locked at the knees. The gendarmes reacted to the catcalls from two prostitutes on the corner and turned their horses towards the lane.

Just before they reached him, a silver Renault Nervastella swerved in front of the gendarmes. Steffan jumped back into the lane as it came to halt, blocking the entrance.

A small man in an immaculate suit emerged out of the driver's door.

'I do apologise for frightening your horses,' he said. 'I've only picked this vehicle up for my employer and I'm just getting used to it.'

The nearest gendarme looked him over top to toe and asked, 'Who is your employer?'

'The honourable statesman Monsieur Édouard Herriot.'

It was only then that Steffan recognised Potiev.

The gendarmes sat a little straighter on their mounts. 'We were sorry to trouble you. May you deliver the vehicle without incident.'

'I will try my very best.' Potiev tipped his hat and the gendarmes continued down the road.

Steffan stuttered out a thank you.

'Looks like I arrived at the right moment, just before they came down the lane.'

Steffan took a deep breath. 'We have over twenty injured men in the Guildhall, some in a very bad way. Ashlam thinks they will be in danger if we take them to hospital.'

'He's right. They will be.'

'Will the gendarmes come back here?'

'No, I don't think so. My employer's name should be enough to keep them away.'

'Can your employer help with medical supplies?'

'I'll come up and see what you need.'

As they walked up the stairs, the men's groans and cries were louder than before. Ashlam and Daniel had organised them into four rows, six men to a row. It made it easier for them to assess the injured.

'Someone's done a good job sewing them up.' Potiev tried not to appear too impressed.

'That was me.'

'Useful,' Potiev said, as if Steffan were the actual thread and needle, not the stitcher.

Steffan continued, 'The men need morphine for their pain. I'm sure a couple received blows to the head from the horses. Unless we get them a doctor, they won't last.'

'We can do morphine.'

'I've seen head wounds like these before. Two men died. But we got one – my cousin – to a doctor in time. The doctor drilled a hole in his skull to relieve the pressure inside and reduce the swelling.'

'We could take the worst ones to Les Invalides. My brother is on tonight and won't ask any questions.'

'Can we take them in your vehicle? Can we come back with the medicine?'

'*Oui* to both things.'

Shovel-face cradled each unconscious man like a small child as he ferried him to the car. The two injured men could fit together across the Renault's back seat. Steffan made himself comfortable in the back seat footwell until Potiev insisted he join him upfront in the passenger seat.

'It won't look suspicious if we get stopped. We can just say they overindulged.'

Potiev drove so smoothly Steffan could have rested a full glass of brandy on the dashboard and not lost a drop. He wished they'd brought some with them. His nerves jangled and his stomach was tight.

Steffan glanced at Potiev who seemed to be enjoying himself. At any moment he expected him to whistle a cheerful little tune. At least the roads were quiet, and they didn't pass any gendarmes or checkpoints. Potiev slowed down as they neared the back wall of the Hôtel des Invalides. He turned between two large trees where a small gate nestled.

'Can you get out and open that?'

After the Renault purred through, Steffan shut the gate and hopped back into the car. Potiev dimmed the lights and crawled along beside the building.

'There, where the light is.'

Potiev tucked the vehicle close to the wall then ran up a small set of steps to knock on the door. One of the injured men had come round, and his groans turned into cries that rose in pitch and volume. Steffan slid over into the backseat footwell again.

He made soothing noises and stroked the man's arm. It seemed to calm him down, but not Steffan.

What was taking so long? The sooner they got the men into the hospital the better.

When feet crunched on the gravel outside, Steffan prepared for the worst. He had nothing to defend himself with apart from his fists.

To his immense relief, Potiev called out to him before he opened the door. 'We have to carry them up.'

The first man seemed to weigh as much as the horse that had kicked him. They struggled to get him up the stairs, and he probably received extra bruises on his back where they scraped him over the steps.

A gurney waited in the doorway, and they eased the man onto it. By the time they returned with the second, another empty gurney waited in the comforting light.

Potiev motioned Steffan back to the Renault where he had enough time to smoke a cigarette before Potiev returned, dumping a bag in his lap. He opened it to find several glass bottles of morphine.

'You struck gold.'

'My brother said we brought those two in just in time. He can still help them. Tomorrow would've been too late.'

Steffan should have been pleased, but he was too tired to feel anything. He could only manage to say, 'The morphine will help the others.'

Potiev parked the Renault in a defensive position across the alley. Steffan staggered up the stairs, handed the morphine over to Ashlam, and finally lay down on a bed of banners to rest. It reminded him they hadn't got their banner back yet. Maybe Potiev could drive them there. Not tonight, though.

Through his fatigue he heard Daniel and Ashlam arguing, but he couldn't even raise his head to find out what was going on.

THIRTY

Yvette

Paris, October 1933

Mornings were getting colder, and Yvette had taken to stoking the fire in the pot belly in their apartment before she went down to collect the water. Normally she'd run down the stairs to fill the jug from the pump in the backyard without putting on her shoes. When she opened the door, cold air from the hallway would rush in.

Today, she congratulated herself on her decision to put on her shoes and coat before joining the line waiting for the pump. She was fourth.

She murmured good morning to her fellow residents as they passed her with their containers of water. Their breath was visible in the cold air as they greeted her in return.

When it was her turn, she pumped the water into her jug, gasping when the cold water splashed on her legs and hands. She'd been ready for it, but it was always a shock on a cold morning.

When she got back to their room, she pushed the door open with her hip. Janie had heaped at least six pastries onto the table.

She must have snuck out to the patisserie while Yvette was getting water. The little fool – they could not afford to eat like that.

'What are you thinking, you nonce?'

The door swung open and a male voice said, 'Let me help you with that.'

She was so surprised she stepped back into the hallway, as the strange man tugged at the bucket in her hand.

'Yvette, just give it to me.'

That voice, she knew that voice, then the man looked up and Eric's face came into focus.

'Eric, what are you doing here?' Her voice rose at the end. She couldn't hide her surprise.

She let him take the bucket. 'How did you know where we live?' What she really wanted to ask was how he got in, as the concierge, Madame Bissette, would consider a man in their room as a serious crime. One so serious, they might be asked to leave.

He smiled and shrugged his shoulders in a way that suggested it was the easiest thing in the world to find out.

'I thought you might like breakfast.' He pointed to the table where he, or Janie, had arranged the assortment of pastries on a plate.

Janie wasn't in the room. Yvette's stomach clenched. 'Where is she?'

'Janie's gone to change in the washroom.' He spread out his hands in a conciliatory gesture.

She must have come across as defensive. 'You took me by surprise. I wasn't expecting to see anyone in our rooms.'

What would he think of their humble dwelling? They had barely anything, and his offering of pastries sat on a cracked plate. They didn't even have enough plates and cutlery for the three of them. He might not think she could pay him.

'I can give you your first franc now. It will save me posting it.'

He waved her suggestion away. 'That's not why I'm here.'

'Why *are* you here, then?' Yvette was finding her feet again.

Janie arrived back, her face bright and grinning. 'Isn't he the gentleman, bringing us breakfast?'

It wasn't exactly what Yvette would call it. Not gentlemanly, more invasive.

To hide her discomfort she said, 'I'll make us coffee.'

She didn't have to contribute to the conversation as Janie kept up a constant stream of questions. What were his lodgings like? Would he stay there every time he was in Paris? How often would he be in Paris? Had he been up the Eiffel Tower, on the Seine, to Notre Dame?

Eric patiently answered each one. Lodgings good. He'd stay overnight once a fortnight with his uncle, who held an important position with the government. He'd be in Paris every second day but going straight back on the train. No to the Eiffel Tower. No to the Seine. Yes, to Notre Dame – only once, with his grandmother.

'We could go today. I'm not due back at Gare du Nord until evening.' Eric turned to Yvette for the answer.

'We could take the day off, couldn't we Yvette?' Janie focused on her too.

Yvette turned around with the freshly made coffee. 'We must go to work. Perhaps we can be tourists if Eric can be here on our Sunday off.'

Eric gave a sigh. 'At least let me walk you both to work, then. Rue de Paradis. What a romantic name. A place where all your dreams come true.'

'It is only Janie who works at the foundry. Today I am working again with Monsieur Chiparus. They live in the opposite direction.'

'What a dilemma. Which beautiful sister should I accompany to work?'

Before meeting Steffan she would have relished him accompanying her to work. But now, Eric seemed too polished, like everything he said was practised. She didn't want him accompanying either of them. Just how was she going to get rid of him?

'I walk with Janie to her work, then I go across the city to work with Monsieur Chiparus. If you come with me, you will become completely lost and miss your train.'

Eric drew a breath, but Janie interrupted him.

'Eric can accompany me to work, then you won't have to. You can go straight to Monsieur Chiparus.'

'I would be delighted,' Eric said.

Yvette didn't want that either, but Eric had delayed their departure this morning. If she walked Janie to work, she'd be late. Janie seemed so happy to see him, so what was the harm?

Eric and Janie kept up non-stop banter, bouncing the conversation between them like a rubber ball.

He didn't seem to notice they didn't have enough plates.

Janie was at ease with him in a way she wasn't with Steffan. But Yvette had no intention of being his 'girl in Paris'; one of those pretty faces he had all the way to Nantes and back. She didn't have to worry about any of that, though, as she'd made her choice. Steffan was here in Paris.

Suddenly she understood why Janie got on so well with Eric. He knew how to put girls at ease. He had a way about him, enhanced by his smile and fine-tuned by his attentive manner.

As they readied to leave, he turned that charm on her again. 'Please let me accompany you to work next time. I would like to see some more of Paris.'

Did this man never give up? She readied herself to brush him off, but Janie butted in.

'Next time you must come with me too, Eric. There's been some trouble around Rue de Paradis and Yvette's worried about me being alone.'

'That's settled, then. I can escort Janie to shield her from any misfortunes.' Eric shrugged on the coat he'd left on the back of one of their chairs.

'Can we keep it down as we go through the foyer?' said Yvette. 'I don't want get in trouble with Madame Bissette.'

Janie and Eric ignored her as they thundered down the stairs, stopping abruptly as the concierge scuttled out of her room.

To Yvette's relief, her ancient face lit up when she recognised Eric. She stroked his jacket and spoke in a French dialect Yvette had never heard before. When Eric replied, the concierge purred like a cat, or maybe she chuckled. She finally released him and returned to her apartment without scolding Yvette.

'What just happened? How did you do that?'

'I happen to be good at languages.' Eric said.

'Among other things,' Yvette muttered under her breath.

Janie gave her a sharp look.

They walked together to the Metro station where Yvette left them. She watched as Eric swept men out of Janie's way, clearing a path for her little sister to walk without being pushed or bumped, until they turned the corner and were lost to her.

Chiparus's studio was colder than usual, and the flimsy dress didn't help, but three hours posing in a simulated mid-air ballet leap sped by quickly as Eric's impromptu visit consumed her thoughts.

Monsieur Chiparus treated Yvette like an artist now. Her part in the process was boring and tedious but she relished every opportunity to get near the turntable, study Monsieur Chiparus's work, and receive his tutorage. All those freezing hours paid off when she placed her hands on the clay as Chiparus's calm voice instructed her on how to carve the material.

Madame Chiparus's attitude towards Yvette had thawed. She'd even started bringing a woollen throw for her to wear during breaks. She came more often and stayed for longer. She didn't seem worried about anything unsavoury happening between artist and muse. Like Yvette, she was mesmerised by the sculpting process.

'Would you like to join us for luncheon?' she asked Yvette at the end of her session.

Yvette accepted. If the morning tea was anything to go by, then luncheon would be something not to miss. The luscious and lovingly tended vegetable garden hadn't escaped her notice.

She dressed quickly and intercepted Monsieur Chiparus before he left the studio. He nodded towards the turntable, and she moved closer. She got the impression her image danced out of the clay.

Chiparus could stop now, and it would still be a work of art, suspended between being and unbeing, her image both immersed in and clambering out of the clay.

She'd accepted the luncheon invitation because she wanted her hands in that clay more often. She wanted her fingers caressing the scalpel as clay curled back on itself like hardened butter, the earthy smell rising from the work.

Yvette counted eight dishes laid out on the table, including a quiche Lorraine, buttered potatoes, crumbed eggplant, and her favourite – broccoli with almonds. If she opened her mouth, saliva would dribble down her chin.

'Thank you for inviting me to eat with you, Madame Chiparus.'

'Please call me Julienne,' she said, gesturing towards Yvette's place setting at the table.

'Thank you, Julienne. You have made such a lovely luncheon. Please thank the kitchen staff.'

Julienne and Monsieur Chiparus laughed and Yvette wondered what she'd said that amused them.

'I am the kitchen staff,' Julienne replied.

'There are so many dishes. Surely you must have help?'

'Julienne is a very self-sufficient person.' Monsieur Chiparus squeezed Julienne's hand.

'I like things just so.' She straightened her placemat a millimetre, so it lined up with the quiche dish.

As Julienne offered her another bowl, Yvette brought the conversation around to what she really wanted to talk about. 'Do you sculpt, like your husband?'

'No, I don't have an interest.' Julienne kept her gaze on the food she was serving.

It was a lie, though. Dealing with Papa had taught Yvette how to spot a lie. All the 'stolen' money, the missing vases, and the endless promises to give up drinking.

For a man immersed in detail, Monsieur Chiparus didn't seem to pick up on his wife's tiny giveaway movements.

The couple looked at each other, then looked at her.

'I'd like to do more than an hour's sculpting per week. I'll pay you for two additional sessions a week.'

The pair continued to look at each other, saying nothing. But they were communicating in a way Yvette couldn't understand.

To break the uncomfortable silence, she said, 'I would pay for clay and any materials.'

The silence stretched out and she said, 'I feel alive when my hands are on the clay.'

Monsieur Chiparus nodded. 'I would be pleased to accept this arrangement.'

'I am so pleased too. It is such an honour.' She felt a deep sense of relief, like a part of her she hadn't known was caged had been freed.

On her way back to the Metro, her heart was so light she felt her feet weren't touching the cobblestones. She'd never have thought she could do anything as creative as sculpt. She'd never thought she'd do *anything*. If Papa had still been alive, her whole being would have been consumed with finding the next rent payment and keeping the money from him until she could get it to the landlord.

As she stepped out of the train onto the platform, she saw another Croix de Feu freshly painted in silver on the wall. Under it was a strange drawing of a skull sitting on a cross and two crossed swords.

When the conductor entered the carriage to clip her ticket, she remembered. Eric had a badge on his jacket with that pattern. Surely, he wasn't a member of the Croix de Feu?

THIRTY-ONE

Yvette

Paris, October 1933

When Yvette arrived at the Blum Foundry to pick up Janie, Steffan and Daniel were waiting for her.

'Janie's going to have dinner with the Blum's and stay the night. You can come out with us tonight,' Steffan informed her.

'We'll shout dinner,' Daniel added.

How could she turn down a free dinner?

'We're going to take you to our favourite place – Claude's.'

They fell into step as Steffan directed them to the tram stop. 'I know we could go by Metro, but I like to see the city around me.'

Yvette nodded in agreement. 'It gets very confusing under the streets. I like to see the city too. Every day I find another market or a dressmaker I'd like to visit. Today I came across a book shop with more books that I've seen in my life.'

Steffan helped her onto the tram and sat beside her. Daniel stood at the front and struck up a conversation with the driver.

'I've been here a little over a year and I am still making discoveries,' said Steffan. 'Just last week I found a shop that only makes leather belts.'

'Our village blacksmith did all the leather work too. Do you think about your home village?'

'I miss my sister and watching her family grow up. Apart from that, no.' Steffan shrugged.

'I worry about what they might think of me. How I'm earning my money.' She hated how the words sounded coming out of her mouth. Why did it always come back to her worrying about what those people thought?

Steffan scooped up her hand. 'You are making a respectable living helping artists improve their craft. How can that be wrong?'

Yvette squeezed his hand. 'Thank you. It means a lot.'

'Do you want to go back to your village? Are you homesick?'

'Oh no. I miss my cousin and my neighbour. And maybe Madame Jervois. The rest of them can go jump in the river.'

'I'll help you push them in.'

She enjoyed the warmth from his leg as it jostled up against her thigh. She couldn't help wishing there was no clothing in between so they could savour the touch of each other's skin. As the tram slowed for the Fontaine Saint-Michel stop, she nearly sighed in frustration that they'd got there so quickly.

Daniel leapt from the still-moving tram and rushed ahead towards a red-canopied café surrounded by tables with matching, red-checked cloths. Those seated at the tables shouted greetings at Daniel.

As she and Steffan strolled towards the entrance, a stocky, balding man with a beet-red face pushed his way out the door. He had an accordion strapped to his chest. She recognised the proprietor, Claude, from Steffan's description.

The outside tables erupted in a chorus of a song she didn't know, but Claude did. He picked up the accompaniment, shouting out a greeting to Steffan and stepping towards Yvette, pretending to serenade her.

'Your revolutionary comrades are inside,' he sang as he squeezed the accordion together.

Steffan hesitated at the door, perhaps unsure of whether she knew about their political leanings. Of course she knew. Janie kept her fully informed.

From what she could see through the swirls of smoke, the café's interior walls were dark mahogany and covered with autographed serviettes, and photographs of Claude posing with customers. The booths on one side of the room were packed with groups of revellers. Daniel sat with an older man at a table near the booths. His companion had an olive complexion and curly black hair, and Daniel introduced him as Ashlam. He kissed her hand in a theatrical manner.

A moon-faced waitress came over to take their order.

'Is this your girl?' she asked Steffan, all the time scowling at Yvette.

Daniel jumped in before Steffan could speak. 'Margot, this is Yvette, my cousin.'

Margot's scowl changed to what passed for a smile. 'So not your girl, then,' she said to Steffan, after taking their order.

Daniel shook his head as she left. 'As you may have noticed, Margot's quite smitten with Steffan.'

'Very painful,' Ashlam said. 'We have to play along or we're lucky to get anything to eat or drink.'

'What about me? It's a very fine balancing act being friendly enough to keep the drinks coming but not too inviting,' Steffan complained.

When Margot returned, she leant over Steffan as she placed the drinks on the table. Her ample bosom pushed into his back like a sack of summer hay.

Ashlam and Daniel tried their hardest not to laugh until Margot left.

'Was that fun?' Daniel asked.

'I am swapping places with you when we order the next round, so you can get smothered.'

Daniel's expression became stern as he looked across the room. 'Excuse me for a moment, I need to talk to someone.' He approached a neatly dressed man. The two embraced and Daniel came back to the table. 'News isn't good. The two comrades we took to Les Invalides were compromised and taken by the gendarmes.'

'That's a death sentence,' Ashlam said.

'Were they injured in the protest?' Yvette asked.

They all stared at her. 'You forget that Janie works at the foundry, and you can't keep anything from her.'

Two men approached their table. 'Can you come and help us at the Guildhall? Some of the wounded aren't doing well.'

Yvette said, 'I will come to help too. I've changed my fair share of bandages in the village.'

'Thank you, Yvette.' Daniel squeezed her hand.

'Do you think it's a good idea she comes with us? It could be dangerous. At any time the gendarmes could raid the hall,' Steffan said without looking at her.

'Is that because you think I'm naïve and know nothing because I've just got here?' Yvette asked him.

'Not at all. I'm just concerned about you. You have Janie to look after. I have a sister I looked after too, so I wouldn't want to compromise you.'

Yvette frowned and Steffan threw his hands up in defeat. 'Okay, forget I said anything.'

Ashlam motioned for them to drink up.

'Looks like I still owe you a dinner,' Steffan said to Yvette.

'Yes, you do. And I will really be looking forward to it.'

THIRTY-TWO

Yvette

Paris, October 1933

The wine churned in her stomach as she followed Daniel down the dark alleyway. Steffan's calm breathing behind her reassured her they weren't likely to be attacked or robbed.

The alleyway ended at a mildewed, multi-storey stone building in need of attention. Daniel hammered on a door which flew open, and she stepped back into Steffan when a man who looked like he'd been hit in the face with a shovel appeared in the doorway. He ushered them in, then up a set of rickety stairs that creaked under their weight. She gagged halfway up as the smell hit her. It was worse than overripe blue cheese.

The source of the stench was the twenty or so men in various states of injury who covered the hall floor. Some of them writhed in pain and others were so still she feared they were dead.

She hadn't wanted to acknowledge it at the café, but Steffan was right. She shouldn't be mixed up in this. What if a raid happened right now? She wanted to turn and run down the stairs and out into the fresh air. She could use Janie as an excuse. Both Daniel and Steffan would be aware Janie would have been fed at the Blum table and sent off to sleep in Rosie's spare bed. Yet she'd made such a fuss about being included, so she couldn't just walk out now.

Yvette had only one option – to help. She covered her nose and mouth with a handkerchief. 'Can we open some windows and let air in?' she asked the man standing guard at the top of the stairs.

He shook his head. Yvette wanted to smack that stubborn head with the nearest piss pot.

What an imbecile he was. Fresh air helped the healing process, and these men were in severe need of healing.

Daniel walked away with a slender young man so fatigued he was struggling to remain upright. She could see his knees trembling under his trousers. He returned with a steaming bucket of water, a tray of bandages and a bottle of rubbing alcohol.

At least they had all the right equipment. 'Give it here.' Yvette took the tray from him so he could better hold the bottle.

He passed the bottle over to Steffan. 'Not for drinking,' he warned him.

'I do know that.' Steffan pretended to drink from the bottle.

Daniel laughed at the joke. Steffan didn't look his way, instead seeking out Yvette's approval. It was sweet that he wanted to impress her. What *would* impress her would be how he treated the wounded.

He gently removed a blood-soaked bandage from a young man's arm. The patient moaned when Yvette swabbed the wound with the rubbing alcohol. Thank goodness the wound didn't appear infected. What troubled her was the young man's groggy appearance. She checked his head for signs he'd been bashed. At the back of his skull she felt a depression and the sticky feel of partly dried blood.

'Head injury,' she said to Steffan.

He beamed and patted her shoulder, a strange reaction to sharing news about a head injury.

She followed Steffan over to the next injured man and worked on removing the bandages from his forehead.

She took the opportunity to look around, and a gasp caught in her throat. A red velvet banner covered the back wall. It showed a picture of the Lady Liberty holding a hammer in one hand and a sickle in the other. The words 'Communist Party of France Artisan Guild' formed a ring around the picture.

'Are we in some political headquarters?' she asked Steffan.

He shook his head, not looking at her, but continuing with his work. 'It's the Artisan Guildhall. They allow us to host our meetings.'

'Communist Party meetings?' She indicated the banner.

'I wasn't sure if you knew that about Daniel, and myself.'

Anger bubbled up and threatened to spill over. 'I have responsibilities. I can't be associating with communists.'

'You did want to help these men.'

'I didn't know they were communists.'

Steffan bristled. 'They are people and workers first. They've risked their lives for what they believe in.'

'And I am risking my life and Janie's by being here.'

Steffan gave her a sad smile. 'Now you know the whole picture, you are free to leave. You don't have to stay if you don't want to. I won't think any less of you.'

His understanding made it harder. She should leave, protect herself and Janie. She looked about the room at the injured men.

'I will stay and help with the wound dressings, then I'll go.'

He leaned forward and kissed her on the lips. It surprised her, yet she liked the taste of him, tobacco, beer, and a hint of almond. Just as well they had a concussed man between them, or things might have gone further.

They worked well together. Steffan removed the soiled bandages, she cleaned the wound and replaced the dressing with fresh bandages. Within half an hour they'd redressed the wounds of the men on their side of the hall.

Steffan called over the slight man she'd met when they arrived and said, 'There's only one man on our side we are really worried about.'

Yvette guided his fingers so he could feel the back of the man's head.

The slight man sighed. 'He needs a doctor. We can't get one to come.'

'He really needs to get help.'

Steffan straightened up. 'We could say he works for Blum and got hit in the head at the foundry.'

The slight man straightened up as well. 'You could do that?'

'Yes, I don't see why not.'

'Daniel and I can come tomorrow with the truck and take him to the hospital.'

'If you think you can manage it.'

'I am certain. We should be able to bring more bandages and other medical supplies too.'

Yvette started to ask how he would get his hands on those supplies, then decided it would be better not to know.

They helped Daniel and his nursing partner finish the last few patients, then washed their bloody hands and accepted a drink of brandy from Ashlam.

Although she wasn't used to hard liquor, Yvette enjoyed the harsh warmth that spread throughout her body. It numbed her to the point where she didn't feel anxious. Not feeling had its temptations, but she couldn't make a habit of it. Her father was proof of that.

When Daniel suggested it was time to go, she was truly ready. Kisses over injured communists, more wounds than she'd ever seen in one room, and a brandy induced euphoria. Her emotions were all jumbled as though they'd been thrown in the air like winnowed wheat.

Daniel insisted on escorting Yvette home, even though she'd have preferred it to be Steffan. It gave her time to go over the night as they travelled home by tram.

Steffan cared for the injured like he would a sick child or a valued pet. He seemed kind, loyal, and he had secure work and a strong family. He had plenty going for him, as well as being a good-looking man.

As the tram slowed, the conductor called out the stop. He wore the same style hat as Eric. For some reason that made her stomach tighten. She'd pay off the 20 francs as fast as she could. She didn't want any more impromptu visits from someone involved in hurting other people.

THIRTY-THREE

Steffan

Paris, October 1933

When Steffan let himself into the Guildhall, the stench of rotting flesh was so strong he could taste it. The place smelt so foul, he couldn't bring himself to continue up the stairs. He gagged and stepped back outside into the fresh air.

Someone up there needed him and if he didn't go up right now, the man wouldn't last the night. He took some deep breaths and swallowed the saliva pooling in his mouth. He wouldn't be found outside the Guildhall spewing up his guts like some coward. He wrapped his neck scarf around his face then strode inside.

He gagged all the way up the stairs. The nausea settled when he saw Daniel sitting at the bar reading *L'Humanite*.

Did Daniel not care that someone in the room was dying from gangrene?

He pulled down his scarf. 'Can't you smell that?'

'Smell what?' Daniel glanced up from the paper.

Steffan didn't trust himself to speak. He shook his head and looked at the six men lying on the stage. Their feet pointed towards them as if they were already dead.

Daniel shrugged. 'You're the one who knows about injuries, not me.'

'We're checking them now.'

Daniel sighed and followed him to the stage. It didn't take him long to find the smell's source, a boy no older than Rosie. He'd helped Ashlam splint his leg after the march when his break had seemed straightforward.

He placed a hand on the boy's cold and clammy forehead. His closed eyes tracked in their sockets like he was dreaming, but Steffan was sure he was unconscious.

'He seemed fine last night.'

'It was your job to check him.'

Daniel shook his head, truly puzzled as to why the boy was so ill.

'Can you really not smell anything?'

'It must be working in the foundry. Lots of men say they can't smell things like they used to.'

'Did you take the splint off yesterday and look at it his leg?'

Daniel shook his head. 'No, no one told me I had to do that. I will do it now.'

Steffan wasn't fast enough to stop Daniel pulling at the splint. The boy woke up screaming and Daniel flinched away from him.

Steffan positioned himself between Daniel and the boy.

'I will do it. You get him some brandy.'

Daniel left the stage.

Steffan should have tended to the men instead of leaving it to Daniel, who wouldn't have known what to look for. He'd seen enough injuries to pick when a wound could become gangrenous.

They plied the boy with brandy until he slipped back into unconsciousness. Steffan took his time unwinding the wrappings, careful not to jostle the boy's leg.

The boy cried out and tried to pull away as he peeled off the last bandage. The smell overpowered him. He held his breath as he examined the wound; the boy's shin, mottled purple and black, had swelled to twice its size and oozed foul-smelling pus. The mottling stopped just before his knee. They'd have to act now to save the rest of the leg.

'Is that smell from my leg?' the boy sobbed.

Steffan nodded, not trusting himself to speak. He would not vomit in front of Daniel, or the boy.

He held the brandy glass up to the boy's mouth while he gulped it down, then poured him another. How unfair that the boy had gone on the march for a laugh, and now he'd probably lose his leg – if he was lucky.

Steffan left the wound uncovered and joined Daniel at the bar where he'd retreated to nurse his glass of brandy.

'I'm sorry, I didn't know it was so bad–'

Steffan cut him off. 'We need to get him help. Go get Ashlam, I'll stay here and check the others while you're away.'

'Ashlam's gone for the night,' Daniel said with such finality that Steffan knew he wouldn't be going looking for him.

'Can you get Potiev to take the boy to Les Invalides?'

Daniel shook his head.

Steffan wanted to shake him until his teeth rattled. 'If we don't get him help tonight, he's going to die.'

Daniel sighed. 'I'm not sure how to contact Potiev. I'm not on the Party Committee yet. We don't get to know a lot of stuff.'

For a communist, Daniel certainly wasn't good in a crisis.

'We'll just have to take him ourselves, then.'

Daniel stared at him open mouthed. 'That's not safe.'

'If we do something now the boy will keep his upper leg. If we wait until tomorrow, he'll lose his whole leg. But most likely he'll die.'

Steffan remained quiet while Daniel swirled his drink. He

knew Daniel well enough now to know that he needed time to mull over their options.

'We can't carry him. We can't take him on the tram. We could get a doctor to come over here.'

'His leg needs to come off. We don't have anything here. We'd still have to convince a doctor to come.' Steffan shrugged, trying not to show how helpless he felt.

'I could get the truck from the foundry,' Daniel suggested.

Steffan shook his head. He couldn't do that to his father.

Daniel gulped down the rest of his brandy. 'I'm going to Claude's to find Potiev.'

'Thank you. You will be saving the boy's life.'

Daniel clattered down the stairs. The whole building shook when he slammed the door.

The boy remained unconscious while Steffan splinted his leg in readiness for his trip to hospital.

He turned his attention to the big man at the end of the row, who'd been trampled in the crowd. His breathing didn't rattle in and out of his body anymore, but he hadn't regained consciousness. They would need to take this man to hospital, along with the boy.

He smiled at the empty plates near the two men in the middle of the row. At least they were eating.

'Are you taking us to hospital tonight?' asked the man with the broken arm and leg. He was around the same age as Steffan, and said his name was Yves.

'Yes, we'll take everyone if we can.'

'I'd like to have a shave before I go.' Yves rubbed his face with his good hand. 'My wife brought my shaving gear, but she couldn't stay to give me one.'

'I can help you with that.'

'Can you give me one too?' the man beside him asked.

The two other conscious men chimed in.

'Shaves all round then.' At least they felt well enough to care about their appearance.

Steffan heated the water on the pot belly then poured it into a basin. He found some soap behind the bar and sharpened Yves's razor on the leather strap.

Concentrating on the shaving calmed Steffan. The balance between the pressure on the blade and the downward movement took all his focus. Too firm, he'd cut Yves, too soft and he'd pull on the hairs as the blade dragged his skin.

Every time he wondered whether Daniel had found Potiev, he pulled his focus back to shaving. He didn't have room to fret if he was on his way back. He could just be in the now, concentrating on the task before him. Carving bone was like that, requiring complete focus with no room to drift off into the worry zone.

An hour later a familiar-sounding truck engine rattled into the alleyway outside. Surely Daniel hadn't collected the Bierlet?

He raced outside to discover that was exactly what he'd done.

Daniel jumped out of the cab. 'I couldn't find Potiev, so ...' He held up his hands in surrender.

Steffan fought the urge to punch him. 'You idiot! Father will be furious.'

'I'll take responsibility. I'll tell him I did it.'

'He'll throw you out.'

Steffan paced up and down by the truck. The sensible thing would be to take it back to the foundry. But if he did, and they waited until morning, the boy would die.

He stopped pacing and turned to Daniel. 'Let's just get them to hospital. We'll sort out Father after that.'

'Them? Weren't we just taking the boy?'

'They all need treatment.'

Daniel opened his mouth to say something, then changed his mind.

The injured boy cried out as they moved him down the stairs, and again as they hoisted him onto the truck bed. Steffan left Daniel arranging sacking over the boy while he returned for the other men.

One could walk and another could stand, so Steffan asked them to help Yves to the truck, while he tried to rouse the fifth patient, the man with the head injury. 'Come on, we're getting you some help.'

He found a carpet behind the stage curtains and unfurled it next to the man. Steffan's shoulder screamed at him as he manoeuvred the man's limp body onto it. The man groaned as he bumped down each stair, but Steffan managed to control his descent.

Daniel fussed about, making sure the men were comfortable before Steffan brought the flatbed's sides up, locking them in place. He got into the driver's seat and slid the window behind him open.

'You ready?' he asked Daniel.

'We'll have to get our story straight for the hospital,' Daniel replied.

'Aren't we just dropping them at Les Invalides?'

'We don't have Potiev to help us.'

'We'll take them to the workers' hospital in Montparnasse. Controller Kubrek sent a worker there when he got burned during a pour.'

'We'll say they were hurt at the foundry, and we tried to look after them in the men's quarters.'

'A finished cast rolled the wrong way when we opened up the shell.'

'And it fell on them.'

'We thought we could look after them. Then this one's leg started festering.'

'We decided to bring them all in.'

'Your father could get into trouble,' Daniel said.

That hadn't occurred to Steffan. 'Will the hospital ask where they work?'

'They'll expect the foundry to pay for their treatment.'

'We'll tell them another name and pass the hat or ask the Party.'

'Potiev could put his hand in that very tailored pocket.'

Steffan pulled out into the silent street, driving as slowly and smoothly as he could. He pretended there was a glass of brandy balanced on the dashboard that he couldn't spill. Going over the tram lines rattled his teeth, and he hoped the men were faring better – he couldn't hear anything from the back over the sound of the engine.

The empty streets added to Steffan's growing sense of dread that what they were doing would harm his family. A shadowy man walking a large dog turned to look at them.

It's only because it's a loud truck, Steffan reminded himself. It wasn't because he thought they were loaded up with injured men. Even so, his skin prickled with relief as the hospital's white façade grew larger. He parked directly outside the front door and ran inside to find a medic.

An older man wearing a white coat looked up as he walked towards him. The man's face drooped with tiredness made worse by his red-rimmed, bloodshot eyes.

'We have some injured outside in my truck.'

Steffan rushed back outside, only to have to wait as the medic ambled down through the entrance.

Daniel helped the medic onto the truck bed. They hurried through their story about the falling cast while the medic checked pulses, opened eyelids, and listened to breathing.

The medic stood up to stretch his back. 'You did well to bring the young one in. He wouldn't have lived if the infection had got more of a hold on him.'

He waved away Steffan's help as he clambered down from the

truck then sauntered off into the hospital to find gurneys for the boy and the unconscious man.

They helped the others into the building, where they slumped into seats in the waiting area with a dozen other injured and ill people. It was a miserable place that stank worse than the spittoons at Claude's. Injured and ill patients had left their vomit and blood on the floor where they'd sat. Steffan avoided touching the walls, stained from countless leaks, dented and smashed by angry fists and addled heads.

The medic returned with two ancient gurneys. 'It's ten francs for each man,' he said. 'We can't treat them until you've paid.'

Steffan pulled out 20 francs from his wallet, and Daniel emptied his pockets, counting out 10 francs.

'We'll come back with the rest later today,' Daniel said quickly.

'Which three would you like us to treat until you return with the money?' The medic moved his hand about as if he could magically conjure up treatment for all.

Daniel's body tensed, and Steffan thought he might yell at the medic, or even hit him.

The medic took the cue and had the good sense to apologise.

'The two on the gurneys, and Yves – the one inside with the broken arm and leg,' Steffan answered.

He drew Daniel back to the truck before the medic further enraged him.

'Capitalism's clamped everything within its jaws, even healthcare,' Daniel ranted as they drove back to the foundry. Steffan estimated it was about 5am, which meant they could sneak the truck back into the loading bay before it was missed.

'We'll pass the hat around before work so we can get the others treated,' Daniel said. 'I can invent a reason to drop something off or pick something up so we can get back there by mid-morning. We don't want the men having to stay in that filthy place longer than they need to.'

Steffan swung the truck into the foundry entrance, ready to jump out, but the gate was open already. It must be later than he'd calculated. The courtyard was full of men from the single men's quarters.

'We thought they'd stolen the truck,' one shouted at them.

Steffan realised what the men were doing – cleaning the courtyard and sweeping up broken glass and moulds. They'd been attacked again. The bastards who'd scrawled their hate on the outside of the building had gotten inside. Even after all their cleaning he could make out *DEATH TO JEWS, JEWS STEALING OUR WORK,* and the skull and crossed swords of the Croix de Feu.

'I forgot to lock the gate,' Daniel said, so quietly Steffan almost missed it.

'You didn't forget to do anything.'

They parked up in the loading bay and joined the other men tidying up the mess and scrubbing hate from the walls, just as Father and Philippe appeared in the courtyard.

Daniel took a deep breath, but before he could confess to anything, Steffan turned to Father and said, 'This is my fault. I took the truck and forgot to lock the gate.'

Father stood taking in the graffiti, the broken windows and the men cleaning the walls.

'I will call for you later this morning when I am ready,' he said without looking at them.

He headed towards his office, Philippe trailing behind. Steffan had an overpowering urge to run after him to beg forgiveness, but as Father disappeared into his office, Steffan's feet were rooted to the ground.

Steffan

Paris, October 1933

Steffan looked up when the carving room door opened. The young apprentice Trieste, his chest puffed out with self-importance, stood in the doorway. It could only mean one thing – Father was ready to talk. With a sinking stomach, Steffan put down his chisel and stood up. Daniel kept carving.

'Le Directeur wants to see you and Daniel in his office. It's about this morning and you two having the truck.' He paused to take a breath. 'Why did you have the truck?'

Daniel didn't acknowledge Trieste and showed no emotion as he hung up his smock. Wasn't he the least bit nervous? Steffan's heart was hammering in his chest, as the last thing he wanted was to see the disappointment in Father's eyes. Shouting was fine, even Father hitting him, but if he'd fractured his trust he'd be crushed. His throat tightened and tears tickled behind his eyes at the thought of Father or Martje treating him differently, after he'd been accepted into the family.

Trieste wasn't one for picking up on cues. He took a breath.

'Think you'll be really for it. Philippe and Le Directeur yelled at each other. Philippe threw a chair across the room.'

'That's enough, Trieste. You can go now. We don't need an escort,' Daniel said.

'I don't want him being angry with me. What if you ran off in the truck again?' He laughed at his own joke, then stopped when Daniel cuffed the back of his head.

Trieste was right, Steffan did want to jump into the truck and drive as far as he could in the opposite direction. But that wasn't an option.

He kept his head down as they passed three workers in the courtyard sanding down a cast.

'You're both for it,' one called out. They laughed and continued their work.

It seemed everyone knew about the truck. Before they reached the office door, Steffan moved past Daniel. 'I'm going in first,' he said as he opened the door.

Father's angry voice boomed above them as Steffan scuttled up the stairs, not in the least bit ready to face Father. Last month, he'd seen him lose his temper when a cast cracked because a worker forgot to add enough copper. He'd thrashed the man, not in an impassioned melee of swirling fists, but slowly, meticulously, as if he'd slipped into a meditative state while beating the dust from a carpet. He'd only stopped when Controleur Kubrek threw a bucket of freezing water over him. Father had then seemed to come back into himself, letting out a small cry when he saw the bloodied man cowering by his feet.

They reached the landing, and Steffan searched the courtyard for Controleur Kubrek, just in case. Martje emerged from her office. 'Just nod and agree with everything he says.'

Steffan had every intention of doing that; he couldn't even muster a squeak his throat was so dry. His heart hammered in his chest, the blood swishing by his ears so loud he couldn't hear their footsteps, let alone Martje's knock on the door.

'Le Directeur?' she called to Father. Her voice was tentative.

'*Entrez*,' he barked.

Martje led them into the room like she was an advance scout, checking the terrain for booby traps and snipers, all the time avoiding eye contact with the ticking time bomb that glared at them from behind his oversized desk.

They lined up in front of him as Father's cigar smoke swirled around them like lethal gas.

He let them stew as he observed them. Steffan controlled his breathing, taking his time to draw it in and out. He didn't want to faint or show panic.

Father shook his head. 'Are you both stupid?'

Steffan followed Martje's lead and kept his head down while Father ranted. He suddenly stopped mid-sentence. Steffan looked up. Father stared at him, clearly expecting some response.

'Well? What were you doing?'

Steffan toyed with lying, telling him they were moonlighting, or cruising, or getting an early order of marble. But Father wasn't a fool – he'd see through it.

'Some of our comrades were injured in the latest march. We hid them in the Artisan Hall because the gendarmes were arresting injured people at the hospital.'

Father rubbed his face and sighed.

Steffan rushed on, the words tumbling from his mouth. 'One was about to lose his leg, so we needed to transport him to hospital. We tried to care for them at the Guildhall, but they got worse. We said they were hurt here at Blum Foundry so the hospital wouldn't know about the march.'

Father face turned an even deeper shade of red. 'You told them that?'

Steffan stomach knotted. 'We couldn't risk them knowing about the march. It would be a death sentence.'

Father's expression hardened and Steffan's mouth went dry.

'Is that why they came today? Did those fascists know about you two hiding the men?'

Of course, they must have. But how? Steffan forced himself not to look at Daniel.

'We never meant to bring the foundry into this,' Steffan said.

'But you have.' Father leaned back. He puffed on his cigar and stared into the distance above their heads.

To fill the silence, Steffan said, 'We don't know why they came here.'

Father didn't answer; he kept staring into the distance as the cigar smoke pooled around him. Finally, he spoke. 'You never grew up Jewish. I think it's difficult for you to grasp that our position is worsening.'

'Oscar, please don't burden him.' Martje held her hand up to stop him speaking.

Father mirrored the gesture back at her. 'He must understand this, Martje. The tide is turning against us. Some in our community refuse to see it. But I do. This is the beginning of the end–'

Martje cut him off. 'Stop this talk, Oscar.'

'Do not interrupt me.' Father raised his voice.

Martje took a step back as if Father's rebuke had pushed her off balance.

'Surely things will calm down,' Daniel said.

'You are naïve and idealistic, and you are not Jewish,' Father shouted.

Daniel lowered his gaze.

'What will we do when the hospital comes asking about the men?' Father asked.

'I don't think they will,' Daniel said.

'You don't know that. They want us gone, and they'll use any excuse to get rid of us.' Father was so worked up his spittle flew into the air as he formed each word.

Steffan's heart began to race. Father was about to lose control.

'We're raising money for the men. Once we've paid it to the hospital, they won't ask any more questions,' Steffan said.

Father went back to staring above their heads. Finally, he spoke. 'How much is owed?'

'Thirty francs – ten per man,' Steffan said before Daniel could answer and become the target of Father's anger.

Father rubbed his face. 'Three men?'

'Six men. We could only pay for three of them.'

'Martje, get thirty francs from the strongbox.'

She gave Steffan's arm a little squeeze as she left the room. Father fixed his gaze on Daniel.

'I will give you the money for the men, but you must pay me back by the end of the week. And I will only give it to you if you promise you will never involve the foundry with your political affiliations again.'

Daniel looked at Father and said, 'Thank you for your assistance, Le Directeur. I promise never to involve the foundry in anything to do with our party.'

Father focused on Steffan. 'I want the same promise from you.'

Steffan parroted Daniel's answer, all the time hoping he could fulfil the promise.

Martje returned with the money and held it out to Father. He shook his head and motioned towards Daniel.

'You can take it to the hospital. If you haven't said our name already, don't say it. Please go now. I wish to speak to Steffan alone.'

Martje went to leave with Daniel, but Father indicated she should stay and find some chairs. Steffan helped her bring in the two straight-back chairs that sat in the hallway for when Father wanted to intimidate the staff by making them wait.

They placed the chairs in front of Father. He sighed, covering his face with his hands.

Martje reached over and patted his hand. 'There, there,' she said in a voice she might use for a baby or small child.

Father took his hands away from his face and looked at Steffan with an expression of sadness. 'You have responsibilities to your family, and you must finish with the Communist Party. You have put us in danger with your recklessness. It must stop. I have no control over what Daniel does, but he is your responsibility now. If he brings danger to the foundry again, both of you must leave here.'

There was no contest, Steffan would not lose his family. 'Of course I will put the family first. I love you all. I would never do anything to harm you.'

Martje stood up, anger radiating from her as she faced Father. 'That's not what we agreed. We need Steffan to be focused on us, not running around trying to stop Daniel doing whatever he is going to do. Ask Daniel to leave.'

Father shook his head. 'Daniel has principles, and he fights for us. I won't throw him out. If Steffan wants to protect the family and stay with us, then he's going to have to make sure Daniel doesn't do anything to threaten us again.'

Martje let out a clenched jaw growl. 'Steffan is our means of protection. Don't make things more complicated.'

Father threw up his hands. 'So, I tell him now, then?'

Steffan felt like he was back in his grandparents' kitchen. They had fought over his and Liselle's heads every time Grand-mère received a letter from Father. Grand-père usually won by snatching the letter and burning it in the stove.

Steffan braced himself for what would come next. Father regarded him for what seemed like an hour and said, 'I would like you to begin referring to yourself as Ossler again, not Blum.'

It was far worse than he'd expected. 'Is what I did so bad that you wish to disown me?'

'You misunderstand me. You are my son and under our protection. You were adopted by your grandparents, which makes you a Gentile on paper.'

Steffan had no idea where Father was going with this. He appealed to Martje to make sense of Father's ramblings.

'What your father is trying to say is that soon, we will transfer the business into your name as your papers do not identify you as Jewish,' Martje said, her tone as neutral as when she ordered the next day's bread.

Steffan shook his head, hoping he could dislodge this strange conversation. 'I don't understand. Why would you do this?'

'This is the only way we will be able to stay in business, because things will get very much worse for us.'

'But the government isn't anti-Jewish.' He thought of Potiev, who always greeted Ashlam like a friend.

Father threw up his hands. 'Things change quickly. And it looks likely the government will not last much longer. We must be ready for that.'

'Philippe won't like it at all. He expects to inherit the foundry.' It was out before Steffan could stop himself.

Martje smiled and nodded. 'Yes, he did expect that. He never expected you to return. He never expected his homeland to turn on him.'

Father leant forward towards him. 'We need you to keep this to yourself. We didn't want to tell you until we were ready.' He shrugged and gave Martje a sad ghost of a smile. 'I guess we are ready.'

As Steffan left the office, his thoughts were whirling as if he'd had more than his fair share of a brandy bottle. He wanted to get out of the foundry, clear his head, make sense of what Martje and Father just told him. His feet led him out the archway and down Rue de Paradis.

Would the midnight scrawlings on the foundry walls develop

into what had happened in the Haberdashery Quarter? Father, and the normally calm Martje, seemed to think it was possible.

And what about Philippe? Once he knew about Father's plan, Steffan would have to look over his shoulder for the rest of his life. If only Philippe didn't see him as a threat.

The sting of rejection knotted his stomach, even though he understood Father's reasoning for changing his name back to Ossler. Yet he'd come here to find his family and reclaim his family name. Father had fought to keep him and Lisette – he'd seen the court papers, and how he'd petitioned the judge. His life would have been very different if Grand-mère and Grand-père had not come to claim them. He'd be here with Father by right, not forced to sidle back into his life like some interloper.

He would leave the Communist Party too. It was an easy choice between family and comrades. But Daniel was another matter. He'd have to watch him closely and make sure nothing he did from now on would come back on the foundry.

His chest tightened as the responsibility for the foundry weighed down upon him. He just couldn't see himself as Le Directeur, telling workers what to do, deciding what they would manufacture and paying wages. He closed his eyes and pictured the wheat field next to the farmhouse, the yellowed stalks rippling together in the breeze like a sleeping animal breathing in and out. He concentrated on the field until he calmed down.

By the time Steffan had walked around the block, Daniel had returned from the hospital and was back in the carving room.

'Did you keep the foundry name out of it?' Steffan asked.

'No one cared once they got the money. They're all being treated now. The boy's had his operation. They took off his lower leg.'

'I expected that. At least we got him there in time.'

'We need to pay those Croix de Feu bastards back. They can't get away with smashing up the foundry.'

Steffan said nothing. He'd have to tell Daniel soon that he was leaving the party, but he wasn't ready yet.

Daniel continued, apparently not needing a reply. 'They have that rally on Sunday. They will be expecting us, so we have to get to them beforehand.'

'Shouldn't we just let things lie for a bit?'

'We need to track a few of them from Figaro's. We could borrow the truck again.'

'Absolutely not.' It came out as more of a shout than a comment.

Daniel looked up. 'Absolutely not to Figaro's, or the truck?'

'The truck. We got ourselves in more than enough trouble.'

Daniel laughed. 'The Figaro tomorrow night, then?'

Steffan sighed and nodded.

Daniel smiled. 'Knew I could count on you, comrade.'

He didn't have a choice. Keeping Daniel from doing anything reckless and protecting the foundry were Steffan's prime concerns. Hadn't his father said so?

THIRTY-FIVE

Yvette

Paris, November 1933

Yvette woke early and smiled down at Janie sleeping peacefully beside her. She'd changed since their arrival in Paris; her features were more defined, the adult version of her was emerging, her face refining as she grew into womanhood, as if life were an expert sculptor that shaved off a sliver of flesh to highlight her cheekbone, then moulded in the excess to plump out her chin.

She resisted touching her, to trace with her fingers how nature had transformed her features from a gangly girl into a beautiful young woman.

Yvette sprung out of bed, sucking in her breath when her feet landed on the freezing floor. She rose onto the balls of her feet to minimise contact with the floor as she dashed across to the potbelly. She even balanced on one foot while stoking up the fire to warm the room.

She found her shoes under the table, where she'd shucked them off last night. She sighed with relief as she slipped them on, then crept about the room laying out their breakfast. The water in the coffee pot spluttered and she opened the coffee jar to find it empty except for the exquisite aroma.

Damn, she'd forgotten to replenish it yesterday.

She stuffed the jar into her string bag and threw on her despised threadbare coat. Thankfully it was the last day she'd have to wear the ugly thing. Her new blue coat was ready for collection tomorrow afternoon.

She couldn't stop grinning as she imagined how the coat would feel swishing around her legs as she ran down the three flights of stairs.

The cold hit her bare legs as she opened the building's front door to step out into the street. The first rays of the day caught the frost on the pavements, and they sparkled like Lalique glassware. Steam puffed out behind pedestrians as they strode out to meet the day.

A young man at the bottom of the steps, obscured by a haze of breath and cigarette smoke, called out her name. He crushed the cigarette under his foot and took a step towards her. Eric.

What on earth was he doing here at this time of the morning? She opened her mouth to say the concierge liked the steps to remain tidy, then thought better of it. Her beautiful blue coat just got further away. She braced herself, ready for him to ask for his money back.

'Yvette, I'm so glad to catch you. No one answered when I knocked on the door.'

'It's very early.'

He didn't seem to notice her discomfort, beaming at her like she was the best thing he'd seen all morning. Admittedly she probably was. Perhaps he wasn't here about the money. She wouldn't bring it up if he didn't.

'I just wanted to give you this.' Eric pulled out a folded flyer from his inside his coat and held it out.

She took it and started to unfold it.

'No, no.' He waved at it as if it were on fire. 'Open it when you're inside.'

She slid it into her string bag. 'I'm going to get coffee,' she said, hoping she didn't come across as too testy.

'I'll walk with you.'

She led off in the direction of her favourite café. It wasn't as if she could shake him off. It was up to him to explain himself. As the silence stretched out between them, Eric couldn't seem to contain himself.

'It's about the rally we're having.'

'The flyer?'

He nodded.

'So, you've just told me what's on the flyer, but you've asked me not to read it until I'm inside?'

He shrugged, either ignoring her tone or misinterpreting it.

'I'm just excited. I'm helping Uncle with the arrangements. I'd like you and Janie to be there. We must be careful who we ask and who knows about it.'

She took in his eager expression. He really wasn't here about the money.

'If you're asking me to come because you like me, you must understand I am with Steffan.'

Eric nodded and ran his hand through his hair. She'd forgotten how his fingers made hair rivulets over his scalp, a not unattractive habit that he seemed to adopt when he was nervous. He was quiet for a time, then he stopped walking, so she stopped too.

'I'm worried about your association with Steffan.'

So that's what it was. He was jealous.

'I'm not sure my association with Steffan's got anything to do with you.' She emphasised the word *association*.

At least he had the decency to look contrite. 'You're correct to point that out. I'm only concerned that you're consorting with a Jew.'

She couldn't believe what he'd just said. She started walking again, as if movement could distance her from his comment. Soon he was by her side again.

'What does it matter?' she said. 'Steffan's mother wasn't Jewish. Judaism passes down the matriarchal line. So, he isn't Jewish.'

Eric ran his hand through his hair several more times. He wouldn't look at her when he spoke. 'His family is Jewish. You should distance yourself from them.'

'I don't see any reason to do that.'

He continued to stare at the ground. 'The Jews' tight grip on France's finances and industry will soon loosen. I don't want your future tied up with theirs ...'

'And why is that?' she snapped.

Finally, he looked up at her. 'Because they no longer have one in France.' She'd never seen that look on his face before. At first, she thought he was upset, then she realised he was feeling guilty about something.

'What do you know, Eric?' She grabbed his arm.

Eric said nothing and looked down again, unable to hold her gaze.

'If you know something about the Blum family, then you need to tell me.'

Finally, he shook his head. 'I don't know anything about them or anyone wanting to hurt them.'

She wasn't sure she believed him. He continued, his voice quiet and pleading, 'Come to the rally and you'll hear what the Croix are saying. Not only the Croix, the politicians, and lots of the French intelligentsia.'

'If you know what they are saying, why don't you just tell me?'

Eric looked up at her directly. 'The French people are turning against the Jews. They want them out of France.'

A coldness expanded in her stomach and prickled her skin.

He'd finally said it, and she wasn't surprised, because she'd known all along this was building up. She didn't want him to know how fearful she'd become for her friends, so she covered it up by saying, 'And why are you worried about Janie and me? We're not Jewish.'

Eric stared at her as if she were stupid. 'Janie and Daniel work at a Jewish foundry, and you are involved with Steffan. Of course, I worry about you both. I don't want anything to happen to you.'

Perhaps he was concerned, but she'd reached the end of her patience with him and all she wanted to do was unleash her worry and fear onto him like a winter blizzard. But she wouldn't allow him to make her lose control. She chose the moment to walk away. 'I have to get the coffee, or I'll be late.'

He moved towards her as if he were trying to embrace her, and she automatically stepped back out of his reach. She couldn't help but notice his hurt expression. Too bad, he deserved it.

'Promise me you will come to the rally. At least you'll hear first-hand how Paris feels about Jews.'

'Only some of Paris,' she corrected him.

'The loud and influential part,' he reminded her.

On impulse she said, 'If I do come, will you release me from the twenty francs I owe?'

He stared at her, then answered, 'Of course, I never intended to hold you to that. If you come, we'll never speak of it again.'

'Let me think about it.'

She entered the café, resisting the urge to turn and see if he was still outside. She paid for the coffee, and he was gone when she came back out onto the pavement.

As she hurried back to the apartment building, the leaflet felt like a burning coal in her bag. She wanted to throw it away, yet she also wanted to read it.

When she was back in the building's foyer, she opened the

leaflet. It advertised the rally with a sketch of someone she assumed was Eric's uncle orating from a podium. Under the picture was the caption, '*A must for anyone who worries about the fate of France. Our renowned speakers will tell you their plans for a better and prosperous France.*'

She'd seen some ugly caricatures of Jews drawn on walls and billboards, but this leaflet didn't use the word Jew and there was nothing anti-Jew on the page.

Perhaps they really did have some ideas on how to make France better and more prosperous. It surely needed to be. Places like her village were only a season away from starvation. But Eric could be putting his own spin on things to discourage her from seeing Steffan.

Either way, she needed to see for herself. She would go to the rally and find out whether Steffan and his family were in danger. Eric clearly knew more that he was letting on, and he wouldn't tell her willingly. She'd play him at his own game by finding out exactly what the Croix were planning.

By the time Yvette returned to their room, Janie was up, washed and dressed and she'd set the table ready for breakfast. Janie took the pamphlet out of the bag while Yvette made the coffee.

'Where did you get this?' Janie asked.

'Eric was waiting outside and he gave it to me. He wants me to go to the rally.'

Janie let out a squeak and jumped up so quickly Yvette wondered if she'd seen a spider. 'You can't go! You know he belongs to the Croix de Feu.'

'How do you know that?'

'Daniel said they are bad people and behind the attacks on Jews.'

'I'm not going because I agree with them, I'm going to help Steffan and his family.'

Janie sat down. 'Oh, that makes sense. I'll come too.' She took a bite of her croissant.

'Absolutely not.' Yvette banged her coffee mug down in front of her.

'When is it?'

'Sunday afternoon.'

'Perfect, neither of us are working.'

'You are not coming.'

'Why not? If we are spies, we'd be more credible together. Did he ask just you, or me too?'

Yvette sighed; she had a point.

Janie giggled. 'I knew it. He asked us both. He wouldn't do that if he thought it was dangerous.'

'All right. We'll go together.'

'As spies.'

'Yes, as spies. You'll have to make sure you don't tell Daniel or Steffan. They would never agree to this plan.'

'Not because Steffan might be worried about you going somewhere with Eric?' Janie asked, a coy smile playing across her lips.

'I don't think that would bother Steffan. I think he'd worry we weren't safe.'

Although she couldn't be sure. Steffan might be jealous if he found out, not that she would be telling him.

'Eric might be trying to wear you down, just being nice to you until you end up with him.'

'He knows I'm with Steffan. I made it very clear to him this morning.'

'Still, he seems persistent.'

'I'm not sure that's his master plan. It seems more like they want to take over France.'

'Best we stop that, then.' Janie took a final gulp of her coffee.

'Yes, best we do.'

They both readied themselves to leave for work.

THIRTY-SIX

Yvette

Paris, November 1933

Yvette's gnawing worries about whether she should let Janie attend the rally left her when her feet touched the worn step at the entrance of L'Académie. She entered through the blue door into a world of possibility, where creativity crackled in the air like a brewing thunderstorm.

Ahead of her she had two hours of modelling, then another two glorious hours to herself to work on her self-portrait.

She stuffed her bag into her locker and heard the swish of Felicity's silk robe against her limbs as she walked down the hallway.

Felicity wore her hair loose today. Dark brown and lush, it cascaded down to her waist, so thick the weight pulled out any remaining curls. She must dye it, as Yvette couldn't see any grey speckling through the brown.

Felicity unconsciously made every movement a pose, even as she stopped to greet Yvette. She stood with one leg crossed in front of the other with her left hand touching the wall.

'We are celebrating Tave's birthday tomorrow night. Please say you'll come. We'd love to introduce you to some more of our artists.'

Yvette had said no so many times; out of habit she opened her mouth to make her apologies then surprised herself by saying, 'What time are you going?'

Felicity's face lit up. 'Oh, you will come? Wonderful. We'll go after the last session.'

'It depends where you're going.'

'Just to our usual, Café de la Rotonde, in Montparnasse. Please say you'll come.'

Yvette had heard about the model Le Bonbon who frequented the café. Le Bonbon kept a white mouse as a pet and fed it sugar cubes all night long. She wanted to meet that girl, who was so free that she could while her time away on a mouse.

Janie was staying with the Blums tomorrow night, and Yvette had nothing planned with Steffan, so she nodded. 'I'll come.'

'Wonderful.' Felicity touched her lightly on the cheek then swished her way down the hall towards Tave's office.

Yvette hurried in the other direction, to the larger life-drawing studio. The wall of glass certainly let in the light, but now it was turning cooler, the room stayed cold. She left it to the last minute to disrobe, position herself on the chaise, and arrange the shawl over her body.

Every time she modelled, she revealed a little more of herself, and exactly what that was depended on who stood behind the easels. The class today were mainly older women with a smattering of grey-bearded men. It gave her confidence; she was less inhibited than when she was modelling in front of younger men. Maybe it was all those years of trying to remain unnoticed in the village.

Yvette lowered the shawl to expose her breasts. No one gasped or whistled. The only reaction was from her skin, which goose bumped in protest at the cold air. She glanced down so she could remember the shape of her nipple pointing up to the ceiling, and the soft sweep of her breast as it joined her ribcage. Closing her eyes, she drew herself in her imagination, sensing how the charcoal felt between her fingers, the pressure on the paper, and the scent of scorched willow.

Yvette was so caught up in her internal world, she was taken by surprise by the scrape of easels being placed against the wall, and the rustle of smocks being removed and hung on the hooks near the door.

She threw on her clothes so she wouldn't miss a second of working on her self-portrait. The artists for the next session trickled into the room and it was time for her to rush across town to model for Monsieur Chiparus.

When Yvette arrived at Monsieur Chiparus's workshop, he'd lined up three completed sculptures on the bench.

She recognised herself in two.

The sculptor pointed to a likeness of her, standing on the tips of her toes with her arms outstretched. On each arm were several rings with fabric attached that cascaded to the ground behind the statue.

'This one is Semiramis.'

She remembered the hours she'd spent in that pose. It seemed miraculous he could turn her likeness into something so intricate and graceful. Even though it was still only plasticine, she recognised her kiss curls peeping out from under the headdress just above the ears.

'Who is Semiramis?'

'She's the ancient Queen of Babylon, and she's called the Queen of Heaven.' He held a magnifying glass to the sculpture's shoulder to make some adjustments to the costume with a tiny scalpel.

'She's very regal.' Yvette was also grateful she hadn't stood for hours with a heavy curtain on her arms.

'It's not difficult to create these works with you as a model.'

A little glow inside her bloomed into pleasure; all the hours of standing about in the freezing studio were worth it when she saw the result.

She recognised the second sculpture's pose and her arms ached at the memory of holding them up above her head. She'd worn a halter top and a pair of bloomers. Monsieur Chiparus had turned those ordinary clothes into an exotic costume.

'What's this one called?'

'That's the Scarab Dancer,' he said, not looking up from his work. 'Egyptian.'

She became aware that Julienne wasn't in the studio.

'Shall I find Julienne and get into my costume?'

He replied, still not looking up. 'She is in the house. I am letting these beauties go today, so I won't need you.'

'Will I still get paid?' The words tumbled out of her.

Monsieur Chiparus's fingers tightened on the scalpel, but he said nothing.

'Should I talk to Julienne about that?'

He didn't look up from the sculpture, and when she'd decided she'd just go and find Julienne he said, 'Yes, Julienne. She manages the finances.'

Yvette went into the house and found her in the kitchen. Julienne seemed genuinely pleased to see her and set about putting the coffee pot on the stove.

'We are very excited to have the next batch of sculptures ready. Blum Foundry are picking them up this morning.' Julienne seemed flustered. She fussed with the coffee pot, moving it about the stove top because nowhere appeared to be the right place. The cup and saucer chittered in her trembling hand.

'Are you not feeling well?' Yvette asked.

'I'm nervous, I suppose. We're hoping that these sculptures sell well. Demétre's been slow getting the work out, and we don't have much money.' Julienne looked around the big kitchen, focusing on the sideboard with its shelves of fine, hand-painted porcelain and the glass-fronted cupboards displaying elegant glass and silverware, as if she could see it disappearing from her.

'Oh, I was going to ask you about payment for today.'

'That wasn't what I was talking about. Of course, we will pay you. We contracted you for the ten weeks. We've still got another two. Demétre's got plans for another three sculptures. He loves working with you. I meant money in general.'

'I appreciate that. Janie and I are still not quite set up yet.'

Their room was practically empty compared to Julienne's kitchen, where grace and wonder filled every shelf and cupboard.

'I have asked Demétre about referrals to other artists, and he's making some enquiries.'

With a respected artist like Monsieur Chiparus recommending her, she was bound to get more work.

Julienne poured the coffee and came to sit with her at the kitchen table.

Yvette took in the well-appointed kitchen, which had more crockery than Madame Sorve's café and boarding house put together. She especially admired the copper-bottomed pots and pans that hung from a frame above the long bench.

'I wouldn't think someone like you would worry about money,' Yvette said.

'It's always on my mind but never on Demétre's. His family circumstances meant he didn't have to worry about money. He's unconcerned that his inheritance is almost gone. He spends like there's no tomorrow. If we don't make money from these sculptures, we will need to move somewhere a little more modest.'

Yvette's perception of Julienne changed in that moment. She became more real, more like her, an equal just trying to survive.

'Will it be hard to give up all this?'

Yvette looked around the kitchen that was bigger than their tiny cottage and filled with many more possessions. This was just one room of many.

Julienne shook her head. 'You would think so, but my family are not well off and I am from a very ordinary background. It doesn't worry me. What worries me is that Demétre wouldn't be able to sculpt. He's not much good for anything else, I'm afraid.'

Yvette couldn't imagine Monsieur Chiparus working in a bakery or smelting metal in a foundry. He really was made to do only one thing.

'I am sure you will sell plenty of pieces.'

Julienne sighed then stood up to fiddle with the coffee pot again.

Suddenly feeling awkward, Yvette decided to change the subject to take Julienne's mind off her problems. 'Have you heard of the Croix de Feu?'

Julienne nodded. 'Yes, I have. Why are you interested in them?'

'A friend of mine belongs to them and he's asked me to attend a rally.'

It wasn't entirely the truth, but Julienne didn't need to know what they were really planning.

'And you want to attend?'

She'd caught Julienne's attention. She sat back down at the table, her usually serene face rumpled by a frown.

'I am interested in what they have to say. My friend says they have a plan to help France.'

Julienne stared at her for what seemed like an extremely long time. She sighed and took a sip of her coffee. 'Their plan is to rid France of people they don't think should live here, like foreigners, and Jewish people.'

'Is that so bad if they are hurting the country?'

A look of disappointment settled on Julienne's face. Yvette didn't want Julienne to think less of her, but she couldn't tell her the truth without getting Steffan and Daniel in trouble. Julienne might pull their pieces from the Blum Foundry, and then the Blums would be the ones wondering how to make ends meet.

'Yes, because that would be people like the Blums. Your young man Steffan and my Demétre. Jews and foreigners. People who are just trying to make a living get caught up in their net.'

'You don't think I should go?'

'If you want to hear them rant hate and push for violence, then go.'

'My friend doesn't seem like that.'

'Yet there he is, involved in an organisation that promotes violence against vulnerable people.' Julienne visibly shook and tears welled in her eyes.

'I didn't mean to upset you, Julienne. I am sorry, I don't want anyone to get hurt.'

Julienne smiled tentatively at her.

She found it difficult to consider Eric a violent man, but people could allow violence by turning away from it and not stopping it. How many men in her village had beaten their wives? The answer was always that it was none of their business. Yet it *was* their business, because it happened right next to them.

Julienne left the room and came back with her payment. 'For the sake of the Blum family, you should stay away from the Croix.'

'Even if I could find out what their plans are?'

'I can tell you what they are up to. They want violence and mayhem. They think they are better than the rest of us and you'll just get trampled in their rush to hurt others.'

She accepted Julienne's money. 'Thank you for your wise words.'

They may have been wise, but they wouldn't deter her from going. She needed to know what their plans were and how that might affect Janie, the Blum Foundry, and Steffan.

Yvette placed her hand on top of Julienne's. 'I will tell my friend I won't go to the rally,' she lied.

THIRTY-SEVEN

Steffan

Paris, November 1933

When Steffan arrived at work the next morning, Daniel was already at his bench, with pieces of the Rudolph Valentino and Natacha Rambova's prototype statuette laid out in front of him on a black cloth. He'd arranged the heads, arms, legs, and hands where they would be fitted onto the sculpture. The display took on a surreal appearance, as if unseen forces had pulled the body parts away from each other. On the other side of the bench, he'd done the same with the Dolly Sisters pieces and the book girl.

'Chiparus is coming today to inspect the pieces and the bronze casts,' Daniel said.

They'd worked all month carving the ivory pieces while Chiparus readied the moulds for casting. Yvette had described how the artist sanded, filed and finetuned every bevel, the patterns in the statues' clothes, each bead on the dancers' shoes, and even mimicked the embroidery on collars and cuffs.

Two weeks ago Chiparus had rejected the initial bronze casting of the three statuettes. It wasn't anything they'd done – Chiparus saw improvements no one else would think important and wanted to enhance the designs. They'd taken the original moulds back so he could do more work on them.

It meant another delay.

Father had taken it rather well, just raising his hands up as if to say, artists – what can we do?

They'd picked the moulds up last week and the foundry workers had re-cast the pieces.

'Is there anything I can do to prepare?' asked Steffan.

'Sweep the room again, then finish the piece you're working on.'

Steffan used a small brush and pan to go over the spotless benches, then swept the floor. He sat down at his workbench and positioned the large magnifying glass to etch the outstretched fingers of a model's hand. Not Yvette's. Her hands and fingers were long and slim, while this woman's palms were smaller and wider.

He became so absorbed in the work it seemed like only a few minutes had passed before Father ushered Monsieur Chiparus into the carving room. A muscle in Father's jaw twitched, the only sign he was apprehensive about the inspection. Trieste trailed behind them, his arms straining from the weight of the heavy box he carried. Father directed the apprentice to place it beside the carved pieces, then sent him away. He laid out the cast bronze pieces next to Steffan's and Daniel's work.

Steffan and Daniel stood together to the side of the workbench, backs straight and hands loosely clasped. Monsieur Chiparus greeted them respectfully, but his focus was entirely on the work. He picked up each piece to study it under a magnifying glass he produced from an inside pocket of his jacket. He must have given the tailor specific measurements for the depth and size of the pocket to house the tool.

Mostly Chiparus nodded and placed the piece back. He frowned as he inspected Natacha Rambova's hands, referring to a magazine photograph of Rudoph Valentino embracing his ballerina wife as she leant into him. Her feet were en pointe, and the camera had caught the movement of her skirt, ready to flair out the moment she spun away from her husband.

'Her little finger needs the knuckle more defined,' Chiparus said, still staring down the magnifying glass.

They all nodded while he continued to pore over the pieces.

Steffan compared the bronze pieces to the photograph Chiparus placed beside him on the bench. The sculpture would look like this once he'd secured Rudolph's ivory head onto his perfectly cast body. Somehow Chiparus had scored every crease and drape of the satin jacket he wore. Steffan couldn't wait to stroke the diamond-shaped pattern that ran up the statue's leg, to feel the change in texture and depth.

Another hour passed until Chiparus seemed satisfied with the bulk of their work. Father flashed them a half smile, a sign of his approval, as he escorted Chiparus out.

Daniel rubbed his hands together. 'Nearly there; we've only two minor adjustments to make – Natasha's pinky finger and the book lady's bicep.'

'Would you like me to do one?' Steffan asked.

'I'll refine Natacha's finger and you can start assembling their statue.'

Steffan attached Natacha's cap to her crown, and her deliciously graceful neck to her shoulders. Daniel hovered over him as he secured Natacha's arms with tiny screws using a tool so small he held it with a pair of tweezers. He gladly let Daniel intervene to fit the fiddly bracelets and metal armbands on Natacha's arms. It had taken him two days to re-carve the statue's right arm after he'd snapped it trying to fit the bracelets.

Father and Trieste came and went, bringing in the hefty marble plinths, lining them up on the carving bench next to the corresponding statue.

While Steffan put together his sculpture, Daniel completed Chiparus's requested adjustments and assembled the girl holding a book behind her back, and two other pairs of Dolly Sisters sculptures.

Father drilled small holes into the base of the plinths ready to pin the sculpture's foot to the marble. Steffan loved the ingeniousness of that pin, which would open into a Y-shape held in place by the small hollow inside the foot.

Steffan went to help Father attach the pins, but Daniel stopped him. 'It's a little tradition. Le Directeur does this part.'

'Position the Dolly Sisters,' Father said, still concentrating on the pins.

Reverentially, Daniel lifted the dancing sisters, one in each hand. Father slid the first sister's foot onto the pin and tripped the mechanism. The statue danced alone on the plinth waiting for her sister, who soon joined her. The pair were caught mid routine, their skirts raised in an arc around legs that kicked as high as their shoulders.

In the next sculpture, the sisters' right legs pistoned behind them as they lunged forward, their mouths open in song, their arms raised above their heads. Steffan hoped they were as energetic in real life as they were in these likenesses. Perhaps he and Yvette could see them perform one day soon.

Steffan was relieved that his clumsy mistake smashing the book lady's prototype hadn't stopped Chiparus making her. She clasped the book behind her back, still ready to abandon it for something more exciting. Steffan marvelled at how Chiparus had captured her impatience and desire for something more than reading.

Then it was Steffan's turn to present Rudolph and Natacha. Father eased Natacha into Rudolph's arms where he cradled her, and she rested her head lightly on his chest. He lowered the whole piece onto the four pins.

Steffan held his breath, as if that would help Father line it up. Father didn't need help, though. His steady hands slid their feet onto the pins where they stood on the plinth, ready for their next steps.

It was the best sculpture of the four. Not that he was biased or anything. It seemed miraculous that he scraped away at bone, the metal workers smelted bronze, and the masons chiselled the marble separately, but together they created something so beautiful. None of it would be possible without the artist, though.

'Let's get them into the shop.' Father said.

They carried them in a procession across the courtyard, like villagers with a statue of the Madonna on feast days. All the workers put down their tools and followed them towards the shop.

Janie jumped up and down, clapping her hands as they entered. 'They are beautiful!'

'We will sell so many of these,' Sarah said, kissing Father as he passed by her.

Philippe came in with the other men and Steffan tried not to let his presence dampen his good mood. Philippe ignored him and he found that annoying, and wished he would acknowledge their hard work.

'The ballet dancers will be very popular,' Sarah said to Steffan as he placed the sculpture on the display table.

He kept his expression neutral as Philippe's discreet glance towards Steffan's statue revealed his anger and jealousy. Only Steffan saw it. And Philippe knew he'd seen it as he raised his eyes momentarily to look at him. No doubt Philippe would make him suffer, but he wasn't going to let it affect him now. The other workers crowded around, praising him for the quality of his work, studying the curls coming out from under Natacha's headdress, and how he'd carved her eyes.

Father's hand came down on his shoulder. 'Great work, son. If this is what you can do in your first year, you are destined for great things.'

'Thank you, Father. That means so much from you.'

He meant for calling him son.

'We'll organise for some buyers to come in later in the week,' Sarah said to Father. She turned to Steffan and said, 'You'll be sick of the sight of Rudolph and Natacha's faces by the time you've carved two hundred of them.'

Steffan laughed, then stopped as he realised, he'd have to make hundreds of these things. What an idiot not to connect this up. Philippe noticed the penny dropping and laughed.

Chiparus entered the shop, sweeping the spotlight away from Steffan, and a new round of inspections, assessments, and compliments whirled about. Steffan hoped his ignorance would be forgotten by Father and Sarah. He had no doubt Philippe would never forget and would milk this for all it was worth.

Back in the carving room, Daniel said, 'Did you really not work out that we'd be mass-producing the sculptures?'

'Not really. I suppose I got so caught up in the process I didn't really think about it.'

Daniel shook his head. 'We'll really need to keep an eye on you, in case your empty head causes you to float away.'

Steffan's head was far from empty. He was always preoccupied, but maybe not with the things most people thought about.

He'd have to pay more attention, especially with Father's plans for him to take over the business. And he didn't want Philippe being chosen over him. No way was that going to happen.

THIRTY-EIGHT

Steffan

Paris, November 1933

As usual, Steffan topped up Madame Bruist's wine glass every time she left the table to bring something from the kitchen. He wished he could just dispense with the charade and go out, but he couldn't risk her telling tales to Father. Last week she'd almost caught him coming home at three in the morning. Eventually she'd seemed satisfied with his explanation that he'd heard a noise outside. If he wasn't careful, Father would insist Steffan moved into the single men's dormitory, or worse, in with them.

As usual, he settled her by the fire after dinner and did the dishes.

'You're such a good boy, just like a son,' Madame Bruist slurred as she slid further into the seat closest to the fire. She was fast asleep by the time he'd finished drying the pots.

When he arrived at the Guildhall, Daniel and Ashlam were sitting close together, whispering in each other's ears, their heads touching. He expected one to reach up and cup the other's face, drawing him in for a kiss.

They pulled apart when they saw Steffan.

'We've been waiting a long time for you. We didn't think you were coming,' said Daniel.

'I had to wait for Madame Bruist to fall asleep. Can I knock back a drink before we go?' He'd spent half the evening filling Madame Bruist full of booze without touching a drop himself. All he wanted was a drink.

Ashlam shook his head. 'They're meeting soon at the Figaro Building, so we've got to find a café with a good view of the front door.'

Steffan trailed after the pair as they raced down the stairs. Each step felt like a betrayal of Father's wishes. If only he'd stayed home.

They swung onto the tram as it was leaving the stop. Steffan let its momentum take him further down the aisle, where he sat down two seats behind Ashlam and Daniel. He could change his mind at any time, just get off the tram at the next stop. But he didn't.

Five stops later, they got off at Boulevard Hausmann and Ashlam led them to a café across the road from the Figaro Building.

Steffan ordered a beer.

The waiter looked him up and down. 'We only serve high class wine and spirits here.'

Steffan fought the urge to smack the waiter's tray up into his face.

'A carafe of your house red and three glasses.' Daniel stood between him and the waiter.

Ashlam motioned them to sit. 'We need to watch the entrance.'

Steffan moved his chair so he could see better.

'Stop it,' Ashlam hissed. 'Don't draw attention to us.'

'I'm moving a chair at a café. How is that going to draw attention?'

Outside the entrance of the Croix du Feu's headquarters, the large doorman, kitted out in his royal blue sash, greeted men as they approached. Ten had passed through the double doors since Steffan had sat down.

Finally, the waiter brought the carafe. Steffan gulped down his first glass and helped himself to a second before the other two had got through their first.

'You make me sit with my back to the action. I might as well make use of the time and get totally plastered.'

'You *are* in a mood.' Ashlam stood up. 'Swap with me. I don't want to have to carry you home.'

As they settled into their new seats, Daniel said, 'Potiev'.

The subject of his attention had the loose-limbed walk of someone who'd never had to toil in the fields.

'Is he going in?' Ashlam hissed. Steffan tried not to smirk as Ashlam squirmed in his seat.

Potiev chatted to the doorman with a familiarity that convinced Steffan he came regularly to the meetings.

'That's strange. Why would Potiev be here?' Daniel said, more to himself than to them.

'Maybe he's here incognito?'

Daniel laughed. 'Everyone knows who Potiev is. He can't go unrecognised.'

Ashlam couldn't stand it anymore. 'Swap places, Daniel.'

'Don't draw attention to yourselves,' Steffan scolded, and was rewarded with a glare from Ashlam.

'He's a communist. What's he doing at a Croix de Feu meeting?' Daniel shook his head like he was trying to dislodge an angry wasp.

'It's obvious. He's playing both sides.' Ashlam took a gulp of his wine.

'But he helped take those men to hospital,' Daniel said.

'And he stopped the gendarmes coming to the alleyway,' Steffan said, trying to piece it together.

The expression on Daniel's face told Steffan he'd made a

similar connection. 'Surely Potiev wouldn't have handed in those men? They were taken away from the hospital.'

'If it was Potiev, why didn't he lead the gendarme to us when we had a hall full of injured?'

'Might have looked a bit too obvious.'

The waiter came by and Steffan ordered another carafe. He was pleasantly numb, the crushing guilt miraculously gone. More wine would make it even better, good enough even for him to tell Daniel he was leaving the party. Something nagged at him. 'Does Potiev know where we work?'

Daniel straightened up. 'Do you think he could be behind the attacks on the foundry?'

'I don't think he did it personally, but he could have let slip where you work, or that it's a Jewish business,' Ashlam answered.

Daniel nodded and studied the Figaro Building. 'Especially if he's trying to get into the good books of that lot.'

Steffan sighed. 'That's a relief. It means the foundry wasn't attacked because we went on the march.'

'Make it all about you.' Ashlam's expression hardened.

'I know it's not about me. I thought we might have led them to the foundry.'

'You did. Or should I say, Daniel did.'

'Oh, come on. You can't hold me responsible for this bunch of idiots full of hate turning up at the foundry.'

A less well-dressed man slowed down by the building's entrance. Something about him was familiar. When the man lifted his head, Steffan recognised him.

He nudged Daniel. 'Look, it's Eric.'

'Who?' Daniel asked.

'Eric, the conductor. From near your village.'

Daniel turned in his seat to get a better look.

'Be discreet,' Ashlam hissed.

Daniel made a face.

'Eric? From La Montagne? Not surprising. His uncle's neck deep in fascism. How do you know him?'

'He turned up at the foundry looking for Yvette and Janie. He helped them when they were travelling.'

Eric shook hands with the doorman, had a smoke with him, then went into the building.

'This is an opportunity, then.' Ashlam lit a cigarette.

'No. That is not a good idea.' Daniel shook his head.

'An opportunity for what?' What were they talking about?

'Yvette.' Ashlam and Daniel said together.

'Because Yvette knows Eric?' Steffan didn't like where this was going.

'Yes. She will help us.' Ashlam seemed to have decided she would because it was his idea.

'I don't think we should be doing anything dangerous.' What Steffan really wanted to say was that he didn't want Yvette anywhere near Eric.

'Surely she'd want to help us stamp out fascism.'

Daniel shook his head. 'So revolutionary, Ashlam. Let's tell her about Eric and see if she'll help us get information from him about what the Croix du Feu are planning. Remember, Janie does work at the foundry, and she might not be safe.'

'We could ask Potiev,' Steffan said. He wanted to shut down any ideas about Eric and Yvette seeing each other again.

'He's an eel. We need to deal with a bigger fish.' Ashlam could be cryptic and annoying. But there was no point pushing him because he'd tell them nothing more.

Daniel diverted back to Yvette. 'I will ask her about Eric.'

'Ask her what?' said Steffan. 'I don't want her put into the middle of this.'

'She won't be in the middle. She'll just be asking him questions about what he's doing with the Croix.'

How could Daniel even think about putting Yvette in danger? 'It's a bad idea and I'm going to tell her not to do it.'

He hadn't expected Daniel to laugh at him. 'Good luck with telling her to do anything,' he said. 'You haven't met Mademoiselle Ane Tetu, Little Miss Stubborn Mule. It made her so angry when we called her that. It's really her, though.'

Steffan's chest tightened. He wanted to know everything about her, more than Daniel, more even than Janie. That he didn't know she was stubborn distressed him. He needed to walk. He threw his drink back in one gulp. 'I have to go,' he said, trying to keep the emotion from his voice.

'*Salut*. We will stay and keep France safe from all who would harm her.' Ashlam raised his glass.

'Very noble of you.'

As he walked to the tram, he had an impulse to go to Yvette and ask her not to put herself in danger. Then the practicalities of getting into her building, dealing with the grumpy concierge, and trying to explain himself to a half-asleep Yvette dowsed the urge.

It could wait. Daniel wasn't going to gallop around there tonight and ask her to save France. Steffan would see her tomorrow at L'Académie. Of course, she would listen to him.

It wasn't that late, and he really needed a beer, so he took the tram back to Claude's.

THIRTY-NINE

Yvette

Paris, November 1933

The bell tinkled a welcome as Yvette stepped into the tailor's shop. The tailor nodded in her direction, occupied with pinning together panels of a jacket around a young man's torso. The tailor's wife, a red scarf wrapped around her head, glided out from the room behind the counter to greet Yvette.

'Your coat is ready, mademoiselle.'

With a flourish, the tailor's wife pulled the coat from a rack behind her. True to its sky-blue colouring, it lit up the room. Even the tailor stood up to admire the garment.

Yvette handed over her hard-earned 15 francs and the coat was hers.

'You must wear it now,' the tailor's wife insisted. She motioned her to take off the shapeless brown coat, then expertly stood behind her to slide the coat onto her frame. She spun her around to button it up, then stood back and sighed, a look of pure bliss on her face.

Yvette made to move towards the mirror. The tailor's wife shook her head.

'Not yet. I forgot the beret.' She rushed behind the counter.

'But I didn't order a beret,' Yvette called after her. She only had enough money to pay for the coat.

The tailor's wife returned with a beret made of the matching wool. 'We had some left-over material, so I made you one.'

Yvette reached for her bag, but the tailor's wife shook her head.

'No charge. I remember getting my first coat and how I wished for a matching hat.'

'That is so kind of you.' Tears welled up in her eyes at the thought of this stranger's kindness as she fussed about fitting the beret on her head. She led her over to the full-length mirror.

'Now you can look.'

It was her reflection, but Yvette didn't recognise herself. She was transformed, just like the little grubs in her garden back in her village that turned into jewel-like beetles. The awkward girl from a tiny village had disappeared, replaced by a Parisian woman.

She couldn't stop the tears spilling down her face. 'I can't believe it. You have made me beautiful.'

The tailor and his wife exchanged a glance, and both laughed. 'This is why I love our work. We just provide the stage for your beauty to shine through. You were already beautiful.'

Before she'd put on the coat, the young man being fitted by the tailor had barely looked at her. Now he seemed transfixed. The tailor noticed and turned the young man away from Yvette to work on the back of his jacket.

The tailor's wife wrapped her old coat in brown paper and tied it with string so it was easier for her to carry. 'Go out there and dazzle the world.'

Yvette left the shop, enjoying every step she took as the satin lining slid against her legs. Before donning her new coat, everyone had rushed by in a hurry. Now men slowed down to wish her a good morning. One even stopped on the pavement to stare at her.

She felt powerful, in control, and ready to meet new artists tonight.

Her newfound visibility hadn't worn off when she reached L'Académie. Other models commented on how pretty her new coat was. Tave even stopped to greet her, instead of rushing by to speak with a preferred artist.

Felicity swept down the corridor in a whirlwind of exclamations to gather Yvette up in a cloud of perfume and compliments. She spun Yvette around to look at her from every angle.

'You are an angel, a muse, a true asset to our establishment.'

'Stop it, Felicity. It's only a coat.'

Felicity shook her head. 'Your beauty was always there, but this colour, how you wear it, how you move in it, enhances everything about you.'

'Felicity, please don't exaggerate.'

'We will be finding you plenty of work tonight. Your dress must be even more spectacular than your exterior garments.'

She ushered Yvette down the hallway into her office, where Yvette had only been once before. The room was a jumble of colour, enhanced by the red and green full-length leadlight windows that faced the street. Felicity's desk was nearly invisible under the pile of shawls, dresses, shoes, and wigs. On the far wall, a built-in wardrobe held at least fifty dresses and over a dozen coats in a rainbow of colours. Yvette had never seen so many clothes in one room.

'From now on, you will hang your coat in the wardrobe, so it doesn't get damaged in your locker. We will also find you a dress for tonight.' She strode over to the wardrobe to sort through the dresses and stopped to pull out an emerald green, chiffon, drop-waisted dress embroidered with lilies in a darker green. She thrust it at Yvette. 'Try this on.'

Yvette took her new coat off and eased it onto a hanger. She had a moment of anxiety that she might return to find the coat given out to another model, but she didn't let it show. Felicity was trying to help her.

Yvette wriggled into the underslip, then put on the dress. It was longer than her other dresses, falling almost to her ankles. She looked herself over in the mirror. The green suited her skin tones and the V-neck worked for her. The material flowed around her body in a way that hid her curves until she moved. It made her feel mysterious, as if the dress was hinting at her femininity.

Felicity nodded her approval. 'That will do well for tonight. I'll find you some matching shoes while you finish your shift.' She waved at a large box.

'Thank you so much for helping me,' said Yvette.

'It's a pleasure. Now off you go, before you're late.'

Yvette changed back into her day dress to hurry into the main studio before the artists arrived.

At the end of the day, Yvette returned to Felicity's office to find her in front of her dressing table preparing for their night out. She'd lined up three pairs of shoes for Yvette to try on. The black pair had buckles on the top; another pair was plainer but in a shade of grey that would work well with the dress, and the last was tan with butterflies embossed in the leather.

'The grey pair are the best match, but I thought you might like to see the others.'

Yvette picked up the tan pair to trace her finger over the butterflies. 'These are my favourite, but I agree the grey will match better.'

'Now come over here and we'll do your makeup.'

Yvette had never worn makeup before. Her mother hadn't had any, and they never went anywhere they could dress up.

Church was their only social outlet, and they were even on the margins of that because of Papa's drinking.

Felicity took her time, selecting the correct shade of foundation for Yvette's skin, matching eye shadow to the colour of her dress, carefully applying kohl to outline her eyes, and choosing a lipstick far brighter than seemed quite proper. She brushed out her hair, twisting it this way, pinning it that way, until she seemed happy with her styling.

Felicity rummaged in a container of jewellery and found a pair of green cut-glass drop earrings. She clipped them onto Yvette's earlobes. 'This will finish off the look.'

She spun Yvette to face the mirror, and for the second time in a day, Yvette didn't recognise the person looking back at her. This woman was as sophisticated as any she'd seen in the Chiparus's well-to-do neighbourhood, or shopping at Place de Vendome.

'Thank you so much, Felicity. You have transformed me.'

'It's a pleasure. Now I'd better see about transforming myself too.'

By the time Yvette had put on the green dress, wedged her feet into Felicity's shoes and put on her new coat, Felicity was dressed and ready to go.

They met Tave and two of the other models in the foyer; Cila, a buxom woman in her thirties, who was Tave's lover, and Pepi, a stick thin woman in her twenties with a long face that reminded Yvette of a donkey.

They launched themselves into the street then into the Metro. It was a first for Yvette, to go anywhere with a group of friends, without Janie, Daniel, or Steffan. She had never felt this free.

They came out of the Metro near Café de la Rotunde, which was sprawled on the corner of a busy intersection, its name emblazoned on a large neon sign above the awning. The outside tables were all full, but Felicity had reserved a table for their group. It took them an age to be seated as they stopped at almost every table to greet people and introduce Yvette. Her head spun with all the names, including two well-known ones – Pablo Picasso and Peggy Guggenheim.

'It's a veritable who's who, here tonight,' Felicity whispered.

'Would Picasso be a good person to approach for modelling?' Yvette asked.

'Not that old letch. He thinks far too much of himself and pays next to nothing. Once we've got ourselves settled, we'll see who else is here.'

The concierge took their coats, and Yvette was conscious she'd attracted the attention of some of the diners nearby. Even Picasso stopped conversing with his party to gaze in her direction. She suppressed a smile. It was exhilarating, being noticed.

'Do you think Le Bonbon is here tonight?' she asked.

'She's a regular here. She's usually inside at one of the booths, with that mouse.' Cila made a face.

'I think I saw Mendiot inside. Such a fine artist but down on his luck. We'll pay for his dinner.'

'That's very kind of you, Felicity,' Yvette said.

'Mendiot will succeed one day, I am sure of it. Once he does, he'll remember that we were kind to him.'

Felicity ordered a bottle of Champagne, and while they waited for it to arrive, she hustled Yvette inside. Felicity surveyed the room for potential artists while Yvette took in the plush red velvet seating, the rich mahogany fittings, the floor-to-ceiling mirrors, and the artists' sketches and paintings covering every available bit of wall.

'Come along, Yvette, I see Cadieu and his followers over in the corner.'

She hurried after Felicity, who rattled off introductions so quickly she didn't have time to absorb any names except Cadieu's. He was a slight man with a walrus moustache and bright blue eyes, and he stood to greet her, making a great show of kissing the back of her hand, while appraising her as to her value.

'Yvette is a serious artist and supplementing her income by modelling,' Felicity informed him, in a tone that implied there would be nothing extra on offer.

'I need a model soon. Please contact me next week,' Cadieu said. He flipped open a holder and passed her one of his cards, then turned to his male companions to encourage them to follow suit. A man who introduced himself as Adrienne Bonmie handed his card to her.

'Thank you, gentlemen. I just saw Vernod over there. I want to introduce Yvette to him before our drinks arrive.'

Felicity marched across the room with Yvette almost running to keep up with her. She stopped at a table where a middle-aged couple were eating their meal. They reminded Yvette of the Chiparus's, and she relaxed a little.

'Oh, my favourite couple,' Felicity gushed over the pair.

'Felicity, always a pleasure. How is L'Académie?' Monsieur Vernod asked.

'Well indeed. I wanted to introduce you to our newest model, Yvette. She is a serious artist and looking for some additional work to fund her tutoring with Monsieur Chiparus.'

The husband and wife appeared interested.

'Are you a sculptor?' Madame Vernod asked.

'Yes, my mother was a sculptor too. Perhaps you knew her – Loriene Provon?'

'I did. I met her through your grandfather. Is she well?'

'She passed last year, after a short illness.'

'I am sorry, my dear. She was a lovely person.'

'Perhaps I could visit you, and you could tell me about her earlier days. She never talked about it.'

'Of course. We would be delighted. Give Yvette your card,' Madame Vernod said to her husband.

Yvette followed Felicity back to their table, her head held high. The three cards in her hand were the bridge to her freedom. If she could get work from these contacts, their lives would be secure in Paris.

Just as she reached the terrace, Eric and an older man, who could only be his uncle, entered the restaurant.

'Yvette! What are you doing here?' Eric stared at her like he couldn't believe what he was seeing.

'I'm here with my friends from L'Académie, celebrating a birthday.'

Not that she owed him an explanation, but she didn't want to be rude, seeing as she still owed him 20 francs and she looked like she might be spending that amount tonight.

'I would like you all to meet my uncle, Monsieur Edward Granger.'

Monsieur Granger's dark coat fitted him well and was cut to give the impression of wider shoulders than he had. The coat must have been worth more than two years of Yvette's earnings. The Croix de Feu badge caught the light and twinkled – a reminder of what this man stood for.

'Yvette is from Mont-Saint-Louis, and I met her and her sister while I was working on the train.'

Yvette was relieved he didn't mention the incident with the pistol or the purse.

'I have asked Yvette to join us on Sunday to hear you speak.'

Monsieur Granger smiled at her. 'I hope you will come.'

'I will be coming, along with my little sister Janie. I want to check that we will be safe. There's been so much trouble lately.'

'You will be perfectly safe with us. We will consider you our special guests.'

The maitre d' arrived to show the pair to their table.

'Until Sunday.'

Monsieur Granger clipped his heels together like an old-fashioned viscount and made his way inside. Eric turned to look at her, his expression giving away his desire to be with Yvette and her party, rather than his straight-laced uncle.

FORTY

Steffan

Paris, November 1933

When Steffan and Daniel arrived at the Guildhall, Ashlam left his usual stool by the bar and joined them at a table.

'We've agreed we're not asking Yvette to attend the rally,' Steffan said with force, just in case Daniel disagreed with him.

He didn't, so Steffan continued, 'I think we should attend ourselves, not as protesters but as observers so we can identify sympathisers.'

Ashlam shook his head. 'We do not fraternise with Jew haters.'

Daniel shrugged. 'It's a great opportunity for us to confront the Croix. We need the whole Guild so we're writing a recommendation to the Party Branch Committee.'

Ashlam swirled his brandy and said, 'They will say no.'

'Steffan and I could go. We need to know what Potiev is planning. He's playing both sides.'

'I have a plan already forming. We will be much more effective if we do this covertly,' Ashlam said.

Daniel smiled and mock saluted. 'I'm all for a side mission, Comrade Ashlam.'

Ashlam stood up. 'Let me show you something.'

Steffan and Daniel followed him into a storage room behind the stage curtains. He pushed some rolled up banners out of the way to reveal a crate of empty brandy bottles.

Steffan wondered if Ashlam had drunk too much.

Daniel clearly didn't get it either, as he asked, 'So, what are we looking at here? Are you wanting us to refill them?'

Ashlam nodded. 'Not with brandy, though.'

'Vodka?' Steffan suggested.

Ashlam shook his head.

'Schnapps?' Daniel asked.

Ashlam laughed, their guesses clearly amusing him.

'We wouldn't waste anything like that on those fascists.' He stared at them intently. 'You really don't know?'

Steffan shook his head, as did Daniel. Anyone who captured Ashlam and tried to torture him for information would be wasting their time – he only divulged things when he was ready. And today he was ready.

'Bottle bombs.' He pulled a bottle out of the crate. 'We fill it with petrol, push in a rag. The rag absorbs the petrol. We light it and throw it at the enemy.' He paused for effect, then continued, 'It smashes with a boom, spreads accelerant over everything its path, then sets it on fire.'

'Are you going to use these on people?'

Ashlam nodded.

It horrified Steffan that Ashlam could consider doing that to another person.

'You can't be serious. That is barbaric.' Steffan pictured a street of protesters turning into burning, screaming candles of death.

'Fascists are not human, Steffan. They deserve nothing less than death, and definitely a painful one.'

Steffan tore the empty bottle from Ashlam's hand. 'They *are* people, and we're not going to throw petrol bombs into a crowded street.'

Ashlam spread his arms wide and shrugged.

Steffan thrust the bottle back at Ashlam. 'Come on, Daniel. We're not listening to this anymore.'

He strode out of the storeroom and fought his way back through the curtains. Daniel hadn't followed him, and anxiety clenched Steffan's stomach. Daniel wouldn't do something so awful as go along with Ashlam's plan?

Just when he decided to go back and get him, Daniel reappeared.

'I wasn't sure you were going to come,' Steffan said.

Daniel shook his head. 'I was trying to talk him out of doing something stupid.'

'Do you think you did?'

'I don't know. Let's get out of here and go to Claude's.'

Steffan gladly followed him down the stairs. When they were out on the main street, he asked, 'Do you think he's serious?'

Daniel nodded. 'Yes, I do. Ashlam's suffered and lost a lot. He wants payback.'

'We can't let that happen. I'll come back tomorrow and get rid of the bottles.'

Daniel touched his shoulder. 'It's a nice thought, but if Ashlam wants to do something, then he's going to find more bottles.'

'Would he try it if we attended the rally?'

'I don't know. I don't think we should risk it.'

'Even more reason for us to go, then. I'm not saying I like these people, but I don't want to see them burnt up either.'

On the tram ride down to Claude's, they sat side by side in companionable silence.

'I guess that settles it. We'll have our own side mission – to look after Yvette – and we'll see what else we can find out from Eric.'

Claude's was heaving with patrons, but once Margot had satisfied herself there were no women with them, she squeezed the pair onto a tiny table just inside the door. They were bumped and jostled, mostly by Margot's massive cleavage, and the atmosphere was jolly as Claude played his usual medley of songs they could sing along to.

After his first beer, Steffan felt more distanced from Ashlam's violent suggestion. How much did he really know about the man? He lived near the Figaro Building in a fancier part of town. He didn't really know what he did for work, or even much about his life. Ashlam had said Potiev was playing them, but maybe Ashlam was? What could he hope to achieve?

He was about to ask Daniel more about Ashlam when he grabbed Margot in some mad little dance. She squealed with delight as Daniel rubbed his face in her cleavage. Margot pulled away from Daniel and dragged Steffan up to dance. Before long the whole café was up on its feet, dancing, clapping and singing like tomorrow would never come. And suddenly Steffan felt okay. He didn't have to worry about Ashlam or Eric or Yvette. He could be here, now, dancing, singing and enjoying this evening, this moment and this place, because this was his life.

FORTY-ONE

Steffan

Paris, November 1933

Steffan and Daniel arrived at the Chiparus studio to collect the final three sculpture moulds. Monsieur Chiparus had them out on his bench and was fussing about, checking them over with his magnifying glass, then making seemingly invisible corrections with a brush with bristles so fine, they could have been made from eyelashes.

He recognised Yvette in two of the sculptures, and the other was a ballerina at the Paris Opera Ballet.

'We'll wait outside until you're ready,' Daniel said to the artist. He moved towards the door, but Monsieur Chiparus was so engrossed in his work, he didn't answer.

Steffan's mood lifted as a familiar voice said, 'You can come and see my work of art.'

Yvette was here, and maybe she was wearing one of those skimpy costumes that showed off her legs and the shape of her breasts. He hurried past the large block of marble to find her hunched over the sculpting turntable, wearing a voluminous artist's smock. He stopped himself from uttering a disappointed groan.

Out of the clay block in front of her was emerging an arm and an excellent likeness of Janie's face.

'What do you think?' she asked without looking up.

'It's shaping up well. I can definitely see Janie.'

Daniel came around the marble obstacle and bobbed down beside Yvette to better view the sculpture. He nodded his approval.

'Chiparus better watch out. You'll be out-selling him soon.'

'He didn't need me today so I put my free time to good use.' She motioned to the clay turntable.

'If you're finished, do you want a ride back into town with us in the bone rattler?' Daniel asked.

Steffan wished he'd asked her first. 'Yes, we'd love to have your company,' he said, hoping it sounded like they'd always meant to offer her a ride.

They smoked and watched Yvette continue to sculpt.

'Be careful you don't make her arm too thin, or it'll break,' Daniel said.

'I'm lucky that hasn't happened to me yet,' Steffan reassured her. 'It's come close, though.'

'It happens to everyone. That's how you learn,' Daniel said.

That may have been the case, but Father was an unforgiving man. Steffan didn't want to make a mistake if he was there to see it.

Monsieur Chiparus announced the pieces were ready. They wrapped the sculptures in canvas and carefully packed them into the crates. By the time they'd loaded them onto the truck, Yvette had appeared beside them in a green skirt and white pintucked blouse, and her serviceable brown coat.

Steffan didn't mind that Daniel always drove when they were together, because today he sat in the middle with Yvette's leg nestled up against his. Every bump jostled her against him, so he took the opportunity to put his arm around her to hold her in place. She patted his leg and he almost shot through the roof with the thrill of her touch.

'Are you going to help us by going to the rally–' Daniel asked.

Steffan cut him off before Yvette could answer. 'She's not going.'

The silence stretched out until Yvette finally spoke. 'I want you both to understand that I make my own decisions. Janie and I won't be going.'

Daniel drew a breath to speak, but it was Yvette's turn to cut him off. 'That's the end of the matter. I've made my decision, so don't push it.'

'I'm glad,' Steffan whispered in her ear.

She squeezed his leg, then turned towards him again. Her lips were so close to his ear, he could feel her warm breath on his face. 'I didn't want you to be upset.'

He gasped when she reached over and squeezed his inner thigh, close to his groin. He felt himself grow hard. She gave him a cheeky grin.

They dropped her at the turn-off to her apartment, and Steffan put his hand on the warm depression her bottom had left on the seat next to him.

He wanted more of that.

'Now we know she's not going,' said Daniel, 'I've got a couple of ideas for how to disrupt the rally.'

Steffan's stomach clenched. He didn't want to be of use in that way, but if the Croix really were threatening the foundry, then he needed to do something.

'You can count on me,' he said, but with a feeling of dread.

They arrived back at the foundry to a heroes' welcome. The men helped carry in the crates and let Father unwind the canvas. When Yvette's likenesses were revealed, the men wolf-whistled and slapped Steffan on the back.

'Lucky bastard,' one said.

'Would like a piece of that myself. What the hell does she see in a scrawny bugger like you?'

'He'd be lucky if he knew what to do with her.'

Steffan laughed it off. He knew what to do, all right. And very soon, if what had happened in the truck meant anything. He was sure Yvette would give him the chance to find out.

His moment of pleasure evaporated when Daniel signalled for Steffan to follow him towards the single men's dorm. Instead of going up the stairs, they squeezed through a small door he'd never noticed before into what appeared to be disused stables.

Daniel led him down a dank corridor and opened a side door. Steffan coughed as the overpowering smell of petrol hit him. Inside, Ashlam was sitting on an upturned crate filling brandy bottles with petrol and stuffing cloth in the necks.

'We're having a party tonight,' he said, taking a drag on his cigarette.

Steffan felt as if he were in a dream. This couldn't be happening – Ashlam here, making bombs to hurt people.

He snatched the cigarette out of Ashlam's mouth and crushed it under his boot.

'I need to talk to you,' he said to Daniel, pulling him out of the room, closing the door. 'What is this? Why is he here?'

'It's not safe for the Guild to make them there.'

'And you think it's safe here? Even if he doesn't get caught, he could burn the place down. The idiot was smoking.'

Daniel waved his hand dismissively. 'He's fine. He's done this plenty of times.'

'That's not exactly the point I'm making. This is so irresponsible. You're putting everyone in the foundry at risk.' He sounded like his father. When had he suddenly become so responsible?

Daniel shrugged. 'We'll be out of here in an hour. When it's darker.'

'I can't believe you, Daniel. He needs to leave now.'

Daniel shrugged again. 'If we go while it's still light, you'll have to drive us out in the truck.'

He couldn't just leave Ashlam here, making petrol bombs. He wanted to shake some sense into Daniel. What was he thinking?

'Okay. I'll drive you both away from the foundry. Can you get out into the street behind from here?'

'How do you think we got in?' Daniel led him to a set of barricaded double doors where at one time, carts must have entered and left. He wiggled a board, twisting it away from the door, leaving a sizable gap. Steffan poked his head out to work out where to bring the truck.

'Get him ready,' he said, and made his way back into the courtyard.

Think casual thoughts, he told himself as he swung into the driver's seat of the truck. He saw no one as he glanced behind him at the loading bay, then groaned as Phillipe strode out of the shop. He glanced at the truck but didn't walk towards it, engrossed in something else.

Steffan eased the truck along the crowded street and around the block, slaloming around the coal man's cart parked outside the theatre, idling past the brush seller whose wares stuck out into the middle of the road, and giving way to a knife sharpener and a flower seller.

He pulled over where he thought the exit to Daniel's bolt hole was.

After thirty nervous seconds, Daniel popped out between the boards. He reached in to retrieve the crate, which was covered in canvas, then tucked it behind the driver's side of the cab. Steffan heard him run a rope around it to keep it in place. They wouldn't want it crashing off while they made their way around a corner.

Ashlam's head appeared out of the hole and stayed there until Steffan got out of the truck to help him through. He stunk of petrol and appeared unsteady on his feet. He'd probably drank at least one of those bottles of brandy and had breathed in too many petrol fumes.

Daniel jumped into the middle bench seat, receiving Ashlam as Steffan shoehorned him into the truck. Daniel put an arm around his shoulders to stop him swaying into Steffan as he drove.

'Where to?' Steffan asked Daniel.

They glanced at each other when Ashlam replied, 'We're going to hit the Figaro Building.'

'Let's take you home. You don't live far from there.'

Ashlam nodded, still struggling to stay upright.

'Where does he live?'

Daniel shook his head at Steffan. 'Somewhere close to the Figaro Building. Let's stop there and see if we can get any sense out of him.'

The closer they got to Boulevard Hausmann, the wider the streets became and the classier the vehicles. Their clunky workhorse stood out at this time of night in such an upmarket area. Steffan ignored the disapproving scowls from the pavement and pulled over in a loading area next to the Figaro Building.

'Can he make it out by himself?' he asked.

Daniel let go of Ashlam, and he wobbled about like a jelly. 'I don't think so. You'll have to help.'

Steffan sighed, and for the second time that night jumped out of the cab and took up position outside the passenger door ready to catch Ashlam as he slid onto the pavement.

'Whoa there.' Steffan steadied Ashlam before he toppled into the side of the truck.

'I'm fine.' Ashlam swatted away his arm.

The fresh air must have been doing him some good, because he straightened up.

'Do you want us to take you home now?'

He shook his head. 'I'll have a little tipple at the café first.'

'Don't you think you've had enough? You are really befuddled.'

Ashlam stared at him as if he'd confessed to joining the Croix de Feu. 'I haven't had anything to drink today.'

There was no point in arguing with him when he got this contrary.

'We're by the Figaro,' Ashlam said, implying he was the only one clever enough to work that out.

Daniel got out of the truck. 'Will you be all right to get home if we leave you here?'

Ashlam nodded.

'What about the crate?' said Steffan. There was no way it was going to stay on the truck.

Daniel reached into the back, fumbled about under the cover, then pulled out the crate which was deftly tucked inside a burlap sack. 'Which café are you going to? I'll carry it over for you.'

Steffan stopped him. 'You can't let him take that into the café.'

Daniel sighed. 'You said they weren't to stay in the truck. So, what's it going to be? Back in the truck or with Ashlam?'

'Back in the truck. We'll get rid of them.'

Daniel covered the crate again. He escorted Ashlam across the road to where they'd watched Potiev enter the Figaro Building all those weeks ago.

Ashlam tried to come back towards the truck, but Daniel held his arm. They stayed on the pavement arguing. When the Figaro's doorman stepped towards the pair, Daniel pushed Ashlam in the direction of the café.

The doorman watched Daniel run back to the truck. From his expression he guessed the man was at the end of his patience with the untidy truck chugging fumes towards the hotel.

'So much for being low key and going unnoticed,' Steffan said when Daniel jumped back in the cab. He forced the truck back into the traffic.

Steffan caught a fleeting glimpse of Ashlam talking animatedly to the waiter.

'We're going to drop that crate in the Seine,' Steffan said.

When Steffan stopped beside the river, Daniel stayed in the truck. The crate splashed into the water and sank straight away. Steffan hoped that would be the end of the bottle bomb idea, but he suspected Ashlam wouldn't give up that easily.

FORTY-TWO

Yvette

Paris, November 1933

Eric must have been back in the concierge's good graces, as he was waiting in the foyer when Yvette and Janie walked down the stairs. The blue dress Yvette had borrowed from Felicity accentuated her slim waist, and the flared skirt rippled around her hips and legs. She saw it working its magic, registering the hunger in his expression.

But when she reached the bottom of the stairs, she realised Eric hadn't been watching her – his gaze was fixed on her sister. Janie was wearing a green dress Sarah had grown out of. Her boyish figure was filling out in her hips and bust, morphing into a woman's. No one who saw her now would think she was a thirteen-year-old girl.

Still, thought Yvette, at least this would make it easier to draw out of Eric what he knew about the Croix de Feu's plans. She needed to tease out the detail, like she would in a sculpture, capturing the fineness of a muscle, or a fleeting expression.

Eric *must* know the whole plan; he had to, with his uncle being so involved with the Croix.

Yvette wasn't wearing her new coat today, as she couldn't afford to get it dirty. It was also very bright, and she didn't want to stand out in the crowd. Janie's coat was still being made, so they both carried their old coats, draped over their right arms.

'You both look beautiful,' said Eric. 'No one will be listening to Colonel de La Rocque, they'll all be mesmerised by the beautiful sisters.'

Janie held out her hand; Eric obliged and kissed it. Janie giggled, saying, 'That tickled.'

They took the Metro to Place de la Concorde, Eric staring at two young men until they gave up their seats. Eric stood in front of them.

'I'm planning to leave my job in the rail service to work with my uncle,' he said, his words staccato, as if his thoughts were coming in waves.

'What would you do for him?' Yvette asked.

'He has political ambitions. He says I would be an asset to the Croix.'

So, Eric had political ambitions too.

'I didn't realise Croix de Feu had political aspirations,' Yvette said. She was being disingenuous but wanted to hear what Eric had to say.

He nodded, and he began to speak. 'Uncle advises Colonel de La Rocque. They're setting up a political arm to run in the next elections.'

Yvette smiled at him. He would think she was interested in him, but she was pleased she'd found an interesting piece of information for Daniel and Steffan. Steffan's fussing about her safety would seem silly now she had something concrete.

She could leave now, return to Daniel and Steffan with her news, but she wanted to continue on to the rally and find out more.

The mountain of Metro steps emerged onto the edge of the

vast square, the Luxor Obelisk dominating the space, the Eiffel Tower in the distance.

As they moved towards the obelisk they passed the Fontaine des Fleuves, and Yvette paused to admire the textured scales of the gilded fish held by a triton.

Eric made a small impatient noise, and Janie shook her head.

'It's impossible walking with Yvette now,' she said. 'She gets distracted by everything, not just sculptures. Yesterday she even stopped to study how some railings were constructed.'

'It's just so interesting,' Yvette replied.

'Only to you. Not to us normal people whose heads aren't stuffed full of art. Come on.'

Yvette set off again. She could come back later to study how the scales were formed and how the metal workers had combined the fish and the triton, to see whether they were two separate pieces joined together or had been made in one casting.

Eric hurried on ahead, appearing eager to get to the rally to meet his uncle. As they grew closer, he spotted a group of men with blue, gold and red armbands, and rushed towards them.

Eric's uncle was standing beside a distinguished-looking man with immaculate hair that sat tightly on his skull. He radiated power. This could only be Colonel de La Rocque.

As Yvette approached, she noticed a gold Croix de Feu emblem, complete with a grinning skull, stitched onto the men's armbands.

As Colonel de La Rocque noticed them, disapproval flickered briefly across his face.

They shouldn't have come. Yvette scanned the crowd for any other women and only saw a couple. Had Eric misread the situation; were women not welcome?

Eric's uncle greeted them cordially and introduced them to Colonel de La Rocque.

Le Colonel kissed her hand, then Janie's. His expression was welcoming, and held no hint of the disapproval she'd seen a moment ago.

Apparently sensing her anxiety, he said, 'We are grateful you both came with Eric to hear our message.'

'Thank you,' she said. 'What are your–'

Eric cut her off. 'Le Colonel has to prepare for his speech.'

She tried again. 'Could you tell me ...'

Another aide drew the Colonel's attention away.

Eric grabbed her tightly by the elbow and pulled her away, hissing, '*Shut up.*'

It was as if he'd struck her across the face. Tears welled up, threatening to spill over. She squeezed her eyes shut, willing the tears away. She wouldn't cry; wouldn't give him the satisfaction. She should walk away right now, slap his face, or make a scene to embarrass him. Instead, she forced herself to say, 'Where is the best place for us to stand, so we can hear the speeches?'

He let go of her arm, and the charming Eric reappeared. But she wasn't fooled this time. She'd never be fooled by him again.

'Just over here,' he said.

Eric took them to a spot about twenty paces away from the nearest people. He seemed to forget they were with him, squinting as he watched his uncle and Le Colonel talking, concentrating hard on reading their lips. His own moved without him knowing.

Why had he asked them along if he was just going to ignore them? She'd do her own lip-reading, then.

Several more women appeared in the crowd, but they were vastly outnumbered by the men. There were wide gaps between the various groups, and the total number of people at the rally appeared smaller because of the massive square of open space around them.

'I wonder why they chose here,' said Yvette, thinking about how much space would have to be filled to make the rally seem successful. She wasn't expecting Eric to answer; she'd made the comment mostly to smooth over the awkwardness she felt at being here now, and at being with him.

'They are important people and must have an equally important venue.'

She refrained from saying that the important venue was only impressive if there were the numbers to fill it. Clearly Le Colonel's speech wasn't important to many people.

Two men rolled out the Croix de Feu banner and held it taught behind the Colonel.

He smoothed his immaculate moustache, straightened his tie and began, his voice booming out over the crowd, effortlessly filling the space.

Le Colonel's speech was punctuated by Eric's fist flying up in the air, followed by his chant of 'Vive La France'.

It was tedious and distracting and made it hard to hear what the Colonel had to say.

'I can't hear them,' said Yvette. 'I'm going to move closer. Are you coming, Janie?'

Janie shook her head. 'I'm staying here with Eric.'

As Yvette wove her way through the groups of onlookers, a loud bang rang out from the far side of the obelisk. Yvette saw two vehicles swerve off the road and career into the crowd. Yvette cried out a warning as a man disappeared under the wheels of a truck.

Something hit the banner behind the Colonel, and flames rippled out across the fabric. One man dropped the banner pole, but the flames caught hold of the other, his screams choked off as he was engulfed in fire.

Those in the crowd closest to the stage ran in the direction of the vehicles.

Yvette watched in horror as men spilled out of the trucks, their faces covered in black cloth, their hands clutching bottles with cloth stuffed in the necks.

One man lit the cloth in his bottle and threw it at the feet of a group of four people. The bottle smashed before them spraying them with burning fuel. The four turned into screaming columns of fire, running as fast as they could from the men bringing death. Most only managed a few steps before they collapsed.

Yvette had to get away; she had to protect Janie. She turned to run back to Janie and Eric, but they had gone.

People ran past her, away from the vehicles and the obelisk. Glass shattered to her left, and a man on fire ran towards her. She screamed and sprinted away from him towards Fontaine des Fleuves. They couldn't set the water on fire; she could jump into the fountain away from the flames. If she got there.

She dodged the panicking people until a man, his face covered in black cloth, blocked her way. In one hand he held a bottle with a cloth spilling out from its neck. In the other was a burning rush.

'I'm going to enjoy seeing you burn, you bourgeois bitch,' he snarled.

She knew that voice.

'Ashlam!' she shrieked. 'It's me, Yvette!'

Her world narrowed to that bottle and the naked flame. As he came closer, she shouted at him.

'Ashlam. My cousin Daniel's your comrade and Steffan's my … man.'

She'd hesitated over what to call Steffan. She was about to die, and she was searching for the right term.

The flame moved away from the bottle.

'Have a nice evening, Yvette,' he said, as if they'd met on a Sunday stroll.

Ashlam stepped past her and headed for the next group of people.

'My sister Janie is here! Please don't hurt her!' she called after him.

He turned back to face her. 'I don't kill children, just collaborators.'

He moved off again. She should stop him harming anyone else, but her body wasn't cooperating. It took her onwards, towards the fountain.

The smashing and screaming, and the hideous smell of burnt flesh and fuel swirled around her. She didn't stop at the fountain. She ran towards the Metro, but ran past that too. They might attack there, and she'd be stuck with no way out.

As she sprinted on, she passed people running towards the attack. Someone stood in her way. She tried to dodge past him, but he grabbed her.

As she struggled to get away, she finally looked at the man. He wore a uniform – a gendarme. He repeated something: 'Calm down. Tell me what happened.'

The gendarme wasn't much older than her. His expression was full of concern.

'A group attacked during the Colonel's speech. They ran people over, burned them with bottles filled with petrol.' She started to cry. 'A man I knew was one of them.'

Another gendarme ran towards Place de la Concorde while the one helping her hammered on a nearby door.

'Police! Open up.'

The door opened a crack, and the gendarme shot his boot into the gap, throwing his force at the door.

He thrust Yvette at a startled, middle-aged, balding man in a smoking jacket.

'Provide her with something to calm her. She's in shock. Don't let her go until we have the situation under control.'

The man took her gently by the arm and escorted her into his lounge, where he poured her a large glass of brandy. He sat next to her and steadied her hand, which was shaking so much that the contents of the glass threatened to spill over her.

After a few sips she said, 'A man threatened to burn me alive. I recognised his voice. After I told him who I was, he let me live.'

The gentleman made soothing noises.

'He told me to have a nice evening, as if I was out for a stroll. I should have stopped him.'

'It seems no one could have stopped him. You were very brave to do what you did.'

'My sister was there with me. We got separated. I asked him not to hurt her. He said he didn't kill children, but she doesn't look like a child.'

'I am sure your sister is fine. He may have hurt you if you'd tried to stop him.'

After the brandy, he made them both a strong coffee. A loud knock on the door startled them, and the gentleman left the room to answer. He returned with the gendarme who'd helped her. He offered him a seat.

'When I stopped you,' said the gendarme, 'you said you knew one of the attackers.'

Yvette nodded. 'His face was covered, but I knew his voice. It was Ashlam. I met him through my cousin, Daniel. My cousin has nothing to do with this.'

The gendarme wrote the information down in a small notebook. 'What's your cousin's name and how does he know Ashlam?'

'Daniel Foucart. I don't know Ashlam's last name. They are both members of the Communist Party.'

'Where can we find Daniel?'

The memory of the hall full of injured men stopped her telling him about the Guildhall. 'They meet at a café called Claude's, near the Fontaine Saint-Michel.'

'I would like you to accompany me to Claude's to find your cousin.'

Her beautiful blue dress was streaked with soot, and she

stank of smoke. The last thing she wanted to do was go with the gendarme. But she was desperate to find Janie.

'If I go with you, will you help me find my sister? She was at the rally too.'

The gendarme said he would. 'Let's go then.'

She thanked the gentleman for helping her, then followed the gendarme out into the street.

FORTY-THREE

Steffan

No sooner were Steffan and Daniel settled at their table at Claude's, than Daniel sprang out of his seat again. 'I'm just going to have a quick word with a comrade who said he'd go past the Croix rally,' he said. 'I'll be back soon.'

While he waited, Steffan scanned the booths for anyone he knew. Margot carried a fully laden tray past him. The way she swayed among the tables reminded him of a bullock wading its way through mud. She had none of the Yvette's grace and poise.

Suddenly she stopped, staring at the door, and the café fell silent.

In the doorway stood a gendarme, and behind him was Yvette. But this wasn't the poised version.

Her hair had escaped from her clips and her dress was marked with sooty streaks. It was cold outside, but she wasn't wearing her coat; it was still captured in the crook of her arm.

What had happened to her? His heart clenched. Someone had hurt her, and he hadn't been there. He rushed towards her shouting her name. 'Yvette!'

When she saw him, her hand flew to her mouth. He opened his arms and she threw herself against him, burying her face in his shoulder. When she spoke, her voice was muffled, and wobbly with emotion.

'I went to the rally. I lost Janie. Ashlam attacked us. He only recognised me at the last minute, otherwise I'd have gone up in flames too.'

He struggled to make sense of what she was telling him.

'Is Janie hurt?'

'No. I don't know. Maybe.' Yvette sobbed into his shoulder.

The gendarme came up behind Yvette, and Steffan braced himself for bad news about Janie. Instead, the gendarme asked, 'Is a man called Ashlam here? If not, where can I find this young lady's cousin Daniel Foucart?'

Steffan indicated towards Daniel.

'Why does the gendarme want Daniel?' he asked Yvette.

'He wants Ashlam, and I told him I met him through Daniel.'

'Did you mention the Party or the Guild?'

'Just the Party.' She looked up at him, and he saw her wondering whether she'd made a mistake. 'The gendarme said he would help me find Janie if I helped him find Ashlam.'

'You said you wouldn't go to the rally. So, what were you doing there?' It came out sounding more accusatory than Steffan would have liked.

'I didn't want you to worry, so I said I wasn't going. But I wanted to help. I knew you'd tell me not to go.'

'I didn't want you to put yourself in danger.'

Suddenly Yvette pushed him away, and her face twisted with anger. 'Ashlam's your friend, your comrade. How could someone you know have done this?'

He was complicit – he'd known Ashlam was planning something, yet he'd done nothing. He'd even taken the bombs from him. Yet he'd known he'd just make more.

Before he could answer, the gendarme came back with

Daniel in tow. He didn't look pleased to be assisting in the enquiries.

The gendarme addressed Yvette. 'We will go to your apartment to check on your sister, then Daniel and I will continue to search for Ashlam.'

'If Janie isn't there, how will we find her?' asked Yvette.

'We will decide our next steps then.'

The gendarme directed them to the back of his Renault, with Yvette seated between Steffan and Daniel. Tension radiated from Yvette, making for a quiet and uncomfortable trip that seemed to last longer than the twenty minutes it took.

When the vehicle pulled up outside the apartment block, Yvette shoved Daniel, saying, 'Get out now,' then raced into the building. They followed at a slower pace, up three flights of stairs into a corridor with at least five doors on each side. Daniel disappeared through the door Yvette had left open behind her.

Steffan followed and found Yvette cradling Janie on the bed. They sobbed together, Janie clinging to Yvette like she was afraid she'd disappear.

Eric was sitting at the table smoking, his expression unreadable.

'It's good to see your sister safe,' the gendarme said.

'Thank you for your help,' Yvette managed to say between sobs.

'We must go,' said the gendarme.

Daniel hesitated, moving towards his cousins. But the gendarme took him firmly by the arm and led him out of the room.

'When the attack started, I couldn't find you two,' Yvette said to Janie.

Eric answered. 'I couldn't see you in the crowd. I needed to get Janie to safety. One of the Colonel's security cars was near us, so we went to them.'

'And you just left without Yvette?' Steffan couldn't keep the anger out of his voice.

'What about your uncle and the Colonel?' Yvette asked, ignoring Steffan's outburst.

'They were shaken but not harmed,' Eric replied.

Steffan couldn't believe what he was hearing – Eric had callously made the decision to protect Janie and abandon Yvette. It was clear where his interests now lay.

'You could have at least looked for her. Yvette's badly shaken. She nearly died.'

Yvette stiffened and said to Steffan, 'Your friend was behind the attack.'

'What friend? Did you know about this?' Eric asked Steffan.

'Of course not. Ashlam's not my friend. I met him through Yvette's cousin.'

'He's Daniel's friend?' Eric said to Yvette.

'Ashlam's a party member. That's why the gendarme wanted Daniel's help. He would never be involved in anything like that,' Yvette replied.

Steffan nodded in agreement, yet he wasn't so sure. Daniel knew a lot more than he was letting on.

'You will never go back to that foundry, Janie,' Eric said.

'Ashlam doesn't even work there,' she replied. 'Are you going to ban me from seeing my own cousin?'

'No one will come looking for Ashlam at the foundry,' Steffan said, with a confidence he didn't feel. He pushed away the memory of Ashlam making bombs at the back of their foundry. How could he have been so foolish as to think he wouldn't make more bombs?

'You're being ridiculous, Eric. Janie will be fine at the foundry,' Yvette said.

Eric sat quietly, appearing to think over their conversation. 'I will tell Uncle this news. The Croix may have heard of Ashlam.'

Steffan was hit by an overwhelming urge to check the

foundry, in case Ashlam was hiding there. He needed an excuse to leave.

'I'll get you both something to eat. It will help you all recover from the shock of what you've been through.'

When he arrived at the foundry, the place was secure. He unlocked the side door and headed for the room under the stairs. He didn't know what he'd do if he found Ashlam there, but he had to protect the foundry. The room was empty, apart from a few rags Ashlam had left behind. He collected them up and stuffed them into the bin. They would be burned tomorrow.

He checked the back wall and found the broken board that had allowed Ashlam to leave through the gap. He'd bring some planks tomorrow to shore it up from the inside.

On the way back, he bought bread and cheese and cured meats from a nearby delicatessen.

At the apartment building, Eric was preparing to leave.

'Will you stay and eat?' asked Steffan.

Eric declined. 'I need to meet with my uncle to discuss any developments.'

Yvette walked Eric to the door, then to Steffan's dismay, placed her hand on his arm.

'If you hear anything that could affect Janie or the foundry, please tell us,' she said.

'Of course. The safety of Janie and you is foremost in my mind.'

Except when it came to saving his own skin.

After Eric had left, they ate the simple dinner Steffan provided. No one spoke. The sisters were exhausted, and Yvette hadn't changed out of her stained dress. It was time for him to leave. He also didn't want to be responsible for getting them into trouble with the concierge.

'I will let you both rest. It's been an awful day.'

Yvette walked him to the top of the stairs.

'I'm so sorry about what happened,' he said. 'I hate it so much that you were in danger.'

'We shouldn't have gone. I didn't know it would be so dangerous.'

'People are pretty riled up. It makes us do horrible things to each other.'

'Do you think Daniel is okay?'

'Yes, I do. He wasn't involved with what Ashlam did.'

'Can you go and check on him for me?'

'Of course.'

They kissed then, and it was slow, lingering, soft and sensual. He didn't want it to stop. But someone was coming up the stairs, and the last thing they needed was being reported on to the concierge.

'I will go and check on Daniel. If he's anywhere, he'll be at the Guildhall.'

He kissed her once more then rushed down the stairs.

Steffan arrived to find Daniel at the bar nursing a drink. 'What happened with you and the gendarme?' he asked.

'I was helpful,' said Daniel, 'but not enough for them to find him.'

'Do you know where he is?'

'No.' Daniel took a gulp of his drink.

'If you do know, you should tell the gendarme. Ashlam's dangerous.'

'I don't betray comrades.' Daniel kept staring into his drink, as if the bottom held the answer to his problems.

'He nearly murdered your cousin and he's killed a whole lot of people. It's not betrayal, it's protecting others.'

Daniel shrugged. 'He didn't hurt her, though.'

'I can't believe your attitude.'

Daniel stared at him for a while before saying, 'I don't agree with Ashlam's methods. However, we are in a war, so we must fight any way we can. Our loyalty must be to each other.'

Steffan shook his head. 'My loyalty is to my family, and I must protect the foundry.'

'Then you should hand back your Party card if you can't put us first.'

'Fine. I will.' Steffan pulled the card from his wallet and slammed it down on the bar beside Daniel. 'Perhaps you need to reassess your loyalty, as it won't be long before I'm in charge of the foundry and there might not be room for you there.'

Steffan stormed down the steps and out into the street. He couldn't believe how foolish Daniel was being, protecting Ashlam to the detriment of them all.

He ran down to the Seine to sit by the water until he was calm enough to return to his lodgings.

FORTY-FOUR

Yvette

Paris, November 1933

Yvette checked their mailbox in the apartment foyer and found a letter from Madame Jervois. She continued up the stairs as she opened it. Madame's lilac perfume tickled her nose.

Her staccato handwriting filled the three pages with gossip about the new boarder at Madame Sorve's, and an encounter with Eric on a journey to La Montagne. On page two, Madame expressed her concern for Monsieur Rhodes and Lila:

> During my last visit the pair took turns hacking and spluttering until I feared for my wellbeing. Fortunately, Baby Joseph appears in good health. I do worry about Lila. Her lips and fingertips are tinged blue. Monsieur Aubert's been sniffing about Lila again. I have kept him away from her so far.

Monsieur Rhodes is in not much better health. I haven't seen him in the village since you left. He creaks about the house. Winter's been hard on his joints.

The Doctor frowns his way through any conversation concerning Lila and mumbles about a new medication that could help. It's VERY expensive.

You must come back soon to make further arrangements for the pair.

Yvette sighed and folded the letter back into the envelope. She would deal with it, but today was her day. She arranged the flowers she'd bought into a jar and sat down ready to complete her art homework.

Part way through the sketch, she was interrupted by loud knocking on the apartment door.

'Yvette,' Eric called out.

When she opened the door, he rushed inside.

'A mob's forming at Gare du Nord. They are planning an attack on the artisan quarter. Rue de Paradis is on their route.'

'We must get Janie,' Yvette said, throwing on her coat.

They flew down the stairs and out into the street, where everything was calm and quiet. There was not a hint it could become a battleground. They ran all the way to Blum Foundry. The businesses they passed were already boarding up windows, barricading doors, and lugging buckets of water upstairs as fire protection.

Philippe and Steffan were outside the foundry, working on protecting the galerie windows.

'I'm here to get Janie,' Yvette said.

Steffan glanced at Eric. 'Did he tell you he's already been here? And that she said no?'

Yvette turned to Eric. 'You didn't tell me that.'

'I thought you could talk some sense into her.'

Trieste came running down the road, calling out, 'They're on their way! They'll be here in a few minutes.'

'It won't be safe for you and Janie to be on the streets,' Steffan said. 'You'll have to come inside.'

'Janie's coming with me. We won't be staying for your stand-off.' She didn't want anything to do with their fight.

'You'll be safer here. It's too late to go anywhere.'

'We'll go in the other direction,' Eric said.

'They're coming in two directions. They might be coming in others too.'

Even Eric seemed uncertain now, but all Yvette wanted was to go.

'They are nearly here!' called Trieste.

Yvette didn't want to go into the foundry with Steffan, but she didn't want to get caught in another attack, either. 'Okay, we'll stay until it's safe to leave, then that's it.'

Janie was inside, and she had to protect her. It wasn't safe anywhere in Paris. The image of a flailing human candle, smelling like cooking fat, flashed into her head. It was so real she almost screamed. She stuffed the memory down inside her like she was swallowing a stale heel of bread.

After this was all over, they were going back to the village. It now seemed ridiculous that she'd been frightened of that old lech Monsieur Aubert – so frightened they'd run all the way here into a bigger mess.

As she followed Steffan through the foundry forecourt into the boarded-up gloom of the shop, it took her a moment to notice the two people moving around inside.

'Yvette's here,' Steffan said to Janie.

Janie kept her back to her and grumped, 'I'm not coming back with you.'

'I know. It's not safe on the streets. We'll wait here until it is.'

Janie turned, her eyes round with surprise. 'Do you mean that? We can stay and help protect the foundry?'

'We will stay.' Yvette stopped short of saying they'd help protect the foundry. But what else could they do? They couldn't huddle in an upstairs room and hope the world would forget about them.

The people who'd been hurt at the rally were now ready to murder her family. And Steffan and the Blum family, who had helped her so much.

'What would you like me to do?' she asked Steffan.

Steffan and Daniel decided the best place for protecting the front gates and the galerie was the room above, a mezzanine used to store boxes of stock, accessed only by a ladder. They assigned Yvette, Janie and Eric to prepare the space. Her back ached and her arms shook as she hauled a bucket of water up the flimsy ladder to place it next to nine others. They had a perfect vantage point from which to toss water to douse any firebombs thrown at flammable parts of the building façade.

Eric had taken charge of preparing the upstairs area against the attack. The irony wasn't lost on Yvette, that he was on their side, protecting the foundry.

Yvette mopped her face with her dress. It was even hotter than normal up here, as the men below welded sheets of metal to the gates. In between the bouts of welding, she thought she could hear the mutter of a restless crowd. Descending the ladder again, she fought the urge to bolt – she'd probably only land in a useless heap at the bottom. Instead she came down slow and steady.

When she reached the floor, Janie held out another water bucket. 'We've only got five more left,' she said.

Yvette nodded. 'I can do five more.'

'Me too.'

She recognised the little falter that crept into Janie's stride as she walked away, a sign she was almost done in.

By the time Yvette came down for the next bucket, the men had finished welding the metal barriers onto the gates. They stood around in clusters talking strategy, their excitement crackling about the courtyard like lightning. They didn't seem scared at all. She didn't know whether her heart was pounding through exertion or terror.

Her muscles shrieked as she took the next bucket up. As she stood looking out of the window down onto the street, Monsieur Blum came into view, shepherding Martje and the children along. They wore their best coats and carried suitcases and boxes.

As she watched them disappear under the arch, she supposed they must have planned to leave but had run out of time.

The men below called the last stragglers on the street to hurry inside. They scurried through the entrance, then the gates clanged shut with the pure tone of a ringing bell. She came down the ladder as the men finished welding them shut. The muttering she'd heard grew into the clomping of boots on pavements, and shouting and chanting. The mob was closing in. Her skin prickled with fear as her chest tightened, and she sucked in little gasping breaths. She didn't want to be at the gates when they arrived, their faces twisted with hate and weapons in their hands. She hurried back to the mezzanine.

Only two more buckets to go. Her leg muscles fought against her as she moved up the ladder; her arm muscles screamed at her to stop. She didn't listen, she had to get that last bucket up. Finally, there were fifteen buckets waiting for flames to extinguish.

She desperately wanted to flop down onto the floor and rest. Steffan scrambled up to join her, and she took Janie's arm to help pull her up the ladder.

There was a loud smash behind her, and in fright she almost let her sister go. Something struck her, and pain exploded in her back, so intense she couldn't breathe.

'Get on the ground! They're throwing rocks,' Eric called up from the ground floor.

By instinct, she threw herself on top of Janie.

'Get off me,' Janie squealed, rolling Yvette off her.

Yvette lay on her side, her breath caught in her body. The pain was intense, and tiny lights danced in her peripheral vision. Something else hit her side, and she crawled across the floor, gasping, out of range of the window.

'Hold your position,' Steffan called to them, as though they were soldiers. Perhaps they were.

The mob was loud now, roaring out insults and death threats. Yvette could hear the *ching ching* of rattling gates. She hoped they'd hold. What would they do if they didn't? The mob would tear them apart. It didn't matter now whether they were Jewish or not, all that mattered to the rioters was that they were on this side of the gate.

Janie clutched her hand. 'I'm scared,' she whimpered, her words barely discernible above the noise.

Suddenly Yvette's focus was pulled to Steffan, who'd hauled out a crate of brandy bottles with rags stuffed in them. The mere sight made her gag, as it brought back the stench of burning flesh and the memory of human torches running, arms flailing, bodies collapsing on the ground.

'You can't do that! You can't burn them,' she screamed at him.

He seemed torn, looking at her and then the mob. 'We can't let them get in.'

He was right. They couldn't let them get in.

She peeked out of the window and saw that the mob had split into two groups, one pounding on the gates, the other kicking at the boarded-up shop windows. Down the road she glimpsed another group enter the street.

'Throw it behind them.' She indicated to the mob below. 'And in front of the next ones coming down the road.'

Steffan nodded and held out the lighter. 'You light them and I'll throw them.'

She flicked the lighter's flint, and a bright flame took hold of the rag. Steffan took his time lining up the shot. She wanted to scream at him to hurry, but he might drop it on the wooden floor, and then they'd be in worse trouble.

He launched the bottle, and it smashed on the ground behind the crowd. The mob beneath them surged towards the building, as if hiding under the arch could protect them. The group coming down the road stopped, waiting to see if it was a one-off, or more were coming.

'Throw another one to stop them coming any further down the road,' Janie said.

Yvette lit the cloth and Steffan took aim.

The bottle smashed in front of the rioters. The flames stopped them. They stood for a moment, then the group swung round and pushed the others back up the street.

The people below them howled and screamed like demons, pounding on the gates and the boarded-up windows. They heard glass shattering.

'That's the shop window,' Janie said.

'They'll be through soon,' Steffan said.

He held a bottle in his hand and looked at Yvette. She knew what he meant. He wanted her approval to throw it at them. She didn't want to give it. She didn't want to be responsible for their screams and their agony. She wanted him to stop looking at her. She covered her face with her hands.

The boards below gave way and voices rose up. They'd made it into the galerie.

Then the sounds outside changed, and the crowd noise subsided. She risked looking through the window, careful to stay out of missile range. The people outside had swung around to face the street past their building, where she couldn't see. She motioned to Steffan to look.

He leant towards the window, and a grin spread across his face. 'We've got reinforcements.'

She moved beside him, and her mouth dropped open as members of the Artisan Guild rained blows down on the protesters. The clubs and pipes smashing their bodies changed the howls of rage into shrieks of pain.

'I've never been so glad to see those bastards,' he said.

In the galerie under them, the muffled shouts and thuds turned into cries of agony, and there was a terrible smell, like burning meat. Yvette gagged and nearly threw up.

'I'll go down and see what's happening,' Steffan said.

He scurried down the ladder to join other foundry staff protecting the door to the galerie.

'Should we go down too?' Janie asked.

Yvette shook her head. 'We'll stay up here in case someone throws something through the windows.'

They moved out of direct range and peered out of the window to watch the fight below.

A looter appeared in the street cradling the Chiparus statuette – the Book Lady – in his arms. She thought it a strange thing for him to steal.

'Stop, thief!' Janie cried.

The man kept running.

'It's just a statue,' Yvette said.

Janie sighed. 'At least we took the best pieces out of the shop.'

Yvette gave her a sharp look. 'Is the Book Lady not a best piece?'

'It's not my favourite. I'd be beside myself if it were Rudolph and Natacha.' Janie shrugged. Then as if to appease her, she added, 'I do like Semiramis, though, and Chiparus's new version of *Lady Leaving the Opera*. It's got your face. We moved those to safety.'

They peeked out of the window again and saw another mob entering the street behind the Artisan Guild.

'Behind you! Look out,' Yvette yelled.

A guild member must have heard her, as he glanced up. She recognised Ashlam. He was here in the crowd. The Guild had been protecting him all along.

Something whizzed by Yvette's head and fire erupted beside her. She screamed and dived away from the flames; her mind full of the image of Ashlam standing in front of her with a lit bottle bomb when she'd been convinced she was about to die.

'Help me,' Janie shouted at her, pouring a bucket of water over the flames.

Yvette picked herself up, ashamed her younger sister could take charge just like that. The fire was nearly out, and Janie pointed to the bucket closest to the flames. 'Use that one.'

Janie's forthrightness surprised Yvette out of her paralysis, and she did as she was asked.

'He's here,' Yvette said.

'Who's here?'

'Ashlam. The one who nearly killed me.'

'Is he throwing bombs at us now?'

'No, he's helping keep the mob away.'

'It doesn't matter. Focus on putting out the fire.'

She was exhausted, but that didn't stop her. The image of Ashlam still whirled about in her head, the memory even more real than what was happening to them now. By the time she'd put out the fire, Janie had lit and thrown four more petrol bombs.

The Guild were gaining ground; the mob had retreated to both ends of the street. The sound of fighting outside died down and Yvette couldn't hear anything coming from the galerie – but the pounding of her heart could have been drowning any sound. Her nerves were still jangling.

Janie peered out the window. 'They've gone. The Guild are protecting the street.'

Yvette jumped as Steffan called, 'You two can come down now.'

She scrambled down the ladder and threw herself into his arms. The tears came; she couldn't stop them. He rubbed her back and hair, made soothing noises like she was an upset child. But she wasn't upset about the fight. 'I saw Ashlam.'

'We'll deal with that later,' he said, then continued to shush her.

She pushed herself out of his arms. 'I don't want to deal with it later. I want to deal with it now. He's outside. We need to tell the gendarmes when they come.'

She stepped away as Steffan moved towards her again.

'Of course, we will tell them when they come. But they aren't here yet, and this isn't over. The mob may come back.'

Janie and Eric entered the galerie.

Steffan turned away from Yvette and she followed him, about to demand he did something about Ashlam, but the devastation of the galerie silenced her. The mob had ripped the boards away, smashed the windows, torn the door from its hinges, and smashed the display cabinets.

She stepped through the broken doorway into the street. About a dozen people lay on the ground near the foundry, as if the mob had come in a wave and left them behind like flotsam on a beach. Some of them were writhing about, crying out for help; others were silent and still. Several were dead from burns inflicted by the bottle bombs. She shuddered. That could have been her at the rally.

The mob had left behind a black tarpaulin that lay crumpled over something on the ground. She went over to it, struggling to understand the twisted pair of legs that stuck out from under it and a hand that reached towards the sky.

A little moan escaped from her. It wasn't a tarpaulin. It was solidified metal. Underneath were the entangled bodies of three people fused together when the foundry workers poured molten metal on the mob.

Steffan moved in front of her to obscure her view. 'I tried to stop them. I didn't want them to do that.'

'You knew they were doing this, and you didn't stop them? Just like you didn't stop Ashlam? You didn't try hard enough.'

Steffan wiped away tears with his sleeve.

'I tried to stop them doing this. They did it anyway. It's so horrible. I can't believe they did it. It stopped them though...'

As Steffan continued to talk, Yvette looked around her at the horror on the street, the broken and damaged bodies. Her stomach twisted and she fought the urge to throw up. She didn't want to listen to Steffan trying to justify what he'd let happen.

'I can't be here anymore. Come on Janie.'

She grabbed her sister by the hand, dragging her down the street. The guild members had dispersed, and the next street was empty.

Eric caught up with them and linked arms with Janie. 'I'm taking you both home.'

Home. Not the apartment – Mont-Saint-Louis. The safe, boring village where nothing ever happened. Where no one got bottle bombs thrown at them or rioted in the lanes.

Lila and Monsieur Rhodes needed her help. At least she could do something there.

'Yes, we would like to go home,' she said.

FORTY-FIVE

Steffan

Paris, November 1933

Steffan called out to Yvette as she ran down the street with Janie. She didn't look back, but Eric did, and Steffan caught a flicker of triumph in his expression.

He couldn't do anything about it now, as Martje was calling to him from the galerie entrance. Trieste and another worker were hauling boards outside.

People from neighbouring businesses were trickling out into the street to check the damage and help the wounded. They stayed away from the three covered in metal. He didn't want to see them anymore, and he didn't want others in the street to have to see them either. He went into the foundry and fetched a large canvas with which to cover the destroyed bodies. Then he helped Trieste secure boards across the windows and barricade the door again.

Back in the foundry, the men's mood was almost festive, as if they'd enjoyed the attack.

Steffan pushed his worry about Yvette and Janie aside as he

raced up the worn stairs to the men's quarters and on up to the planking they'd laid across the roof trusses.

Daniel and Phillippe were directing about ten foundry workers who were hauling smelting buckets up by pullies to tipping points they'd set up across the back windows of the building.

Even though Philippe ignored him, Steffan told them what happened at the front of the building, and about the breach into the galerie. He didn't mention Yvette and Janie leaving with Eric. 'I wasn't sure the Artisan Guild would come and help us,' he said.

'Nearly a third of the chapter work here,' said Daniel. 'Of course they were going to help.'

Daniel took him up a rickety staircase that gave them a view from the roof. The road below was a mess of coagulating metal and under this were the grotesque shapes of fallen men. It was horrific and macabre.

Steffan's stomach tightened, and his face flushed. How could he be part of doing this to other people? They'd murdered men, even if they were rioters who might have killed them all if they'd gained access.

He kept pushing away the practical thought of how they would clean up the mess. Maybe they'd have to wait until the metal set and then just remove all the flag stones under them.

What a callous thought. He was hit with a wave of nausea. To distract himself, he asked, 'How many people got hurt?'

'About thirty. Not all of them are down there. Some took off as soon as we hit the first ones.' Daniel's answer was so emotionless he could have been reporting on how many bronze screws were left in stock.

Steffan's brain buzzed, and he couldn't make his mouth work to form an answer.

'At least we won't get attacked from this side now,' Daniel said. He seemed proud of what he'd done.

Steffan took no pleasure in hurting others, even if they were trying to hurt him and his family. 'Please don't do this again.' He was talking to Philippe now too.

Daniel sized him up as if he were choosing the best calf in a paddock.

Philippe ignored him, and gave more directions to the men.

Hopelessness washed over Steffan. They weren't going to stop. They weren't going to listen to him.

He returned to the courtyard.

Trieste ran towards him, calling, 'The gendarmes are outside the foundry.'

As if on cue, the foundry gates rattled and a loud voice boomed out, 'This is the police. Open the gates now, or we will shoot them open.'

The men in the courtyard turned to Steffan for a decision. He nodded and approached the gates, calling out, 'We will comply. We will open them now.'

'You have one minute,' the voice replied.

The men fumbled with the bolts and smashed open the temporary welds. As they pulled the gates open, the gendarmes pushed their way through.

'Are you the foundry owner?' asked a gendarme with extra stripes on his epaulettes and a smarter cap – presumably their leader.

Steffan shook his head. 'No, that is Monsieur Blum.'

'Get him.'

As Steffan crossed the courtyard, the other gendarmes fanned out to round up the men.

Steffan stepped inside the offices and called, 'Father, you need to come down and talk to the gendarmes.'

He appeared at the top of the stairs. For the first time since Steffan had known him, Father looked scared. His face was pale and lined, and he looked much older than his fifty years. Philippe appeared behind him. Steffan wondered whether Father knew what Philippe and Daniel had done at the rear of the building.

The gendarmes' leader appeared behind Steffan. 'Is that him?'

He nodded, and the gendarme pushed Steffan back outside. Another directed him towards the centre of the courtyard, where the foundry workers were being forced to their knees in two orderly rows.

More gendarmes disappeared into back of the foundry, clearly aware of what the other foundry workers were doing.

Father and Phillippe were brought out into the courtyard at gunpoint. Steffan stepped towards Father, but someone gripped his arm. It was Daniel, who pushed him down next to a kneeling worker, positioning himself on Steffan's other side. He struggled to get away, but Daniel was stronger.

'No heroics from you,' Daniel hissed in his ear.

A gendarme pointed a rifle at Steffan. He wanted to speak to them, to stop this happening, but his brain felt empty.

'I'm not letting you go with them,' said Daniel. 'We need you here. The family needs you.'

Martje came rushing down the stairs, only to find her way blocked by armed gendarmes.

'What do you want with my husband and son?' she cried out. 'They've done nothing wrong.'

No one answered her.

The ten workers who had been at the back of the building were marched out of the foundry gates by armed gendarmes and were followed by Father and Philippe.

Steffan wanted to cry out that they should take him instead. He'd set the wheels in motion. He'd brought this down on his family.

When the gendarmes left, Martje called for the workers to shut the gates. 'Daniel will lead the work taking down the pullies at the back of the foundry,' she said. 'Take any metal back into the foundry.'

Daniel hauled him up off the ground. 'Go after Martje,' he said.

Martje turned to go back up the stairs and Steffan followed behind her. He reached her at the landing. Tears streamed down her face.

'I just need time to gather myself,' she said.

Steffan anxiously waited for her blame him, but she said nothing, and gave no sign that she did. 'I will come and find you when I'm ready,' she said gently.

She went into the office and closed the door.

He found Sarah and Rosie, red-eyed from sobbing, in the upstairs tearoom.

'What's going to happen to Papa and Philippe?' Rosie asked.

'We'll go and get them once Martje's ready,' he said.

But he didn't know if it would be possible to get them.

As soon as he'd helped Martje and Father, he'd need to talk to Yvette. He held Rosie's hand while he worked how put things right with her.

FORTY-SIX

Yvette

Paris, November 1933

Yvette ran down Rue de Paradis, away from the horror and chaos. Steffan had called out to her, but the footfalls behind her weren't his. Janie was following her, and so was Eric.

Steffan called again, the distance between them now stretched. She felt only relief that he wasn't coming after her.

'Wait at the corner,' Eric called out. 'They might still be there.'

But they weren't, and she couldn't hear their boots on the cobbles. Still, she slowed so the pair could catch up.

Eric took the lead as they ran towards the apartment building. Staff from shops were boarding up their broken shop windows, and picking up scattered produce. Clusters of shopkeepers and café owners huddled together in the street.

A waiter righting tables and asked in a shaking voice, 'Are they coming back again?'

Eric answered, 'They went the other way.'

When they got to the apartment building, Eric hurried them up the steps into the foyer.

Janie clung to him. 'Don't leave us.' She pressed her face into his chest, and Eric kissed her on the top of her head in a way that implied there was more to their friendship. Yvette's stomach tightened.

'You're safe now,' he said, 'but I need to check in with my uncle. I'll come back in a few hours.'

Yvette wasn't sure she wanted Eric as part of their plans, but it would upset Janie to raise this now. 'We'll leave you a note with the concierge if we are not here,' she said.

'If you want to go home to the village, I'll come by and pick you up tonight as I'm going back to La Montagne on the evening train. I can get you free passage.'

Yvette needed to do something – anything – to get away from the situation. They had enough money to buy return tickets, but Eric would no doubt help them.

'Yes, let's go tonight. What time will you pick us up?'

'See you here at seven. I have use of Uncle's car.'

'I have to tell L'Académie and the Chiparus's we'll be away.'

'Shall I come earlier? Say five thirty? I don't want either of you moving about the city alone.'

They went upstairs to their apartment, where Janie flopped onto the bed. Yvette stoked the potbelly to make them a hot drink. She didn't want to stop moving. Moving kept things swirling around in her head, not settling on thoughts, smells or the screaming. She moved to the table to tidy up her sketching materials. It seems like days ago that she'd abandoned her homework, but it was only hours.

She picked up Madame Jervois's letter and passed it to Janie. 'We received this today.'

Janie read the letter. 'So ... going back's just a visit, isn't it?'

Yvette shrugged. 'When we were there, we seemed to have so many troubles. None of them are as big as here, though.'

'Don't you want to be an artist? You won't be able to do that in the village.'

'I could keep sketching.'

'Don't be ridiculous. Look what happened to Mama.'

Janie was right, yet maybe she was ridiculous thinking she could be an artist. How many women artists had she met here?

She really wanted to distance herself from the images in her head, the screaming, the smell of burning flesh and the twisted bodies. She wanted distance from Steffan and Daniel. She could barely breathe.

But they'd paid their rent for the next two months, and she wasn't going to waste that. 'Yes,' she said, 'we are coming back. I just need to clear my head.'

'And we can sort out Lila and Monsieur Rhodes.'

Yvette loved Janie's faith that things would work out. It settled her pounding heart and steadied her hand enough that she could pour the water into the coffee pot.

'I will go to L'Académie and the Chiparus's, to let them know we'll be gone for a week.'

'What about Steffan?'

Yvette shook her head. 'I don't really want to talk to him right now.'

Over the next few hours, she wrote notes to Felicity and the Chiparus's. She started a letter to Steffan, screwed it up and threw it into the fire. After the fifth attempt, she gave up. Her head was still in too much of a whirl to find words that fitted together on a page.

Janie went downstairs, with strict instructions to stay in the foyer, to find out information from residents as they entered the apartment building.

Eric arrived promptly at 5.30pm in his uncle's sleek black automobile. The driver opened the rear door and assisted them into the back seat as if they were proper ladies. They drove through the wealthier streets of the city, untouched by the unrest, towards the Chiparus's residence.

It was dark by the time they arrived. Julienne was surprised to see Yvette when she opened the door. 'Is everything all right?'

'We're going back to our village for a little while to sort out the welfare of some family members.' Yvette handed her letter to Julienne.

'We will have some more work for you when you are back.'

'I appreciate that. I want to continue my lessons too.'

'Of course. Is Steffan taking you to the station?'

'Eric has his uncle's car.'

Julienne's jaw twitched but she only said, 'I hope your trip goes well and your family members are too.'

Yvette stepped towards Julienne and hugged her.

Julienne received it stiffly. 'Be careful with that man,' she said.

'I will, Julienne. You needn't worry.'

She returned to the car to be ferried across the city in style. The closer they got to L'Académie, the more the streets were damaged. The driver had to make a couple of detours where roads were blocked off while residents cleaned up.

When Yvette stepped inside L'Académie, Felicity rushed towards her and wrapped her in a perfume-filled hug and a swirl of questions.

'Are you all okay? How are the Blums and Steffan? Was it awful? Oh my god, those fascists are the worst.'

'Everyone was all right when I left them.'

Felicity released her.

'We're going back to the village for a week or so. I need to sort out my cousin Lila and her baby. She's unwell.'

Felicity nodded. 'Your going has nothing to do with what's happened in the last few days?'

Tears prickled in Yvette's eyes. 'I do need some time to think. It's been awful.' She handed Felicity the letter.

'I hope this isn't a resignation.'

Yvette shook her head. 'No, just asking for a couple of weeks off.'

'A couple?'

'Three weeks.'

'Okay, we can do without you for three weeks. But you are very popular. And very talented.' Felicity hugged her again.

For the first time since they'd come to Paris, Yvette finally felt she belonged, and that her dream of becoming an artist wasn't impossible.

'Don't worry, Felicity. I will be back.'

Monsieur Granger's driver held the door open for her as she slipped back into the vehicle. She wound down the window and took great gulps of Paris air to sustain her. Just in case they never made it back.

FORTY-SEVEN

Steffan

Paris, November 1933

It was the third morning Steffan and Martje had been to the commissariat with food and clothes for Oscar and Philippe, in the hope they'd be allowed to see them. They stood outside with the families of others who'd been arrested; their numbers seemed to grow larger each day.

A gendarme appeared in the doorway and told the crowd they would not be seeing any prisoners.

The worry etching a pathway on Martje's face seemed to deepen, along with Steffan's guilt for bringing this catastrophe on his family. If only he'd stopped Ashlam, things might not have escalated.

He hadn't heard from Yvette, either, nor had Janie shown up for work. Not surprising since it would be weeks before the galerie was ready to open again. He'd gone to the apartment building, but the concierge wouldn't let him go up to their apartment. The note he'd left hadn't seemed to work, as Yvette hadn't contacted him.

He escorted Martje back home and circled back to L'Académie to see if he could catch up with Yvette there.

Felicity greeted him with sympathy and an overabundance of perfume. When he enquired after Yvette, she stared at him with such solemnity, his stomach dropped.

'Did she not tell you she was going home to her village for a few weeks?'

Steffan was stunned that she would leave without telling him. 'When did she leave?'

'The night of the riot. Her friend who's the train conductor got them free seats.'

Eric. She'd left with Eric. It was worse than he could ever have imagined.

'Is she coming back?'

'She said it was only for three weeks, and I will hold her to that. She is the artists' favourite.'

When he left, he intended to walk back to the foundry, but his feet took him in the direction of Gare Montparnasse. He stood in the middle of the station as passengers jostled him. He was in the way, but he couldn't have moved, even if he'd wanted to. He was paralysed by indecision; he should be here helping his family, yet all he wanted was to be with Yvette.

He'd hurt her so badly by not stopping Ashlam, and now she'd run off back to her village. With Eric. He had to make it up to her.

He approached the ticket counter and spoke to the attendant.

'When's the next train to Mont-Saint-Louis?'

The attendant consulted a timetable beside him. 'The next train to La Montagne leaves in ten minutes. You can catch a connecting one from there.'

'I'll have a ticket, thanks.'

'Return?'

'No, just one way.'

He ran to the platform and threw himself on the train before he changed his mind. He should be with his family sorting out the mess he'd help create. But one thing he knew – he wanted Yvette in his life. And he wasn't prepared to wait three weeks to put things right.

The train left the station with a screech of metal and hydraulics.

He sat back in his seat and stared at the destination on his ticket. Mont-Saint-Louis. Hopefully it wasn't too big, and everyone knew each other. It didn't matter, because he'd find Yvette, even if he had to knock on every door.

Acknowledgments

Rue de Paradis is the first in the 'Semiramis – Queen of Heaven' series.

I completed the first draft of this book in 2006, as part of Whitireia Community Polytechnic's novel-writing programme. Now, nearly 20 years later, I have finally sent two of the characters out into the world while I continue working on the second in the series.

People often ask me why I chose to write about antiques, and whether I am an expert. I'm not, but as I set out on my research journey, I met someone who was, and to whom I'm indebted.

The first home my husband and I purchased was a little Art Deco house perched on a hill in the suburb of Brooklyn, Wellington. This house got me interested in this period of design, and, thinking I could build my first novel around the subject, I contacted our local auction house, Dunbar Sloane, to ask if they could put me on to an expert in the field. Their inhouse expert, Anthony Gallagher, was keen to meet for a coffee, and his eyes lit up when I asked him what the Holy Grail of the Art Deco world was.

He told me about Demétre Chiparus and the bronze and ivory sculptures he made in the 1920s and 30s. My life was never the same again – in a good way – as I learned about Monsieur Chiparus, his wife Julienne, and the foundries that made his pieces in Paris nearly 100 years ago.

In the early days of writing this novel, I was mentored by Elspeth Sandys and the late Renee Taylor, and I would like to thank them for their input. Many more people helped along the way, including members of the Pheonix Science Fiction Writers Group, who suffered through early versions of chapters, as did participants in our Frances Cherry writing workshops.

Thank you to our now defunct book group. Not only did the group spur me on to read dozens of classics that improved my writing but its members gave me useful feedback on an early draft of the novel.

More recently, Kathryn Burnett's Writing Room kept me focused, and members of the feedback group made solid suggestions for improving chapters. Kathryn agreed to be my writing accountability coach, and I barely lied to her about my progress.

I'd also like to acknowledge my first husband Mike Greer, my kids Leo and Bennie, and our nanny Glenda O'Connor. Glenda kept the wheels on our little family bus for many years, and I am grateful to her for going above and beyond.

I'd also like to thank Barbara Unkovic for her structural assessment of the draft, and Sue Copsey for her detailed and insightful edit of the manuscript.

But mostly I'd like to thank all the artists and writers who 'just have to'. It's the way we make sense of our lives and the world around us.

References

I've referenced two books I frequently returned to during the writing of *Rue de Paradis*.

Pitt, Leonard. (2006). *Walks Through Lost Paris.* Counterpoint, Berkeley

Shayo, Alberto. (1999) *Chiparus: Master of Art Deco*. Abbeville Press, New York, New York, USA

The first long-fiction piece I wrote was a plagiarised version of *Watership Down*, featuring guinea pigs rather than rabbits. At nine, I had no idea about copyright.

As I grew older, I became interested in film, documentary and spoken-word storytelling. Once I started my business and my family, I chose to work with the written word as it was something I could do without needing to collaborate.

My publishing successes include short stories in three anthologies, as well as plays and short stories in the *New Zealand School Journal*.

I have written and produced five *Insight and Spectrum* documentaries for Radio New Zealand. I was also co-winner of a Sir Julius Vogel award for the fan-fiction documentary *Renaldo: First Sheep on the Moon*.

I've completed four novels, but *Rue de Paradis* is the first I've taken through to publication. I put an earlier draft aside to work on other projects, but one of the characters, Deco wouldn't let it go. I kept seeing life through his eyes – a Lalique vase, or a bronze sculpture I knew he'd love to 'rehome'.

After attending a digital publishing series run by the Paraparaumu Library, I found a way to make the story work. I tore up the draft and embarked on a trilogy.

In 2018, I went to Paris to 'continue my research' and get serious about writing this series, and considered using Chiparus as a central character. Chiparus lived a quiet life with a total focus on sculpting. Although he didn't become a main character, he is a useful case study of a person obsessed with their work and a metaphor for the fading popularity of decorative arts in the 1930s. As Chiparus's fortunes declined, and the war in Europe raged around them, he and Julienne ended up living in a shack near the zoo. Julienne spent all day foraging for food and raising rabbits in the backyard so they didn't starve, and Demétre would go to the zoo every day to sketch and sculpt the animals. Their circumstances improved after the war as Chiparus sold some bigger sculptures, but his decorative artworks didn't regain popularity until this century.

Apart from finishing my first novel, the achievement I'm most proud of is fledging my two young adults into the world. They both have active artistic lives and I'm proud to say that they are thriving.

I live on the Miramar Peninsula in Wellington, reaping the rewards of our Predator Free movement, which has enabled us to bring our native birds back into the city. Sitting on my deck watching the all the life around me fills me with hope that if we work together, we can solve our societal problems.

My other passion is workplace health, safety, and wellbeing and I've been fortunate enough to make my living as a health and safety specialist through my business Working Wise: www.workingwise.nz.

———

To sign up to my newsletter
and find out more about the next books in the
'Semiramis – Queen of Heaven' series,
visit: www.jeenamurphy.com

———